IMMORTAL VENDETTAS
BOOK ONE

OLD SCORES

A.J. Harrison

WWW.IMMORTALVENDETTAS.COM

www.immortalvendettas.com

ISBN: 979-8-9886364-3-4 (Amazon Paperback)
ISBN: 979-8-9886364-9-6 (Barnes & Noble Paperback)
ISBN: 979-8-9886364-5-8 (Other Paperback Versions)
ISBN: 979-8-9886364-8-9 (eBook)

Any references to historical events, real places, or real people are used fictitiously. Names, characters, and places are the products of the author's imagination.

Quotes from Niccoló Machiavelli's *The Prince* and Gottfried Bürger's "Lenore" (by way of Bram Stoker's *Dracula*) are public domain.

Cover art by Jeff Brown.

First printing edition 2023.

For Gabriel, Mandy, Liz, and Monica,
without whom this book never would have been finished.

"[T]he Romans, foreseeing troubles, dealt with them at once, and, even to avoid a war, would not let them come to a head, for they knew that war is not to be avoided, but is only to be put off to the advantage of others."

— *Niccoló Machiavelli*, The Prince

PROLOGUE

Tell Hariri, Syria

BAKED BY the desert sun, squinting against its blaze even as it sank toward the horizon, Chris Edgeborn wiped his face with the cloth hanging from his belt and wished for the dozenth time that he hadn't left his bandanna back at the campsite. It would only be a fifteen-minute walk back as the crow flew, but the crow wouldn't be stopped every thirty seconds by every other intern who had forgotten something; he'd need a pack mule to carry it all back.

The salty smell of his sweat mixed with the grease of his layers of sunblock didn't do his stomach any favors, but he couldn't bear to think of going without it. The adjustment from Williams, Minnesota—population two hundred, average high temperature of sixty-eight in the summer—to Stanford University had been rough enough; the Syrian desert felt like an oven on broil. It had Chris rethinking his entire planned career in archeology; if all ancient sites were going to be like this, he'd never make it through field work. The only reason he had toughed it out this long was—

"Chris!"

Her.

"Hey, Chris! You're not tired already, are you? We've probably got another good hour of sunlight!"

"No, just getting a breath of fresh air," he called back with false enthusiasm, the heat . . . well, not forgotten, but less burdensome for a moment. Renee Dent was the real reason Chris was here in this scorching desert digging through the remains of Mari, a civilization so old Hammurabi had put it to rest.

Blaming the desert heat for his flagging interest in the field of classical archeology wouldn't be fair, though sweating out every drop as soon as he drank it certainly wasn't helping. If Chris were forced to be honest with himself, he would admit that three years of lectures, slides, text interpretations, and learning languages that hadn't been the native tongues of men since before Christ walked the earth had been a far cry from adventure archaeology and old mummy movies. A glimmer of the old love for ancient history still flickered in his mind, but by and large he'd kept the major because he couldn't change it and still graduate in four years. But he need not have journeyed out to central Syria to meet his major requirements.

No, that was Renee's doing. Unlike Chris, her time in Stanford's Classics Department had only sharpened her desire to make this endless landscape of sand and the painstaking brushing of artifacts her life. And it was infectious, too, a happy contagion that made Chris wonder if the heat was really so bad in the grand scheme of things.

Renee brushed a lock of ebony hair away from the dark curves of her cheeks and jogged up the smooth stones of what had once been a royal palace wall. She stopped in front of Chris, saw the cloth still in his hand, and gave him a scandalized look. "You're not using that as a sweat rag, are you?"

Chris cleared his throat. "Well, I left my bandanna back in the tent . . ."

"Chris!" she snapped in a whisper. "We're only supposed to use those on the artifacts! Patterson's gonna freak if he finds out."

"Yeah, well, then it's a good thing Patterson's not our professor, isn't it?" Chris quipped back, trying not to smile at her. It was hard—she was so beautiful, even when she was mad—but he didn't think she would see the humor.

Renee's deep brown eyes rolled. "Well yeah, but Dr. Baxter's still new, remember? We can't mess this up for him!"

Chris frowned. She had him there. Newly hooded, Dr. Elliot Baxter—fresh from postdoc and not even thirty—ostensibly shared command, but his "partner" from the University of Chicago, Dr. Patterson, had been running the dig for half a decade now.

"Yeah, you're right," he sighed, tucking the artifact towel back into his belt and wiping the sleeve of his T-shirt across his brow instead. "And something tells me Patterson won't think much of taking breaks, either."

"So, back in?" Renee asked, smiling her dazzling smile.

Chris swallowed, smiled back, and nodded. "Back in."

Ducking into the covered dig chamber made Chris remember why he had walked out into the scorching sunset in the first place. The enclosed, dusty space was a dry sauna, and the tarps covering the chamber gave it a strange orange tint. Patterson had explained the first day that clear tarps would only make it hotter, and so at first the interns had lavished praise on the orange. But now, with dusk encroaching, the shadows of the chamber stretched nearly to the opposite wall. Knowing Patterson, the ancient mining lanterns would come on soon.

The thought alone made Chris parched, and as Renee went back to work, he took a swallow compulsively from his canteen.

"Careful with that! I don't want you contaminating anything!"

Chris sighed, but he kept it quiet. Across the chamber, cleaning a small piece of rock with a brush, Renee pressed her lips together between her teeth to keep from smiling. Chris shot her a covert look and then nodded. "Sorry Dr. Patterson."

Mitchell Patterson waddled into view, face indignant. Half as wide as he was tall (and he barely came up to Chris's chin), Patterson was balding rapidly, and only a few strands of sweat-slicked hair rested on his crown. Dressed head to toe in various shades of khaki, he fanned himself irritably with one fat hand and patted his paunch absentmindedly with the other. The half dozen pockets on his vest bulged with notes and pictures (all digital, no flash), and the swell of his belly almost hid the camera in its protective case on his belt.

Patterson shook his head, jowls wobbling, and spoke over his shoulder to two men Chris didn't recognize. "Not all our interns are quite as prepared for field work."

Chris gritted his teeth. He resented the criticism in front of strangers, of course, but the comparison had to mean he was nearby—and there he was, trailing just behind the two strangers. Lawrence Warwick IV—of the New London Warwicks, as he would tell anyone who would listen long enough—Dr. Patterson's protégé and graduate research intern at Chicago.

"Decided to put some work in, Chris?" Lawrence asked with an arched eyebrow.

Renee stuck her tongue out at Lawrence behind his back, and Chris didn't try to conceal his grin this time. "Miss me, Larry?"

His face turned a rich shade of puce even in the gloom. "Lawrence."

Patterson rolled his eyes and threw his arms up into the air. "Ugh! Can we cut and redo that?"

Only at this did Chris look more carefully at the men following Patterson. The one in front, a smallish sort of man, clean-shaven and with a sternly combed haircut, nodded once to his companion, a tall, blond man built like a diesel engine who turned off a shouldered camera with the press of a button. The smaller man looked excited, but the cameraman looked around disinterestedly, half-frowning, as if he wasn't sure what to do now that he wasn't working.

Once he saw the camera's red light wink out, Patterson rounded on Chris, who tried to keep a straight face at the wriggle of stomach accompanying the movement. "All right, look. Can you keep the games to yourself while our guests are here?"

"Actually, I don't think he's met them, have you Chris?"

Chris turned gratefully to Dr. Elliot Baxter. Taller than all of them but the cameraman, his shock of russet hair tousled like that of a movie star coming off the set, Dr. Baxter seemed out of place in the dreary business of cataloguing artifacts and brushing away eons of dirt. His five o'clock shadow highlighted his rugged good looks. Alone among the crew, he had the stoicism to wear long pants, which he'd tucked into his sand-coated boots. A smile played about his lips.

"No, I haven't, Doc," Chris called back, sidestepping Patterson to get a better look at the men Baxter was walking toward.

"Didn't think so," Baxter said lightly, though he snuck in a glance that said he knew quite well that he had just saved his pupil. "Mr. Fritz Kalten and Mr. Hans Richtein, of the Deutsche Presse-Agentur."

Chris had to smile as he shook hands with Kalten, the short reporter, who pumped his hand and beamed at him. The cameraman, Richtein, was still holding the camera with his right hand, and just waved with his left.

"So good to meet you!" Kalten enthused, his bright blue eyes drinking in Chris's features before looking over the chamber again. His German accent was noticeable, but his English was flawless. "We are here doing a piece on the excavation of this site! The original dig was conducted by the French, yes?"

"Um . . ." Chris hesitated. It sounded right, but then, he'd only glanced once at the pamphlet Baxter had given them about Mari, and that was five weeks ago.

"Yes, that's correct," Patterson jumped in, frowning once at Chris before turning a fleshy smile on Kalten. Nodding encouragingly, the newsman snapped his fingers at Richtein, who turned the camera back on. "Syria was under the control of the French at the time, of course, but the site's been opened to dozens of nations' archeologists since then . . ."

As the three meandered in the direction of the tented area's exit, Chris breathed out in relief and started toward Renee. Baxter put a hand on his shoulder, grinned, and said in a low voice, "I saved your butt there, kid. You owe me one."

"Yeah, I know," Chris said sheepishly. "Thanks, Doc."

"Dr. Baxter," Lawrence interrupted, his high, nasal voice making Chris wince. "I can only get some of the meaning out of this tablet I found. Can you help me with it? Oh, did I mention I found another one?"

Clearing his throat, Baxter turned away. "You did, Lawrence, but yeah, let me have a look . . ."

With all the others occupied, Chris turned back to where Renee had been crouching, dusting at artifacts, but found the area empty. He stepped out of the main chamber into the smaller side corridor from which Baxter had come, following it around and down. Insulated now from the natural light, the tunnel was lit by a strand of lamps, and as predicted, it was even hotter than the outside. The tunnel dead-ended with a ladder. "Renee?"

"Down here," came the reply.

Of course. Chris swallowed; he'd never much liked heights, and it didn't help that the steel ladder was wedged into a rock face that looked like it might crumble if breathed on wrong. But Baxter had been up and down the thing all day, and if Renee was down there, what could it hurt?

Twelve disconcerting feet later, Chris looked around and found Renee crouched in a corner of the room, face scrunched up in concentration, her dusting brush in one hand. She did not look at Chris as he knelt beside her, following her gaze to the wall. She frowned and traced it with her fingertips. "This doesn't look right . . ."

"What do you mean?" Chris couldn't see anything strange; it was a wall. Then again . . .

"The discoloration—see this?"

He spotted it an instant before Renee spoke, and now wore the same puzzled expression. Most of the room, and the corridor and main chamber above, consisted of block after block of the same stone, bleached by the sun and sandblasted long enough to become smooth and white long before the sands of time had buried them. But a four-foot-square patch of wall in this corner was a much deeper shade of stony beige, nearly the same as the sand on the desert surface, and its texture remained coarse. Both students traced their fingers across the rough rock, confused.

"This is so weird," Renee began, taking a pencil from her shirt pocket and scratching behind one ear with it. "Why would—"

"Ah!" Chris cried out, looking at his forefinger. The lancing pain had not deceived him; a rivulet of blood ran down his finger toward his palm, and a matching smear stained the stone in question. He grimaced. Patterson wasn't going to accept a sharp rock as an excuse for more "contamination."

"You okay?" Renee asked, concerned.

"Yeah, it's just a cut . . ." Chris began, but even as he spoke the blood flowed more freely. He frowned, looking back at the unusual bricks. They hadn't been that sharp . . .

"Geez, that looks pretty nasty," Renee said, digging around in her fanny pack for a moment before producing a bandage. "Here, let me."

Extending his hand to her, Chris momentarily forgot the mystery of the out-of-place, aggressive brick. Despite the oppressive heat, Renee's fingertips were still cool; they felt soothing against Chris's hand. He smiled despite himself, and when she met his eyes, Renee smiled too. She held his hand after the bandage had been applied, her thumb unconsciously massaging the bandaged part of Chris's finger.

"Want me to kiss it and make it better?" she asked lightly, but without laughing.

Chris kept himself from swallowing, determined to keep it cool. "That'd be nice."

She had just begun to lift his bandaged finger to her lips when the ladder clanged, making them both jump. Renee dropped Chris's finger, and he looked up in irritation at the interruption.

"What are you guys doing down here?"

Chris gritted his teeth. "Putting some work in, Larry, what does it look like we're doing?"

"Lawrence!" the older intern hissed as he took the final step down and dug his heels into the sand. Eyeing Chris's bandaged finger, he pinched the bridge of his nose and added, "Oh lord, you haven't contaminated anything else, have you?"

Chris rolled his eyes—hearing Patterson's words in Lawrence's voice struck him as unbearably sycophantic—but, in fairness, the blood stain would be a bit of a problem. He sighed and pointed over his shoulder. "It's just a scratch . . ."

Grumbling in irritation, Lawrence stalked over to them. "Where?"

"The corner brick."

Lawrence knelt down between Chris and Renee—Chris found himself resenting the forced separation as much as the intrusion—and glared for a moment before his expression relaxed infinitesimally. "Where?"

Chris turned back and pointed with his bandaged finger, only to stop and ask himself the same question. The brick was perfectly dry, not a hint of red, unique only in its difference from its fellows.

Wondering if Renee had cleaned up for him behind his back, Chris looked across Lawrence's shoulders at her, but her puzzled expression mirrored his own.

Shrugging, he ventured, "Must have taken the worst of it on my finger."

"Lucky for you," Lawrence replied, but he sounded too intrigued to be snide. He was frowning now, taking his glasses from his face to wipe the lenses before replacing them. He pointed, but didn't touch the brick himself. "This brick?"

"Yeah, that's the one."

"Look at the color! And the texture! This chamber must be almost four thousand years old, but this . . . it looks like they put it here last week!"

"Renee had just mentioned that . . ."

"DR. PATTERSON!" Lawrence yelled, cupping his hands around his mouth to make the sound carry. "COME SEE WHAT WE FOUND!"

"We?" Renee asked with narrowed eyes.

Lawrence smirked without looking at either of them, keeping his gaze on the brick. Chris's right hand balled into a fist as his lips curled back from his teeth. Lawrence caught the look, shrugged, and said, "Publish or perish."

"I swear to God, Larry . . ."

"Lawrence!" Lawrence snapped back, turning to face Chris. Temper cracking, Chris started forward, and Lawrence took a crouching step back. He bumped into Renee and, off-balance, both toppled to the sand. They smacked into the curious brick on the way down, one after the other, and both cried out.

Chris's face paled. Renee had put out a hand to steady herself, and it scraped across the brick, leaving a smear of blood. Lawrence had hit his head, and a nasty gash spilled blood down his face and onto his glasses, the tiny distributaries branching out across the lenses. Renee flexed her hand and whimpered at the sting.

"Renee!" Chris reached out a hand. "I'm so sorry!"

She turned her hand over to look at the wound, and they both gasped; it looked like someone had taken a knife to her palm. Renee groaned at the sight.

"Renee . . ."

"It's okay, just gimme a minute . . ." she said breathily, as if dizzy from the sight of the blood. She looked to her side, eyes lighting up with worry. "Is he okay?"

Chris heard voices and muffled footsteps above him as he glanced at Lawrence. He bent to check the other man's pulse when something caught his eye and his blood chilled.

The bloodthirsty brick looked for all the world as if it had just been cut from the quarry. Again.

"The brick," he began, his voice heavy with confusion. "What happened to the blood?"

Renee shifted up into a sitting position to stare, eyes wide. "I dunno . . . ah!" She winced again at the pain in her hand, grabbing her wrist convulsively this time. She stared at the wound, still dripping blood on the sand, which stayed red. "There must have been a stain."

"There was . . ."

Before either could speak again, air hissed past the brick's edges, like a puff of steam escaping a vent.

"Did you just see that?" Chris asked, convinced his eyes were playing tricks on him. Maybe the dust on the wall had been dislodged; Lawrence and Renee had certainly hit it hard enough.

Renee nodded nervously. "There was . . . what was that, smoke? Something behind the brick."

"Yeah." Chris was surprised to hear himself whispering. Suddenly, the excavated room felt claustrophobic, as if the smooth brick walls were crushing in on him like the booby-trapped rooms in old mummy movies. He swallowed.

Then Renee screamed.

Only shock kept Chris from screaming too. Untouched by either of them, the brick slid back an inch into the wall. A low, grating rumble accompanied the movement, the same sound a pyramid door would make as it slammed shut on hapless explorers . . .

Stop it. Chris was working himself up for nothing.

"What's going on down there?"

The voices above were now impossible to ignore. Patterson couldn't move too quickly, but he sounded close. The scuffle of footsteps and chatter of a foreign language suggested the news crew was with Patterson, so Baxter wouldn't be far behind.

"Crap," Chris muttered. Patterson would kill him when he found out that Chris had knocked out his prize pupil. Sighing, he raised his voice to call out, "We had an accident, Dr. Patterson. I think—"

"AGH!"

Renee's shriek cut Chris off and made his heart skip a beat. He turned in shock to see her disappearing in a shower of sand. The floor in the room's corner had vanished, leaving behind a black void, into which Renee and Lawrence tumbled. Chris caught a glimpse of fear in Renee's umber eyes before she fell from sight.

"RENEE!" he screamed, extending his hand after her on instinct before he forced himself back. The collapsing floor had stopped inches from the toe of his boot, and if he leaned much farther forward he'd disappear after her. He choked at the sound of two loud thunks far below, like bags of salt dropping onto a sand pile.

"What happened?"

"Chris!"

Patterson's voice bounced off Chris's conscious mind, an arrow deflected by the armor that terror had created for him. But the second voice, Baxter's confident but concerned tenor, pierced the fog spreading through Chris's thoughts, and he forced himself to look up.

Baxter and the cameraman, Richtein, stood at the top of the ladder, shoulder to shoulder and staring down. Chris pointed desperately at the hole. "The floor gave out. They fell!"

Without a word, Baxter put on a pair of work gloves, took two steps onto the ladder, placed his hands along the outside rails, and slid the rest of the way down. He was at Chris's side in an instant, as Richtein took his heavy camera in one hand and started down the ladder with the other. Even in shock, Chris found a moment to be amazed at the thick bands of muscle bulging under the German's shirt. He carried the camera like it was a flashlight.

"Chris," Baxter said forcefully, returning his student's attention to the matter at hand. Chris stood up and pointed, trying to keep his voice calm.

"There. They . . . they just fell, Doc . . ."

Nodding, Baxter stepped to the edge of the hole, taking his flashlight from his belt and flicking it on. Chris squinted down; the beam had very little effect, as if the darkness itself was a fog, preventing any light from penetrating its secrets.

"Renee? Lawrence?" Baxter called, concern evident even in his controlled voice.

"I'm here!" The sound of Renee's voice relaxed the icy hand that had clamped around Chris's heart. "I'm okay. I think Lawrence landed on his arm, though. He's still out, but he's breathing okay. I can feel his pulse."

Baxter sighed once in relief, glancing behind him. Richtein had joined them now, setting aside his camera and extending a hand to help Kalten, the reporter, down off the ladder. The burly cameraman then glanced up, saw Patterson testing the ladder with one foot, gave Chris a covert smirk, and braced the ladder, elbows locked. Chris smiled back despite himself; if a Buick climbed down the ladder, Richtein would probably only have grunted.

Thick hands clasping the top of the ladder rails to anchor himself, Patterson grumbled, "What happened, Elliot?"

"The floor gave out," Baxter said, sounding as curious as he was concerned. "There must be a subterranean chamber."

"Are they all right?" Kalten asked. His excited professional demeanor had taken a backseat at last.

"I think so . . ." Baxter began. Looking back into the hole, he angled the light down again and whistled. He raised his voice again. "Renee, that must be twenty feet at least. What broke your fall?"

"I did!" came the quick reply, and Chris heard a note of smugness in her voice. "Three summers of Judo camp."

Chris's sigh of relief turned into a hysterical laugh. Baxter just grinned and shook his head before his expression sobered. "We'll need to get down there and take care of Lawrence. Chris, grab the rappelling kit."

It had been placed off to the side of this room weeks before; Baxter had insisted on giving the three interns a crash course in rappelling when they had first come to Mari, though the twelve feet from the tunnel above hadn't been much of a challenge. Chris dragged the heavy equipment case across the sand, ignoring Patterson's scandalized look.

"Don't do that!" Patterson hissed. "You'll damage the—"

"Not now, Mitch," Baxter cut in, and though his voice was still calm, there was a note of command that Chris had never heard him use before with his senior. Patterson noticed the change too, and he looked up indignantly. Upon catching Baxter's expression, though, he let the matter drop with only a whimper as he watched Chris's progress.

Baxter opened the case and began to set the anchoring bolt in the rock, not even looking up as Dr. Patterson made more choking sounds while chips of rock flew. Sliding back across the room to give him space, Chris was surprised to see Richtein setting a second anchor, working even faster than Baxter. Baxter seemed surprised too, and when Richtein looked up, his disinterest had given way to a smug grin.

"Where did you learn?" he asked; it was the first time Chris had heard him speak. His voice was very deep, almost rumbling, and his accent was thicker than Kalten's.

"I did some climbing in college, and we had to rappel at Megiddo," Baxter replied. He looked interested. "You?"

"*Die deutsche Armee*," he replied, still grinning, and Baxter smiled back. Looking up at Chris's uncomprehending face, Richtein added, "German Army."

"How'd you wind up at dpa?" Baxter asked as he worked, but this time Hans Richtein's face clouded, and he did not reply.

Once they had the bolts anchored, it was the work of a moment to set the rappelling rope. Baxter tied a lantern to the end and lowered it down to Renee, the thick nylon hissing as it slid through the leather of his gloves.

"Got it!" she called from below. "Gee, it's dark down here . . . but you're clear, Doc, nothing underneath."

Baxter nodded, slipped on his rappelling harness, and lowered himself down from the lip of the hole without another word, the rope wrapped around the back of his waist, veins standing out in his arm muscles as he disappeared. Richtein made to follow, but Kalten put a hand on his arm and turned to Patterson.

"Herr Doktor," he began, sounding excited again now that the immediate danger had passed. "May we film? An action sequence, if you will?"

"Er . . . I suppose so," Patterson allowed with a wince.

Kalten either missed the look and tone or ignored them, instead turning to his cameraman with a positively glowing expression. "Hans, *bitte hol mir die Kamera*."

Richtein rolled his eyes, but set the rappelling rope back down and went to grab his camera. Kalten nodded approval, then gestured to the hole in the ground, his bright eyes now on Chris. "After you, sir, after you!"

Chris swallowed. Twenty feet on a rope was quite different from twelve on a ladder. But he stepped up, trying to think of Renee—who might need his help—and not the fact that falling that very distance had possibly broken Larry's arm . . .

Hooking the rope through the carabiner on his belt, he started to tie the rope into a seat, but when he hesitated over the knot, Richtein came to his aid, tying the Swiss seat with practiced ease. Chris smiled, took a deep breath, and lowered himself down into the darkness, eyes closed for fear that he wouldn't be able to resist looking down. The rope slid through his hands bit by bit, and he knew he didn't look anywhere near as graceful as Baxter had, but at least he was moving.

"That's it, Chris," Baxter called up. "Almost there."

Then, with a few more slides of the rope, Chris's booted feet hit sand. He slid the rope free gratefully, opened his eyes, then drew in a surprised breath. The darkness was so crushing that opening his eyes hadn't made much difference. He stepped back as the rope swayed, Kalten coming down now. "Renee?"

"Over here."

Turning toward her voice, Chris saw there *was* light. The lamp's dim glow threw Renee into focus; she was kneeling beside Lawrence's unconscious body. Baxter stood holding the climbing rope, and though he was only ten feet from the lamp, he was shrouded almost completely. Even the light from the room above seemed to dissipate a few feet below the hole.

Unnerved, Chris jogged over to Renee's side, kneeling down next to her. Without thinking, he put an arm around her shoulders. "Are you okay?"

Her warm smile erased his tension, and she put her uninjured hand on his side. "I'm fine. Just a couple scrapes, really."

They moved simultaneously to hug each other, then parted after a few seconds, smiling. Renee gestured down at Lawrence, and her expression became concerned. "Not sure about him, though. He hasn't woken up, and I don't want to slap him or anything; he might have a concussion. But his arm looks pretty bad."

Chris's stomach turned. Lawrence's forearm was bent at an angle at which Chris was certain forearms were not supposed to bend; he was probably better off unconscious. Nodding uneasily, Chris looked back to the much safer view of Renee's face. "Yeah, that does look nasty. Should we try and set it?"

"Better let me," Dr. Baxter's voice cut in from very close. Both students jumped; the sand had muffled his footsteps, and the dim light had thrown no shadows to warn them of his approach. As he knelt beside his injured student, probing the broken arm gingerly with his fingertips, he asked, "Renee, can you turn the light up at all?"

"Sorry, Doc, it's on maximum already."

Baxter paused, eyes narrowed. "I could have sworn I just put a new battery in that thing . . ."

They all looked at the lanternThe bright, intense white of the new bulb forced Chris to turn away after a second, but in that movement he saw the bright light smothered by the dark. It was surely a trick of the dust motes in the air, but the light itself seemed to bend like mist, keeping the lantern's glow bottled up in its immediate surroundings.

Without warning, a thin band of light cut through the air above them. The three turned as one to find Fritz Kalten and Hans Richtein standing side by side. Richtein had mounted a flashlight on his camera, and its beam, weaker than the lantern but narrower in focus, projected a few feet farther into the dark.

Renee's breath shook. "You scared me!"

"*Es tut*—" Hans started, but caught himself and said instead, "Sorry."

As Baxter went back to Lawrence, Kalten began to speak in German, and Richtein followed him with the camera, stepping slowly to be sure of his footing. Chris had just turned back to Renee when the cameraman's bass voice cut over all the other sounds.

"*Was ist das?!*"

"What's what?" Baxter asked, raising his head from his work, eyes narrowed. He looked over Chris's shoulder, then inhaled sharply. The widening of his eyes showed Chris how incredibly green they were, even in the gloom. "Whoa . . ."

"Wha . . ." Chris started, but when he turned it was obvious "what." In the middle of the room, illuminated by Hans's camera, was a large stone sarcophagus.

Chris stood warily, dimly aware that Baxter and Renee had done the same. Renee picked up the lantern and walked up to the sarcophagus, looking curious. Sudden misgivings kept Chris from sharing her enthusiasm; he didn't like the way the others all walked forward as if summoned.

"Renee . . ." he started, then clamped his teeth together. What would he say?

"What's going on down there?" Chris had forgotten about Dr. Patterson waiting above them in the excavated room. They had left him behind in case they needed help summoned—not that he could've climbed back up anyway.

Clearly, Chris wasn't the only one who had forgotten about the senior archaeologist. Baxter started, but didn't look away from the sarcophagus when he called back, "We found a sarcophagus, Mitch. It looks—"

"A burial chamber?" The irate tone vanished from Patterson's voice, replaced by interest and more excitement than Chris could ever remember there. "Really? With an intact sarcophagus! Mr. Kalten, are you getting this?"

Chris rolled his eyes but had only an instant for disdain before his attention returned to the sarcophagus. The others all kept advancing, their eyes distant, hands outstretched as if to touch it and make sure it was real. Lawrence's injuries seemed forgotten.

The unpleasant feeling returned, but now it was overpowering, and he couldn't keep his cry inside. "Don't! Don't touch it!"

Baxter shuddered as if shaken, but when he spoke, he did not turn away. "Why not?"

"I . . ." Chris hesitated. What could he say?

But now he wasn't the only one unsettled. Hans Richtein had stopped moving forward, and in the glare of his camera's mounted flashlight, Chris saw that his eyes were narrowed. His free hand twitched forward, as if to grab his boss by the back of his coat, but he seemed to think better of it and his fingers tightened into a fist.

Renee set the lamp down on the sarcophagus lid. "Can you read this writing, Doc?"

Baxter set his hands on the lid as well, and Chris's heartbeat accelerated. What was wrong with him?

"Some," Baxter said, and though his eyes narrowed in concentration, his voice was flat and emotionless. He lifted one hand off the lid and started to point to some characters, but his arm trembled, and he lowered his hand back to the lid. "Let's see . . . 'rest' . . . 'sleep' . . . 'king' . . . and 'blo—'"

"'King'?" Patterson's voice echoed down. If he had been excited before, he was nothing short of giddy now. "Could we . . . Elliot, a royal tomb! A Mari royal tomb! Elliot, we're going to be set for life with this! Mr. Kalten, you'll be the first to report the discovery of an ancient Mari royal tomb!"

Chris turned to Kalten, but from what Chris could see of his half-shadowed face, it was as vacant as Baxter's voice. Nodding absently, the reporter placed his hands on the sarcophagus lid next to Baxter's, a moment before Renee did the same on the professor's other side.

Chris saw their intent and gasped. "No!"

"*Nein!*" Hans echoed him, lowering his camera and reaching forward, but they were both too late. The three at the sarcophagus shoved in unison, and with a harsh rumble the lid moved aside several inches. Renee's lantern tumbled off the other end, crashing to the ground and giving a few spastic, feeble winks before dying.

Chris grabbed Renee by her hips and tried to draw her back, but she had latched her hands onto the rim of the opened sarcophagus and held on with desperate strength. Richtein had seized Kalten by the collar, and Chris saw the surprise in his face when he was unable to pull his boss away. The swell of muscle on the cameraman's arms should have allowed him to throw the reporter across the room.

"Renee," Chris moaned. "Renee, please . . ."

She lifted her left hand, and Chris nodded encouragingly, half-smiling. "That's right, now let go . . . come on . . ."

He never saw the blow coming. Renee's elbow drove hard into his stomach, winding him. Coughing, Chris released her and staggered back. The light from Hans's camera barely kept her silhouetted, even this close.

A grunt drew his attention. Kalten had tried the same thing on Richtein, who took the blow without a blink and struck back, his palm connecting with the side of the reporter's neck. Felled by the attack, Kalten toppled forward into the sarcophagus and slid into a gap just wide enough for his body—as if it had been made for him. He lay there, buried in the gloom up to his elbows, his hands draped over the sides of the sarcophagus and his rear hanging comically in the air.

Then he shuddered.

And then his body began writhing, his hands clawing at the stone, an anguished choke echoing from inside the sarcophagus. Chris cried out in horror, and the light on Kalten wavered as Richtein took a shocked step back. Kalten's fingers scrabbled uselessly against the stone, drawing blood as their tips and nails ground down with the effort. The reporter's whole visible body jerked as if electrocuted, then shuddered and lay still. Kalten slipped a bit, then slid back out of the sarcophagus to collapse on the ground. Richtein tracked him with the camera light.

This time, Chris couldn't bottle his scream. Even in the gloom, he saw the dead glaze on Kalten's eyes, glassy as a wax sculpture's. Chris's scream continued as he looked past the vacant eyes, past the mouth twisted in horror, and found the mutilated gash where Kalten's throat had been. The white of his spine shone through.

"What?" Patterson was obviously concerned and agitated, as he could not see anything for himself. "Christopher, what's happening?"

A scuffle drew Chris's attention away from Kalten's body before he could begin to formulate a reply. He looked back in time to see Baxter's upper body disappear into the sarcophagus.

Chris grabbed Renee a second before Baxter started twitching, one hand knotting in her hair and the other on her collar. He wrenched hard, and she came away from the stone this time, blinking as if she had just woken. The clouds in her eyes parted, and she blinked again in confusion before she finally noticed Kalten's body and shrieked, nails digging into Chris's arms. "CHRIS!"

He pulled at her desperately, shoes slipping on the sandy floor. "Renee, we need to go."

Baxter's body shuddered, grew still, and fell to the floor.

An iron hand on Chris's shoulder made him cry out, but Hans Richtein used it only to push him aside as he stepped past with a look of icy focus. The muscles across his barrel chest bulged. As he passed the pair, his hands tightened into fists and he grunted, "Run. Now."

Chris needed no more encouragement, and he dragged Renee toward the patch of dim light in the ceiling, the rope invisible. He clawed for it blindly, one arm around Renee's waist, the other swinging through the air. He tripped on the camera Hans had dropped and landed on his chest, the air driven from his lungs.

Another grunt caught his attention. Hans Richtein spasmed on the ground, though nothing was near him. Renee pulled Chris back to his feet, and they both spun as a breeze slashed across their backs, but nothing was there.

"Kids? What happened?" Patterson asked, his voice empty of anything but worry. Chris looked around and saw the rope at last. He laid a hand on it and Renee wrapped her arms around his neck. Did he have the strength to pull them both up? Could Patterson be of any help? Chris looked up at him.

Chris's lips moved, but horror had paralyzed his voice. Patterson leaned over the hole, a hand on the wall to steady himself as he peered through his glasses into the gloom.

And behind him . . .

Chris screamed anew, but it was too late for any of them now.

PAIN FLARED in Lawrence Warwick's arm as he awoke, blinking groggily. His head ached—what happened? Chris had come at him, he'd fallen—or had that little slacker pushed him? But why was it so dark? And sandier than he remembered; he had put a lot of effort into cleaning off the floor in that room; where had all this sand come from?

"—are mine now."

Lawrence didn't recognize the voice, but his head turned in its direction. A nauseating wave of disorientation rolled over him, but he managed not to cry out. Far too undignified, that, and what would that obnoxious Stanford kid think if he was whimpering about a fall?

"When I speak, you listen," the throaty voice continued. It was like nothing Lawrence had ever heard. Echoing on itself, some-how, with an aura of unquestionable authority. "When I command, you obey."

"Yes, Master."

This voice was more familiar, and Lawrence tried to push him-self up to see. Pain lanced up his left arm, and this time he could not smother his anguished cry. He landed on his stomach, his bro-ken arm under him, and the agony of that sharpened all his senses for an instant.

Looking past the smears of red on his glasses, he drank in the room with a glance. Not five feet away lay the reporter, Mr. Kalten, and Dr. Baxter, their throats carved out. In the light from a hole in the ceiling, Lawrence saw Dr. Patterson's corpse hanging upside-down from some sort of rope, its fatty folds of flesh deflated like balloons, his head barely attached for the rip across his neck. Below, on the ground, were two more bodies, their limbs akimbo. In the light of Mr. Richtein's camera, Lawrence saw Chris's face— but the rest of his body was facing the other way. His girlfriend lay beside him, still clutching the fabric of his shirt in death.

Beside them, two pairs of eyes had turned at Lawrence's cry. Hans Richtein's were manic, glaring, his well-built body tensed to react. And the other . . .

The shriek had only begun in the back of Lawrence's throat when that horrible red glow crossed the room and was upon him.

Many Years Later

ONE

Chicago, Illinois, USA

COLD, FAT raindrops splattered off the pavement and everyone caught outside. The damp smell of worms hung in the air. Potholes filled and overflowed onto the old streets as a bolt of lightning tore through the sky, illuminating the gray afternoon. The few cars hurrying through the neighborhood kicked up streams of water in their wake. Groups of two and three clustered together in doorways with hoods pulled over their heads or faces hidden behind their arms, their ragged sweatshirts and holey jeans whipping in the gale. A man waited under a bent street sign with his head down until someone walked past. The walking man slipped a sandwich baggie into the first's hand, then pocketed a twenty in return.

The few windows not covered by boards or bars were stained with grease almost to opacity or cracked open by errant baseballs hit from the park across the street. Here and there the holes were smaller, more focused.

Every third streetlight functioned on the best roads, and passersby sometimes wondered whether the thick construction rent-a-fences strategically placed around the edges of the neighborhood—for planned efforts that never seemed to get to the construction stage—were to keep the denizens of the projects in, or simply to make them less visible to the rest of the city.

A sharp step disturbed a puddle, splashing water and mud aside. The few droplets that plopped back onto the boot slithered off like rats deserting a sinking ship. A few heads rose, eyes focusing through the hazy rain on the figure, blurred by the downpour but still recognizable. Bodies pressed closer together, heads lowered again, muttered conversations silenced, and all eyes turned away.

All but two.

A man in a faded Bears sweatshirt started forward, an unsprung switchblade materializing in one hand and a small, confident smirk growing on his lips. He made it two steps before a hand seized his sweatshirt, dragging him back. The smirk curled into a sneer as he regarded the friend who had grabbed him.

The other man's eyes were wide beneath the brim of a baseball cap so soiled the team was unrecognizable. He shook his head.

"Man, he's right there," the first one complained, tapping the knife just below the spring button with his thumb.

"Naw, man, don't do it," the second said. When the first looked back to his would-be target, the restraining hand tightened. "Man, *don't*."

"One scrawny guy?"

"Bro, you remember Lenny Nelson last year?"

The thumb tapping the knife froze. "Yeah . . ."

"You remember what happened to him?"

"What about it?" The voice was a whisper this time, barely audible over the rain.

The second man just tilted his head toward the subject of their argument. The first pair of eyes went as wide as the second, and the switchblade was gone as quickly as it had appeared. The two friends stepped back onto the sidewalk as one, arms crossed and eyes down, reluctant to even have the hazy figure in their peripheral vision.

The figure, a young man, was dressed all in black. His pants were pressed and his dress shirt buttoned all the way to its banded collar. His sleek leather duster hung to his calves and tight-fitting black gloves sheathed his hands; a bitter gust billowed the coat back and molded his clothes to his tall, slender frame. Chicago had not seen the sun in weeks, but its light might never have touched the deathly pale face; his dark eyebrows glistened in the rain. His long, black hair was tied into a neat ponytail, though the wind whipped it about his shoulders, and the contrast against his pallor framed the slight points of his ears. He kept his face forward and his steel gray eyes focused, meeting no gaze. The rain smacked off his face with no more effect than the cold—no turned head, no shielded eyes, no wiped brow. He stalked more than strode across the street.

A few people had clustered on the porch of one building, taking cover under what remained of the roof. Their shoes scraped on the concrete as they scrambled out of the young man's way. He might have walked right through them had they held their ground, but instead he passed by without a glance and batted the cracked front door open with his fingertips.

The carpet of the front hall was stained a dull brown; even the original architect could not have found traces of the original royal blue. The young man strode up the sagging stairs, the echoes of his bootsteps muted in the vacant halls even when he stepped on bare wood; only the water dripping from his clothes marked his presence.

A small child cringed on the landing between the third and fourth floors. The young man reached the landing and paused, the only movement the flexing of his gloved fingertips. After a moment, he took a silent step and knelt beside the cowering boy, grasped the child's hand in his iron grip, and pulled it away from the boy's face. Black and purple bruises covered the child's jawline and upper chest, visible under the collar of his T-shirt. The dark-garbed man stood without a word, his cold expression unchanged. He was halfway up to the fourth floor when a woman appeared at the top of the stairs. "Tom, where did you—"

She saw Simon and cut off abruptly. She had a distinct shadow on her cheek and a swollen lower lip, and her left arm was held up in a makeshift sling. The pale man's face might have been etched in stone as he motioned the woman aside with a flicking gesture, as if shooing away a bothersome insect. She shuffled back, lowering her head, and the young man moved past her.

She spotted her son on the landing below; he had turned his shadowed face up at the sound of her voice. The woman's expression crumpled as she gazed at her son, and her face turned to the young man again as he laid his hand on the next railing. Her eyes widened, but she looked at her boy again, then blurted out, "Simon!"

Simon—the only name the young man had ever supplied to the residents and squatters—paused, one foot on the stair. Water continued to drip from his coat onto the floor. He turned his head enough to look at the woman sideways, and when he spoke she shivered. "What do you want?"

Her words fell out of her mouth uncontrolled. "My husband, he . . . when he's been drinkin' he . . . well, look at my boy!" She gestured with her good arm at the lower landing; Simon did not look. "If it were just me, I'd . . . I wouldn't ask . . . I'd never want . . . but my little guy . . . he ain't never done nothin' wrong. I just wanna help him . . ."

She lost her composure then, falling to her knees and starting to cry. Her good hand pawed at Simon's coat as a cold November wind whistled down the hallway through a broken window on the landing. "Can you . . . is there anything . . . ?"

Words failed her. Simon's expression flickered—a wince of the muscles in his eyelids. He looked down at the boy, then back at her. The silence dragged on as he stared. He finally reached down with one gloved hand and took the woman's uninjured arm in a vicelike grip, pulling her to her feet. He gestured with his free hand down the hall of doors. "Which one?"

Trembling, the woman pointed to a door that stood ajar. Simon's empty voice again cut the silence. "May I enter?"

She whispered, "Go in," and Simon tapped open the door with the toe of his boot and stepped over the threshold. The apartment held almost no furniture, save for an old TV and a small refrigerator. A feculent smell coming from a half-closed door identified the bathroom. A few pieces of cardboard sheathed with newspaper and scraps of cloth were stretched out on the floor to serve as beds. A mattress with several holes in it was situated across the room, surrounded by pulled-out stuffing and broken beer bottles. The rank smells of stale alcohol, urine, semen, and blood wafted throughout the room. Dark stains covered the rotting floor, and the wallpaper on the one finished wall had peeled to shreds; the others were pockmarked drywall. A slightly dented wooden baseball bat leaned against the wall next to a pile of unfolded clothes. Simon watched a pair of cockroaches scuttle across the floor, then retreated seconds after he had entered, nose wrinkling. He resumed his journey toward his room, pausing only once to look the mother in the eyes; she opened her mouth as if to speak, but quailed under his piercing gaze.

Simon finished the trek to his room on the fifth floor and drew a key from his coat pocket to unlock the door. He entered his room, closing the door behind him, and the clicks of many locks sealed him away.

RED, GREEN, blue, and yellow streams of light cut through the endless sea of black, always moving. Faces were illuminated for a second, and beads of sweat on intertwined bodies glowed with residual light for a second more. Lips pressed together and bodies locked in sensuous embraces, all before the hungry eyes of a hunter.

Simon sat in the shadows, the mad scene of controlled chaos below lost on him. The smells of sweat and alcohol mingled in his nose, the intoxicating fragrance of life. He closed his eyes, and still he could almost taste the pulsating energies of the people around him. He felt their excitement, their eagerness, their passion and desire.

And he heard their heartbeats.

They pulsated in his ears like a living percussion ensemble, the quick and high-tempo beats of the dancers intermingling with the slow, relaxed beats of those resting on the sidelines. Had they been real drums, the discord would have been impossible to follow, but he could pick each heartbeat out individually if he concentrated hard enough. Every rhythmic pulse put pressure on his eardrums, and his fingertips tingled as if he could touch their quivering veins as blood rippled through them.

Simon sat alone in the Blood, Sweat, and Tears club, far from those he watched. Painfully, patiently, he forced himself to wait, spinning a dry shot glass on his table and surveying his surroundings. It was good to practice self-control, and it made the reward all the sweeter when it came.

The battle between the air conditioning and the sweating bodies raged on, neither side ever to be victorious. Hundreds of bodies crowded a dance floor meant for half their number fifty feet below the swirling lights. The DJ's stand towered over the floor, accessible only by a ladder. A terrible fire hazard, to be sure, but Simon imagined it gave the DJ a sense of power and control as he looked down at the masses dancing to his tune.

From his own vantage point, Simon shook his head. *Pathetic.*

The bouncers at the door, he granted, were an upside to the club. He had seen all that Chicago had to offer, and it got better than this, but the bouncers kept the riffraff out, and that kept the attendance to those who had a way with people.

Simon had his own way with people. His eyes flicked toward the door; the bouncer had been adamant that Simon could not enter . . . and then Simon had met his eyes. He smiled briefly at the memory, lips curling back. His teeth glimmered in the passing light.

The lights dimmed to a haze, then died. The speakers fell mute. Simon felt a ripple of eagerness wash over the assembled masses, and he watched their movements. He could almost see better without the light, the flashing beams no longer hindering his eyes, which pierced the darkness and the mist that had begun to seep from the cheap fog machines below the DJ's stand. The smoke that belched forth had the distinct odor of burned wet leaves, but the partiers still shivered as the cold mist coursed over their bodies, a ghostly caress in the dark.

Simon snorted and spun his glass again.

Whirling, deep purple lights blazed back to life, projected not only from the overhead lights but from small, wall-mounted systems as well. With a hiss of hydraulics, the ceiling lights descended, spinning in slow, deliberate circles and arcs. The bass line of a haunting heavy metal beat pounded from the speakers and rattled the glass tabletop under Simon's hands. Fingers laced through the hair at the backs of skulls, nails clawed at exposed flesh, arms tightened around bodies, and they were back to it.

Simon rolled his eyes—and then stopped mid-roll, his entire body freezing so totally that he seemed a lifeless corpse propped up in the chair. The glass slipped from his fingers and cracked against the tabletop. He leaned forward, and all others in the room faded from his sight as he stared at her.

Tight leather pants clung to her form, tied together by two dozen knots up each side. Her halter top cut off above her midriff, and a ring pierced the skin of her belly button. Shining black leather boots matched the unusual sheen in her long ebony hair, tied into dozens of small braids with a single thicker strand in the middle. She swayed with the music, beckoning men to her and pushing them away again after a moment of contact, a second's euphoria before the return to the real world. Her tongue traced her painted lips, leaving a hint of glittering blue on the tip.

Simon's breathing became shallow and rapid. His steel eyes tightened hungrily, and his lips parted, molding themselves to a phantom vein in the air. Her heartbeat rang clearly in his head above all the others, a snare drum amidst basses, and he drew a deep breath through his nose. Her scent seasoned the mist and the air-conditioned breeze. Staring hard and deafening his senses to the rest of the world, he saw and felt her pulse, measured and lusty.

Simon rose from his chair and took to the stairs, ignoring the people who lurched out of his way or squawked in protest as he brushed them aside. The club had overdone the fog, as it often did, and it obscured and distorted even those figures closest, but Simon's other senses had not misplaced his target, and he entered the crowd. Bodies slammed against his, long fingernails traced the smooth leather of his coat, and soft skin caressed his strong cheekbones, only to be withdrawn again, startled by the unnatural cold of his flesh. He never shoved but never broke pace, letting people slide off his shoulders like waves against a rock, slipping through sheets of neon mist until the last tendrils coiled away and he found her.

Perfect though his vision was, she was even more desirable point-blank. He could count the individual beads of sweat on her bare back, her top tied only by a string at her neck and another midway down her spine. Her eyes, an inviting shade of sparkling green, were vivid and alive. Simon stepped into her gaze, and she was transfixed. The dancers around her, expecting her to move sinuously on, came to an awkward halt as she froze in their midst, but Simon couldn't spare them the attention to care.

They stared for a moment, her charms fighting against his preternatural attraction. Then he held out a hand covered in a form-fitting leather glove. She took it and stepped into his embrace.

Her body pressed against his, her warm skin separated from his only by her thin covering, and the equally thin layer of black he wore. His eyes half-closed as he drew a ragged breath, momentarily overcome by the sheer vitality he inhaled, before he fixed her with his gaze again. He traced his gloved hands up her back, his senses so attuned that he felt every muscle in her body even through the tight leather. She ran her hands up his chest and behind his neck, locking one behind his skull as the other slid down his thigh.

The inescapable hunger seized him; he tried to suppress it, as before, but as she could not escape him, nor could he escape himself. His desire grew as she pressed her body to his, and the vessels in his hands, neck, and face contracted. He closed his eyes, struggling against the unstoppable urge, and his hands clung to her form, holding her so close that his cold body grew tepid, nearly warm. But then he felt the familiar pokes of two tiny pinpricks on the inside of his lower lip.

Simon spun her then, moving in a slow but deliberate circle. He touched his lips to her neck and she quivered. It was all too easy to direct her across the floor, ignoring the envious looks from those they passed, and vanish into the fog-shrouded semidarkness under the staircase that Simon had descended only a moment before, where shadows reached out to enfold them.

The woman's nails slid down Simon's chest as she kissed his neck. Her other hand took his wrist and slid his hand along her side, brushing easily under the flimsy fabric of her shirt. One leg slid up against Simon's thigh. The pounding metal beat faded to a whisper in the young man's ears with his head so close to hers. He squeezed his eyes shut, breathing hard, but he was so attuned to her now that her pulse tickled his lips as each heartbeat disturbed the air between them.

Opening his mouth to breathe hot air against her skin and clasping the back of her neck with his free hand as she shuddered against him, he sucked air in past teeth far too long to be a man's. The taste of her scent stung the back of his throat and the shreds of his restraint burned to cinders.

Her body lurched as his sharp teeth sank into her neck, her fingers digging into his skin as she managed a choked gasp. Simon withdrew his teeth quickly, then lowered his lips to her bleeding throat and took in the warm fluid. It coursed down his dry throat, bringing rejuvenation to the dried-out husk his body had become. A second after the initial shock, his victim's spasming muscles relaxed, the overwhelming magic of his killer's kiss consuming her.

He would need to stop soon, keep her only wounded. They were a chance spotlight away from being illuminated for all to see and surrounded by people who would not remain oblivious forever. Simon knew all this, but the rush of hot blood lured him on. He drank more, then more, draining her life force to feed the ceaseless fire of his thirst. What difference would it make, one swallow more or less? His face warmed, and his body tingled with power . . .

Simon felt a small nudge on his lip. He opened his eyes and withdrew from the woman in shock. The veins all over her body stood out, and her stunning features were masked beneath the powerless horror that had become her expression. Her skin had paled from rich mocha to waxy beige, and the color had faded from her eyes. His empty form had changed places with hers, his body now rich and strong while hers was almost drained, withered, and dried out. He let her slide out of his arms, and her chilled body sunk to the warm floor.

Simon's mouth hung open a shade, unconscious of the dribble of red sliding from the corner of his lip toward his chin. She was not dead, but the weak strain of her pulse assured him the moment was not far off. How many heartbeats did she have left? Half a hundred? Fewer? Her gasps for breath were so weak even Simon strained to hear them. For a moment, he wondered if she had come alone . . . why she had chosen this club, this night . . . what her name was . . .

Seconds passed, and Simon knew he could spare no more time. He looked over those too close for fog to obscure, but the darkness masked murderer and murdered alike; even those who had envied Simon his conquest had let him pass out of their minds. No one was coming; no one had seen.

A single careful flick of one finger split the skin between the two puncture marks, though precious little blood remained to seep from the broadened wound. A knife strike, certainly; all but the most careful examiners would think so. Simon hesitated, then brushed the lids down over the girl's pale, emptily searching eyes. A moment premature, but inescapable nonetheless.

He rose in a whirl of black leather and slid through the narrowest spaces between dancers, turning his face from every light that flashed his way as he brushed the blood from his chin with the back of one hand. He was through the side exit door before anyone's eyes could fix on him.

The alleyway leading from the nightclub to the street was dark. Mist rose from sewer covers, and the afternoon's freezing rain had become quiet snow. Amidst the silent, countless crystals of falling white, Simon strode away from the club, hands in his pockets. His steps were a bit rushed, quickened by the knowledge that eventually some other couple would stagger into the darkness beneath the stairs, intoxicated with each other; it would take only seconds for horror to overtake lust. As his tongue traced the inside of his teeth, Simon's fangs slid back up into his head. A newspaper wafted by on the wind, and Simon snatched it from the air with delicate grace, wiped the bloodstains from his mouth, then crumpled the paper and tossed it aside. He breathed in, then exhaled, a small fog passing his lips as his still-hot breath met the air and the last evidence of his handiwork was borne away on the chill breeze.

Alert for the sound of sirens, Simon emerged onto the sidewalk and nearly collided with a tall man who was laughing as he scooped a toddler up from where the boy had been kicking up tufts of snow while giggling.

"I'm sorry," the man said to Simon with a sheepish grin. The vampire took a single step back as the man's wife came up on the other side and took the boy. Their son had apparently concealed a chunk of snow in one of his blue mittens, because he clapped it immediately on her head and squealed as the woman shook the snow from her hair and feigned a glower at the boy that gave way to a smirk.

Still chuckling, the father gave Simon a chin nod and a smile before he and his family moved on. Stepping onto the sidewalk, Simon watched the man put his arm around his wife's shoulders. The little boy looked over his mother's shoulder, locking eyes with Simon for a second. As snow collected in his long hair and he heard at last the first, faint screams from the club, Simon watched the family go until they rounded the corner.

HOURS LATER, Tricia Corley sat in a corner of her apartment, her son Tom in her lap. They could hear the heavy, staggering footsteps on the stairs, and the boy started to squirm. Tricia kissed his forehead and brushed his hair with her uninjured arm while whispering empty words of comfort.

The door wobbled twice, the handle jiggering, then burst open. Tom Corley Senior stumbled through, a beer bottle in his right hand, the dregs swilling around the bottom. His tank top undershirt, stretched thin over his gut, was stained with sweat that Tricia smelled across the room. His work shirt hung over one shoulder.

"Bitch of a shift," he started, but then peered around, his expression turning contemptuous. He spat on the floor. "Dammit, didn't I tell you t' clean this place? How many times, huh? How many fuckin' times I gotta tell you?"

Tricia clambered to her feet, reaching out to him, but he shoved her down to the floor. As he did, his shirt slid down his greasy arm and into a damp patch of mold on the floor. "Jesus, now look at this!" he snapped. "What am I suppose t' do, wear that shit to work tomorrow?"

"I'm sorry," Tricia whispered, reaching to pick the shirt out of the mess, but her husband drove her back with a kick that missed by several inches. He rolled his eyes, picked up the shirt in a ball, and threw it at her.

"Sorry my ass, just fix it!"

She raised her arms instinctively to catch the shirt, then cried out when she moved the broken one. She bit her lip, but the boy saw the pain on her face and began to cry.

Tom sneered. "What's his problem? Didn't you get him food today?"

"Couldn' afford it," Tricia mumbled, adjusting her sling to keep herself from flinching again.

"What? Bitch, what do I work for? What do I give you money for?"

The response came to her lips before she could control it. "You don't; you spend it all at the bar."

Her eyes widened and her good hand flew to her mouth, but the words were out and the damage done. Tom's angry expression froze over, and with a shake of his head he reached for the baseball bat. The bottle he had carried in his hand dropped to the floor and shattered on an already dark spot. Tricia scooted over to her son and shielded him with her body.

As Tom laid the bat over his shoulder and advanced, a black-gloved hand seized the business end from behind and levered it down. Taken by surprise at the force and abruptness of the attack, pain lancing through his shoulder, Tom roared and dropped to his knees. He turned awkwardly to swing the bat around, and the same gloved hand caught it.

"Oh fuck!" Tom said, eyes widening as he took in the ferocious expression on Simon's face. All the blood drained from his own face as he half-screamed, "Motherfucker, it's him! Trish, it's him!"

Simon jerked the bat out of Tom's grip and slammed the blunt end into his gut. As the man coughed and choked, Simon whirled in a blur of his dark coat and smashed the handle of the bat across Tom's chin. Tom dropped, screaming and holding his mouth, which was leaking blood. Three teeth lay on the floor, and his jaw bloated where it had broken in several places.

Simon stared at the bat for a moment as Tom scrambled back, spitting blood and clawing his way toward his wife and son. Then, as if he had awoken from a daze, Simon took the bat in both hands and snapped it in two. Tom looked back at the sound, terror flashing over his face before he lurched into the corner, pushing Tricia and little Tom in front of him.

"Ta' 'em!" he slurred as much as his swollen mouth allowed. "Ta' 'em! Lemme 'lone!"

Simon started forward, and little Tom screamed and hid his face in his mother's chest. But Simon just reached over them both and grabbed Tom Senior by the wrists he'd held up to cover his head. Lifting the man bodily into the air, Simon slammed him back down on the other side of his family, then kicked him hard enough to send him skidding across the floor and into the doorframe. He spared Tricia and her son one emotionless glance, then stepped into the hallway, dragged Tom Corley out, and closed the door behind him.

For an instant there was quiet, punctuated only by whimpers and hard breathing. Then the horrible screams started, a twisted soprano melody with the flat slaps of hard strikes meeting flesh as the bass counter. Tricia held her child's head against her breast with one hand covering his other ear, quivering at the force she had called into work. She had been terrified and despairing when she spoke to Simon, but now . . . but if it saved her son . . .

The thunks continued, even as the screams died into whimpers. A few times, a heavy thud rattled the door on its frame; the final time, the jamb pulled away from the splintering wood. Wet cracks issued from the hall twice, each followed by a piercing shriek of agony that rattled Tricia's teeth. Then the door fell open and husband and wife locked eyes as he toppled through. Tears streamed from Tom Corley's eyes, swollen almost shut already. His arms were mangled in strange directions and discolored with bruises around the elbows; one wrist pointed back toward his face. He managed a whimper, blubbering through lips no longer fully attached, and tried to drag himself back in with his elbows.

A gloved hand grabbed him by the hair and dragged him, moaning, back into the hall.

It was several long minutes before Tricia could force herself to set her son on the mattress and crawl to the door to close it. She listened at the crack, knowing everyone else on the floor was doing the same thing, but there was nothing to hear now. She couldn't muster the nerve to stick her head outside the door, and she knew that even if she found the courage, no one else would.

Listening intently, she jumped as the fifth floor door above her closed with a soft creak.

TWO

Newark, New Jersey, USA

THE WAVES on the Kill Van Kull lapped against the MS *John Polidori* as it sailed toward Newark Bay, the murky water opaqued to a green sheet by the thunderclouds that threatened overhead. The day was still waning, but the sun had long since been obscured in the distance. Fog swirled in the *John Polidori's* wake like ethereal tendrils probing at the hull, and a heavier mist that threatened to congeal into rain had forced the ship to run with all lights on; the glowing torch of Lady Liberty was a vague smear of orange across Upper New York Bay.

Only seven days out of Marseilles, the *John Polidori* was set for a December 5 arrival in Newark, three days ahead of schedule—luck almost unheard of in the choppy waters of the North Atlantic in winter. The days had seen their fair share of waves and chill, but every night they had calmed so thoroughly that the *John Polidori* slid through the water like a toboggan down a hill. Though more than a little confused at his sudden good fortune, Captain Roger McClarren wasn't going to question it.

Forty-seven years old and gone slightly to seed, though the arms of his faded sea jacket strained at the bulge of muscle beneath, McClarren had a face tanned to the consistency of leather. His sharp blue eyes were recessed deeply into his skull and a bit covered by heavy flesh, but they missed nothing. He gritted his teeth as the wind lashed his cheeks, though no sea breeze had stung in a decade.

"Damn fog," he growled.

At a hundred and forty feet wide, the *John Polidori* was nothing even close to the thousand feet of the Kill Van Kull that separated Staten Island from New Jersey, but more than enough to smash to rubble any smaller craft that drifted into her path. McClarren had seen it more than once; some fisherman or pleasure yachter listening to his damn headphones or i-whatevers, obliterated under the unforgiving bow of a tanker or carrier like an egg smashed with a rock. Though the crew and their GPS on the *John Polidori*'s bridge would ensure the ship never drifted too close to the shore or any of God's obstacles, there was no technology to keep the ship out of the way of other men's stupidity.

McClarren growled aloud.

"Making good time, Skipper," the first mate ventured, standing a few paces back. Wearing only an insulated vest despite the winter's chill, tattoos inked up both massive arms, the mate ran a hand over his bald head, shaking it with a small, disbelieving smile. "Best I've ever sailed."

"Me too," McClarren conceded grudgingly. He and Lorraine, the mate, had sailed together a dozen times now; each man had the measure of the other, and they made a good match. McClarren had already decided to offer Lorraine a contract for another five trans-Atlantic trips—once he talked the company rep at Newark into the deal. McClarren sighed. *He may be French, but he's still one of the best.* And besides, the man had been sailing since he was fifteen; he belonged to a country no more than the gulls above them.

As the *John Polidori* sailed deeper into the channel, McClarren reflected that the voyage, despite its swiftness, had not been without its share of debacles. They had missed the Azores completely. Of course, the Azores weren't on their offloading schedule, but with the pace they had set, McClarren had considered giving the men a day's worth of liberty on the little Portuguese islands. But a claustrophobic blanket of fog and the threat of lightning on the horizon had cancelled that diversion straightaway. It had been all the new navigator and his crew could do to avoid crashing into the islands themselves. They had been forced to sail completely around, though they had somehow managed to make up time in the process.

More irritating were the crew shortages. It was a fact of life that at least one crewman would jump ship at every port, but there were no ports between Marseilles and New York, and yet an unusual number of crewmen had gone missing. A few had missed roll call after inspection at Gibraltar, and Lorraine was of the view that they had slipped off on one of the customs boats; certainly it was too far for the average seaman to swim to shore. But then more had vanished by the time they hit the Azores, and Captain McClarren was not convinced by the half-hearted suggestion that those men had been so desperate for shore leave that they'd swum to islands eight hundred miles from the mainland.

Searching the ship was a useless endeavor; even if they hadn't been short half a dozen men, the container ship was simply too big, with too many towers of container crates, to find a man who did not wish to be found. Perhaps they were hiding out and planning to jump ship in Newark? McClarren gritted his teeth. He'd have a word with the harbormaster to have security on alert; the men wouldn't escape to the mainland unless they *literally* jumped ship . . .

"Post a secondary deck watch," he barked. "Eyes on the sides. I want to know if anyone tries slipping off before we dock."

Lorraine frowned, brushing at the mustache that curved down past his mouth. "I went through the ship myself with two of the men. Unannounced, you know. We didn't find a trace of anyone, sir."

He hesitated, and McClarren narrowed his beady eyes. "And?"

"And . . ." Lorraine looked disconcerted for a moment. ". . . and O'Banion's gone now too, sir."

"O'Banion?" McClarren's eyes seemed to pop into existence on his face. "What the hell's happening on my ship?!"

Though third mate Aaron O'Banion had a mouth so foul he alone could have carried on the stereotype of sailors for a generation, he was also loyal and hardworking. He would never jump ship.

"I don't know, Captain," Lorraine said, perturbed. "Maybe we lost him in that storm two days back? I haven't seen him since."

"No, I saw him last night, he took the watch," McClarren said, running a grease-coated hand through his hair. He shook his head. "What the hell . . ."

They stood in silence for a moment, the roar of the *John Polidori*'s engines echoing as they passed under the rusty Bayonne Bridge. As the fog before them thinned, the lights of Port Newark glowed ahead. McClarren shook his head and glanced over his shoulder.

"Set that watch. We'll deal with the O'Banion thing once we've got Port Authority around to keep some order."

"Aye aye, sir. Who do you want on the watch?"

McClarren almost snapped off "anyone," but thought better of it; if his crew really was jumping ship, he needed good men to watch them. "Take Reese, he's solid. Tierney. Chekhov, if he's out of sick bay. And the new guy, I like him. Big blond."

Lorraine needed no further explanation. From the crew on the cargo carrier, there was only one person who would be specially noted as "big."

"Right. Hans Richtein."

"SO WHY are we here again?"

The two Port Authority police officers looked at each other, wearing identical expressions of exasperation. Kyle Warren, of the Immigration and Customs Enforcement office, lounged on the hood of the Port Authority's modified Jeep Cherokee, looking bored. In contrast to the two uniformed officers, Warren wore plain clothes, his badge on a neck chain beneath his dark T-shirt, and his gun in a shoulder holster. He also wore stylish sunglasses, despite the fact that the day was growing more overcast by the minute.

"The captain of the *John Polidori* wanted some men here when his ship docked," Nick Rossini, the senior of the two Port Authority cops, replied with strained patience; it was the third time he'd given this same speech. "He's had problems with men jumping ship on this trip. Wants us to watch for stowaways, too."

Warren brushed his sunglasses down to the tip of his nose, exposing the skeptical look in his brown eyes. "Okay, rephrase. Why am I here?"

Rossini's mouth tightened into a hard line, so his compatriot spoke instead. "Don't you think people jumping ship into the United States without registering *might* come under the jurisdiction of Immigration?" Charlie Page asked in a scathing tone. He had taken the Port Authority job after narrowly failing the ICE exam, hoping the practical experience in such a major department would help his next application. That was three years ago, and the bitterness lingered.

"Yeah, probably," Warren sighed.

Before them all floated the *John Polidori*, its massive anchor chains disappearing into the murky waters at the bow and stern of the ship. A strong gust blew in from the bay, and Warren winced theatrically. "Nothing like the smell of fish in the afternoon . . ."

At first, the Port Authority officers had stood ramrod straight, identical models of stoicism as Warren threw punches and kicks in the air, paced back and forth, and whistled to himself. Charlie had twitched when, ten minutes into their vigil, Warren drew his pistol and took to sliding the magazine in and out, but Nick remained unmoved, as if to demonstrate how a professional should behave.

Hours later, though, Warren had taken to reclining against the hood of the Jeep, and even Page and Rossini were leaning on a nearby stack of containers and staring blankly at the *John Polidori*. The cranes, striped red and white like horizontal candy canes, continued to shift the cargo containers from the ship to the dock, a never-ending rainbow of steel boxes carrying who knew what. Like clockwork, forklifts came for the majority of the containers, those that did not have flatbeds ready and waiting and were not bound for additional screening. Other Port Authority and Customs officers had already gone up and down the gangway twice to attend to the cargo manifest and speak to the captain.

The fog grew thicker, and the nauseating odor of oil mixed with the Hudson River drifted with it. The skyline in the west had all but claimed the hazy bright spot that passed for sunlight.

Warren opened his mouth at the same time an orange cargo container crashed to the ground fifty yards away; his words were lost amidst the scraping shriek of steel on concrete. All three officers winced, then Nick Rossini looked over. "Say again?"

"How—much—longer?" Warren repeated loudly and slowly, as if to a small child.

Rossini grimaced, but said, "There shouldn't be many more, it looks like the deck's mostly—"

"Hey, look!"

Charlie Page drew their attention back to the ship. On the *John Polidori*'s deck, one of the sailors was screaming at the crane operator so loudly that those on shore could hear every word, his cursing so vicious that all three police officers recoiled in surprise. The sailor then charged to the gangway and was on the ground before anyone reacted.

"Hey . . ." Warren started, frowning now.

Charlie looked at Nick. "Isn't that what we're supposed to be stopping?"

"Yeah," Nick grumbled, straightening his gun belt and placing one hand on his handcuffs. The radio at his hip crackled to life.

"*Unit three, crane operator reports one of the deck crew has left the ship.*"

"We see it, moving to intercept," Nick said, even as the ICE agent slid off the hood of the Jeep and Charlie ran around to the driver's seat.

"*Copy. Handle as you see fit, but if you can, try to get him back on the ship peaceably. Might just be a misunderstanding.*"

"10-4," Nick said, but he frowned. *Yeah, misunderstanding.* He climbed into the back of the Jeep; Warren was already in the front passenger seat, his SIG in hand. When the lights of the Jeep illuminated the scene, Nick's mouth fell open. The sailor already had the cargo container that had fallen up on a forklift, and even as the Jeep's engine growled to life, the forklift scooted forward and out of sight.

"Gun it!" Warren cried. Nick found himself surprised that anything had cracked that arrogant, bored veneer. But Charlie Page needed no encouragement, and the Jeep roared off in pursuit. They rounded the corner the forklift had taken in seconds and saw it disappearing down a towering alley of crates.

"Misunderstanding my ass." Nick shook his head, then pointed farther down the harbor. "Cut him off at the next junction. No, keep 'em off," he added as Charlie reached for the emergency light switch. "And kill the headlights. Don't warn him where we're coming from."

The lanes of crates were not long, but even a single crate was taller than the Jeep, so they had no trouble remaining stealthy with the lights off. The forklift drove deeper into the harbor, ambling away from both the ship and the exit. Nick glanced out the window, and noticed with a frown that they seemed to be leaving *everything* behind, though the fog was so thick he couldn't be sure.

The Jeep took the next corner so quickly that the back tires fish-tailed out, but Charlie compensated and zipped forward to obstruct the narrow lane between the container stacks, boxing the forklift in. He was out the driver's door a second later, turning on the spotlight and angling it toward their quarry.

The forklift screeched to a halt and the container slid forward precipitously on its teeth. Even from the other side of the Jeep, Nick heard the sailor scream. Nick and Warren jogged around to join Charlie, Warren aiming his pistol down the alley. The blazing bright of the spotlight lit the forklift; the crates on either side were so high that the miserable gloom that passed for daylight was absent, and deformed shadows played out behind the stopped vehicle.

Waving a discouraging hand at Warren's drawn weapon, Nick raised his voice. "Port Authority Po—"

Mechanical squealing cut him off. The forklift's teeth lowered until they clunked against the gravel of the alley. The container wobbled for a moment, then lay still.

Gritting his teeth, Nick tried again as Charlie advanced a step. "This is the Port Authority Police! Step out of the vehicle with your hands up!"

The sailor appeared from one side of the cargo container, his hands raised and a calm smile on his face. His shock of blond hair was windblown, but he looked otherwise quite at ease. Nick wondered if the man's flannel shirt had billowed out; could his arms really be that big? The fog swirled around the sailor, the vapors blinding white in the spotlight's glare.

"I'm so terribly sorry officers, has there been some sort of misunderstanding?" the sailor inquired. His tone, businesslike but courteous, was such a change from the bellowed profanities of a moment before that the police officers looked at one another in confusion.

"Er . . ." Charlie began, squinting against the illuminated fog, then recovered himself. "The captain gave orders that the crew were to remain aboard the ship."

The sailor chuckled, his head tilting to one side. "Oh, I see the issue," he said with a good-natured smile; his German accent was only barely noticeable. "I'm not a sailor—or rather, not a crew member. I was with the ship only to transport my cargo."

He gestured to the crate, then raised an eyebrow so blond it was almost transparent; only the contraction of his brow betrayed the expression. "May I lower my hands now?"

"Yes," Nick grunted, stepping past his colleagues. "What's your name?"

"Hans Richtein," the sailor said as he lowered his arms.

"Check it against the crew registry," Nick said to Charlie.

Richtein's bright blue eyes widened for just a second before he brought his expression back under control. "Excuse me!" he said, still polite, but with enough force that Charlie froze with his hand still a few inches from his radio. "Is there a problem?"

"No . . ." Nick began, though he had a growing suspicion there might be a rather terrible one.

"We need to verify your identity and the status of your cargo," Kyle Warren snapped, speaking at last and taking a step forward so he stood beside Nick. "And we'll need proof of your right to transport said cargo from—"

"Ah, why didn't you say so!" Hans replied, though there was an edge to his tone. Nick thought his accent had become a bit more pronounced. "I have my passport here, and . . ."

"You'll still need to go through customs and have your visa approved," Kyle cut him off, eyes narrowed. He still had the SIG in one hand. "And we'll be searching your cargo."

The smile evaporated off Richtein's face. "I'm afraid that will be difficult. My cargo is . . . sensitive in nature."

Nick and Kyle traded a look.

"Oh, don't misunderstand me!" Hans added, becoming more flustered as he took a step forward. Charlie laid his hand on his baton. "Nothing illegal, you can be sure. But there is sensitive film equipment; light can damage it."

"We'll be careful," Kyle said bitingly.

Hans turned his head to gaze right for a second, then glared at the wall of crates to the west in apparent frustration. Nick glanced that way as well, confused. *Well, what was he hoping to see? They're crates.* Beyond was the New York skyline, but the view must have been better from the deck of the ship. And it wasn't like the impending sunset could be seen through the thunderheads that seemed to thicken every time Nick looked back up.

Kyle took a step toward the container, and Hans tensed. Kyle's eyes narrowed. "Sir, I'm going to need you to step aside."

"I . . . I can not," Hans replied, his eyes darting from one face to another.

"Excuse me?"

"I must . . . warrant! You have shown me no warrant!" Richtein's face was wiped blank of its crazed look, but the newfound calm did not reach his frustrated eyes as he glanced again at the stack of crates.

Nick and Kyle exchanged another grimace before Kyle stepped forward again. Now only three feet separated him from the sailor. Kyle's earlier joking bravado had vanished, and his voice was one of cool command. "Customs has the right to search any inbound cargo. Stand aside."

"You must not interfere!" Hans insisted, throwing his massive arms wide, each bicep the size of Kyle's head. The fog swirled around him with the sudden movement.

The ICE agent glowered, then looked back at Nick. "Cuff our friend while I—"

That turn of the head cost him any chance of defending himself. Hans seized his gun hand with one enormous hand and struck him full in the chest with his forearm. Kyle flew back, slammed into the container wall with a clang that echoed off the dozens of other containers, then crumpled to the ground, insensible.

Nick's hand had already closed around the handle of his service pistol, but Hans Richtein launched himself at the officer and tackled him back. They plowed into Charlie before he could move aside, and all three crashed into the side of the police Jeep. Hans wrapped his thick hands around Nick's throat. "You will not interfere! He does not will it!"

Several things happened at once.

Charlie slipped out from under Nick, drew his baton in a single fluid motion, and struck Hans between the shoulder blades. The German sailor crashed forward with a cry of agony, smothering Nick between his bulk and the Jeep. One of his arms struck the spotlight, which winked out.

In the west, invisible behind the cloud cover, the sun set below the horizon.

The fog around the men billowed, reaching up to face level.

A peal of thunder rattled the containers, its boom sounding from directly overhead.

And as Kyle Warren struggled to his feet, his gun on the ground beside him, his fingers clasping his head, the door of Hans Richtein's stolen orange cargo container burst open.

All four men froze, staring at the container. With the spotlight out, almost no illumination reached into the corridor. The dim shape of the container loomed in the dark, silent and still.

"CUFF HIM!" Kyle snarled again, though Nick and Charlie were already wrestling their struggling quarry's arms behind him to do just that. "And call for backup."

Kyle's vision swam, hazy even without the weird fog. He squinted against the dull, throbbing pain radiating from the back of his head to his eyeballs. *What the hell! What's worth attacking a federal agent over? He has to be smuggling something bad. Too smooth for a gunrunner, though. Drugs, maybe? Some terrorist weapon?* It was time to check out the container the big jag was so protective of.

The ICE agent clicked on his flashlight; the bright light contorted around the fog, and it lit barely three feet in front of him. But the ground came into view, and his fallen SIG P229 was visible, the silver slide glimmering against the dull gravel. He grabbed it and advanced on the container, flashlight and weapon aimed forward. Taking a deep breath to steady himself and clear the lingering stars from his head, he stepped around the corner and aimed into the container.

"What's he got?" Charlie called. His voice was tight with strain; Kyle assumed he was still trying to wrestle the smuggler into submission.

He peered into the gloom, eyes narrowed, head still aching. "Two containers. Sand, by the looks of it."

So it was drugs. Any of those biological weapons needed special conveyance and air-locked chambers. The container housed two crates, one wooden, the other steel. The wooden box had splintered at some point on its journey; the lid was cracked open, and coarse, sandy soil had spilled over the floor of the container. Kyle had a second to marvel at how clean the container was inside, aside from the sand—not an oil stain or a spot of grease, nor even the smudges of workers' footprints—before his attention was captured by the other case.

Where the wooden crate had opened due to external shock, the steel one seemed to have been opened deliberately; latches along the lid marked where it would click tightly shut. The layer of sand in it was thinner, barely covering the interior. For that matter, the interior was oddly plush. Why such a nice getup for sand? And why the long rails instead of handles?

"Jesus Christ!"

"What?" the call came back.

"It's a coffin!"

And so it was. Kyle staggered back, eyes wide, glancing around the container again though he knew it to be empty. He pointed his flashlight in every direction but down, where soupy mist slithered around his feet.

"Bring the prisoner in here," he called out, his voice still shaky. The sounds of scuffle accompanied the two Port Authority officers as they brought Hans, struggling every step, to the mouth of the container. He glared at Kyle, his manic blue eyes beyond reason.

"Release me! Now!"

Had his accent been that thick before? "You'll be lucky not to go to federal prison, pal. Now, what are you transporting in here?"

He turned his flashlight on the two sand crates. The sailor's eyes followed the light's path, then he froze in shock, his mouth wide and face paling. His lips worked soundlessly for a few seconds before he gasped out a sentence.

"No . . . No! Where is he? What have you done with him?"

"Who?" Kyle demanded, alert now, looking around the container yet again. The mist was coiling away from the entrance and toward the back of the container.

"He . . . he can not have left me!" As tense as he was, Kyle felt a second's pang of sympathy for the insane sailor; the sheer torment in his voice was crushing. The booming bass shrank to a whisper as he said, "He would not *leave* me . . ."

Kyle turned toward the entrance again, taking a step forward. "Who?"

Hans shuddered a second longer, then grew still again. Despair dropped off his face as suddenly as it had come, so quickly that Kyle wondered whether it had ever even been there. He stared in confusion as the burly prisoner's expression turned smug, his lips parting to reveal a triumphant grin. His eyes proclaimed victory.

Kyle's eyes turned to the two cops, who wore identical expressions of utmost horror. It was now Charlie Page's mouth that opened and closed without sound, and now Nick Rossini who shook. Lowering his SIG to his side, Kyle rolled his eyes. *What, do they think I'm going to shoot them? Why are they looking at me like that?*

Then he looked closer and saw that they were not looking at him, but past him.

The last thing Kyle Warren saw before the container door banged shut was the handcuffs dropping off Hans Richtein's wrists, and the last thing he felt before the darkness took him was the iron hands clamping down on his shoulders.

WHEN THE door of the container opened again, Nick Rossini and Charlie Page lay dead at Hans Richtein's feet. Hans cracked his knuckles and took the radios from the officers' belts. He already had their guns tucked through his belt. "We spoke with the sailor," he said into one of them, pitching his voice higher. "We'll escort him back to his ship."

"*10-4, unit three.*"

Hans smirked and smashed the radios together, dropping the useless pieces to the ground. When the container opened, he fell back to his knees, hands flat on the ground.

"Master!" he exclaimed, tightening the muscles in his face so he would not cry and reveal himself weak. The Master had not left him! He knew it had been impossible, knew the Master would never leave him, but when the arrogant agent had said the container was empty . . . that no one was there; if he had been abandoned . . . Hans shuddered.

The hem of a black cloak came into view, and Hans scrabbled forward to kiss it. "Master!"

A hiss from above caused Hans to shrink back. The voice was even and calm, but frosty. A shiver slid up the German's spine. "You have denied me further sustenance."

How foolish he had been! Hans cursed himself. What was he thinking, taking these two lives? Why did he not save them for the

Master? Now the Master had only consumed the loudmouth federal agent; he was not sated, and Hans was to blame.

He looked up piteously. The Master's face was hidden by the shadows of his cowl, but his hands were curled into claws, their razor-sharp nails gleaming in the beam from a dropped flashlight. The mist had vanished.

"I'm so sorry, Master, I did not think! I meant only to remove them from your path . . ."

"Because they were *obstacles* to me?" The voice dripped sarcasm.

"No!" Hans said, turning pale. "Of course not, Master! But I did not wish you to trouble yourself with such as them!"

"Hmm." The voice lost some of its judgment, becoming apathetic. The cowled head turned in the direction of the ships. "They will be missed. We must go."

Turning to face the Jeep, the Master waved at it with a clawed hand. It rolled forward, clearing their path. The Master spoke again, cruel reproof back in his tone. "Are you at least capable of eluding further pursuit without my aid?"

"Of course, Master!" Hans replied, drawing in a breath. He would not be punished! The punishments were terrible, of course, but worse, they showed how he had failed the Master. "I can get the container to a truck bed, and from there—"

A single flick of the clawlike fingertips silenced him. "It does not interest me. See that it is done."

He turned, and Hans nodded, already rising. He paused halfway in a strange sort of bow when he saw that the Master had not retreated to his sanctuary. "My lord?"

"The container of my earth was ruptured."

The blood drained from Hans's face. "P-perhaps the sea, Master, the rough s-s-seas . . ."

"It was not so last night." The voice was cool, insidiously collected. "My earth has been risked through your carelessness."

Hans did not see the blow coming; he simply felt the agonizing impact against his gut. Before he could even fall to his knees, a second strike lifted him off his feet and crushed him against the wall of cargo containers. He slid an inch toward the ground before a hand like a vice tightened at his throat, and he could not breathe. His big feet dangled in the air.

From within the cowl came two matched red gleams, glowing as if a light shone through a diamond dipped in blood.

"It will be weeks before more of my earth arrives. You will remember your duty in the future."

Without waiting, the Master dropped Hans back to the ground, turned, and vanished into the container. The orange door banged shut with finality.

Hans Richtein struggled back to his feet, trying to force breath to his lungs. The pain was dreadful, and yet it was a blessing in disguise, for it reminded him of the deeper pain of *before*—that dark, lost time before he had known the balm of the Master's voice. The details of *before* became muddier with each passing year, but Hans knew the Master had saved him, and that he never wanted to go back.

He was in the forklift's seat after a few seconds. After igniting the engine and raising the teeth again—carefully, so very carefully, so the Master would not be disturbed—he shifted into gear and drove back to the main road, angling toward the harbor entrance as the thunderheads erupted at last into a downpour.

THREE

Chicago, Illinois, USA

A CRUSH of students flooded the concrete paths that spider-webbed through the campus of the University of Illinois at Chicago. The snow had halfway melted from the campus, leaving wet puddles in some spots and clumps of resilient white in others. Despite the lingering December chill, clusters of students had knotted together, backs to the wind and talking excitedly. Others leaned on the numerous light posts and skeletal trees for some marginal cover. A great many had cups of coffee in their hands, steam escaping from their lids, but even the students without seemed alert for the early morning.

The last day of the semester had come.

In the summer months, the hundreds of trees at UIC's campus could shadow thousands beneath their voluminous leaves, but winter left the campus bright, the leaves long since fallen and the trees not to bloom until April at the earliest. Most of the students saw this as a good thing; the last thing the Chicago winter needed was shadows to make it even colder. Leaning against the concrete pillar of an academic building in the slim shadow available and trying not to think of himself as hiding there, the vampire Simon found himself missing the more arboreal seasons.

The sun did not harm him, per se—not this late in the morning, anyway—but he wasn't eager to rush back into the mild disorientation and weakness that accompanied direct exposure. He tried to keep himself well-fed enough that the sunlight would be only uncomfortable, rather than a true liability. However, a vampire who prided himself on independence and self-reliance had to shun every threat. The moment he dismissed the daylight's effects on him was the moment he'd catch a stake through the heart.

Simon laughed aloud at that, the empty, echoing sound startling a pair of passing freshmen. He had been taught better than to completely dismiss the idea, or to discount any human as a threat, but the thought of being destroyed by any of these people was comical. So much of the student body came and went without any notice of those around them that Simon expected, unless he killed someone in front of them (and he thought with a quieter, disdainful snicker that it would have to be *directly* in front of them), no one would ever suspect what he was, much less be prepared to handle the matter.

He had selected UIC for this very reason. With its tens of thousands of students, the school was large enough that Simon could disappear into crowds at will and seldom have the same class with another student twice. He never hunted at the school and never spoke to anyone beyond cursory answers to direct questions; there was nothing to cement him in anyone's memory. He could not avoid being noticed, but he was never *known*.

Why come at all?

Regarding a retreating shadow warily as the sun climbed, he sighed at the old internal argument. To learn, he supposed, would be the normal response, but learn what? Philosophy, literature, history, and the sciences were not going to improve his hunting technique. He had thought that at least language classes might be practical, but screams sounded the same in every tongue.

He frowned. Surely there was something to be said for learning in its own right? What was supposed to be said, he didn't know, but something. Of course, the last days of class were always devoted to review for finals, which meant he would learn nothing new, and might as well have slept . . .

Or was it them?

The vampire gritted his teeth. The humans; it always came back to the cursed humans. It was not that they interested him on an individual level, really, and he felt no pity for them. But something about them collectively drew him—some invisible lure kept him coming to class and lurking around the commons in the day when he should have slept, sitting and learning what he could have gained from a book, feeling like a wolf curled up in a sheep's pen for a pleasant rest. He had haunted the shadows of a dozen of humanity's environments, but the college had a unique draw—a riot of contradictory personalities forced by circumstance into uneasy interactions, at a stage of life when potential was just becoming actual.

At night, his strength reborn with prey in his hands and hot blood in his throat, he could deny the strange attraction. But on campus, surrounded by lives he might on another occasion have ended, it seemed almost . . . appropriate that he was here.

He laughed again to himself. He expected the humans, if they knew the truth, might have a different view, and knew he should as well. Laughable threats became deadly serious when idle curiosity became recklessness, as he well remembered . . .

Don't grow too fond of your food, Simon. It makes dinner needlessly difficult.

This time the voice in Simon's mind was not his own, because it was not thought but memory, and it brought a host of others with it: the heat of flames around him, the crunch of bone and the scent of blood, wide brown eyes staring into his as his fangs closed in on her throat . . .

Eyes snapping open, the vampire pushed himself off the concrete building, refusing to let his thoughts wander down that path. It had been bad enough living through it the first time; he had no need to indulge in the memory now. Trudging out into the sunlight, his shoulders slumping slightly, he started across the campus.

It was, Simon thought, the worst aspect of his "hobby" of school attendance, or any other diurnal activity. He found night classes too distracting, what with the heartbeats in his ears and the constant urges to kill his fellow students, but he could not sleep at night, and only at dawn or noon could he fall into his deathlike sleep—and once he was out, that was that. Missing either deadline meant another day without rest.

Oftentimes his annoyance with the humans and his paranoia about being detected as an aberration in their midst led him to return to the schedule he should be keeping. For weeks or months at a time, he would prowl the night and sleep in the day, seeing no living people except those about to become dinner. But without fail, whether a few days or a few months later, he found himself drawn back. So it had been these five years.

Idly, he wondered how it felt for humans to go without. During these periods of rebellion to his natural schedule, enough blood could keep him moving and upright until nightfall, but it was awkward and uncomfortable on the best days. Another reason to forego his "hobby."

"Hey Simon."

And yet another reason . . .

Simon opened his eyes with a quiet growl, offering no comment to Miguel Vargos as the other man walked past, wearing an endearing smile. He was accompanied, as Simon had expected, by a handful of his friends; none of them ever seemed to go anywhere alone. Several were dressed in dark colors, and a few were nearly as pale as

Simon—some naturally, others by artifice. They wore enough steel and silver rings, necklaces, and bracelets that the combined reflection in the bright sunlight made the vampire cringe.

Miguel's smile dimmed, and he stayed facing Simon, walking backward, for almost ten feet more before shrugging and turning back to converse with his companions, none of whom dared more than a glance in Simon's direction, and furtively at that.

The vampire shook his head. Miguel and his coterie of misfits. Close with one another, but distinctly not with anyone else. Though he appreciated the irony of a monster among mortals considering anyone else odd, he couldn't deny finding them strange, and Miguel's perennial attempts to bring him into the fold, such as it was, were becoming maddening.

With a grumble, Simon stalked off in the opposite direction of Miguel, even though it would take him away from his ultimate destination. The sarcastic distaste of the majority of the humans was annoying on a surface level, but their dismissive attitude also meant they didn't pay real attention, so in the end it was a benefit. Miguel, on the other hand, seemed so interested—no, more than just interested, intrigued, as if he knew Simon had a secret he wasn't sharing and was determined to unearth it. If Simon passed alongside the overwhelming majority of lives around him like a wraith in the dark, Miguel Vargos had developed night vision. It gave the hunter the uncomfortable sensation of being hunted.

He glanced over his shoulder, and in his distraction failed to sense the girl's approach until it was too late. While turning around to face the way he was walking, he walked right into her, her forehead smacking into his teeth and nose. The vampire's head snapped back, stunned for an instant, but his left hand shot out on reflex, catching her by the arm as she started to fall even as his right curled into a fist and pulled back for a punch. Steadying herself with his grip, she goggled up at Simon.

"Edgy much?" she asked, too loudly but with a fledgling smile. The vampire noticed the earbud headphones just before the girl reached for them. She looked at his cocked fist but did not recoil, seeming sure that Simon would not lash out at her.

Once he was sure of that himself, he took a second to calm his reflexes and unfold the fingers of his right hand. Making sure his companion was secure on her feet before he released her, he said, "I . . . I'm sorry. You startled me."

The answering smile was warmer this time, if a little sheepish, as the young woman turned off the MP3 player on her arm. "It's fine, me too. I wasn't watching where I was going." She tilted her head to one side, expression curious. "You always this jumpy, though?"

"I . . ."

Simon hesitated, taking a step back to get a good look at the girl, but when he did, his train of thought jumped the track. She was several inches shorter than him, athletically thin without appearing unhealthy. She wore a black T-shirt under a denim coat and faded blue jeans that she had rolled up to her knees despite the day's chill. Her green and white striped socks extended all the way up to her cuffed jeans, and over them she wore shiny black combat boots, a chain of plastic beads around one. She had bracelets on both wrists, along with a plastic watch on her right. There was a dull shade of pink on her nails, but she wore no makeup, and her chestnut hair was tied into two pigtails.

Simon could not honestly say he had never seen someone look quite so tacky, but it had been a while.

All this brought his dark eyebrows up, but what silenced him were the girl's eyes. Slightly overlarge to her soft face, they were big and bright, a warm shade of light brown, and darted here and there, noticing details and taking in the scene. There was a soft, roguish gleam in them, a lively and peppy alertness that almost masked a small flicker of uncertainty. Simon was good at reading people by their eyes, but something lurked beneath it all, something he couldn't quite place.

Noticing the movement of his eyes, she looked him over in turn, taking in his dark appearance with no hint of either judgment or approval, merely curiosity. When she was done, she rested her hands on her hips with a jingle of bracelets and looked into his eyes while drumming her fingers until he finished. When their gazes met, she inquired, "Like what you see?"

Startled out of his reverie, the vampire searched for words, but only managed another, "I—"

"Well, take a picture, it'll last longer," she interrupted, the corners of her mouth tugging up a bit. "But until you do, you'll have to make do with what you see."

Realizing that a few people nearby had stopped when they ran into one another, and that he was on the verge of incoherence, Simon took a second to rally himself, smoothing his expression back to cool control. "Won't I be the lucky one, then?"

"Aww, aren't you sweet," the girl replied, a bit of sarcasm in her tone, though her smile spread anyway.

"Not generally, though the appropriate stimulus can make me so."

The young woman looked at him for a moment, processing that. "I'm pleased to have catalyzed your infrequent flirtatiousness," she replied, her tone nearly as formal and controlled as Simon's, though the effect suffered when she giggled a second later. As the vampire studied her, his steel eyes narrowed, she added, "Don't I feel special."

There was a heartbeat's pause, and then Simon looked her over again and smirked back. "I can only imagine."

The girl laughed again, but there was a hint of color to her cheeks now. Around them, passersby had continued on their way, content that Simon was not about to hit her. Seeing the chance for his escape, he asked, "You're all right, then?"

"Oh yeah, I'm fine," she reassured him, folding the cord of her headphones over her MP3 player to free her hands. Before Simon could take a step away, she added, "I'm still getting used to this place, I guess."

"You're a freshman?" Simon guessed, the words escaping his lips with no thought behind them. He winced; a question would demand an answer, and that meant further conversation . . .

The girl noticed the wince, misinterpreted it, and rolled her eyes. "Nothing wrong with being a freshman!" she replied sternly, trying not to smirk. Then she shook her head. "But no, sophomore. I'm a transfer."

"From where did you transfer?"

The girl hesitated, then confessed, "Northwestern."

Simon frowned, confused. "You transferred from Northwestern . . . to UIC?"

"Yep."

"Why?"

"It's kind of a long story . . ." she equivocated, biting down on one side of her lower lip. Before she could say anything else, a breeze slipped through the crack between two concrete buildings and rushed along the half-covered grass of the common area. The girl shivered, clutching her denim coat around her. "Hey, do you mind if we step inside? It's a little cold."

Her warm brown eyes flicked up to Simon's gray ones and steadied there, waiting for his reply. He found her gaze disconcerting; those intent eyes kept him from focusing. But here was the chance to escape—to excuse himself in a way that guaranteed he would be a pleasant, untroubling, and fleeting memory.

What he actually said, as he gestured toward the nearby Student Center, was, "Why aren't you wearing something warmer?"

The words just fell out of his mouth of their own accord. Simon's eyes widened and his mouth hung open, but the girl missed the look of dismay; she had already started jogging toward the Student Center. It was all the vampire could do to trail after her. *What am I doing?*

Holding the door for her robotically, he followed the girl inside, struggling to pull his expression together as she relaxed in the warmth.

"Well, I drive to campus, so it's not usually a problem," the girl admitted, rubbing her red nose. "I just get out and run to my first class."

"Ah."

Simon managed to smooth his pale features just before his companion looked up at him. She smiled again, and thrust her left hand out to him. "I'm Anita, by the way."

The vampire took her hand awkwardly in his own gloved left. "Simon."

"Nice to meet you, Simon," Anita replied, and the easy friendliness on her soft features showed that she meant it.

"And you." Simon's tone was more hesitant as he tried to catch up to himself, and his answering smile less confident. Hoping to cover, he was about to ask again about Anita's transfer when she spoke first.

"So, what has you wound up so tight, Simon?" While the vampire searched for an answer, eyes looking this way and that, she added, "I mean, you don't usually almost punch someone you bump into, right?"

"No," Simon replied, eager to dispel that line of thought, if nothing else. Taking a breath, he added, "Just a reflex; I didn't see you coming. I was . . . distracted."

"By what?"

Simon stopped himself from glancing out the glass doors to make sure Miguel hadn't tailed him and witnessed this bizarre scene. "Oh . . ." He reached for the first, most stereotypical answer his mind could latch on to. "Finals."

"Gotcha." The girl nodded seriously, looking down for a second before her eyes turned back to Simon's. "Are they tough here?"

Having never taken one, the vampire could not say, but he managed, "I guess it depends on the class."

"Touché. I'm not looking forward to my history final." Anita's voice had little in the way of hope as she added, " I don't suppose you're any good with European history?"

Again, Simon knew that a gentle dismissal would be the best way to extricate himself. But he found himself saying instead, "Decent enough."

"Really?" A flicker of optimism returned to Anita's eyes. "Would you have time to help me study?"

Simon considered the request, brow furrowing. This woman made him far too unsteady; he was unused to being off-balance in any way, and the sensation was deeply disturbing. It seemed best to rid himself of her and be done with it before she had the chance to become a real threat. And yet . . .

At the same time, was it not wise to investigate? To determine the source of the aberration, find out what about this bizarre girl had hooked him like a fish on a line? Could he responsibly leave such a question unanswered? Curiosity killed cats, but complacency killed vampires.

The vampire debated with himself so long that Anita waved a hand in front of his face. "Earth to Simon? Do you read us, Simon?"

Blinking, he shook his head to clear it. "I'm sorry, I was just . . . thinking about my schedule," he offered weakly. *It's not like last time.* Trying not to grimace, he added, "But yes, I can help you study. When?"

"Hmm . . ." Anita paused, crossing her arms over her chest. Simon noticed that she seemed to almost be hugging herself with the gesture, and wondered if she could still be cold. "Well, I'm not doing anything now . . . ?"

Simon had enough presence of mind to save himself from that, at least. Too exposed already, he needed time to recover. "I'm sorry, I have plans at the moment. Perhaps tomorrow?"

She considered, then nodded. "Okay. How about we meet at the library at, say, noon?"

The grimace reached his lips this time. Hibernal solar noon was after twelve, and he needed at least half the day's sleep to prepare himself. "How about three? I'm something of a . . . late sleeper."

"Yeah, me too," Anita said, looking relieved. "I only said noon because normal people like to be up and moving by then, even on weekends."

She affected a shudder, then smiled, and the vampire had to keep from laughing. "I fear I'll disappoint you if you're looking for normal . . ."

"Oh good," Anita replied, unfazed. "Normal's boring. So tomorrow at three, then?"

"I'll see you then."

Nodding, Anita turned to go, then looked back at Simon. She gazed at him long enough that he narrowed his eyes and opened his mouth, but then she just shook her head, smiled, and headed back out the glass doors with a determined look.

Simon stared after her. It had been his longest conversation in five years with someone who was still alive, and even more unusually, she had left the conversation that way. Always in control of what terse conversation he indulged in—his inhuman eyes and the strange, haunted sound of his voice usually unnerved those who tried to speak to him—he was unused to being at a loss for words, but Anita had him out of step, wide of his usual mark, and flailing.

He was unsettled. Troubled. The hunter again had the disturbing sensation of being the prey.

He required an explanation. A resolution. Security and peace of mind.

Never let a danger exist when you can eliminate it, Simon.

The voice from his memory again, but this time he nodded to himself. Allowing Anita a few moments to get clear of the Student Center and watching her until she was nearly lost in the crowd, Simon pushed open the doors and followed.

HOURS LATER, Anita stood on the sidewalk and clutched her arms around herself in the night's chill until the familiar BMW rounded the corner. "Hey! HEY!"

Rolling to a smooth stop at the curb, its door unlocking with a muffled thump, the sedan idled as Anita jogged over. Pulling the door open, she moaned in relief at the warmth. "You have no idea how good that feels right now."

Crouched on a rooftop several stories up, Simon watched her duck in and close the door, then followed the car with his eyes as it made a U-turn and angled north. Rising to his full height, he backed up two paces, then took a running leap and launched himself into the night.

FOUR

Evanston, Illinois, USA

"SO YEAH, the bio final's gonna suck, but at least I'll be done with my science gen eds when it's over," Anita said half an hour later as her car took the final turn into the cul-de-sac, the lights of her house dominating the dark at the end of the road. "And Simon said he'd help me study for Western civ, so maybe that won't be so bad."

Driving one-handed, her elbow resting against the window, Marion de Santos glanced over at Anita speculatively before turning her eyes back to the road. "That's good. Lord knows your parents and I can't help you there."

Anita laughed. "Yeah, two doctors, and not a fact between them. Wish Uncle Tim was here."

"Mmmm. He's lived in Europe what, twenty years now?"

"Something like that, yeah. Moved before I was born. And he goes everywhere; he must have picked up something about a king or two."

Without looking at Anita, Marion slipped in, "So, is Simon cute?"

Anita rolled her eyes and grinned over the gear shift. "Thinking the third try's gonna be the charm?"

Marion laughed. "Just testing you, kid."

The BMW rolled up onto the Rothard driveway, and though the cul-de-sac was carefully maintained, the ride became even smoother as they passed the three-foot-high brick boundary wall that bordered the property. The car came to a graceful halt beside the house's side patio.

"I'll get you to talk eventually. Hop out, I'll go park."

"You sure?" Anita asked, but Marion just rolled her eyes, so Anita stepped out, crossing the driveway once Marion had driven on. She skipped up the few steps onto the covered patio and drew open the glass outer door, letting it rest against her hip as she rummaged in her backpack for her key ring. Unlocking the interior door, she stepped into the warm hallway with a contented sigh and kicked her snow-covered boots onto the mat.

Anita glanced habitually to her left, but her father's study door was closed, so she set off down the hall, letting the hand carrying her backpack fall to her side so the backpack itself bounced on the floor with every other step. She made it to the entry foyer without incident, and was just beginning to congratulate herself when a deep, rumbly cough behind made her start; she almost walked into the volute at the end of the banister. Gritting her teeth behind clenched lips, she did not turn.

"Anita Joy."

She winced; both names never meant anything good. Pivoting on the spot and leaning back on her heels to rest against the banister, she frowned dramatically and tried to lower her voice as deep as her father's, producing a guttural, "What?"

Richard Rothard's eyes narrowed as he turned away from the grandfather clock he had been adjusting to face her. He stood several inches taller than his daughter and looked as if he carried twice her mass in a belly that hung several inches over his belt. The lobes of his ears drooped almost to his jaw, and his voluminous chin flowed into his chest with little distinct neck in the way. His jowls were heavy, but his fleshy face took nothing from his hazel eyes, which were clear and fixed even behind his thick-rimmed, circular glasses. His brown hair was graying, and though it shrouded the tops of his ears, he kept it carefully combed away from his eyes, which left him with a great deal of shiny forehead.

Glancing over his daughter's appearance, his frown deepened. "Please tell me you didn't wear that in public."

Anita followed his eyes and noticed a toe sticking out of a hole in one green and white striped sock. She wiggled it before looking back up and saying brightly, "No, of course not. I had boots on!"

For a moment Dr. Rothard just stared back, then he groaned as he pushed his glasses up onto his forehead to cover his eyes with one hand. Shaking his head, he waved his free hand in Anita's direction. She seized the opportunity and vanished up the stairs, backpack thumping on the steps in her wake.

She crossed the hall to her room, threw open the door, and slung her backpack with practiced ease over her bed and onto the half-pulled out chair at her desk. She pulled off her denim coat and, with one sleeve turned inside-out, dropped it unceremoniously to the floor. With a running dive, she collapsed onto her bed, shins hanging off into space, arms spread out as she smiled into her sheets.

"I know that you're *so* going to miss classes, honey," said an amused voice behind her, "but try to rein in your devastation; it's indecent."

Anita's smile broadened, and she pressed her face into her comforter before flipping over onto her back and sitting up. She pulled her knees up to her chest and looked at her mother. "Geez, what's up with you guys? Dad snuck up on me too!"

Nancy Rothard rolled her eyes and crossed her arms over her chest as she leaned against the doorframe. "I hate to break it to you, sweetheart, but you're not exactly subtle. I think I could have heard you coming up the stairs from the pier."

As unlike her husband in looks as she was like him in intellect, Doctor Nancy Rothard was no taller than her daughter, though her figure was fuller. She had the same warm glow in her brown eyes, though her hair was a bit darker, and it had been dyed to fend off the first scouts of the inevitable invasion of gray.

Anita glanced at her backpack on its chair. "Oh. Yeah."

Nancy laughed, shifting her weight off the door and walking into the room to sit beside Anita on the bed. "So, how are finals looking?"

"Well, bio's gonna suck . . ." she repeated.

"Your father could probably help you study," Nancy offered, but Anita gave her a pained look.

"It's Intro to Bio, Mom, not brain surgery. I don't think he can dumb himself down enough for it," she replied, shaking her head. Then she smirked. "Besides, back when Dad was learning the introductory stuff, it was by cutting open brontosauruses to see how they—"

"Watch it, missy, your father's only three years older than me," Nancy replied sternly, though the corners of her mouth twitched upward. "Well, at least ask him if you have any questions. It's been sixteen years since I saw a patient, but I got you through psych, didn't I?"

"Yeah, but that's psych, Mom, it's not a *real* science." Anita's grin widened and she laughed at her mother's stony look and narrowed eyes.

"Uh-huh. Keep it up, smarty."

She glowered for a second more, then grinned back and put an arm around her daughter's shoulders. "Okay. So what about the others?"

"Well, Spanish should be a breeze. U.S. government too. Statistics is all plug-and-chug; as long as I don't forget the formulas, I should be okay."

She hesitated, and Nancy nodded knowingly. "And Western civ?"

"Well, there are a lot of dates to remember. Our professor even said, 'In higher level history courses, it's more about seeing trends and patterns. But you can't do that if you don't know your basic facts, so you'll be doing a lot of memorization in this class,'" Anita grumbled, putting on another deep voice to mimic her professor before reverting to her own. "That midterm was hell."

Her mother shrugged. "You'll just have to struggle through it and memorize, I guess. Make sure you put in plenty of study time."

That reminded Anita, and her face brightened. "Oh, yeah! I met a guy today; he said he's good with history, so he's going to help me study tomorrow. Maybe that'll help."

Nancy's eyes widened and she turned to face Anita. "Oh? How did you meet him?"

"Well, I kinda walked into him . . ." When Nancy raised her eyebrows, Anita looked up at the ceiling as though fascinated by its sky blue color and added in an offhand way, "Kinda literally . . ."

Nancy shook her head with an indulgent smile. "Let me guess. Headphones in, eyes closed, head banging, paying no attention at all to where you were going?"

Anita looked scandalized. "Mother! I am stunned and hurt by that careless accusation." She paused, then smiled and added, "My eyes were open at least half the time. At least."

They both laughed, then Anita went on, "But yeah, Simon and I got to talking, and he said he was pretty good at history, so we're gonna study tomorrow."

"I'm glad to hear that. It's good that you made a new friend."

Anita tensed slightly, but before she could respond, a deep voice rumbled from down the hall. "A new friend? Do tell."

Both women's eyes turned to Richard Rothard, who lumbered down the hall wearing a skeptical look. She sighed, then said, "I just bumped into a guy today, and we started talking, and—"

"'Bumped into' him?" Dr. Rothard interrupted, eyes narrowing. "Were you walking around with your headphones in again?"

Anita sighed. "Yeah, but—"

"Anita, how many times have we told you, you need to be more careful?"

Anita grimaced. "Anyway, so Simon and I are getting together tomorrow to study history. I guess he took it before; he says he's good at it."

"And what time are you meeting this young man?"

"Three."

Dr. Rothard raised one bushy eyebrow. "In the afternoon? Bit of a late start, isn't it?"

"I offered noon," Anita said defensively, "but he said he likes to sleep in too, so it works better for both of us . . ."

She trailed off, looking at her father's frown. Richard Rothard tended not to think much of sleeping in past ten, or the people who did it.

"Western civ is your last final, isn't it?" Nancy put in.

Grateful for the change of subject, Anita nodded. "Yep."

"Well, if tomorrow's study session goes well, maybe you could have Simon over for dinner sometime next week." Noticing the deepening frown on her husband's face, Nancy added smoothly, "I always thought it was best to have something to snack on while I was studying. Didn't you, Rick?"

One of Richard's hands settled on his belly, seemingly of its own volition. Clearing his throat, he managed, "Er . . . yes, I suppose so . . ."

Seeing that he was unconvinced, Nancy continued, "And you haven't had Christine over for weeks. You could have them both for dinner."

Richard's face relaxed a bit more at this suggestion, and Anita jumped on it. "Yeah, that's a good idea! And she took Western civ too; she might be able to help us study."

Thinking for a moment, Richard leaned against the doorframe, which creaked. "When are you planning to do this?"

Anita thought for a moment. "Well, Western civ's on Thursday, so . . . Wednesday?"

Nancy considered, then nodded to her husband, who nodded back. "Wednesday it is, then. Let Marion know." Yawning magnificently, he covered his mouth with one fleshy hand, then added, "Well, I'm done for tonight. I have a consultation tomorrow, so I'm going to head to bed. Good night, ladies."

They returned his good night. When the door of the master bedroom down the hall clicked closed, Nancy tried to look innocent as she asked, "So this Simon . . .what's he like?"

Anita rolled her eyes. "You and Marion. 'Is he cute?' 'Is he hot?' 'Do you wanna jump him?' I swear . . ."

"Marion said that to you?" Nancy inquired, looking surprised.

Anita waved her hand. "No, of course not. He's pretty quiet, doesn't say much. He seems nice, though. But I met the guy today! We talked for like, five minutes. I barely know him."

"Still . . ." her mother replied calmly, searching for the right words. "Nice of him to help a stranger—especially one who walked into him."

Anita's mouth trembled as if she was resisting a smile, though she kept her arms crossed over her chest.

"That speaks well of him. Depending on how things go tomorrow, see if he wants to come over for dinner."

Anita said nothing, but nodded thoughtfully.

"It'll be good for you to have a new friend," her mother pressed on, "and if he's the shy type, maybe he could use a friend too."

"Mom, it's a study"—Anita almost said "date" but saved herself at the last second—"session, we're not doing therapy together."

"I know," her mother said, "I just . . . want to make sure you're doing all right. And not just academically."

Anita set her jaw. "I'm fine, Mom. Really."

Nancy Rothard looked at her daughter for a long moment, but she finally rose and said, "Okay. I hope it all goes well tomorrow. You'll let me know?"

"Yeah, of course," Anita said, looking at the deep navy blue carpet.

"All right. Good night, sweetie."

"Night, Mom."

With a last concerned look, Nancy stepped out the door.

EYES CLOSED in concentration, Simon picked out Mrs. Rothard's footfalls as they headed down the hall; he presumed their carpet was thick, for he could barely hear her steps. Her pulse was a bit clearer, though glass and walls muffled that too. A distant door opened and closed, leaving silence in its wake except for Anita.

Her heartbeat echoed in Simon's head as if someone had put a bass drum in his brain. Even with both her parents near her, he had been able to isolate Anita's pulse without effort. Her father's had been strained; though he dared not look around the corner, Simon felt sure the man was well overweight. The mother's pulse was stronger, though it carried the almost inaudible hallmarks of age; if forced to guess, Simon would have put both the Rothards in their late forties or early fifties. Anita, on the other hand, had been like a beacon, her heartbeat strong and clear, flaring up when she was excited or stressed. If the mother could have heard Anita blundering up the stairs from the pier, Simon was confident he could have found her heartbeat from the same distance.

Pressed against the cold wall of the house like a lizard, the flesh of his hands and the toes of his boots adhering to the brick as easily as the tiny spider picking its way past his thumb, Simon glanced down at the yard. It was matted with snow, though a curving path of flagstones had been shoveled clear. The path led from the massive wooden porch to the pier Mrs. Rothard had mentioned, which jutted out into Lake Michigan at the end of the lot. The porch itself stretched almost halfway across the yard to the water. Off to one side was a simple hedge maze, the tops of its evergreen walls covered in a thin layer of white.

A slight shift in Anita's heartbeat refocused Simon on the house. It had been almost double tempo at the end of her conversation with her mother; whatever Anita had said to the contrary, the vampire was certain the older woman's words had gotten to her. But now it grew fainter, and Simon dared a glance. Leaning just far enough to put one eye past the upper corner of the window beside her glass balcony doors, he saw Anita vanishing down a staircase at the end of the hallway.

Considering for a moment, Simon crept back down the wall. He had no fear of falling, but the very last thing he wanted to do was make a sound. He lowered himself until he was directly under Anita's balcony. He heard muffled voices through the window below and closed his eyes again to help him concentrate.

"I'm just gonna grab a sandwich before bed. I only had some Twizzlers since lunch."

"You want me to fix you something, kiddo?" It must have been the woman who had picked up Anita. Her heartbeat was even stronger than Anita's; he guessed that she was older, perhaps her late twenties, and in good health.

"Nah, don't worry about it, I'm going right to bed anyway." Refocusing on Anita's heartbeat, Simon found to his mild surprise that it was more enticing than her companion's.

"Okay, if you're sure." There was a pause, then, "So, is Simon cute?"

Raising his eyebrows, Simon leaned forward in spite of himself.

"You're never gonna give up, are you?"

"It's why you love me."

"Yeah, I guess."

"You guess you love me, or you guess he's cute?"

"Oh, come on, you know I love you," Anita said dryly, but Simon heard the smile in her voice. "But yeah, he's kinda cute."

"I knew it!"

"What, I can't accidentally walk into ugly guys too?"

"Oh, no, you walk into everybody." They both laughed. "But you've got a study date tomorrow with him . . ."

"It's not a date!"

"Uh-huh."

The skepticism in the woman's tone was obvious even to Simon. The silence that followed was longer than the vampire would have expected, broken only by the sounds of Anita making her sandwich and then starting on it, and he was not surprised to hear the older woman's curious tone when she asked, "What?"

Anita sighed. "Well, he may come to dinner on Wednesday . . ."

"Ha!"

"It's not a date!"

"Uh-huh."

"It was Mom's idea!"

"Uh-huh."

"I haven't even asked him yet! It depends on tomorrow."

"Well, good luck then, stud-ette."

There was a sound of crumpling paper, then its faint impact on flesh; Simon guessed Anita had thrown something at her friend. They both laughed.

"All right, I'm heading to bed. Good night, Marion."

"Good night, kiddo. Sleep good."

"You too."

Climbing back up the wall, Simon made it to his former spot beside Anita's balcony door in time to hear her heartbeat approach, then bank down the hall. But she opened a door much closer than the one her parents had, and a light came on through a window on his other side. He hesitated, listening to make sure Marion was still downstairs, then risked sticking his head past the window to get a real look at Anita's room.

Like Anita herself, its appearance was so strange that for a moment all Simon could do was stare. One end of a desk sat directly beneath him. The dark navy carpet went well with the sky blue walls, but both made the queen size bed with lurid orange sheets and a hunter green comforter stand out even more. A dreamcatcher hung on one of the posts of Anita's headboard. Beyond her bed and its nightstand, beside the door, was an artist's easel with a half-used pad of paper on it. Beside it was a five-level bookshelf crammed to capacity, and beside that the door.

On the other side of the room, past the door, was a white dresser with all four drawers opened, revealing various pieces of clothing inside. The southern wall was devoted to two bifold closets, the doors of which all hung open too. A small telescope was tucked in the last corner of the room, with a pair of binoculars hanging from it by their strap. Another bookshelf was pressed against the wall next to the telescope. The floor was strewn here and there with piles of clothes, textbooks, and the occasional magazine.

Simon heard the toilet next door, and then the sink running, and ducked back into hiding. Sure enough, he sensed Anita coming back into the room a few seconds later, moving here and there, opening and closing drawers before the lights went off at last and she sat back on her bed. Simon heard nothing but her heartbeat, and, his curiosity tugging at him, he stepped down onto the balcony. Anita had brushed the snow off here too, though half-heartedly, and the vampire selected spots where his boots would leave no prints. Balancing in place, he looked through the window.

Overhead, hundreds of glow-in-the-dark stars shone neon green on the ceiling. The light of a laptop computer on the edge of the bed cast a mild blue glow on Anita, who sat cross-legged while watching the screen. She had changed to a loose T-shirt and sweatpants, discarded her jewelry, and adopted a relaxed posture, leaning forward with her chin on her laced fingers. Her elbows rested on her knees, and she seemed to be drifting off to sleep sitting up. She stared at nothing, her face lit by the glowing laptop screen.

Simon had tilted his head to one side in curious contemplation when he felt the pokes on his lips.

Unbidden, and even unrealized, his fangs had extended upon seeing her, tired and alone. He fought the impulse, but even in the darkness he could almost see the arteries in her neck pulsing, and her heartbeat serenaded him. She was young and healthy; her blood would be not only delicious, but rejuvenating. Simon could almost taste its ambrosia on his lips already.

It would be so simple. She'd see him for a moment, but before she could cry out, she'd meet his gaze, his hypnotic steel eyes, and he'd have her. She would open the door and step out to meet him, and her life would be his.

She closed the laptop screen with a quiet sigh, picked up the computer, then turned to place it back on her desk. Facing the window, she glanced up and saw the vampire's face. She started and opened her mouth to cry out. Then she saw his eyes, and she was his. His eyes glowed with fierce delight as he moved toward her . . .

ANITA SNAPPED out of her daze and stared at the balcony. There was nothing there, but she could have sworn . . .

She groped under her bed, never diverting her eyes, until her thin fingers found the comforting chill of an aluminum baseball bat. She hefted the makeshift weapon and edged toward the balcony door. When she was within a foot of it, she turned the lock very slowly, then yanked the door open and rushed out, bat poised to strike.

Nothing. Only the cold night air greeted her. Shivering, she slid back inside, making sure to secure the bolt on her door. Still uneasy, she laid the bat at arm's length by her headboard and snuggled under the protective warmth of her covers. She soon fell asleep, and the incident became no more than a dream.

ANITA'S DISQUIETING dream was Simon's waking nightmare. He leaned on the Rothards' chimney, whence he had watched her come out and seen the puzzlement on her face when she found no prowler. Nothing would have been easier than drawing her out the door and into his arms, but instead he had spared her, and he had no idea why.

Had it been the curious light in her eyes? No, he'd seen all manner of looks in the eyes of his victims and never given them a second thought. Their faint mistiness, then, imperceptible to a human but like a burning flare to his gaze? No, that wasn't it either; plenty of his victims had wept openly just before he took them. Perhaps he just preferred to choose his victims than have his instincts choose for him . . .

But Simon could barely complete that thought; he was adept at lying, but not to himself. Try as he might, he couldn't solve the riddle, and he was coming more and more to the realization that, no matter how profound his fury or deep his confusion, he would find no easy answer. His troubling thoughts accompanied him to the edge of the roof, where he stepped off without breaking pace and vanished into the night, Anita Rothard safe behind him.

FIVE

Outskirts of Akron, Ohio, USA

THE RENTAL truck trundled into a gas station just as the sky in the east began to turn blue. Sitting at the wheel, which was tiny in his massive hands, Hans Richtein beamed to himself. Though he imagined the Master would not see the humor, and was therefore careful not to mention it aloud, it pleased him to travel west, as it had on the *John Polidori* and a dozen other journeys before. It thrilled him to race against the dawn, to travel away from the sun; it gave him a few more moments each night with the Master's comforting presence in the back of his mind, directing him subtly, safe and secure.

Even the Master, however, could not magically produce gas for the truck, so Hans resigned himself to pulling off the westbound highway and allowing the sun to creep up on him again. Trying not to think of the long, lonely day ahead—the feeling reminded him too much of *before*—he pulled up to the pump and parked. As the numbers clicked by, Hans surveyed the area. At least it was off the beaten path. Next door was a shabby building with the flickering neon sign: PACO'S TACOS: AUT_ENTIC MEXICAN CUIS__E. Beyond was a parking lot with several semi tractors, most with trailers attached, a few without. Across the street was a brick building with TIRES in black block letters across one side and a number of those very objects on a rack outside.

Breathing in the smell of rubber and gasoline, Hans glanced back across the road while his truck continued to fill up. A billboard stood in the dense grass behind the tire store, emblazoned with a curvy woman's silhouette on a purple background and an ad for adult entertainment nearby. Hans felt a stirring of interest, and almost looked to see the exit number before remembering that the Master had not told him to be entertained. His instructions were very clear. Nodding to himself, Hans turned back to the pump just as the numbers clicked to a stop.

He took in the total with wide eyes, then dug out the wallet that had so recently been Charlie Page's and found that he still had more than enough cash. Walking briskly across the lot, he stepped inside the gas station, a bell chiming above the door as he entered. Stifling a yawn, the small cashier looked up—and up—at Hans, eyes widening.

"Pump six," Hans said shortly, looking down at the man.

"Um . . . good morning," the cashier mumbled, shaking his head as he typed at his computer.

Hans surveyed the eastern sky with dismay, and when he spoke, his voice was not far from a growl. ""Do not say such a thing. There is time yet before morning!"

"Um . . . right. Very true," the clerk noted uneasily, staring a moment before punching a few more keys. "Total comes to $82.37."

Hans grumbled to himself, but handed over the money and took his change without a word, ignoring the cashier's wish for a good day as he stepped back outside. As if any day could be good!

But the poor fool lived outside the notice of the Master; if anything, he should be pitied. Hans had lived a similarly empty life, *before* . . .

He clambered back into the driver's seat and reached for his seat belt when he had a thought that was not his own.

I thirst.

Immediately, Hans looked out over the area again. His first thought was the cashier . . . but no, he had already been inside and recorded on the security monitors. A death could be connected to him, and that might cause inconvenience for the Master. After thinking for a moment, Hans turned the engine over and pulled out onto the road, then swerved again into the truck stop. He let the truck roll with his foot off the gas, looking around until he spotted a single tractor parked away from the others at the back of the lot. Backing in so the hood of his truck was even with the back wheels of the semi, Hans parked again and got out.

He made a show of dragging his large feet on the gravel as he walked to the back of the rental truck, throwing open the lock on its loading door as loudly as possible. Ambling over to the semi as if drunk, he took care to bump hard into the driver's door before straightening up and facing its front tire, which barely came up to his hips. Unzipping his pants, he began to urinate on the wheel.

"H-hey, wuzzgoinon out there?" came a sleepy voice from inside the cabin.

Hans smiled at his own brilliance, but bellowed in a slurred voice, "Shut up! Issa free country!"

"What's going . . ." the voice repeated, now closer, at the window. Then, sharper and much louder, "Hey! What the hell do you think you're doing?"

"Shut up!" Hans repeated, spitting in the direction of the window.

There was an incensed roar from inside the semi, and the door clunked open. Hans quickly zipped his pants and backed off as the trucker hopped down, looking livid. He was smaller than Hans, as most men were, but he had a gleaming knife in his hand and a furious look on his face. Hans almost reached for Kyle Warren's service pistol, tucked at the back of his belt under his flannel shirt, before remembering that this man was the Master's.

Instead, Hans darted toward the back of the rental truck, and the trucker charged after. "Come back here you dirty son of a bitch! I'm gonna—"

What he was going to do, Hans never found out. When the trucker rounded the corner, the back door of the rental flew upward. There was a half-second in which the trucker, distracted, glanced up into the darkness inside. Then, in a motion so fast it was a blur to Hans's eyes, the trucker was snatched by his heavy winter coat and dragged up into the back of the truck. The door slammed shut again with a resounding bang, muffling the scream that started and stopped within a second.

Hans peered around the lot, making sure no one had noticed, but he saw no movement. The other semis in the lot were still, the lights in their cabins dark. He waited, shifting from foot to foot as he looked past the truck to the eastern horizon, which had begun to pinken, until at last the rental truck's door opened again, and Hans made haste to kneel in the gravel.

"Was he to your satisfaction, Master?" he asked.

"It will suffice," came the voice from above, cold and hard.

Hans looked up, crestfallen. "If you prefer another, Master, I could—"

"Fool!" the voice said, and Hans shrank down as far as his enormous frame would allow. "Do you not feel the dawn's approach? And you must not leave a larger trail behind us. This one must remain with me until we can dispose of them all."

Hans chanced a glance inside the truck, where the trucker's body lay atop the decaying remains of the three policemen they had killed at Newark. He knew, of course, that they had already attracted some attention; they had stolen the rental truck, and rather than have the police hunting a missing truck, it had seemed far better for the Master to consume all the attendants on duty and smash their computers to destroy any convenient record of the vehicle itself. Now the New Jersey police would be concerning themselves with three missing policemen and a triple homicide, and never even notice that a truck had been stolen.

"Of course, Master!" Hans moaned. How could he not have realized? The killing in New Jersey was an isolated incident, but if a slew of bodies was discovered when a matching rental truck had so recently passed through? Someone might make the connection, and they might be pursued. And the Master had made it very clear that there were to be no delays.

The cowl above the shadowed face dipped, as if the Master sensed Hans's thoughts. "When will we reach Chicago?"

Hans thought quickly; just before pulling off the highway, he had seen the signs for Akron. "With a few hours off the road at midday . . . by tonight at the latest, Lord."

The darkness within the truck made no sound, and Hans asked carefully, "You still believe he is there, Master?"

Again, there was no sound, but a chill ran down Hans's spine; the air around him might have dropped twenty degrees. When the voice spoke again, it was laden with menace. "I am certain he is there." It became even harsher, an inhuman hiss as it demanded, "Certainly you do not doubt me?"

"No, Master, never!" Hans said, horrified at the idea. "But I do not wish you to be delayed in your quest to—"

"No more delayed than you have already made me? 'Please, Master, a few hours of sleep,'" the voice mocked with a snort. "I have already been far more tolerant of your frailties than you have any right to expect. I quite agree, you must not delay me further."

Hans trembled. "If you wish, Master, I need not stop today?"

After a second's silence, the Master spoke, sounding disinterested again. "No. I will not move in the day regardless, and I need you fit to provide what meager service you can. By all means, sleep, eat, whatever you desire, so long as you are certain that we *will* reach Chicago by nightfall."

Hans understood the implied threat, and he looked up and nodded. "Have no fear, Master."

"I have none," the voice replied coldly. "Nor will I have mercy if I do not see the lights of Chicago when next I open this door."

The door slammed down.

Swallowing, Hans locked the door, then darted around the side of his truck, closing the driver's door of the semi on his way before he climbed back into the cabin of his own vehicle. He waited a moment to ensure that the Master had time to settle himself, watching with resignation as orange tinged the eastern sky, then turned over the engine, pulled out onto the road, and drove toward the on-ramp to I-80 West.

JUST AS the sun reached its zenith, Simon's steel gray eyes opened. He saw only darkness, but he had no need for his night vision here, with his back comfortable on rejuvenating earth and the close-fitted walls of the wooden crate that served as a casket surrounding him like an embrace. He knew every inch of the box even in perfect darkness. The routine of this semiconscious wakefulness at midday, too, was only a mild disruption. A few more seconds and he could return to deathlike, dreamless sleep.

And that was fortunate, for at least he was not pursued by dreams of . . .

Anita. She flashed back into Simon's memory, and with a half-articulated groan—muffled, as his lips were still paralyzed—he remembered the planned "study session." For one of his few remaining seconds, he considered breaking the date, thinking that it might be best to avoid the girl from now on and preserve himself from whatever bizarre power she exhibited over him. But in the next second he realized that, even more than yesterday, he could no longer dismiss his curiosity as idle.

The second after that, control of his limbs returned, and he moved.

Pushing open the lid, Simon blinked in the sudden light, eyes narrowed to slits as he sat up. The box was little more than a reinforced wooden shipping crate, but if any of his neighbors dared to break in while he was gone—and got through the door—it would excite less immediate suspicion than a casket. He had no need to brush any of the precious dirt off his back, for after years of total immobility, it was so matted down that nothing less than picking up the box and shaking it could dislodge it. Thinking longingly of sleep, the vampire got to his feet and staggered toward his coat rack.

He had stretched out a pale hand toward his dull black boots when it occurred to him that the sense of brightness had not dissipated. Frowning, he glanced at the lone window of his hovel. To his intense displeasure, it faced east, but no other apartment had been free when he moved in, and the window provided an important means of departure. Simon had taken care to install two layers of dark blue fabric over the window for a makeshift curtain, so no light seeped in during the day, and was methodical about replacing the curtain every time he returned home.

The room seemed so uncomfortably bright because both layers of curtain hung limp from one of the nails Simon had put in the wall, flooding the small room with midday light.

For a moment Simon only stared, frozen in the act of reaching for his boots, steel eyes wide with alarm. Then, with a sinking feeling, he looked across the room. With the sun overhead, the earth crate was shadowed, but at daybreak . . .

Unable to help himself, Simon shuddered. Only twice had he ever been caught in dawn's light, and each time for only a split second. But the excruciating sizzle as his flesh roasted down to bone on his hands, the bone itself charring black, was etched indelibly in his memory. Last night he had arrived home early and lain upon his earth in the dark even before oblivion could come, alone with his frustration. He had finally fallen into his trance when dawn arrived, but if he had foregone sleep and opened the lid . . .

There were no shadows to dodge into in the box, and he could not have sprung out of it to hide somewhere else. He would have burned, incinerated without ever even leaving his place of rest. Simon's hand shook as he replaced the curtains, shrouding the room in dim again. He had never forgotten before.

Gritting his teeth as he pulled on and laced his boots, he was forced to admit that he knew why he had forgotten. *Anita.* He had returned home from her house annoyed, confused, and so lost in his own mind that every movement was mechanical. But to have missed something that had such severe consequences . . .

As he pulled on his heavy duster, which seemed to add twenty pounds to his slight frame, the vampire shook his head, trying to return to cool calm. It was a single incident that had fortunately been a lesson rather than a punishment for his carelessness. It would not happen again, not now that he was on guard for it. Even Anita could not trip him up in such a way twice . . .

Simon fastened the snaps on his leather gloves, flexed his fingers, and stepped to the cracked, dusty sink. Once there, he took his customary swig from a bottle of mouthwash, swished the foul-tasting liquid in his mouth for a few seconds until he was sure it had wiped away the smell of blood from his breath, then spat it out. Crossing the room, he undid the locks on his door, the only things in the room apart from the crate that looked remotely well cared for. He laid his hand on the door, then paused.

Anita . . .

With a grimace, he turned back, slammed the crate's lid closed, and dragged the box to the opposite corner of the room, as far from the window as it could go.

NOT LONG after Simon stalked out of his apartment building, muttering darkly to himself, Anita Rothard shuffled into her kitchen in her pajamas, eyes still half-closed and smothering a yawn with the back of one hand. She poured herself some cereal and sat down on one of the bar stools at the kitchen counter. Marion walked in before Anita had taken her third spoonful, took one look at her face, and went to the refrigerator as well. After a moment, she set a glass of orange juice down in front of Anita with a smile.

"Long night, kiddo?"

"Mmmm," Anita replied, sipping the orange juice, her other hand holding the spoon over the counter instead of the bowl, dripping milk. Marion reached across the counter and moved Anita's wrist over her cereal again.

"Mm-mm." Anita's grunt had the inflection of "thank you."

Marion frowned. "You all right, Anita?"

Taking another bracing swallow of juice, Anita set the spoon down this time, then rubbed her eyes for a moment with the heels of her hands. "Yeah, I guess. I just . . ." Her face scrunched up as she tried to remember. "You ever think you woke up, and see something scary, but then you *really* wake up and know it was all a dream, but you still feel edgy?"

Marion raised her eyebrows. "No, but it sure doesn't sound fun."

Anita's responding, "Mmmm," had a decidedly negative ring to it, but she returned to her breakfast, and Marion left without pressing her. Anita chipped at her cereal, unable to shake the unsettling disquietude that had been with her since she woke up. She remembered feeling frightened, but not of what, and the more she struggled to remember, the blurrier her recollections became, until she had only a vague impression of a fiery red glow and the sense of impending danger.

When she came downstairs next, skin reddened from a hot shower and pigtails put up still wet, Anita was more composed and much more alert, and when she tracked down Marion in the parlor it was with her usual easy smile in place. "Hey, Marion, you still good to give me a ride to school?"

Marion rolled her honey-colored eyes. "Nah, I figure I'll just let you walk. Wear a scarf."

They both laughed, and Marion teased, "Of course I'll give you a ride. Can't have you miss your date . . ."

"It's not a—"

Anita cut off, surprised, as her father walked around the corner with his eyebrows raised. She blurted out, "What are you doing here?"

Dr. Rothard's eyes seemed to sink into his fleshy cheeks as they narrowed. "This is my house."

"Well, yeah, I meant . . ." Anita floundered for a moment. "Aren't you supposed to be at the clinic? You said you had a consultation today."

"Some of us get up at a decent hour, Anita," her father replied in a withering tone. "I've been to the office and back already."

Looking at him more carefully, Anita noticed that her father was indeed wearing his suit pants and a collared shirt, with a tie loosened around his neck. That alone should have been a giveaway, she realized; from the moment it went on, Richard Rothard never loosened his tie until all his work was done for the day. All she managed was, "Oh."

Shaking his head, Dr. Rothard pulled back the sleeve of his left arm and glanced at the gold watch on his wrist. "Traffic was nasty this morning, you'd better get dressed and leave soon if you want to be on time."

"Okay, I—" Anita stopped, frowning. "What do you mean, 'get dressed'?"

Gesturing at his daughter with one hand, Dr. Rothard said, "Well, you're certainly not going out looking like that, are you?"

Anita glanced down at herself. She was wearing blue denim overalls over a tie-dyed sweater, but the cuffs of her pant legs were rolled down more conventionally today, so only the gleaming steel rings on either side of her motorcycle boots identified them for what they were. She looked back up at her father, eyes narrowed. "What's wrong with this?"

"The boots, Anita."

Anita supposed she might have felt grateful that he wasn't attacking her sweater too, but she didn't. She said defensively, "I like them."

"I don't. Take them off before you go."

"Well, it'll be pretty cold walking through the snow in just my socks, but I suppose a little frostbite won't kill me."

"Anita, you are not leaving this house looking like a hoodlum. And I don't need the attitude."

Anita flinched, but pushed past him down the hall to the side door, calling over her shoulder, "Would you look at the time—I have literally anywhere else to be. I'll be back later."

As Dr. Rothard swelled up, Marion slipped past him, heading for the closet across the foyer. "Just a minute, Anita, I'll get my coat and—"

"I'll drive myself."

"Anita, wait . . ."

But Anita was already outside, and the door slammed behind her, echoing down the hall. For a moment, Dr. Rothard and Marion looked at each other, then he shook his head with a disgusted expression, threw up his hands, and thundered down the hall in the same direction, disappearing into his study and closing the door with almost the same force. Marion crossed her arms, leaned on the banister, and shook her head as the sound of squealing tires screeched down the drive outside.

DUCKING INSIDE the library with a quiet sigh of relief, straightening and drawing up shoulders he hadn't realized were slumped until he stepped out of direct sunlight, Simon spotted Anita sitting nearby, and his eyes narrowed curiously. Though she was obviously waiting for him, she sat with her knees drawn to her chest and her arms wrapped around them, looking disconsolate. Still regretting his spur-of-the-moment decision to meet her today in the first place, Simon wondered whether she might just send him away, thinking sourly that he could have used the sleep the second half of the day would have provided. But as he gazed at Anita for a long moment, he found himself hoping she wanted him to stay.

Not at all cheered by that sudden sentiment, Simon took a moment to control his expression before he walked over. Anita was staring vacantly forward, and Simon had to nudge her with the toe of one boot before she started and looked up.

"Simon! Whoa, I'm sorry, I didn't even see you come in," she apologized, scrambling to her feet.

Simon raised an eyebrow, but said nothing.

"Um . . . I kinda forgot my stuff . . ." Anita started, looking embarrassed, and Simon noticed at last that she indeed had nothing with her. She looked Simon over. "I guess you didn't bring anything either?"

Simon hadn't considered this and found, in a second of reflection, that he also had not been thinking about the studying portion of the meeting at all; his thoughts centered on Anita herself.

Anita seemed to notice Simon's hesitance, for her face fell. "I'm really sorry, Simon . . ."

Forcing himself to focus, he replied, "No, it's nothing. We're in a library; there must be books here we can use."

"Reassuring" was not a tone with which Simon was well-practiced, but Anita relaxed a bit, so it must have gone over well enough. "Yeah, that's true," she said more optimistically, then gestured across the lobby. "Hey, do you mind if I get some coffee first?"

Simon shook his head, trying to look nonchalant as he fell in step beside her. "Tired?"

"Yeah . . . I didn't sleep too well. Bad dreams."

Simon's steel eyes widened, but Anita was focused on the coffee shop and didn't notice. Though he wanted badly to ask what she remembered, he was afraid of triggering her memory himself. There had been no burst of horrified revelation when she saw him, so he counted himself lucky and left it alone.

"Can I buy you one?" Anita asked as they fell into line, refocusing Simon's attention on her.

"No."

"Hey, come on, you're helping me study, it's the least I can do," she pressed, but Simon shook his head, trying for an answering smile that felt alien on his lips.

"Really, I'm fine. But thank you for the offer."

Shrugging, Anita paid for a coffee and accepted a cup so large it looked like a miniature thermos. Simon drifted after her, and they made their way up to the third floor and began wandering through the reference section. Anita picked out a few thick books, her grip on them becoming more precarious as she tried to slide each off the shelf with two fingers while holding her giant coffee cup with the other three.

"Maybe I should carry them?" Simon offered dryly, taking the stack out of Anita's arms as she grinned sheepishly.

"Thanks."

They picked out a few more, Simon holding them all against his side with one hand and tossing additions onto the pile with his other hand. When Anita looked back at the stack, her eyes widened. "Wow. Think we've got enough?"

She smiled, so Simon smiled back and replied, "Somehow I think we'll manage. Shall we?"

They found a pair of padded armchairs, low to the ground, and Simon dumped the pile of books on the floor between them as Anita pulled her chair around to face Simon's. She kicked off her motorcycle boots and sat cross-legged in her chair, balancing her coffee cup on one of its arms. She was wearing mismatched socks, one intricate paisley blue, the other simple but jarringly bright yellow.

Simon stared. "A bit cold for motorcycles, isn't it?"

"What? Oh, I don't ride. Not yet, anyway," Anita added, her eyes lighting up, an adventurous grin on her face. "I just like 'em."

Simon hesitated, but it seemed the logical thing to do, so he slid his leather duster off and draped it over the back of his chair. He caught a fading look of surprise on Anita's face, and though he could not be sure, he suspected she was caught off guard by how thin he was. Clearing his throat to help dodge the question, he sat and gestured to the books. "Where should we start?"

But Anita was giving him a curious look. "Aren't you warm with those gloves?"

Simon could hardly remove them; the points of his clawlike nails pressed against the inside fingertips of his gloves. He floundered for a moment before trying to smile. "Do you *really* want to get into fashion choices?"

Anita smirked but let it go, and Simon breathed a quiet sigh of relief. He picked up an encyclopedia and asked again, "Where should we start?"

Anita sighed, taking a long swallow of coffee and running her fingers through her hair. Simon found himself watching the way her hair fell around her face, and refocused on her warm eyes only when she grinned and said, "Um . . . 'Let there be light'?"

Simon flinched and his teeth clamped together. Anita looked startled, and added hastily, "Kidding! I was kidding; I'm not that lost."

Swallowing, trying to force his expression to relax, Simon sat back up. "Good," he said, his voice faint. He cleared his throat, then added, "We'd be here a long time if you were."

"Sheesh, give me a little credit!"

"Right," Simon said, blinking his reflective eyes twice, then shaking his head and looking down at the books. "Right."

Shaking her head with a smile, Anita bent down and began sorting through the stack of books, pressing her lips together between her teeth as she searched for the best place to start. Simon moved to copy her, but even as his gloved fingers brushed aside a tome here and there, his eyes never left Anita.

SIX

Chicago, Illinois, USA

HOURS AFTER the sun vanished behind the horizon, Hans Richtein piloted a small speedboat along the Calumet River toward Lake Michigan. He tried to keep as far from the opposite bank as possible, glancing over his shoulder every twenty seconds or so toward the shore from which he had departed. He saw the outline of the rental truck parked beside a derelict steel mill. Heavy darkness lay on the riverbank, and the functional lights on the mill were few, but Hans thought he could almost see the dark-cloaked figure awaiting his return, watching over him. The thought comforted him, though going so far away was disconcerting.

The river was murky enough to have hidden the bodies in the shallows, but the Master insisted they be discarded farther out in the deeper water of the lake. So Hans drove the boat toward where the banks dropped away and open water waited, keeping his pace slow so the engine would attract no attention. He had already broken the running lights on the boat, just as the Master had broken the man from whom they'd stolen it.

When Hans glanced back and found even the steel mill's lights growing fainter, his sense of unease deepened, but as if in response to his concern, fog rose around the boat, shrouding it from view. Overhead, the wispy clouds thickened, stars disappearing one by one behind their veil until even the moon was but a hazy glow. The misty walls on either side of the boat rose higher, and they closed in behind the boat as it moved, like a tidal wave pursuing it without any particular rush. In contrast, the mist before the prow retracted as the boat slid forward, and Hans grew calm, the thick bands of muscle in his shoulders relaxing as the Master made his way clear.

A mile out into the lake, Hans let the boat glide to a smooth halt, easing back the throttle until it bobbed in the water. Even the waves stilled, the murky water barely trembling, as if afraid to defy the power on the distant riverbank. Hans grinned down at the water. *As well it should be.*

Then he turned to his work. The boat owner's corpse still wore its look of stunned surprise and was pleasantly pliable; handling him took only a moment. Hans tied a length of nylon rope around the body's neck, fixed the other end to a pair of cinder blocks, and with a grunt of effort pitched all three over the side. The trucker the Master had killed just before dawn followed a moment later.

Storage in the cold truck had kept Kyle Warren, Charlie Page, and Nick Rossini from bloating, but the smell coming from their bodies made Hans retch in spite of himself. When he had opened the back of the truck at the riverbank, only his intense desire not to offend the Master had allowed him to keep a straight face. The breeze did little to drive the smell off, and in the short time it took Hans to drag their hideous remains down to his stolen boat from the truck he had choked back vomit twice.

Now, away from the Master, the impulse overcame him, and some of the greasy pizza he had consumed in his short midday stop in Indiana plopped into Lake Michigan. Wiping his mouth on the back of his hand, Hans turned back to the bodies, gritted his teeth, and tied them to more cinder blocks. As he tossed them one by one into the water, they vanished into the depths, vacant eyes staring upward until the darkness consumed them.

Hans rested only a moment, the muscles in his upper arms aching slightly, before he went back to the controls to turn the boat in a tight half circle and accelerate back toward shore. He knew a moment of fear that he might not be able to find the way—heading out, his only destination had been "away from the shore"—but the mist that had ushered him out recoiled again as the Master guided him home. More confident, he picked up the speed as much as he dared, letting the wind blow some of the foul corpse odor away onto the breeze and returning to his master all the sooner.

When he again passed between the two riverbanks, however, he slackened his pace, determined to draw no attention. He had just begun to see a faint glow before him—perhaps the headlights of cars on a bridge?—when the mist stopped recoiling and formed a solid wall in front of the boat. Pulling back the throttle, Hans directed the boat toward a grimy, blackened seawall until its fiberglass hull bumped gently into the steel. He looked up expectantly, and was not disappointed.

Perched at the edge of the wall above, the hooded figure waited with its fingers steepled, tapping the index fingertips against each other. Planting one foot on the edge of the boat, Hans leapt, grabbing the edge of the seawall and ignoring the pain as the rusted metal bit into his palms. He started to pull his bulk up, but then the Master moved, grasping Hans by the wrist with one icy, skeletal hand and heaving his heavy servant onto land as if lifting nothing more than a feather.

"Thank you, Master!" Hans said, getting to his feet and wiping the grime off his hands onto his jeans.

The robed figure did not respond, instead turning its attention back to the boat. He flicked his fingers, and the boat immediately sank, as if some unseen hand were pressing it down, until the murky water poured onto the deck. But when the vampire lowered his hand, the boat sprang back up like a cork, filled to the gunwales with water but floating resolutely. Emitting a low hiss, the cowled face turned to Richtein. "What is this?"

Swallowing, Hans ventured, "Modern boats are made not to sink, my lord, even if you put holes in them."

The vampire snarled, and Hans tried unsuccessfully to shrink back; his broad frame was not made for cowering in on himself. But after a second, the Master fell silent and looked northward. Though nothing of downtown Chicago was visible from their position on the docks, the Master still seemed content, and Hans felt brave enough to offer, "He is here, my lord."

Desperate not to offend again, he did not make it a question.

"Oh, yes," the icy voice agreed, unwonted satisfaction in its sepulchral tones. "Yes, I'm quite certain he's here."

The Master glanced back at the boat and raised both hands. The craft shuddered, water spilling over the sides as it rocked back and forth. With a series of loud cracks and snaps, it broke into pieces. The engine dragged a chunk down into the depths while the other pieces drifted away toward Lake Michigan on the river's current.

In a voice laden with such cruel amusement that Hans shivered and drew his thick winter jacket tighter over his chest, the Master added, "But not for long."

"WELL, I think I'm definitely up to a passing grade now!" Anita said, giggling a bit as they made their way back down the stairs and toward the exit. "Thanks again for studying with me, Simon, I know you must have a lot of studying to do yourself."

A step behind, Simon nodded and made a noncommittal noise in his throat. It was a good thing Anita had started to catch on to the historical trends they had gone over, because, since sunset, he had been finding it increasingly difficult to concentrate on anything but Anita herself. He had a new, predatory appreciation for her beauty, more than what he had seen in the day. At the moment his full powers returned, it had taken most of his control not to spring out of his chair at her, and the rest to keep his fangs retracted.

He could almost see the blood in the twin carotid arteries in her neck as the warm liquid pumped up to her brain. He detected no obstruction to the flow, though when she became excited or frustrated it picked up pace and Simon struggled not to twitch. Her heartbeat rang in his ears, so close that all the other humans they passed faded away like background noise. Following her outside, he almost walked into a doorframe before twisting sideways to dodge it at the last second.

Stepping into the chilly night was a relief; though Anita's body heat stood out even more while surrounded by frigid concrete, it also radiated less through the air; it was distracting, not all-consuming. Simon found himself able to think a bit more clearly, and so he noticed Anita shivering in the cold, arms clutched around her chest and rubbing the sleeves of her sweater against her biceps.

"Wow, it got really c-c-cold," she stammered.

Simon shrugged out of his leather coat and held it out to her. "Please."

"Oh n-n-no, I don't want you to be c-cold too . . ."

"Trust me, it's not a problem," Simon returned dryly, drawing the coat open with both hands now and shaking it at her. "I insist."

Anita did not protest again, slipping her arms through the sleeves of the coat as Simon helped her into it. The tails reached her heels and the sleeves covered her hands, but she wrapped the front tightly around herself nonetheless. Wearing it himself, Simon would have left no warmth in it, but they had been inside the library so long that it had picked up some heat anyway, and Anita sighed contentedly.

As he settled the collar on her shoulder, one of Simon's gloved fingers brushed Anita's neck, and for an instant, the rhythm of her pulse radiated up his hand and through his nerves. He took a deep breath through his nose to control himself, clamping his jaw shut behind his lips to force his fangs to stay retracted. Anita's hair had fallen down her back while they studied, though it was still crimped where the pigtail bands had been, and Simon almost brushed it out so it would drape down the back of the coat before he thought of how easy it would be to break her neck if he got it in his iron grip.

He drew his hand back, clenching it into a fist. Best not to chance it.

"Thanks!" Anita said, waving the long sleeves and laughing. "Your arms are really long."

"Happy to help," Simon said, smiling while opening his mouth no more than necessary to talk. "I'll walk you to your car."

"Are you sure?"

"I am going to want the coat back eventually."

Anita laughed, and Simon tried to as well, though it sounded flimsy to his ears. They walked in silence for a moment, keeping a brisk pace; she was obviously intent on getting out of the cold as quickly as possible, coat or no coat. Simon focused on Anita herself so he would not envision the parking lot at the end of their walk, and how many dark places there might be to pull her into, or how quickly he could clap one gloved hand over her mouth so she wouldn't scream, or how his glowing red eyes would prevent her from making any sound at all . . .

"Man, that looks pretty bad."

Focus. Simon followed Anita's gaze east, where thunderheads had gathered over Lake Michigan. Even miles away from the waterfront, the storm did indeed look ominous, and overhead the cloud cover was already thick. The only illumination came from the campus lights and the cars passing on the highway.

Simon frowned. "Yes, it does. Is it supposed to snow?"

"I dunno; I didn't check the weather today."

The vampire glanced back, still frowning, and his eyes narrowed. "Speaking of which, this is the second day in a row you haven't worn warm enough clothes for the weather."

"What? Oh," Anita said, and she blushed, avoiding Simon's gaze and staring straight ahead. "I forgot to grab my coat this morning."

Simon glanced sideways as he picked up a heartbeat, but it was only a campus security officer heading in the opposite direction. Trying to stay focused, he pressed, "Your coat and all your study materials?"

"Er . . . yeah." Anita bit down on her bottom lip.

"Why?"

She sighed and looked up at Simon. "Just had a bit of a bad start this morning. It's nothing."

"If you say so . . ."

They were almost to the street, and Anita was looking away, clearly not eager to share anything else. But then she straightened as if she'd had a sudden thought, and her brown eyes were lively again as she turned back to Simon. "Hey, are you doing anything Wednesday?"

Though he knew where she was leading, Simon could hardly say that without raising awkward questions, so he just shook his head. "No."

"Okay . . ." Anita hesitated, and Simon wondered why, but before he could press her, she continued in a rush, "Well, if you don't have anything come up, my parents and I were wondering if you'd like to come over for dinner? As . . . you know . . . kind of a thank you for helping me. And we might be able to study some more after, if you wouldn't mind?"

Simon hesitated, his dark eyebrows drawing together so they almost met. Though he had considered little else between overhearing it the night before and meeting up with Anita today, he still had no answer. He could not eat dinner with her anywhere; his body took one nourishment alone. Worse still, inside her home, with only her parents and the servant as witnesses, it would be easy for him to snap and kill them all, for who would come looking for them soon enough to put him in any real danger? He had seen last night that the neighbors' houses were well removed, and with a hedge fence ringing the property, too. No one would hear them scream.

But if he wanted to kill her, why not now, when she was defenseless? No one would ever find him if her parents gave the police his name, and what would appear on the security tapes? Just Anita, walking alone into a shadow with no apparent motivation but curiosity . . .

"I understand if you don't want to." Anita's voice forced Simon's attention back to the moment, and when he fixed her with his steel gaze again his expression became confused. Anita looked . . . what? He couldn't place her expression. Not embarrassed, but more than hesitant. "Or if you have something else to do. I just thought I'd offer . . ."

What to do?

Lost though he was in indecision, even Simon could tell that Anita was worried he was going to turn her down again, and she was going to take it as a personal hurt. Thoughts of the physical hurt he might inflict on her if he agreed drifted out of his mind, and yet again, Simon had the odd impression someone else was speaking through his mouth when he said, "No. I'm sorry, I just . . . had to think of when I'll be studying," he managed before adding, "but I'd love to come over. What time?"

Anita's expression, so near to resignation, suddenly lit up, and Simon was struck again by how intense her eyes were, bulging a bit in her excitement. "Really? Awesome! Um . . . let's say . . . seven o'clock?"

Long after sunset, without even a hope of easing into his nocturnally enhanced senses. Simon fought to keep the grimace off his face, fearing Anita would misinterpret it. "Seven it is."

"Awesome," Anita repeated, grinning, then gestured across the street. "Come on, I'm parked in 5C."

They jaywalked across the road, Anita looking both ways, Simon looking at Anita, his ears telling him the cars on the road were much too far away to pose a threat. With no immediate danger, it was impossible for anything to distract him from her echoing heartbeat, the warmth of what skin was still exposed, and the fact that he could hear no heartbeats in the lot beyond . . .

Skipping under the trees, Anita slid a little bit when she hit an icy patch, and Simon shot out a gloved hand to catch her by the elbow before she fell. His grip was tight, and even through his own gloves, the borrowed coat, and her sweater, he felt the blood sliding through her veins, quickened by her lingering excitement. He drew in a gasping breath through his teeth, both hands tightening on reflex—even though one still held Anita's arm.

She let out a little cry of pain, then looked up into Simon's face with a confused expression that quickly became wary, almost frightened. Forcing himself to loosen his hold on her, knowing that it would be the work of a second to let his fangs lower and bury them in her throat, he tried to sound level when he asked, "What?"

"I . . . you just . . . you looked really intense for a second there . . ."

Blood . . . so close . . . so warm . . .

Simon's hand shook as he commanded his fingers, one by one, to let her go.

"I was afraid you were going to fall," he said quietly, not trusting himself to open his mouth all the way. He tapped the toe of one of his own boots on the hard pavement, looking down at it so he wouldn't have to see the faint movement of blood in her neck, though her pulse was now deafening from her fear. "Not the best place for a landing . . ."

"No. No, that would've hurt," Anita agreed, still sounding wary.

"I'm sorry if I hurt you, but I didn't want you to fall . . ."

Anita took a step closer. Surprised by this movement, Simon looked up and saw that the wariness in her expression had been replaced with concern—but not for herself. "No, it's fine. I mean, thanks. You're right, that would have been nasty."

She gave him a tentative smile, and Simon returned the expression half-heartedly. Anita's brow furrowed, and she looked as if she were still worried about having offended him. He almost laughed at that, but instead cleared his throat and offered her his left arm. "Want a hand?"

"Thanks."

She pulled up the long leather sleeve of Simon's coat and laid her hand on his elbow, putting some weight there to keep herself steady. The vampire found this marginally easier to bear, though he her pulse still whispered through her fingertips. As they walked across the parking lot, Anita's hand tightened on his arm, her thumb absently tracing his triceps. He caught an intrigued look on her face in his peripheral vision, and wondered if the contrast between his thin frame and the iron-hard muscle all along it surprised her.

When they reached Anita's car—not the BMW he had seen her in the night before, but a sleek SUV—the vampire looked for a safe, bland comment and settled on, "Nice car."

To his surprise, Anita looked away, taking her hand back and clearing her throat. "Thanks."

Perplexed, Simon struggled for words while trying not to look at Anita's neck; with her face twisted away, the muscles—and veins—stood out.

"Er . . . I suppose I'll see you Wednesday, then?"

"Oh! Yeah, I'd better give you the address!" Anita snapped out of her abstraction. She opened the driver's door and leaned across to open the glove box, then began rummaging around inside. She was totally distracted, and Simon knew this was the moment to strike. His gloved hands curled into claws without his consent, and he shifted forward, leaning over her back. One strike to the spine would paralyze her, and he could hurl her into the car and drain her blood at his leisure. Once she was empty, it would take only a little work to get the SUV in some horrible accident, fire charring her corpse. A broken back and a lack of blood would hardly stand out in that mess. His fangs descended . . .

Stop! His entire body shuddered as he half-lurched toward her.

Why? He was having trouble coming up with an answer as Anita cried, "Gotcha!"

She turned, and with a supreme effort of will, Simon straightened back up at the same time, covering his mouth with one gloved hand as he did so. He raised his eyebrows, trying to look curious without speaking.

"Sorry, normally I'd just text you, but my cell phone was in my backpack, of course . . ." Anita grumbled as she began to write down the address with the pen and paper she had just produced.

"Mmm," Simon mumbled, trying to sound agreeable.

"Okay, here," she said, tearing off the top note and handing it over. Simon took it with his free hand, keeping the other pressed over his lips. "It's in Evanston. It's quickest to just take Ninety-Four there."

Simon had no intention of traveling by anything requiring wheels—or contact with the ground, for that matter—but he nodded and dropped his right hand as his fangs retracted at last. "All right. I'll see you then."

"Okay. And, um . . . Simon . . ." Anita bit the inside of her bottom lip, not meeting his gaze. "I . . . well . . ."

"What?" he asked, his nerves strained almost to the breaking point. It wasn't difficult to imagine what his teeth could do to her full bottom lip, swollen with blood even in this chill. In a more level tone, he added, "Are you all right?"

Anita floundered for a moment, then said in a rush, "Yeah, it's just, it doesn't bother me at all—I mean, I'm the one with biker boots and stripy socks—but my dad's kinda . . . conservative when it comes to clothes, so . . ."

She trailed off, looking ashamed, and Simon finally grasped where she was going. He nodded, smirking. "And head-to-toe black is probably not the best way to make a first impression?"

Anita nodded back, not looking up, and Simon reached out a hand without meaning to. He laid it gently on her upper arm, and she looked up into his eyes, surprised. Though he could feel, again, the faint pulse in her brachial artery, this time it was easier to ignore, because he was focused on her eyes.

"Not a problem." He smiled. "Though I would like the coat back."

"What? Oh! Yeah, sorry!" Anita said, shrugging off Simon's leather coat and handing it back. She shivered in the sudden cold, but some of her brief melancholy seemed to have dissipated. "I totally forgot; it's so comfy!"

Slinging the coat on with a fluid, practiced motion, Simon nodded. "I'm rather fond of it myself." He took two steps back, the distance paining him as it put more cold air between her hot blood and his eager lips, and worked to keep his face calm as he added, "Good luck with your other finals. I'll see you Wednesday."

"Thanks, you too!" Anita said, giving Simon a warm smile that briefly pacified the violent drive in him. She ducked into the car, closed the door, and turned the engine over, immediately reaching for the heater. Backing out of her spot, she waved once to Simon, who lifted a single gloved hand in farewell as the SUV crept over the slushy ground and out onto the street.

Once he was sure she was gone, Simon darted to the tree line, ducking out of sight of anyone who might pass by. Once he was veiled in shadow, he doubled over beside a tree, gloved fingertips gouging lines into the wood, gasping. His fangs had lowered again of their own volition, and the tree's bark turned red in the preternatural glow of his eyes. Stunned that he had managed to not kill Anita and still baffled as to why, he stood there, shuddering, resisting the impulse to throw himself out of hiding and attack the nearest thing with a pulse.

He reminded himself that there was a reason he did not hunt at the school, and that the murder would be far too easy to connect with him, especially since Anita had seen him here in the lot so recently. She would be sure to provide information about him if the police asked, and he had created that liability himself by sparing her. Gritting his teeth in frustration, he slowly stood back up.

He would not kill here. He could wait. He told himself that until he was certain he would not slip up, then set off into the night.

Here? No. Kill? Yes.

SEVEN

ANITA PACED back and forth, batting her hair out of her face. The smell of simmering tomato sauce wafted down the hall, and she drummed her fingers against the banister whenever she paused beside it, the rings on her left hand clicking together as she did. She glanced for the tenth time in as many minutes at her watch.

It was 6:47 Wednesday evening. Anita realized dinner wouldn't be ready at seven, or probably even near that time, but she wanted a chance to talk to Simon anyway. She had not seen him since their study session on Saturday. It wasn't unusual—tens of thousands of students attended UIC, and even Simon's distinctive all-black ensemble was easily lost in the crowd—but Anita was worried nonetheless. If something had come up, or Simon had simply changed his mind, she would only find out when he didn't show.

Wearing a T-shirt from her senior high school musical, its black front interrupted by the explosion of color that made up the musical's title, her faded jeans and rainbow-striped toe socks not complementing it at all, Anita fully expected that the outfit would draw her father's ire when they were entertaining a guest. However, she had never seen Simon in anything but black, and she wasn't sure what he would wear instead, so she thought it best to divert Dr. Rothard's wrath just in case. Wearing her hair down for once, Anita could not help repeatedly brushing it back over her ears, even though it fell forward again whenever she moved. She looked at the hair band on her right wrist, where it blended in with a cluster of plastic bracelets.

"No," a voice said sternly. "Leave it down, looks cuter."

Christine Stokely lounged on a leather loveseat in the parlor, her arms draped over one end onto a nearby end table, her feet swaying as they hung over the other end. She was watching Anita fret in the hallway, thin eyebrows raised over a bored expression. "He'll be here when he gets here, Anita; quit pacing."

Anita forced herself to stand still, managed it for about five seconds, then grabbed several locks of her hair and pantomimed pulling them out of her head. "Rrrrgggghhh!"

Christine sat up with unconscious grace, her silky black hair sliding like liquid from her shoulders. She brushed a strand of it out of her face with one long fingernail, and unlike Anita's, it stayed put. Her big, sky blue eyes blinked irritably. "Look, what's the boggle? You're just having him over for dinner. You've known him for what, two days?"

"Well, I met him last week . . ."

"That doesn't count, you said you haven't seen him since the weekend. So what's the problem? I thought you weren't calling him your boyfriend yet."

"Oh no, not you too. Look, he's not—"

"Then quit worrying! He's a new acquaintance that you're having over for dinner, so calm down."

She leaned back on the sofa, rolling her eyes and extending her arms above her head, yawning and stretching like a cat. She wore a hot pink tunic top that extended to her thighs, cinched around her waist with a wide, glossy black belt that matched her black leggings and socks. One billowing sleeve of her top draped off her left shoulder. She wore a silver tennis bracelet on one wrist and a sapphire ring on the middle finger of her other hand.

"So, how did Spanish go?"

"What?" Anita asked.

Christine rolled her eyes and made an impatient sound. "Spanish! You know, finals? College? It was today, wasn't it?"

"Oh. Right." Anita blinked, forcing herself to focus. "It wasn't a problem. The oral portion was a cakewalk."

"Hmm. Well, I guess it would be. You do have Marion as your paid personal tutor."

"Hey!" Anita complained. "She helps me because she wants to; it's not part of her job."

Christine sat up, her expression reflecting polite disbelief. "Well, what else is she going to do? Refuse to help her bosses' daughter?"

Anita frowned, but did not respond. Before she could formulate a reply, a wind chime sounded from the hall and echoed through the house.

Turning at the musical sound of the doorbell, Anita's expression lit up, her momentary disconcert forgotten. Christine looked toward the door with interest as she drifted across the parlor toward a recliner facing the back hallway, where she could see Simon before he saw her. She sat, batted back a lock of her shiny black hair, and leaned forward on her crossed legs.

Anita composed herself, brushed her hair behind her ear again resolutely, and opened the door with a smile. Simon stood on the stoop, and the light from the porch lamp shadowed his sharp facial features, except his eerie steel eyes, which seemed to shine with a light of their own. He leaned forward in a bow of sorts, a forced smile on his lips. "Good evening, Anita."

"Hey, Simon! How are you?"

"Fine, thank you."

"I haven't seen you since we studied."

"Well, I have had my own finals to study for." Then, before she could ask, he added, "How are yours going? Are you ready for tomorrow?"

Anita's mouth turned down on one side. "I guess we'll find out . . ."

She shrugged with forced nonchalance, and Simon nodded back, a bit unsure. Anita smiled for a minute before stepping out of the doorway and gesturing extravagantly with one arm.

SIMON MOVED a foot toward the threshold, then stopped as if his foot had hit an invisible brick wall. Thinking quickly, he faked a violent cough, resting one hand against the doorframe to steady himself. Anita stepped forward with a look of curious concern, offering her hand, but he straightened, stretching his neck to one side before nodding. "I'm all right. May I come in?"

Anita nodded. "Yeah, come on in, Marion's cooking dinner."

Simon tried to keep his expression smooth; he had been avoiding the university campus like a plague house for fear of running into Anita again before he had to, worried that his resistance to temptation might falter, but there was nothing for it now, and he stepped through without hesitation. Anita appraised his appearance and relaxed a little; he suspected she was relieved that he had shed his all-black motif in favor of blue jeans and a scarlet dress shirt, unbuttoned at his neck. He still had the same short black leather boots in which Anita had always seen him, but he had acquired a new, brown leather bomber jacket as well.

The vampire himself wasn't altogether happy with his appearance, but he imagined that the two hypnotized clerks at the department store would have been even less pleased than him—if they had any inkling of what had happened. Simon rubbed the fingertips of his right hand with his thumb; it was still odd to feel the smooth curve of short nails instead of long claws. Filing them down with his kukri knife had taken the better part of an hour, and he had also shaved the few hairs from his palms.

Anita herself was looking at Simon, eyebrows raised, evidently waiting on his reaction to her home. He noticed the well-polished gleam of the hardwood floor, and had already judged that there was a basement from the hollow clunks produced by his bootsteps. The entrance foyer was a narrow room, but the ceiling was high, and a long hallway led straight off from the front door. From its end, Simon smelled something cooking—Italian. To Simon's left was a tall, steep staircase, the carpeted steps short but wide enough for two people to ascend them abreast.

Sensing that Anita was waiting for him to speak, he studied a framed landscape of Lake Michigan. "This is lovely."

"I…thanks!" Simon raised an eyebrow, and Anita admitted, "I did that a couple years ago."

She smiled, and Simon gave it his best effort to return it naturally. Then he glanced to the right.

His eyes zeroed in on the other woman, leaning forward with her chin resting in her palm, the elbow of the same arm balanced on her crossed knees. Her hair was long, black, and shiny. Her baby blue eyes were catlike and alert, and they followed his movements. Beneath her laid-back, casual posture, Simon discerned the careful attention she paid to his every motion. She watched him as a hunter watched prey. *Like a vampire*, he thought.

It startled him that he had needed to pick her up with his eyes, though now that he paid attention, her heartbeat offered its own, seductive rhythm. He had been so focused on Anita . . .

Simon forced a detached look onto his face, nodding to her as his eyes took in the room she occupied. It was a small parlor that didn't manage to hold his attention very long, so he turned his gaze back to Anita, furtively keeping the other woman in his peripheral view. "You have other company."

It was a statement, but it provoked a quick response. "Oh yeah, sorry. Simon, this is my best friend, Christine Stokely. Christine, this is Simon, my new study buddy."

Christine lazily rose and then extended one hand and said, "Charmed."

She made it sound bored and uncaring, as if she were making small talk about the dust on a table. Her hand hung in the air limply, and she made a show of being distracted. But when Simon looked directly at her, her eyes narrowed and fixed on his. Her mouth opened ever so slightly, and she looked both confused and intrigued, as if she knew there was something off about him.

Eager to put an end to her speculating, Simon squeezed her hand in his and watched her eyes widen as the icy chill in his touch sidetracked her curiosity for a split second. He shook her hand and held it a second longer than he needed to, letting the cold seep into her flesh before releasing her. She recoiled, clutching her palm with narrow, startled eyes. "Your hand . . . it's so cold . . ."

Simon smiled, a sight that made both Anita and Christine flinch just a bit. "It's chilly outside."

Anita recovered first, and set her hands on Simon's shoulders. "Can I take your coat, Simon?"

The vampire arched his back, shrugging the leather jacket off into her hands. As Anita opened the closet to hang up Simon's coat, Christine leaned against a wall on the vampire's other side, eyeing him again with that curious, speculative look. Her full lips curved into a small, secretive smile when he met her eyes.

When she emerged from the closet, Anita took Simon's hand. A slight shiver ran over her frame, and Simon knew she felt the ice in his grip too, but she did not let go. Instead, she laced her fingers through his and led him down the hall to the kitchen. Christine trailed a few steps behind.

As they approached the kitchen, Anita took a deep breath through her nose, a smile lighting up her face as her warm eyes half-closed. Simon chanced a deep breath as well, and tried not to twitch. Anita's scent, almost like vanilla—so very close, her body actually touching his—was enough to make him clamp his jaws shut again.

From behind him, he caught a more floral scent as well, a mixture of lilies and cream that he assumed had to be Christine's. Different from Anita's, a bit stronger, but just as luscious and appealing.

With both women so near, the vampire was hard-pressed to focus on anything else, but when he looked straight ahead he saw two women working over a stove and quibbling with one another. They were cooking something, and doing it well, if Anita's reaction was any indication. Forcing himself to concentrate, Simon breathed in again and identified the scents of bread and tomato sauce. *Definitely something Italian.* There was another scent mixed in, faint but somehow nauseating. Simon tried to place it, but the conversation distracted him before he made much progress.

"Let me check the breadsticks while you do that, Marion."

Simon glanced at the Hispanic woman, who rolled her eyes as she said, "Really, Nancy, I can handle it."

"I don't mind," replied the older woman.

"Neither do I," Marion grumbled, though she was smiling too. She bumped Nancy sideways with her hip to clear her way to the oven. Simon stared, but Nancy only laughed.

Anita released Simon's hand, skipping forward. He hesitated in the hallway, and Christine came up beside him. He sensed her eyes on him, but ignored her for the moment.

"Hey, Mom!"

Nancy Rothard turned to face her daughter, and Marion seized the moment, opening the stove door and eyeing the breadsticks with a triumphant noise. Nancy laughed again, shaking her head, then her eyes found Simon and she looked the vampire over briefly, her expression showing only curiosity and polite interest.

"Mom, this is Simon. Simon, this is my mom."

Stepping out from behind the counter separating them, Nancy extended her hand to Simon, who shook it. This time he released her quickly, though she still shivered at his coldness. But she did not comment, instead smiling and saying, "Welcome to our home, Simon. We're glad you could join us."

"Thank you, Mrs. Rothard."

"Oh, please, call me Nancy."

Simon frowned, glancing at Anita. Her mother didn't miss the gesture, and her smile turned wry.

"I'm not very traditional about things like that, don't worry."

Trying to compose his expression, Simon tried a smile. "As you wish."

"We're just putting the final touches on dinner now—"

"I'm putting the final touches on dinner," Marion's voice came from behind Nancy, sounding disgruntled. "You're trying to keep me from doing my job."

Anita and her mother both laughed, though Simon noticed that Christine didn't. Closing the oven door, Marion turned and extended her hand over the counter. Simon shook it as well. The woman looked several years older than Anita, though much younger than Nancy.

"I'm Marion. Nice to—hey, you're pretty cold. You want a hot drink to warm you up while dinner's cooking?"

Simon bit his tongue; he imagined the humans wouldn't see the irony. "No, thank you, I'm fine."

"Christine?"

"Nothing for me."

"Anita?"

Anita glanced at her two friends, then shook her head. "No, but thanks, Marion."

Nancy had been subtly backing up behind Marion, and when Anita spoke she seized the lid off a pot, letting out a rush of steam that condensed on her face. "Should be a few more minutes, kids," she noted as Marion turned to give her a sour look. "Why don't you go watch TV or something in the den? We'll call you when it's ready."

"You know, you're gonna have to cut my salary if you keep doing all this, and I'm not gonna like that . . ." Marion complained, trying to reach around her employer for the pot Simon guessed contained the tomato sauce.

As Nancy laughed, Anita gestured with her head across the kitchen, and Simon and Christine followed. The kitchen flowed uninterrupted into a dinette with a small breakfast table. Simon followed Anita into the dinette and through the open door beyond.

A long oak table had chairs enough for twenty, with more in the corners of the room, though only five places had been set. The floor here was hardwood as well, but a long rug of simple, interwoven earth tones stretched beyond the length and width of the table; even if scooted back, no chair would touch the shiny floor. A sumptuous chandelier with more lights than Simon could easily count hung suspended over the table—he averted his eyes before it became a compulsion—and beyond was a stained glass window of a white rose in full bloom facing east.

"This is the dining room," Anita said unnecessarily, already moving toward a door to the left of where they had entered, but she stopped when Simon did not follow.

Christine stepped up on the vampire's other side, crossing her arms over her ribcage and drawing them just slightly upward. Simon wondered if she was trying to show off her breasts. She certainly did not need to; there was no missing them. She gave Simon a smile that he could not read. "Lovely, isn't it? I've always liked that, Anita. We've got the rose window at our place too, but something about the morning light here . . . You should see it, Simon."

Well, I could see it for a second . . . Stained glass would not protect him from the sunrise. "Do you live nearby?"

"Hmm?" Christine asked in a voice that was almost a purr. "Oh, yeah, a couple subdivisions over."

Simon noticed Anita hesitating by the door, looking unsure what to say. He turned away from the window. "It is beautiful, Anita."

"Thanks." Simon narrowed his eyes, surprised by the sudden torpor in the word, but before he could ask, Anita beckoned them both and added a bit more brightly, "Come on, we can chill in here until dinner's ready."

The vampire followed his host through a short hallway and into a room that might have been an octagon had it not been attached to the rest of the house. Simon had noticed it from the outside—it protruded beyond the rest of the front wall of the Rothards' Tudor home. A large, U-shaped couch dominated the center of the room, resting on a more decorative rug that again covered a large section of the glossy wooden floor. Centered in front of the leather couch was a glass table, and mounted on the wall beyond was the largest television Simon had ever seen, a flat screen only inches thick. Several shelves full of movies lined two more of the walls, all fitted to the wall space between ceiling-high glass windows. On the remaining wall was a rack of CDs as tall as Simon himself, a stack of vinyl records, a stereo system with an MP3 jack, and what Simon was almost certain was a record player.

Christine strolled around the couch and took a seat facing the television. Anita followed suit, sitting opposite Christine with a space between them for Simon. She smiled and patted the leather cushion. "Come on, let's see if there's anything good on."

While Anita went for the remote and began flipping through channels, Christine gave Simon that analytical look again. Not sure how to respond, he looked back at her, gray eyes fixed on her icy blue ones. The corner of her mouth twitched, as if she wanted to frown, but she controlled her expression this time, eyes narrowing. She glanced at Anita, pursed her lips, then started to slide over, as if to take the place meant for Simon.

The vampire frowned, hesitated an instant, then acted on the first impulse that entered his mind. He knew it was foolish; so easy to be caught—such a pointless, reckless use of his powers. But he was full of blood—knowing the temptation Anita would pose, and a bit frustrated after the weekend, he had fed more than necessary the previous night to bolster himself—and it gave him a sort of intemperate daring. He locked eyes with Christine, more force in his gaze, and she froze, entranced. Before Anita noticed this bizarre behavior, Simon moved.

Normally, a young vampire was reduced to moving at the speed of his human prey; his reflexes were much better than theirs would ever be, but he still moved from place to place as they did. But when glutted on blood and very well rested, he could occasionally tap deeper powers that matched his impossible strength.

And so Simon crossed the ten feet from the door to the couch in half a second, blurring with the pure speed of the motion. In the time it took to blink, he had gone from a standing position at the door, vaulted over the back of the couch, and landed lightly between the girls.

Though Anita had been focused on the TV, she still jumped when Simon appeared beside her, her warm eyes wide. "Whoa! Eager, beaver?"

Simon cleared his throat, gesturing toward the end of the couch. "Well, you know, it was a long walk . . ." he joked, grinning at her. He knew that exhibiting his powers like that was risky, but it gave him a strange rush too.

Anita tilted her head to one side, but fortunately looked past Simon the next second. "Hey, Chris, you okay?"

Simon looked at Christine too, and saw that she was still gazing blankly at the door, but Anita's voice snapped her out of her preoc-cupation. She recoiled as she found Simon only inches away.

"Chris?" Anita sounded concerned now.

"What?" the raven-haired girl asked, shaking her head, her hair shimmering like oil on water as she did so. Then she blinked, and her wide eyes narrowed again. "Yeah, sorry, must have spaced out for a minute."

Smirking to himself, Simon sat back, turning his attention to the TV.

But after a moment, the smirk was gone, and the vampire was trying his best just to keep from grimacing. The couch was spacious, but Anita and Christine had both slid closer to him; their body heat radiated through the air and whispered across his flesh. Anita's vanilla scent and Christine's, like flowers, forced themselves upon him even as he tried to breathe as little as possible.

Christine leaned back, head tilted toward Simon, and her silky hair spilled out onto his shoulder. His mouth fell open with a shaky indrawn breath. Trying to control himself, he looked over at Anita. She noticed the movement, looking up into his eyes and smiling slowly. He smiled back cautiously, and saw Anita relax a tension in her shoulders he had not previously noticed. She leaned her head back also, her skin flushed, and Simon traced the path of blood in her neck.

His jaw clenched as he looked back to the television, unaware of what he was watching. Unable to help himself, he kept looking at the two women in his peripheral view; Anita, unsuspecting and relaxed, and Christine, occasionally giving him furtive, appraising looks between long stretches of watching the TV. It would be so easy to kill them both. Or better yet, stun one while he drained the other, so he could enjoy their blood without waste. It would only be the work of a moment or two to kill everyone else in the house, and then he could be on his way.

Focus. I fed last night. I am not thirsty.

And he wasn't. He did not need either of them, could get by without their blood—indeed, without any blood tonight. He did not need dinner.

Maybe not, but dessert . . .

Simon almost jumped off the couch when a deep, echoing bass note rang through the entire house.

Anita and Christine both laughed, and Anita said, "You know, I could have sworn you said you *weren't* always jumpy . . ."

Simon tried to laugh, though he cringed at how weak it sounded. "Sorry, just . . . wasn't expecting that."

Anita started to get up, though Christine remained sitting beside Simon. "Yeah, that's our gong. Marion loves it. Breakfast, lunch, dinner, sunset, Tuesday . . . you name an occasion, she'll find a reason to bang the gong." She giggled.

"Oh, like you don't," Christine said, rolling her eyes. "I remember when you got that thing. I felt like I was living in China again."

Both girls laughed.

"But right now it means dinner?" Simon ventured after a second, and Anita nodded. Slowly unclenching his fingers, reflecting that his claws would have gouged into his palms if he hadn't filed them down, Simon got to his feet also, turning to offer his hand to Christine. She took it, and though her jaw tightened, she did not let go as she pulled herself up.

"Thanks," she breathed, her eyes on Simon's face. He noted with some disconcert that Christine wasn't meeting his gaze directly this time.

Trying not to wonder why, he turned and followed Anita around the sofa. "So what exactly does Marion do here?"

"A lot, actually," Anita said. "She cleans, does laundry, cooks— well, sort of, when my mom will let her." She laughed. "A lot of around the house stuff, mostly. And she gives me rides to school sometimes, too."

"So she's . . . what, a servant?" Simon asked, but regretted it as Anita frowned.

"I'd never call her that. She's been with us for ten years now, she's like family."

"Forgive me, I'm just . . . unused to the arrangement."

Anita read his expression for a moment, then shook her head, smiling again. "It's okay, I understand. I just don't think of her that way, ya know? She's almost like my big sister."

Bringing up the rear, Christine made a small noise of disagreement, but said nothing. Anita looked like she wanted to comment, but after a brief pause, she shook her head and led the way back to the dining room. Simon started to follow, but paused, feeling eyes on the back of his head. He turned and saw that yet again, Christine was wearing that incomprehensible expression.

"What?" he asked guardedly. She opened her mouth as if to speak, icy blue eyes examining Simon's features, but then shook her head.

"Nothing. Come on, I'm hungry," she added, and stepped past Simon, her hair swishing through the air.

Me too. Simon looked after her longingly, then shook his head and followed.

EIGHT

SIMON ENTERED the dining room a few steps behind Christine, at the same time Anita's parents came in from the other door. Nancy Rothard smiled at him, and he managed a distracted smile back, but that expression did not long survive a look from Anita's father. With eyes narrowed enough that they looked tiny in his circular glasses, Dr. Rothard studied Simon for a long moment, and the young vampire had the distinct impression of being examined like an object on display. His walk slowed until he was still, and he waited for Dr. Rothard to speak.

Evidently content with Simon's outward appearance, or at least finding no obvious fault with it, the shorter man looked up at Simon and offered one hand. "Simon, I presume?"

The vampire shook his hand, noticing as he did so that Dr. Rothard didn't react to the chill as the others had. Then again, the doctor's fingers were thicker than Simon's; his hand was engulfed as much as shaken. "That's me, Mr. Rothard."

"Doctor Rothard, actually."

Simon couldn't help but contrast this to Nancy's introduction, but kept the observation to himself as he released the doctor's hand. "Excuse me, Doctor."

The doctor nodded, but before he could offer any other comment, his wife put in, "Well, dinner's ready. Let's get settled in."

She shot Simon a supportive smile past her husband's shoulder. Dr. Rothard ambled over to draw out his wife's chair for her. Anita was already pulling out the chair to her mother's right, but Simon darted past her parents with his nocturnal grace to get a hand on the back of the ornate oak in time to slide it in beneath her. For a moment she looked surprised to find him there, but then her face brightened and she said, "Thanks."

Simon nodded and started for the seat on Anita's other side when Dr. Rothard rumbled, "We'll have you opposite Anita, Simon, beside Christine."

The man's tone held no doubt of being obeyed, so Simon rounded the table. Christine, he noticed, was still standing beside her chair. When she caught Simon's steel eyes, she raised one waxed eyebrow expectantly. Though he felt a bit awkward doing it, Simon held her chair for her as well, then took his own across from Anita.

"So, Mr. . . . what did you say your last name was?" Dr. Rothard asked, resting his elbows on the table and leaning forward with a penetrating look.

Simon hadn't said, and there was a good reason. To stall for time, he looked across the table and said, "Anita didn't tell you?"

She raised her eyebrows and held up her hands as if to ward off blame. "Hey, don't look at me, you didn't tell me either." Misinterpreting Simon's obvious discomfort, she was quick to add, "I guess it didn't come up, did it?"

Dr. Rothard frowned and turned his hazel eyes back on Simon. "Yes, well, now it has, and it's . . . ?"

Out of time, Simon seized on the first thing he knew he could remember. "Melas. Simon Melas."

"Your family from Mexico?"

Simon thought he heard the hint of a question behind the question, and the subtle tightening of Anita's jaw reinforced the impression. But he kept his face impassive as he looked back at Dr. Rothard and said, "No, Spain. My great-grandparents were from Barcelona."

The doctor nodded, several folds appearing in his ample neck. "Beautiful city. We went there some years ago, when Anita was still young. My brother works in Spain."

Simon was about to ask after the issue when the door to the dinette swung open and Marion appeared, carrying a dish in both hands, with another balanced on each forearm. Setting the large dish down, she lowered her arms so the smaller plates slid down into her grip, catching them with practiced ease. Anita smiled and shook her head, and even Simon was impressed with her dexterity. "Spaghetti, breadsticks, potatoes. Bottle of wine, Doctor?"

Dr. Rothard nodded. "A bottle of cabernet, thank you."

"Are you over twenty-one, Simon?" Nancy asked.

In more ways than one. "Yes."

"Do you want a glass, sweetie?" she added to Anita, who nodded. "Christine?"

Christine took a second to answer, eyes flicking sideways to Simon and back. "Yes, thanks."

"Some for everyone, Marion, thanks," Nancy said.

As she turned to go, Anita added, "Are you gonna eat with us?"

Marion glanced across the table at Simon and Christine, so quickly the vampire was almost certain he was the only one to catch the look. "No, I'm good, kiddo. Thanks, though."

As she disappeared out the door, Dr. Rothard cleared his throat and said, "Well, let's pray while we wait. In the name of the Father, and of the Son, and of the Holy Spirit . . ."

He crossed himself, as did his wife and daughter, although Anita frowned as she did so. Christine folded her hands in her lap, her expression a bit lofty, but said nothing. Simon, by contrast, was frozen rigid in his chair, gripping its arms so tightly he feared he might crush the wood.

"Bless us, O Lord, and these, Thy gifts. . ."

Simon clenched his jaw to keep it from shaking. He thought that if vampires could sweat, he would be. Across the table, Anita had her head bowed and was moving her mouth, but not actually lip-syncing the words of the prayer.

". . . which we are about to receive, from Thy bounty . . ."

Desperate to distract himself, Simon noticed Christine looking bored. Evidently he had succeeded in keeping his face expressionless, because she gave him a small smile with her full lips and mouthed "atheist" at him.

". . . through Christ, our Lord. Amen."

For a moment Simon lost his composure entirely and tried to cower down into his chair, a shudder wracking his frame. Fortunately, Anita's parents had their heads bowed while crossing themselves again, Christine had shifted her gaze forward, looking polite and attentive, and Anita had reached up as if to sign the cross, but when she saw her father wasn't looking, just brushed one bang out of her face with a conflicted look. None of them saw Simon in his instant of weakness, and he forced himself to straighten before he betrayed himself. Releasing the arms of his chair one finger at a time, he laid his pale hands in his lap to hide the lingering trembles.

As Marion bustled back in, managing to carry a bottle tucked under one arm, five wine glasses, and a corkscrew, the Rothards began to dish out their dinner. Anita uncovered the dish of potatoes, and again Simon flinched at the smell, though he still couldn't place why. Knowing it wouldn't be long before the conversational microscope was back on him, Simon tried to preempt the bullet and observed, "I take it you like cooking, Mrs. Rothard?"

"Nancy," she corrected, giving Simon a narrow-eyed smile, as if challenging him to protest. When he didn't, she added, "And yes, I try to get a hand in now and then. Not that Marion needs my help, of course."

The older woman smiled up at Marion, who gave a proud nod, though she smiled too. As the wine glasses were passed around, Marion set the bottle at Dr. Rothard's hand, then asked, "Can I get anything else for you, Boss?"

"No, I think we're all set. Thanks, Marion. So, Simon," Dr. Rothard intoned as he spooned himself a generous portion of spaghetti, "Anita says you're good with history."

"I'm decent," Simon said, more to avoid a follow-up question than anything else, but Anita wasn't having that.

"He's being modest," she said, smiling across the table at him. "I can actually remember names now. Even some dates!"

Anita's mother laughed, and even her father cracked a smile, but Christine rolled her eyes and said, "Oh, come on, it's not that hard."

"It's everything from the dawn of time to 1648!" Anita replied indignantly. "The Peace of . . . somewhere."

"Westphalia," Christine said dryly.

"That's the one!"

Simon had been absently spooning whatever was handed to him onto his plate, trying to keep the quantities small so it would be less obvious when he didn't eat anything. When Christine handed him the dish of potatoes, though, an nausea and weakness overpowered him. The dish slipped through his limp fingers, clattering hard onto the table. All eyes turned his way as the young vampire leaned as far back in his chair as possible, fighting to clear his clouding vision as the smell finally registered.

"I'm sorry," he said, trying to sound embarrassed rather than defensive and on guard. "I have a . . . very bad reaction to garlic."

"Bad reaction" fell pitifully short of the choking, repulsive haze of the plant in any appreciable quantity, but even laced into food it was quite bad enough. Anita and her mother wore identical looks of surprise, while Dr. Rothard frowned down the table. Christine rescued him, laughing in a way that sounded like she practiced it as she reached over and gracefully took the dish back. As the smell of the garlic retreated, Christine's floral scent lingered in Simon's nose and cleared his vision in a dangerous way.

"Vampire, Simon?" she asked.

She laughed again, and Anita did too. Simon tried to join in to smooth the moment over, though even to his ears it sounded strained and fake. Clearing his throat, he pressed the rim of his wine glass to his lips, letting the liquid brush against his flesh before setting the glass back down. He tried to inhale the bouquet of the wine, but it was impossible to overpower Christine's alluring scent with her sitting right beside him.

Dr. Rothard twirled spaghetti around his fork without looking at it, still staring at Simon. "Is history your major then, Simon?"

"Yes," Simon nodded, unable to come up with a better lie on the spot.

"And what do you hope to do with that when you graduate?"

"I'm . . . not sure. Still thinking about jobs." Simon was terribly tempted to stare Dr. Rothard in the eyes and just overpower the man's mind, but he knew in such close quarters it would never go unnoticed.

The doctor's answering frown made it clear what he thought of that kind of indecision, but Anita put in with a mouth full of food, "Weh, ih uh mayer oo ca' ooze fer lahss uh—"

"Swallow, sweetheart," Nancy Rothard interrupted. Dr. Rothard had taken a bite at the same time, but now his disapproving look fell on his daughter.

Anita either missed or ignored the look and took a massive swallow that Simon could see as it went down her throat. "Well, it's a major you can use for lots of jobs, isn't it?"

"Very true," Nancy agreed.

Across the table, Anita smiled at Simon, and he gave her a grateful nod back. Batting spaghetti around his plate with his fork and wondering whether he could move fast enough to flick it off the table without anyone noticing, Simon tried to pass attention back to Christine. "And you?"

"Economics, with an adjunct major in International Studies," she responded easily, sipping her wine. "Just declared it last week, actually."

"Following in your dad's footsteps?" Nancy asked her with an interested look, but Christine's answering smile was just slightly sardonic.

"Well, hopefully I can aim a little higher, but that's the general idea."

"Your dad hasn't done poorly for himself," Nancy replied, looking surprised.

"No, I suppose not," Christine conceded. "But isn't that the American dream? Every generation building on the last one to become even better?"

Simon thought he was the only one to notice Dr. Rothard's brief glance at Anita, and the following look of mild disappointment, until his wife took his hand and gave it a brief but firm squeeze. Anita definitely caught the gesture, because she frowned and looked down for a moment. In that second, with everyone's eyes elsewhere, Simon snatched the breadstick off his plate with an invisibly fast movement and tucked it under the table.

No one seemed to have noticed, so he asked Anita's father, "You're a doctor, you said?"

"Yes," the man replied, "I'm a neurosurgical researcher. Primarily brain surgery, although I've dabbled in some spinal cord reconstruction too."

Simon blinked, not sure how to respond to that. Nancy averted the awkward moment by adding, "And I was a clinical psychologist. I quit practice when Anita was a few years old, though."

They ate in silence for a long moment after that, Anita apparently absorbed in her food, Christine looking perfectly at ease, and

Simon trying to shift the spaghetti around his plate to make it look like there was less of it. The silence ought to have been welcome; he had never been in this position—*Not that I know of, anyway*—and he realized now that watching humans interact in film or, on those nights when he was glutted with blood and his self-control was at its best, eavesdropping on them from a nearby café table, was woefully insufficient preparation for the real thing. But as he faked another sip of wine, he realized the lull in the conversation brought less relief than he had hoped.

Though having to watch his every word and improvise lies was taxing, at least the consistent chatter had distracted him from the heartbeats thumping in his ears. But now, stuck playing with food he couldn't actually eat while Christine was only inches away, Simon found his mind drifting back to a meal he could enjoy. He wondered if he could throw his utensils with enough accuracy to kill Anita's parents from his chair, or if he would actually have to get up and—

"So!" he said in a bracing tone, hating to call attention to himself but unwilling to commit to a quintuple homicide just yet. He looked from Christine to Anita. "How did you two meet?"

"Funny story," Anita said, pausing with a half-eaten breadstick in her hand. "We were best friends at the end of junior high, and we were all set to go to high school together, but then Chris moved. Then I got to Northwestern last year, and who did I bump into . . ."

She smiled across the table at Christine. Christine smiled too, but in a careful, controlled way, like the gesture was planned and not instinctive. Simon asked, "Why did you move?"

"My father's work," Christine answered. "That's when we were in China. We moved to Hong Kong."

There was a brief silence. The humans were getting close to finishing, and Nancy Rothard was mopping up spaghetti sauce with a breadstick, but the clinking of silverware wasn't as effective at keeping the heartbeats at bay as talking, so Simon forced himself to add, "Was that difficult? Moving so far away?"

"Not really," Christine said indifferently. "I was used to it by then. My father was an Air Force officer when I was younger, so moving wasn't exactly new to me."

"Until you landed here." Anita's smile lit up her face. "Good times."

An answering smile fluttered across Christine's lips, and this one looked genuine. "Yeah."

"What about you, Simon?" Nancy put in. Her plate was clear now, only a faint residue of red on it, and she set her forearms on the table's edge and fixed Simon with an interested look. "What do your parents do?"

"Er . . ." Simon hadn't even thought of this problem, and found he had no ready lie at hand. All eyes were back on him, and his mind froze.

"Well?" Dr. Rothard asked after a moment. "You have parents, don't you?"

Simon almost thanked him for the suggestion; as it was, he had to adopt a pained look to cover his sigh of relief. "No, actually," he said, trying to space the words so as to sound both hesitant and aggrieved. It was a strange emotion to simulate. "They died."

There was a shocked silence for a second, in which Simon reflected that it might have been the truest thing he had said so far. Then Anita reached out one hand, as if she wanted to take Simon's from across the table, though it was too wide for her to reach. Her brown eyes were soft and sympathetic. "I'm so sorry."

Dr. Rothard cleared his throat, looking embarrassed. "Yes, please excuse me, Simon, I had no idea . . ."

"Of course you didn't," Simon replied, wondering if his attempt at a gentle smile was coming across as smug as he felt. *Gentle* was not in his usual repertoire of expressions either. "How could you? It's not the sort of thing I talk about much."

The awkward silence that ensued was broken when Marion appeared from the kitchen as if she'd been called. "All done?"

"Would you like any more? There's plenty," Nancy asked Christine and Simon.

"No, thanks," the black-haired young woman replied. She did not turn her head, but Simon saw her watching him in her peripheral vision.

"I literally could not eat any more," the vampire added, trying not to smirk before chiding himself internally. *Enough. They're giving you plenty of opportunities to slip up; don't manufacture them yourself.*

The others rose, stacking their silverware on their plates, and Simon was quick to copy them, tossing his napkin onto the plate to shield some of the spaghetti for good measure. He had only made it two steps toward the kitchen, however, before Marion came around to him and Christine, shaking her head with a smile. "I'll take those for you, guys."

"I can . . ." Simon started, but he trailed off when Christine handed Marion her plate wordlessly and Marion gave him an exasperated look. He shrugged, handing over his plate without further protest, and the housekeeper spun and vanished back out the door. Glancing around for Anita, it took Simon a moment to realize Christine was leaning on the doorframe, watching him with her baby blue eyes and smiling slightly.

"What do you want to do now?" she asked in a silky tone, eyebrows arched.

Simon returned her gaze for a moment, but she didn't flinch, and something about that made him uneasy. He heard Anita's heartbeat through the door, but thought it would raise awkward questions to advertise that, so he asked, "Where's Anita?"

Christine pointed over her shoulder languidly, and Simon stepped past her through the door, though he couldn't help glancing sideways at her when he drew even. Distracted and trying to recenter himself, Simon pushed open the door with more force than necessary and missed slamming the heavy oak into Anita's head by two inches.

"Whoa!" she said, her big brown eyes widening even further.

Simon winced, drawing a breath in an effort to collect himself. "I'm sorry, I didn't know you were there."

"It's okay," Anita said, shaking her head and making her hair fall back into her face. She blew one strand out of the way with a look of mild annoyance, then looked over Simon's shoulder. "I'm gonna run to the bathroom. Chris, can you guys get set up in the great room?"

"Sure." Christine moved up behind him, close enough that her body heat in the air warmed the air between them, and for a moment the vampire felt trapped between their alluring heartbeats. She inclined her head toward the opposite end of the long dinette and kitchen. Anita vanished down the hall that ultimately returned to the front door, so Christine led the way through a pair of glass doors straight ahead with a careless ease that suggested she was no stranger to the place. Passing Marion and Nancy, who were both washing dishes and quibbling good-naturedly about it, Simon passed into the Rothard great room.

The room stretched to what should have been the second story, and windows rose from the floor to meet the vaulted ceiling. A chandelier was suspended in the center, so bedecked with row upon row of glowing bulbs that it made the one in the dining room look insignificant in comparison. Two couches and a pair of love seats alternated around a rectangular coffee table. A luxuriant Oriental rug with several blues and reds covered nearly all the hardwood floor, and it followed the outline of the room so well—even featuring an indent for the fireplace on the southern wall—that Simon was sure it had been custom made. A piano in one corner was dusted and polished, but the lack of any sheet music made Simon wonder if it had ever been used.

Christine stepped up beside him, and the vampire's eyes half-closed for a second, her heartbeat a gentle, seductive whisper in his ear. "Do you play?"

"What? Oh, no," Simon said, blinking. "You?"

She shook her head, ebony locks swaying. "Only violin. None of them play, either," she confided, a hint of disapproval in her face. "Anita gave it up when we were still in grade school."

Making a noncommittal noise, Simon stepped away from her, holding his breath to keep that hint of lilac and cherry from maddening him. He stepped past a wood and gold grandfather clock and found himself facing a collection of pictures. Anita's parents' wedding picture was there, and Simon noted with some amusement how much thinner Dr. Rothard had been then. There were several pictures of Anita, as well, though only what he assumed was her high school graduation picture looked recent.

"Don't tell me you're one of those people who likes to see his girlfriend's baby pictures," Christine complained behind him.

Simon didn't turn. "I'm not one to think too much on the past."

Farther down, he spotted a picture in a gold frame. Though it was in color, the quality suggested it was very old. He thought he recognized an even younger Dr. Rothard, along with a young man and woman who shared his deep-set eyes, and an older couple who looked very much like all three of the children. Gesturing with one index finger, still surprised to not see a sharp claw on the end of it, he asked, "Dr. Rothard's family?"

"Yeah," came a voice from the door.

Turning around, Simon found Anita there, a few textbooks in one arm, her face uncharacteristically expressionless. Her brown eyes darted to Christine, then back to Simon, and she walked slowly toward him, tossing the books onto one love seat on the way. Stepping up beside the vampire, she said, "That's my dad, obviously, and my Uncle Tim."

"The one who lives in Spain?"

"Yep," Anita said with a half-smile, as if she was pleased he had remembered. "And my Grandpa Mitchell and Grandma Janice. They still live in Upstate New York."

"And your aunt?" Simon guessed, pointing to the girl between Richard and Timothy Rothard in the picture.

Wistfulness touched Anita's eyes. "My Aunt Anne Marie. She died before I was born."

"I'm sorry," Simon said automatically, but even as he did so he felt a faint twinge of genuine sympathy for the obvious longing in Anita's face, as if she was missing this woman she'd never known. The next second he flinched, alarmed that he'd had such a reaction, and gestured to the couches where Christine waited, leaning against one sofa and watching them with her arms crossed. "Would you like to get in some more studying before tomorrow?"

"Yeah, that'd probably be good," Anita agreed, smiling again. She patted Simon on the arm before walking back to a loveseat. The touch of her warm hand through his thin shirt and the smell of vanilla as her hair swished in the air made Simon tense, jaw locking as he fought for control. A blow on the side of her neck would stun her, and he could spring at Christine before she had time to react. Anita would not recover before he was ready for her . . .

Stop. Not here. Not now.

He watched Anita stretch before she sat down, saw Christine's eyes on him as he moved to join them.

At least not yet.

CLOSE NOW.

Hans Richtein heard the whisper in his mind, the sibilant edge of the Master's tone like the gentle caress of a serpent's flicking tongue. He knew a moment of elation that their long search was coming to a close, that the Master's painstaking work and careful planning would be rewarded, as was his due. For a moment Hans was relieved, too, that he might get a chance for some real rest when this last threat was eliminated, but he chided himself immediately after. What was his weariness compared to the countless years the Master had invested in this work? Nothing, that's what it was.

Of course, their search had been difficult. They'd combed the cemeteries, graveyards, seedy neighborhoods, and ruined buildings of Chicago and its labyrinth of suburbs, the Master's faint sense of their quarry's presence guiding them in the right direction. Hans had never dared to think that the Master might be wrong, and even as his wrath and frustration grew blacker and more terrifying at being continually frustrated in their hunt, the Master had never faltered in his own certainty that their target was here.

The past five nights had been spent driving from spot to bleak spot, with frequent detours to feed. The lonely days alternated between scouring maps for other likely locations and catching what few hours of sleep could be had snuggled between the Master's coffin and his case of soil in the back of their stolen truck. And when they found a particularly likely spot, there was always the Master's method of investigation . . .

Despite himself, Hans shivered. Yet another reason to hope that this was indeed their ultimate destination.

Yes . . . very close now indeed . . .

The rental truck's headlights cut into the permanent, protective shroud of fog surrounding the truck. Streetlights ahead were vague, hazy orbs of light hovering in the dark, and there were not many of them. Minimal light shone through the windows of the surrounding buildings, dark sentinels asleep at their posts. Hans drove on, leaning forward as much as his bulk allowed and peering ahead through the fog. After passing one more block of derelict houses, the faint outline of wrought iron bars appeared out of the gloom.

"There."

The Master's predatory, hissing voice filled the truck's cabin and Hans started. The black-cloaked figure had appeared out of nowhere in the passenger seat, his hooded face directed toward the windshield. The burly German could only stare in wonder, though after a moment he noticed a thin trail of mist trickling through a crack between the cabin and the back of the truck as the last folds of the Master's robe took shape before his eyes.

Swallowing, trying to collect himself, Hans asked, "He is here, Master?"

The cowl dipped. "The signs of his presence are unmistakable. Halt the vehicle."

"'Park,' Master," Hans ventured as he turned the engine off. The next second, he doubled over against the steering wheel, eyes bulging as his ribs squeezed in, forcing the air from his lungs.

Still staring forward, seeming to take no notice of his servant, the vampire said, "Did I ask for your correction?"

"Forgive me, Master!" Hans managed to choke out. Such a foolish mistake. The next second, the pressure was gone, and he collapsed backward against his seat, inhaling a desperate gulp of oxygen. Both doors of the truck sprang open untouched, and the robed figure oozed out of his seat and onto the sidewalk, shadow flowing into shadow.

"Come."

Taking another breath to steady himself, Hans hopped down onto the street, ignoring the lingering ache in his sides. The chastisement had been manifestly justified, and it was crucial not to fail the Master at this critical moment. He lumbered off after his liege, whose cloak trailed so smoothly along the ground that he seemed to be floating rather than walking, the mist curling around his dark form like an affectionate pet seeking its master's attention. Though almost jogging, Hans still fell behind, and only caught up with the Master when he paused before the open iron gates. Squinting into the dark above, Hans made out an inscription:

COEMETERIUM SANCTI BRIGIDA

And on a tarnished brass plaque attached to the bars on one side:

SAINT BRIGID'S CEMETERY

THIS LOCAL HISTORICAL SITE WAS ESTABLISHED IN 1841, EARLY IN THE PERIOD OF IRISH IMMIGRATION TO THE UNITED STATES, AND IS THE FINAL RESTING PLACE OF MANY PROMINENT LEADERS OF CHICAGO'S IRISH COMMUNITY. IT WAS NAMED FOR SAINT BRIGID, THE PATRONESS OF IRELAND.

"The smell of death is upon the air," the Master noted, and he drew a long, rattling breath that rasped in his throat for so long that Hans almost shifted uncomfortably before catching himself. Then the sound cut off, and the Master added in a clipped, businesslike tone, "We must be certain. Follow."

The vampire glided off down the main pathway, and Hans jogged to keep up. They passed a sea of faded headstones and a number of bare trees. Birds sat silent in the branches, staring down at the trespassers. A pall of decay and death hung in the atmosphere, and if the Master was right—*since* the Master was right—it was likely a horrific and violent fight was coming, but not even the faintest dread shadowed Hans's eagerness to serve. What enemy could touch him while he stood at the Master's side?

The Master stopped, kneeling beside a spattering of bloodstains on the ground. Hans looked them over, knowing immediately they had not come from a gunshot or a knife wound; the blood had sprayed much too far, even for a shotgun blast, and a trail in one section suggested the bleeding victim had been dragged some fifteen feet. The Master surveyed the carnage, dabbing one long, thin finger into the blood. Scarlet rivulets glistened on his hooked nail and dripped into a rotted scab on his flesh. The finger vanished into the dark of his hood, and he paused a moment before rising and continuing on his way in silence.

The cloaked figure stopped again at a central stone chapel and peered into the darkness inside. He drew another rasping breath, then mused in an intrigued tone, "Eight. Nine altogether. Just indolent in his isolation? Or strengthening himself against my arrival?"

"That won't matter, Master, will it?" Hans asked, though his confident tone made it clear he had no doubts.

"Certainly not," the Master replied coolly. "Come, the final test awaits."

Hans shivered, but did not dare do anything but follow as the Master slid off to the side of the chapel, drifting among the headstones without leaving a footprint in the snow until they arrived at a mausoleum. Parts of its door were rotted away, and through the gaps Hans smelled the reek of death and blood far more recent than anyone who had been buried here in the early period of Irish immigration. Wrapping one long-fingered hand around the door handle with almost loving delicacy, his gleaming hooked nails coming to rest one by one against the pale flesh of his wrist, the Master opened the door. The rotting scent intensified as the vampire gestured to the mausoleum. "Bring one of them."

It was a risky business. Only the Master could discern which body would reveal the most information, but to sift through corpses himself was unthinkable. Drawing a lighter from his pocket, Hans flicked it on, blinking against the sudden glare and gritting his teeth while trying not to recoil at the scene before his eyes.

Eight mangled corpses lay dumped around the mausoleum, some mostly intact, some barely recognizable as human. There was no sign of the ninth. Hans stepped carefully over the bodies, pressing the sleeve of his free hand over his mouth and nose. He ignored the ruined body of a man with half a head left, a handgun still clenched in its rigid death grip, and passed over a girl wearing a look of unfocused panic. Finally, he picked up the stiff body of another young woman, her dead eyes still glazed with fear. Clicking off the lighter, Hans carried the woman's chilled corpse outside.

The Master stood at the edge of a circle of candles he had set up, his arms crossed. Laying the body with its head between two of the candles, Hans pulled out his lighter again, igniting each candle in turn until all glowed orange in the darkness and cast weird shadows on the body's face. Eyes down, he asked, "Is she the right one, Master?"

The vampire did not answer, instead ghosting to the corpse's head and raising his hands. The sleeves of his robe fell back to his elbows, exposing his spindly arms, spiderwebbed with veins that stood out purple and blue and raised shadows against his necrotized flesh in the candlelight. The Master began to chant in a language so ancient Hans knew instinctively that no other being who walked the Earth would understand. His voice was a dismal, funereal monotone, and in the still silence of the cemetery, the all but forgotten words echoed off the tombstones, rebounding upon their source and increasing their power.

Despite himself, Hans shuddered, feeling as if the shadow of death hovered over them—or, rather, retracted from where it ought, by rights, to be. For a moment he felt wrong—deeply wrong—as the intensity of this abomination weighed down on him. *Requiescat in pace*, he had always prayed as a little boy. *Ruhe in Frieden. May the dead rest in peace.* To unsettle that peace was an infamy so foul that—

Then the Master spoke, and the errant thought—a relic of *before*—flittered away.

"The sacrifice."

Hans swallowed, and with trembling fingers drew back the flannel sleeve on one enormous forearm. The Master's ice cold hand caught him near the elbow and pulled him down to the ground until both knelt over the dead body. Without further ceremony, the vampire dug one hooked nail into his servant's flesh and began to cut. Hans closed his eyes and locked his jaw, struggling not to whimper or even grimace as the Master cut deep line after deep line into his flesh. The Master never chose to cut the same lines twice, and by now the German's arms were bedecked with cuts in various states of healing; to reopen an old wound made a less perfect sacrifice. Though he knew almost nothing of the ritual and dared not question the Master's judgment, Hans hoped that this would indeed be the last "consultation."

The blood ran down his palm and dripped onto the dead woman's lips, staining her teeth red as it slithered into her throat. The Master began to chant again, and the drops that had missed her mouth shifted, gliding off the lips and teeth into the void of her throat. The vampire squeezed until Hans began to lose feeling in his arm, then cast his servant backward with a flicking gesture. Cradling his bleeding arm against his chest, Hans watched as the vampire raised his hands over the woman's face.

"You have accepted the sacrifice," he hissed, staring down at the girl. "Speak."

The body remained immobile, expression still rigid, eyes still staring with fear at the sky. But from the open mouth came a whisper, barely louder than breathing, a continuous exhalation like steam escaping. Then, as the flames of the candles cowered down in their wicks, the whisper became words.

"*Cold . . . so cold . . .*"

"Name yourself," the vampire commanded.

"*Name . . . my name . . . Patricia. Trixie. My name . . . it's so cold here . . .*"

"How did your death come about?"

"*I . . . am I dead? Where am I?*"

"Answer! What happened to you?"

"*I . . . we had a party. Jack said it would be fun. I made Mitch and Dana come . . . I'm so sorry, Dana, please, I'm sorry . . .*"

"And then what happened, little one?" Hans blinked in surprise at the change in the Master's tone, now so comforting and persuasive, gentle and reassuring, as if speaking to a frightened child.

"*He came. I was afraid, but no one else was. No, that's wrong. Jeremy was too. Is Jeremy all right?*"

"Of course he is, child," the vampire lied soothingly. "What happened when 'he' came?"

"Looked at me. I wanted to go with him. I don't know why . . . I wanted to go with him. Did he tell me to? No, but I wanted to go with him . . ."

"And when you went with him?" Eagerness was beginning to work into the Master's tone, and it was catching. The pain in Hans's arm faded as he shuffled as close as he dared, staying well out of the circle of candles.

"Held me. He was cold . . . it's so cold here. Kissed my . . . my neck . . . why does it hurt? It hurts! Help me, make it stop hurting!"

"And his eyes. Tell me about them," the vampire demanded.

"So col—"

"Answer me!"

"Eyes . . . red. They glowed. Oh God, what happened to me? Why is this happening to me? Why is it so cold here? Am I—"

"You have served your purpose," the Master said, tone victorious and detached. "Be gone."

"Help—"

The candles extinguished as one, and the voice of the dead girl with them.

For a moment, master and servant sat in silence, Hans unable to control his trembling, the vampire's form so still he might have been another tombstone in the sudden darkness. The silence stretched until it was unbearable, and Hans had to ask in a whisper, "Where is he, Master?"

The vampire was silent a moment more, and the German didn't dare speak again unbidden. At last, the cowled figure rose to its feet, concealed face turning toward his servant. "Not here now. But he will return before the dawn."

Without warning, the vampire strode off through the darkness. He did not deign to yell, but his voice carried as if drawn to Hans's ears. "Put that thing back with the others, then attend me. My trap must be set when the prey walks into it."

NINE

FLUSHING THE toilet in the Rothards' bathroom for the sound effect—*When you lie, be thorough about it*, that voice in his memory said—Simon stepped over to the sink and splashed water on his face several times, looking into the empty mirror with an expression he was sure would be frustrated if he could see it. The water on his face, sliding down his cheeks and onto his neck, was neither cool nor warm; it just was. He clenched his teeth as he patted his face dry with a hand towel, reflecting that it was probably the temperature that made humans say this practice was soothing. He certainly didn't feel soothed.

For the last hour and a half, he had been crammed onto a single decorative sofa with Anita and Christine, slowly losing his mind. Their combined body heat pressed on him like a smothering pillow, making thought almost impossible, and he had taken to speaking only when asked a direct question so he could keep his jaw locked shut and his fangs retracted.

Christine would brush his arm with a gesture too smooth to be a real accident, or Anita would nudge him playfully with her shoulder, and he would force a polite smile while feeling as if someone had set him on fire. He had thought that the searing burn of the dawn's light roasting his flesh away had been the most torturous thing imaginable, but at least that had been involuntary, a mistake; he had done this to himself intentionally. Just as bad, he had made no headway in understanding Anita or her queer effect on him, and while Christine had no similar influence, she was no less enticing as prey.

Stepping out of the bathroom to return to the girls with the air of a man bracing himself to fight a dragon while wearing wooden armor, Simon heard voices from the great room and paused to listen.

"—definitely something about him," Christine was saying.

"Yeah," Anita agreed. "He's got his quirks, but then, everybody does. And . . . well, it's like you said, there's something about him. It's . . ."

"Enticing?"

"I was going to say 'intriguing,'" Anita replied after a second's pause. Simon wondered if he was imagining the almost cautioning tone in Anita's voice. But there was no way to imagine the slight stutter in her heartbeat, the tempo picking up as if she was nervous, or even bracing for a fight.

Christine's tone and heartbeat remained level. "That too."

The conversation lapsed into silence, leaving only the rustling of notebook pages and the ever-present rhythm of heartbeats, Anita's slowing back down. Simon stood motionless for a moment, trying to let the sounds settle into his head and become familiar again, but then the floor creaked down the hall and the heavier, strained heartbeat of Dr. Rothard drew his attention. Not wanting to be caught standing around listening to things he shouldn't be able to hear, Simon forced himself back into the great room.

Neither girl looked up from the books they were studying as the vampire rejoined them. They sat on opposite ends of the couch, as if leaving a spot for him in the middle, but Simon opted to sit on a loveseat instead. Anita jumped as Simon sat down two feet away.

"Whoa! Where did you come from?"

Christine looked up, her expression startled as well before she composed it. Simon smiled, trying not to breathe. "I'm quiet like that. Any progress?"

Anita sighed and leaned back, though Christine kept her eyes on Simon for a moment before following her friend's movement. "Nah, I think I've learned all I'm gonna learn."

She combed her fingers through her chestnut hair, lacing them at the back of her skull and tucking her head down for a moment tiredly. Christine scooted over to pat her back with a dry smile, then looked over Anita's bent frame at Simon, thin eyebrows raised. Simon met her gaze, eyes narrowing, but Christine stared back, her eyes narrowing to match as her smile curved slightly. Most humans couldn't stand to meet his eyes for more than a second or two, and Simon was struck by the horrifying thought that perhaps they could become immune to him with practice. It made him feel naked, disarmed.

Then Anita sat back up in a flourish, hair falling into her face as she drew a deep, bracing breath, then blew it out again. The hot scent of her breath on the air made Simon tense. "Okay, no more work. What do you guys want to do now?"

Christine had opened her mouth to respond when Simon leapt on the opportunity. The temptation to lash out was growing instead of receding; obviously he wasn't becoming immune to them, and he needed the escape. "I should probably be leaving."

Both girls looked disappointed, and Christine glanced over Simon's shoulder at the grandfather clock. "So early? It's only eleven."

The heat of the room had drawn a flush onto Anita's neck and face, and even Christine's porcelain cheeks were colored with a hint of rose. The warmth of blood so close to the surface of their skin was so distracting that Simon lied off the cuff, "Yes, but I have a final tomorrow, I need to sleep."

"What class?" Anita asked.

Simon tried not to wince, cursing himself for the slip. He looked down at the table to distract himself from their faces, though their heartbeats still drummed in his ears. What had he said his major was?

"Simon? You okay?"

The vampire feigned a yawn, catching a glimpse of Anita's confused expression as he tried to think. History, that was it. "Different history class," he managed. Before she could ask anything else, he got to his feet and said, "I really should go."

Anita's look of confusion morphed to concern, and she opened her mouth as if she wanted to say something, then closed it again. She stood as well, nodding. "Okay. Well, I'll walk you out."

"That's not necessary—" Simon started, his only thought escape, but Anita shook her head stubbornly.

"You're my guest," she insisted. Then she rolled her eyes above a reluctant smirk. "Besides, my dad would never let me hear the end of it."

The thought of bumping into the good doctor alone was so unappealing that even the distraction of having Anita with him was preferable, so Simon just nodded helplessly and started toward the door. Both heartbeats kept pace, so he had already resigned himself to the inevitable when Christine said, "I'll walk out with you too."

The kitchen was dark on the way out, only the dinette's overhead light still on, and the chandelier over the foyer was dimmed too. The vampire's night vision was perfect, but both of his companions drew a bit closer to him, Anita at his right side and Christine on his left. When Anita vanished into the hall closet to get Simon's coat, Christine stepped forward and peered up into his pale face, she asked, "Do you need a lift home?"

"No." There was absolute confidence in the vampire's voice on this point; in an enclosed environment, where it would be so easy to make a kill look like a horrible car accident, his resistance would fail him, and she was embedded enough in Anita's life that that needed to be a cold choice, not a crack. Belatedly, he added, "Thank you, though."

"Do you live close by?" Christine persisted. Her blue eyes narrowed inquisitively, and she crossed her arms under her breasts again. "It really wouldn't be any trouble . . ."

"On the South Side," Simon admitted recklessly, swallowing and tucking his hands behind his back so he could squeeze them into fists. Before she could press the point, he added, "But it's not a problem. This time of night you can just fly."

Christine frowned, but shrugged and went to retrieve a pair of glossy leather boots by the door. In the second before Anita reappeared with his coat, Simon's face contorted into a self-castigating snarl. This was not the time to be clever—not when the two women had him so off-balanced that he might make a more dangerous slip at any second.

Then Anita was back and Simon tried to discipline his expression. She held out his coat, and the vampire tucked his arms through it with a word of thanks. Anita pulled the coat up onto his shoulders, patting it in place . . . and left her hands there for a moment, fingers curving around the contours of his upper arms. He opened his mouth, but couldn't think of anything to say. Then Christine finished zipping up her second boot and Anita drew her hands back, just offering Simon a friendly smile when he turned to face her.

"You know, if you want to borrow my coat, you can just ask," Christine said, smirking at Anita.

"What? Oh, sorry!" Anita said, but Christine had already stepped into the closet, returning quickly with a thin leather jacket that Simon felt certain wasn't enough to keep out the cold.

"No problem," Christine replied with a tolerant air. Laying the fingertips of one hand on the doorknob, she said, "Thanks for dinner, Anita."

"Sure," Anita responded.

"Nice to meet you, Simon." The raven-haired woman's voice was still friendly, but softer, closer to a purr. She blinked slowly at the vampire, her long, dark eyelashes accentuating the movement.

"And you," Simon nodded, looking back at her stoically. She pulled open the door and stepped onto the porch, but paused there, glancing back and clearly expecting Simon to follow.

He looked down at Anita, who was biting one side of her lip, and found her uncertainty mirrored his own. Outside was relief, deliverance, cold night air to clear away the lingering fog their scents and the heat of their bodies had wrapped around his mind. And yet, somehow, Simon felt less eager to spring out the door.

I can some and go as I please now . . . but though that made her accessible as prey, it told him no more about *her.*

Christine's porcelain brow furrowed. "Coming?"

"You should get some sleep," Anita said quietly. Simon turned to look at her, and she smiled up at him.

"Yes," he agreed, though sleep was still many hours away. Stepping out onto the porch, it occurred to him to add, "Thank you for having me."

"Thanks for helping me study," Anita returned. Then her face brightened and her eyes widened as she said, "Hey, do you wanna grab some lunch tomorrow after our finals?"

Instinct overtook thought. "Yes."

Before Simon could even consider taking back the word, Anita replied, "Cool. I'm done with my final at eleven thirty. What about you?"

He couldn't rise until noon, plus close to an hour of transit . . . she wouldn't want to wait that long. He was well-rested and well-fed; he could do without sleep . . . "Eleven fifteen. I'll wait for you."

"Okay, great!" Anita beamed. "We'll meet after eleven thirty at Student Center East, okay?"

"I'll see you then," Simon replied, managing a half-smile, and turned to go. Christine had waited for him, and they set off down the shoveled sidewalk together. The vampire felt the young woman's peripheral vision on him, but she didn't speak until they reached the driveway.

Christine glanced back at the front door, as if to make sure it was closed, then gestured over her shoulder with one index finger. "Well, that's my ride." She raised an eyebrow and smiled. "Sure I can't give you one?"

Beyond the side porch, parked in front of the Rothards' garage, was a ruby red roadster. Simon glanced at it, then said resolutely, "I'm certain, thank you."

She covered her look of disappointment quickly. "Whatever. Until next time, Simon."

She didn't smile, but winked once before spinning like a model on a runway and strolling back to her car. Simon watched her go for a few seconds, then caught himself and headed in the opposite direction. On the street, he darted down the road and crouched behind a brick mailbox until the sports car's headlights lit up the Rothard driveway. Watching as Christine drove off in the opposite direction, engine purring, Simon remained immobile until the glowing red taillights vanished around a corner.

Then he began to change. The smallest finger on each hand shrank until it melded with his flesh, and the other three thinned to the thickness of a vein. Tough webbing grew between the fingers, stretching and spreading as his skin darkened from sickly white to charcoal gray. His thumbs shrank into tiny, protrusive claws.

As the world expanded around him, hair sprouted on his face, his eye teeth sharpened, and his actual fangs descended even as they shrank in size. Most of the rest of his teeth disappeared into his gums altogether while his ears grew and grew, their slight points becoming much more exaggerated. As his clothes sank into his body, coarse fur erupted on his torso.

He continued to shrink, legs compacting to a fraction of his body height and his boots absorbing into his feet, which turned into tiny clawed legs. Then, no more than five seconds after it began, it was over. Glancing around at the suddenly enormous world with the keen vampiric sight that fortunately remained constant from form to form, Simon flapped his wings and took a few hopping steps, then launched into the air.

The bat circled once around the Rothard house, then angled off southward into the night.

ANITA WATCHED Christine's red Infiniti vanish down the road, then drew away from the translucent white curtains on the front window with a sigh. She tromped up the stairs, finally tying her hair back in a sloppy ponytail, but came to a sudden stop on the top step. She had been pacing and fretting with Christine long before Simon's arrival, but her bedroom light was on. Exhaling in resignation, she trudged toward her door, wondering which of them it was.

It turned out to be both. Nancy Rothard sat on Anita's bed, running her fingers over the dreamcatcher tied to one bedpost. Her husband stood at the balcony door, holding the curtain open with one hand and looking out onto Lake Michigan. Nancy looked up as her daughter walked in, smiling her small smile. "Hi, sweetie."

Anita gave her a dry look as her father turned around. "Well?"

"Well what?" Dr. Rothard asked.

"Well, I'm a little old to get tucked in, don't you think?" she replied sarcastically. "So you obviously want to talk about something."

The two doctors looked at one another, which put Anita on guard even more. Then her father drew out the chair at her desk. The hardwood creaked as he settled himself onto it. "Mr. Melas."

"What about him?" Anita asked, more defensively than she intended.

"We think—" Dr. Rothard started, but Nancy cleared her throat. He gave his wife a vexed look, but nodded and grudgingly corrected, "*I* think there's something off about him."

Anita shook her head in disbelief. "You only talked to him over dinner! What would possibly make you think that?"

"He was very vague, nothing too clear. Didn't you think so?" he asked Nancy in exasperation.

"I think he was very cautious," she replied, wearing her professional, clinical look again. "Choosing his words with great care."

"Probably because you were bullying him," Anita accused her father, crossing her arms.

"I did not 'bully' him," Dr. Rothard said crossly.

Nancy shifted on Anita's bed to put a hand on her husband's knee. "You can be a little intimidating with new people, Rick."

Grumbling for a moment, he pressed on, "I just don't want you mixing up with the wrong sort of people, Anita."

"The 'wrong sort of people'?" Anita repeated. She shook her head, gritting her teeth and trying not to lose her temper. "You're as unfriendly as you could possibly be to him and you think *he's* the wrong kind of person?"

Dr. Rothard's face became stony at the implication. "Watch your tone, young lady."

Anita closed her eyes and took a deep breath. She wasn't sure why she felt so offended on Simon's behalf. She *did* barely know him. But he'd been nothing but kind to her, if a little hesitant, and she found herself compelled to stand up for him. Like Christine said, there was just something about him . . .

In a controlled voice, she said, "You don't even know him."

Dr. Rothard opened his mouth, but Nancy moved her hand to his wrist to forestall his reply and said, "Maybe we all just need to get to know him better."

"Maybe we do," he conceded. He got ponderously to his feet, taking off his glasses and cleaning them with one sleeve of his shirt.

Blinking myopically, he added in a calm tone, "Just make sure you make good decisions, Anita."

Anita narrowed her eyes, but she caught her mother's stern look and nodded. "Right."

Replacing his glasses, her father walked toward the door. He held out one arm, as if considering hugging her, but just patted her on the shoulder before he walked out the door and down the hall.

Shaking her head, Anita stormed over to her dresser, rifling among the drawers for pajamas. Her mother got off her bed and said, "I'm sorry, honey. You know your father."

"Yeah, I know," Anita snapped, not turning.

"He does mean well."

"I'm sure."

"Anita . . ."

"Mom, I need to get showered and get to bed before this final tomorrow," Anita said. "Can we talk some other time?"

Nancy gazed back into her daughter's eyes for a moment, and Anita had the unpleasant feeling of being analyzed. But her mother just nodded with a weary look. "Sure. Good night, sweetie. Good luck tomorrow, if I don't see you before you go."

She pressed a kiss onto Anita's forehead, then walked out the door. Anita waited until her parents' bedroom door clicked closed, then slipped into the bathroom next to her own room and turned the water on hotter than she could enjoy. She stood in the shower a long time, feeling guilty for being short, but also angry for feeling guilty at all. She felt mad at her father for his bullheadedness, and her mother for her ambivalence, and Christine for the look she thought she'd seen in her beautiful friend's blue eyes when they fell on Simon . . .

Anita sighed, balling her hands into fists and leaning them against the smooth marble of the shower wall. She wondered where that anger at Christine had come from, and whether there was even any justification for being angry. She and Christine had been friends since they were kids, even if they'd only just reconnected this last year; she'd known Simon less than a week. What *was* it about him?

Frustrated, Anita stepped out of the shower and jerked her pajamas on, trading her contacts for her old, unflattering pair of glasses, then trudged back to her room. Part of her wanted to go talk to Marion and vent, but the need to sleep before her final hadn't just been a convenient excuse. Throwing her glasses onto her desk, she collapsed into bed, one hand patting the baseball bat she now kept leaned against her headboard.

But sleep was elusive, and as Anita tossed and turned, looking up at the glow-in-the-dark stars on her ceiling and trying to spot the real constellations she'd put among them, she found herself thinking of Simon. Closing her eyes, she knew the lights she saw were just the residual glow of the stars, but for a second she saw something more familiar there—a reflective, silver gaze looking back at her in her mind's eye.

Her mother was right about one thing—she wanted to get to know Simon better, and to get to the bottom of this mysterious effect he seemed to have on everyone.

FLIGHT WAS effortless, bypassing conscious thought. With his tiny eyes focused on the lights that crowded the Dan Ryan Expressway even at this time of night, Simon enjoyed the clean, crisp taste of the winter air in his nose, still relieved to be free of the luscious, tantalizing scents of the women.

But he could still remember, and without the need to pay real attention to what he was doing, Simon had no escape from his brooding. For a third time, he had intentionally promised to be around Anita for no reason he could justify to himself—the fourth, if he counted not walking away from that first conversation. Exposing himself to Anita, and now her family and best friend, was bad enough, but he couldn't even see an end to it.

Sitting between them on the couch, rattling off historical details and trends, he'd thought of a hundred ways to cover the killings. He had beaten down each in turn as they sprang to mind, but he still could not explain *why*. He had mingled with the students of UIC and never desired their company. Perhaps it was because Anita was the first to offer? No, that wasn't entirely accurate. Miguel Vargos had made more offers than Simon could count, and every time Simon had shut him out and never regretted it.

Why was Anita different? He needed to find out.

Well, we have a lunch date tomorrow. Lucky me. Though Simon still wasn't thirsty, he knew that going without any daytime rest would require some extra strength. He could skip the date . . . but the need to figure out this inexplicable chink in his armor was becoming more irresistible every time he and Anita Rothard crossed paths. She was not unique, exactly, but last time had been so different . . .

He ducked one wing and banked southwest, passing over the ragged ensemble of apartments, worn-down houses, and shady storefronts that was home. He flew until he saw the lights of airplanes launching in the distance and the slim break in construction beyond that was the course of the Chicago River. Tucking his wings into a steep dive, Simon fluttered several times over an area of warehouses and factories. A few had lights on inside, the third shift hard at work, but most were dark.

Simon finally spotted the perfect ambush location: a construction site, full of dark corners and abandoned machinery and surrounded by a tarp-covered chain-link fence. It looked to be the beginnings of a warehouse or an office building; the hole dug for the basement took up almost the entire block, but the plywood thrown down as flooring and the many patches of lingering weeds suggested the project had only just gotten past the digging stage, if that. Between the backhoe parked near the entrance to the site and the stacks of material around the muddy pit, there were so many ways to hide a body or make a death look like a terrible accident that Simon didn't think he could design a better location himself.

And, even better, a solitary target was wandering into sight. Strolling down the dark, deserted sidewalk with a jaunty, carefree step that no sane or sober human would have in a spot like this, the man glanced around himself seemingly at random, as if he was a tourist taking in the sights. As a bat, Simon couldn't smile, but his lip curled back from his needle-sharp teeth as he drifted down to land on the frosty dirt. It took only a few seconds to become himself again. The flesh of his wings smoothed and whitened into hands as his fingers regrew, his face became smooth-shaven and mostly human, and he shot back up, the world becoming its proper size around him.

He listened for the drunkard, but couldn't hear the steps he was sure would be unmeasured and erratic. Frowning, Simon darted up the packed dirt ramp construction trucks used to get down into the site. He stopped at a break in the chain-link fence and waited another second, but heard nothing, not even a heartbeat. Eyes narrowing now, letting his fangs descend, he stepped out onto the street.

There wasn't even a second to process how wrong things had gone. The left side of his face exploded in pain from a punch so powerful that it snapped his head the other way. He had barely begun to jerk to the right when a second crashing blow caught his jaw from that way too. He had a split second to process the blur that had crossed in front of his vision, and realized that they hadn't been strikes from two attackers, but two blows from one impossibly fast assailant. Then a kick caught him in the sternum and he was airborne.

Simon crashed into a mix of dried mud and gravel and skidded several feet before he came to rest, his new leather jacket ripping along the back and sleeves. The pain in his face and chest was bewildering, inconceivable, though he managed to catch a flash of movement as his intended victim charged him. Reacting on instinct, Simon cast about for a weapon until he spotted a shovel stuck business end down in the frosty ground. He ripped it free and spun on his attacker with a two-handed blow that could have killed a rhinoceros.

In a whirling movement, the other man caught the shovel by the shaft and wrenched it out of Simon's grip. While Simon wasted a second staring in shocked incomprehension, his enemy completed the spin, and the spade end of the shovel smashed into the left side of Simon's face so hard something cracked in his skull. As he cried out in startled pain, the man with the shovel spun again, too fast to see, and a second burst of agony consumed Simon's left knee. The blow was so hard that the shovel head snapped off and Simon was struck off his feet again, suspended horizontally in the air for an instant.

He began to fall, but his enemy swung what was left of the shovel and caught him in the ribs. Smacked like a cricket ball, Simon flew backward, spinning in the air until he smashed down onto a piece of iron piping. He gasped as pain raced along his lower ribs and blood trickled down his forehead and into his eye. Somehow, he dragged himself to his feet and seized the nearest thing at hand—a portable concrete mixer, empty but still close to two hundred pounds. Simon grabbed it with both hands, wrenched it from the ground, and hurled it in the direction of his attacker.

The concrete mixer sailed through the air, then . . . stopped. Simon glanced downward to see the legs behind it and almost missed it when his attacker hurled the mixer back at him. He raised his arms on instinct, but wasn't fast enough to move out of the way before the mixer smashed him to the ground. His forearms protected his face, but if his ribs hadn't been broken before, they were now. Heaving a breath, Simon braced his hands on the mixer to lever it off.

And then he froze, becoming absolutely still as a blur of motion came to an abrupt stop at his side and the heel of a black boot came to rest on his throat.

"Hello, Simon, how are you?" asked a bright, cheerful voice.

Simon's eyes narrowed to gray slits and he bared his fangs in a predatory hiss. He grabbed at the leg pinning his neck down, but try as he might he couldn't lever the other an inch. He glared up and managed to gargle, "Salem!"

It was the recollection he always repressed, the voice that sometimes spoke from his memory alongside his own thoughts. Though most of his mind was consumed with shock and fear—pinned, trapped, and very likely about to die—a tiny part of his brain found the time to feel better. Thrashed around the construction yard like a rag doll, at least he had solace in the knowledge that he had never stood a chance to begin with—not against an enemy like this.

The vampire Salem smiled down at him, but mockery and derision gleamed in his emerald eyes, and his long canine fangs were bared as well. His close-cropped black hair had the sleek, lustrous shine that showed the other vampire had fed recently, as did the color in his normally pale cheeks. His clothes—a black T-shirt, blue jeans, and a fraying, black cloth duster—were simple and obviously received little care. And, of course, the combat boots, one of which pressed down on Simon's throat.

Unable to free himself, Simon tried to spot anything useful in his peripheral vision. A screwdriver lay nearby; he could grab it if he was fast, stab the business end through Salem's knee. But he had barely begun to reach for it when the elder vampire seemed to teleport even closer, one knee pinning Simon's other hand, his own hand now at Simon's neck. The sharp claw of Salem's thumb dug into the pale flesh above one of Simon's carotid arteries, and the four nails on his fingers pressed against the other.

"Ah ah ah," Salem said with a remonstrating shake of his head. "I wouldn't go that route, if I were you."

Slowly, exaggerating the movement, Simon pulled his hand back.

"Very wise," Salem complimented him, though his lip curled. He looked around, taking in the atmosphere of their impromptu duel as if he had just noticed it. "Well, as ambushes go, this was a pretty pathetic attempt. But I'll give you points for the location. Too bad you couldn't put up a better fight; this could have been glorious."

He looked around the construction site with a wistful frown, as if he had been cheated out of something enjoyable.

"It wasn't . . . for you," Simon said, pausing to take in a tiny breath between words. Salem's claws were pressed so tightly against the arteries in his neck that he feared breathing too deeply might cause the blood to spill. "Didn't know . . . it was you."

"You didn't recognize me?" The faux hurt in Salem's voice was ruined by the singsong tone of his words. He leaned in closer, fire dancing in his green eyes, and there was nothing singsong in the predatory growl of his voice as he added, "Don't tell me you've forgotten me, my little Brutus."

"Never," Simon swore, glaring back. "Hunting . . . I thought you . . . were a human."

"Indeed?" Salem asked, his sneer open now, and though he leaned back, his clawed hand didn't move. "What gave me away? The human warmth in my flesh? The human heartbeat drumming in your ears? Tell me, boy, have you been abstaining a few weeks? Losing your touch? Did I ever manage to teach you anything?"

He looked back the way they had come, then his gaze returned to Simon. "Obviously not fighting skills."

Simon growled, but with legs and one hand pinned and the equivalent of razor-sharp knives at his throat, his ferocity was empty. Salem knew it too, because he laughed for a long moment, shaking his head with a look somewhere between amusement and pity. "You should be careful when you go out at night, Simon. Someday you might meet an undead less merciful than I am."

Simon stared. "You're going to let me go?"

"Well, I had a delicious, nine-course breakfast tonight, and since nothing could make my after-meal constitutional better except re-paying you a bit for the last time we met . . ." He tightened his grip, and Simon started to panic as the skin split and faint slithers of blood flowed down the sides of his neck. But then Salem pulled his bloody claws away and got to his feet, though he leaned on the cement mixer, pinning Simon down. "Yes, I'll let you go. This time. But my mercy only goes so far, boy. Attack me again, and you'll find out just how short that distance is."

Salem slapped both hands down on the dented cement mixer, levering down on it with all his strength, and Simon writhed under it, jaws locked together and eyes clamped shut against the crushing torment on his torso. Then the pressure vanished, leaving only the weight of the mixer pushing down on him. Simon opened his eyes, but Salem was gone. No dissipating mist, no bat flying away, no shower of dust drifting off on a beam of moonlight . . . just gone.

For a few seconds, Simon just rested his head back against the gravel and mud, ponytail pressing into the back of his skull, sur-prised and relieved to be alive, such as it was. Then he seized the wheel bar of the mixer and wrenched it off himself, though he no-ticed with concern that it seemed far heavier than it had a minute before. He sat up in relief—then sank back to the ground with an agonized gasp, doubling over on himself, wracked by a twisting flare of pain as if his bowels were being tugged in opposite direc-tions while his ribs were dragged outward. He choked and coughed blood onto the snow.

Huddled against the dirt, shaking, he found himself remember-ing Salem's words from long ago. *Daytime you need to be careful, espe-cially in open sunlight. But at night? Unless you find someone carrying blessed weapons, or take a* really *nasty fall or stroll in front of a truck, nothing can break those bones of yours. Well, except another vampire, of course.*

Simon wasn't sure how bad his injuries were, but the unremitting pangs in his gut and face made him afraid to speculate. There could be no question of morphing to another form now; if anything, it would make him even more vulnerable. Forcing himself to his hands and knees and keeping as bent over as he could, the young vampire began to claw his way toward the entrance of the site, wondering if he might not have been better off killed after all.

THE EASTERN sky had long since turned the gray of the waning night and was pinkening toward sunrise when Salem sauntered back through the gates of Saint Brigid's Cemetery. The approach of the light was almost a tangible sensation, his extra senses weakening and the limitless, unbridled power shrinking from his limbs. But dawn was always that way, and by the time daylight hit in earnest, he would be safe at rest.

He wondered idly whether Simon would make it home or burn to ash in the morning's first light, then shrugged, indifferent. The boy deserved it. Bad enough to attack someone he had no prayer of beating, but to let himself be beaten so thoroughly . . . Salem sighed in a melancholy sort of way. Greatness wasn't for everyone, and those damnably determined to court Death could not be forever withheld from its embrace. *You can only lead the wolf to slaughter; you can't make him drink.*

With that first light of the sun only minutes away, many vampires would have been scrambling in a mad dash for their resting places, or at least stepping into the nearest unfailing shadows, but Salem himself was unhurried and not at all anxious. Once Mr. O'Reilly had been relocated, the little corner tomb in the mausoleum had become positively homey, and it was a moment's walk away. Besides, he could walk the entire cemetery with his eyes closed— even in daylight—and was so familiar with it that he could detect anything amiss.

That very sensation started to gnaw at him halfway toward his tomb.

Steps slowing, emerald eyes narrowing and sweeping the frost-covered grounds, Salem strained his fading hearing for any sounds, but the unnatural silence of the graveyard was as heavy and oppressive as it had been since he moved in. He saw the faint trail of blood from where he'd caught that last course of breakfast, the kid who had tried to run, but that was an expected aberration. No wind howled through the bare trees and weathered headstones, and even the lightening sky no longer mattered. The air was pregnant with tension, and the dead held their breath, waiting to see what it would birth.

Slipping with surreal grace through gray obelisks and skeletal trees, silent as a wraith, Salem darted from shadow to shadow, concentrating even though he heard, saw, and smelled nothing. He slowed as he approached his own mausoleum, coming to a stop a dozen paces away. As his eyes darted over the still, silent sea of stones, his right hand drifted beneath his coat and brushed against his left hip before he remembered nothing was there. Frowning, he knelt, never looking down as he clawed up a handful of the cold earth and rubbed it over his palms, the soil sticking under his daggerlike nails and a few tiny clumps catching on the thin hairs of his palms.

Part of him was annoyed; nothing was deadlier than a vampire in the night, and he felt like a child frightened by the dark. But too many years had passed, and following his instincts had rewarded him too many times for him to ignore that quiet, insistent voice now. On impulse, Salem got back to his feet and held out both dirtied hands, face contorting for a second in concentration. The frost and snow seemed to rise from the ground like a solid heat mirage, but the illusion died as the mist spread in earnest, amoeba extensions reaching out in all directions, blanketing the nearest parts of the graveyard in fog and shadow.

In a flash, the vampire was at the door of the mausoleum, and the door was barely cracked before he slid inside. Flicking the door closed behind him, Salem crossed the cramped space in less than a heartbeat, one preternaturally fast hand darting into his purloined grave and returning with a scabbarded sword. He had just gripped the handle of the weapon when he realized he had never heard the door click shut.

His movement was a blur, the shriek of metal following the slash of the sword as it was drawn. Salem caught the briefest flash of black robes retreating like smoke on the wind, then the figure was out the door. Without hesitation, he burst back into the graveyard himself.

Hooked talons nearly clawed his head from his neck; only a lithe, lightning-quick twist kept Salem in one piece. His answering slash of the gladius should have taken the hooded figure's arm off at the elbow, but his enemy was equal to the challenge and slipped back. Salem followed, lunging hard, then spun in a decapitating whirl, hoping to predict his foe's movement and lop off his head. But the other creature flowed like a black storm cloud just out of reach. The mist around them roiled with their movements, and it thickened and swelled until both black figures were dancing their lethal dance invisible to all but each other.

Simon? Salem considered the possibility incredulously as a clawed hand swung so close that it raked four rips into his T-shirt. But that was impossible; even if Salem hadn't beaten the younger vampire to a pulp hours before, there was no way Simon could ever be fast and agile enough to dodge the rain of sword slashes Salem unleashed on his enemy. The fog moved to shield the other vampire from sight, and Salem realized with an uneasy twist that he had been overpowered; the unnatural mist was no longer his to control.

The hooded vampire came in with both claws elevated, looming half a head taller than Salem himself. Salem slashed for the exposed middle, but the blade passed straight through the black robe as if it didn't exist. For an instant he froze, pure surprise overtaking every other reaction. Then an invisible force struck him and he flew backward. He landed on the frozen dirt and backrolled to his feet, blade raised defensively, eyes glowing hell red.

And as his enemy loomed out of the mist, Salem's vision finally managed to pierce the veil of shadow beneath that hood.

"Shafax," he said, voice dripping contempt as he bared his fangs and curled his lips back into a predatory snarl. The name fell off his tongue like a curse, as if he hoped to strike his enemy dead by speaking it.

The towering vampire paused, looking down on his enemy, hook-nailed fingers working in the air as if he envisioned Salem's throat in his grip. "Did you believe you could hide from me forever, Flavius? That I would not find you? That on all this Earth, there is a place I would not go to crush you?"

"Finally come for me in person, King of Vampires?" Salem shot back. He sneered and taunted, "Have you run out of minions for me to kill?"

He peered into the hood of Shafax's robe and his eyes flashed. "Or have you taken to killing them yourself now?"

The voice that issued forth from the abyss of the cowl, though dry and whispery as parchment rubbing on itself, had a distinct note of disdainful amusement. "All will serve me in one fashion or another, Flavius. But you have chosen your path, and that way lies oblivion."

One gnarled hand shot forward, palm out, and again Salem found himself hurled backward by an unseen force. But this time he was ready for it, falling back intentionally and rolling to a crouch. He reversed immediately, rolling forward and slicing sideways with his blade. He had anticipated Shafax's charge, and the other vampire's clawed hand slashed through nothing but air. Salem's gladius, however, struck a glancing blow on the way, and when he sprang to his feet, bubbling, black blood dripped from his blade.

"You shall pay dearly for that blasphemy!" Shafax whispered, and for an instant the force of his gaze had Salem retreating despite himself before snarling and raising his blade. Then, as if it had grown bored of the fight, the mist surrounding the two vampires sank to earth, vanishing into the frosted ground. Salem narrowed his glowing eyes in confusion until he felt the last vestiges of that limitless nighttime power leaving him.

He chanced a glance over his shoulder and paid for it with four more gouges across his chest; this time they split both his T-shirt and the skin beneath. He hissed through sharp, gritted teeth and flung himself backward. But now Shafax had caught the pinkening of the eastern horizon as well, and both vampires understood in an instant that the contest was about to conclude, one way or another.

Salem turned and ran.

The cowardice of it pained him, but there was no way he could master his enemy in time to avoid the sunrise . . . if he could conquer Shafax at all. He sensed more than heard the vampire king close behind him, but Salem reached his mausoleum an instant ahead, vanishing through that tiniest crack and slamming the door shut behind him.

The concussive force of the blow on the door nearly sent Salem flying across the small room to land in Mary O'Reilly's final bed, and he wobbled for a second before regaining his balance. Dropping his sword, he braced his heels on the uneven, cobblestoned floor, levering his shoulder against the wooden door. Shafax's next blow sent a ripple of force down Salem's body so hard that the stones beneath his boots cracked, and the door itself was suddenly woven through with fault lines. One more blow would burst the entire thing to splinters, so Salem reached down for his sword, waited until the last possible second, and rammed the point of the blade through the door.

The startled hiss had only irritation in its malevolent sibilance, and Salem knew he hadn't managed to catch the other undead with his weapon. But Shafax took the hint, and one hook-clawed fist smashed through the stone beside the door instead, long fingers groping for a hold on Salem to rip him back out through the wall. Salem pulled his sword free of the door and cut at the hand, but it dissolved into mist.

The coming of the dawn was upon them, now only seconds away. With a scream of frustrated rage, Shafax roared in a voice that echoed along the tombstones, "Slave! Serve your master! The resting place!"

And then the hated lips were at the hole in the mausoleum wall. "You can not escape me now, Flavius." The words clung to Salem like humidity, making him feel sticky and sick. "Today or tomorrow, your blood will not long be your own."

Then . . . nothing.

Through the broken stone and the shattered door, which now looked as if a strong wind might finish it off, Salem heard the sounds of very human exertion and something heavy being dragged. So, Shafax wasn't working alone or just dropping by Chicago on a whim. Pressing one still-dirtied hand to the bloody gashes on his chest where Shafax had cleaved down to bone, Salem snarled and realized he might benefit from a plan himself.

But that plan could no longer include St. Brigid's. Careful to duck under the hole in the stone where the daylight had at last let its first rays through, Salem took up the worn leather scabbard he had dropped and sheathed his sword. Slinging its baldric over his chest, he glanced at his tomb, then its neighbor, and smirked as he sent the lid of the neighbor to the ground, where it cracked into thirds. Hooking two fingers under the ribcage of a long-bleached skeleton that rested awkwardly on top of another, Salem tossed it back into the grave he had been occupying. One leg dropped off at the knee on the way, but the rest returned to its original home with a dry clatter.

"Thanks for the loan, Seamus," the vampire said with a wink. Then he turned to the broken door and braced himself for the escape that waited beyond.

TEN

E VEN THE wintry chill in the air couldn't dampen Anita's spir-
its as she all but fled one of the campus's towering concrete
buildings. Her Western civilization exam was history, and now she
had nothing planned for the day but her lunch . . . meeting with
Simon. She refused to even think the word "date."

She looked around, clutching her thin purple coat closed; of the
five original plastic purple fasteners, only two remained. Though
a crush of students filled the commons, most hurrying between
buildings or tucked into alcoves away from the wind for manic
last-minute studying, Anita hoped she would spot Simon's tall, dark
figure without trouble; she needed to thank him. While poring over
her exam, more than once she had heard the answer in her head, but
in Simon's dry voice. Clearly, he had done something to make the
material stick. However, she also needed to see how he would react
to her today, after Christine . . .

Before she sank too far into that train of thought, a smooth
voice said from beside her, "Excuse me."

She turned and looked up. Facing her with a disarming smile on his tan face was a man wearing a black denim jacket and a pair of jeans that Anita wasn't sure even she could fit into. His dark brown eyes were penetrating—not in the same way as Simon's, but analytical and clever. A handful of people waited behind him, most of them studying Anita with looks ranging from interest to skepticism, though the smallest among them, a mousy girl wearing heavy white makeup and a clatter of bracelets, had her head down.

Anita raised her eyebrows. "Uh . . . hi."

An amused smirk played about the young man's lips. "Looking for Simon?"

Eyes widening as her jaw dropped, Anita stared for a long moment. "How did you know that?"

He laughed, his smile turning friendly even as his eyes kept their secretive, knowing glimmer. "I'm a little more observant than most of the sheeple. I like to think so, anyway. Someone like Simon makes a friend, it's hard not to notice."

Anita wasn't sure what to say to that, but the young man laughed again and offered her a hand. "I'm sorry, I've forgotten my manners. Miguel Vargos. And you are . . . ?"

Shaking his hand, Anita managed a bit of a smirk back. "You don't know? I'm disappointed."

Miguel winked. "There's a difference between observant and nosy, thank you very much."

Laughing, Anita relaxed as she released his hand. "Anita Rothard."

"A true pleasure, Anita."

"Likewise. So, have you seen Simon?" She glanced around Miguel's collection of friends, as if Simon might be concealed in their midst.

Miguel's smile faded. "As it happens, I have. We passed him up on Harrison Street. He was . . ."

Miguel's voice trailed off, as if he were choosing his words with great care, and Anita tensed. From behind Miguel, a heavyset young man shuffling a set of Magic cards observed, "He didn't look so good."

The girl beside him nodded. "First time I've ever seen him not wearing black, either."

A shiver skittered up her spine that had nothing to do with the cold wind whistling through her thin jacket. "What was he wearing?"

The same girl raised an eyebrow. "Blue jeans. And a red shirt, I think."

A thrill of fear touched Anita's heart, and she took a step back. "I . . . I'm sorry, but I should go make sure he's okay."

Miguel studied her for a second before gesturing to his friends. "We'll go with you, if you'd like."

"No, that's okay," Anita said hurriedly. She had a feeling Simon wouldn't want a huge crowd around him. "Thanks, though. And thanks for telling me."

"Of course," she heard from behind her as she started to jog north across the quad. She felt the eyes on her back, but ignored them as she picked her way through the crowd. She couldn't explain even to herself why she was hurrying; Simon might have stayed up all night studying and come for his final without a chance to change, and if so, he would certainly look exhausted.

As she reached the north end of the quad, it began to dawn on her just how little she had to go on. Half dozen paths led to Harrison Street, and that was assuming Simon was even still there. A flush coloring her cheeks at her sudden impulse, Anita slowed to a walk, clicking the rings on her left hand together.

Then, just as she started to turn back, she saw him, and started jogging again.

Simon was slumped under one of the bare trees along the walkway. His arms were crossed over knees drawn up toward his chest, and his forehead rested on his forearms, long hair loosed from its usual ponytail and twisting in the wind at the back of his neck. As she approached him, Anita noticed he was indeed wearing the clothes in which she had last seen him, though his jacket was missing and his jeans were dirtied and torn at the knees.

Stopping a few feet away, Anita had a sudden terror that he was dead; he had not moved or made any indication that he was aware of her arrival. But when she started, "Simon, are you—" he raised his head, and she had to clap a hand over her mouth to keep from screaming.

A hideous, purple discoloration had spread from Simon's left temple to his jaw, and he had a black eye on the right to match. His lower lip was cut, and there was dried blood around his mouth. His gray eyes were glazed over, and he stared at her without recognition until she dropped down at his side.

"Simon, what happened to you?" Anita asked frantically, reaching for him but checking herself, afraid she might do more damage if she touched him.

Simon shook his head slowly, opening and closing his mashed lips several times before he forced words through them. "It's all right," he said, and his voice was barely a whisper. "I just . . . fell."

"You fell?" Anita exclaimed. "Off what, the Sears Tower?"

Simon's lips twitched, as if he was trying to smile but found the effort too much.

"Stay still, I'll call you an ambulance," Anita promised, digging in her bag for her cell phone. But she had barely gotten it out when Simon lurched forward and gripped her wrist with one hand.

"No, don't," he said, blinking at her as if struggling to focus. Anita remembered him catching her when she had almost fallen on the ice the first time they studied, remembered the iron strength in his hand. His grip seemed so much weaker now.

"Simon, you look like someone tried to kill you!" she said in disbelief. He laughed weakly, then cringed and pressed his free hand to his ribs as he coughed. Anita's eyes followed the movement; just how badly was he hurt? "You have to get checked out."

"No," he repeated, taking a few slow breaths until his ragged breathing leveled out. "I just need . . . to go home . . . get some rest . . ."

"Simon . . ."

"I said no!" he snapped, and there was a flicker of life in his dead voice again. He squeezed harder on her wrist, then placed his other hand against the tree trunk. Arms shaking, tendons bulging in his wrists, he struggled to a standing position.

"What are you doing?" Anita hissed, getting to her feet and pressing her free hand to his chest. He flinched, and she jerked it back. "Sorry. But Simon, you can't just go like this . . ."

"I'll be fine," he reassured her, blinking until some of the glassiness left his eyes. "But I'm . . . going home . . . I'll need a rain check . . . for today . . ."

Anita stared until she remembered why she was meeting him in the first place. "Of course. But Simon, are you sure I can't—"

"Positive."

"Can I at least give you a ride home?"

Simon almost smiled, although his battered lips made the expression hideous. "No. Thanks," he added. "I'll see you . . . sometime . . ."

The conversation seemed to be draining what little life he had left in him. Anita slowly pulled her hand back and returned her cell phone back to her bag. "Give me a call so I know you got home okay?"

"Sure," Simon agreed vacantly, turning and staggering back toward Harrison Street, one arm wrapped around his ribs.

Anita watched him go for a minute, then realized she hadn't given him her number. She opened her mouth to call out to him . . . then paused. Her eyes followed him as he shuffled north, head bowed and shoulders slumped. People passing him did double takes, but didn't seem inclined to stop him. Anita couldn't imagine what had happened to him, who or what could have hurt him that way, but she was sure it hadn't been a fall.

He looked practically dead already. If he made it home in that condition, it would be a miracle.

Hesitating one moment more, Anita looked around herself. Then she took out her cell phone and typed a quick text to Marion: *change of plans. B out late. Will call when I need a ride. Thnx.*

She hit the send button, tucked the phone into her pocket, and started after Simon.

"THIS IS the Green Line train to Ashland, Sixty-Third Street. State and Lake is next. Doors open on the left at State and Lake."

Simon collapsed into a blue-and-yellow seat at the very back of the train car with a faint sigh. Sitting could bring him no more rest than stretching out on a feather bed would without his earth beneath him, but at least it didn't require the effort of staying on his feet. He would not make it home before noon, so it would be another long night without sleep. But unless he had the great misfortune of running into Salem for a second time, he could hunt in the night and sleep the whole next day.

He shouldn't have gone to meet Anita; the simple act of getting on the train and making it a block south to campus had nearly broken him. In retrospect, he was dumbfounded by his own recklessness, but something about just abandoning Anita without a word had seemed so wrong that it pierced even the fog in his mind.

Now, though, he was content to let that fog seep back in, to let conscious thought flitter away. He could not doze off, but he resolved to listen to the station stops and let the rest of the world continue to exist around him.

He was so calmed by this plan, so content with the idea of not moving for the foreseeable future, that he had no chance whatsoever of seeing Anita Rothard slip into the train car behind his, her frightened eyes focused on him through the window.

OWNERSHIP OF the old warehouse in the Back of the Yards had changed hands so many times that, whenever an inquiry was made or a complaint filed with the Chicago Department of Buildings, the reply invariably began with, "To the best of our knowledge . . ."

One in a cluster of similar warehouses south of the Chicago River, the old warehouse was indistinct among its fellows, a community of distribution centers, warehouses, and plants that had grown up in the shadow of the Chicago stockyards. With the rise and fall of the economy over the years, the warehouses often grew dark, only to return to life when the next ambitious company expanded operations. This warehouse's windows were grimed over, and the vast, empty spaces inside had acquired a film of dust since the last machines had hummed within them, but the weeds outside were not overgrown enough nor the condition of the building dilapidated enough to command a detailed investigation.

Slipping through a pair of rusted semi-trailers, Salem studied the warehouse for a long moment, one clawed hand resting on the chilled steel of the nearer trailer, the other on the handle of the sword he now wore beneath his coat. A charter bus rumbled by on the street, and Salem watched it through the chain-link fence until it was out of sight. Then, pausing once to listen for anything amiss, he darted across the concrete parking area. No sunlight pierced the murky cloud cover, so he had no need to hide his lack of shadow; he wondered if it was Shafax's doing.

As he approached the door, he noted a shiny Camry parked outside what had once been the business entrance and growled to himself. Buttoning his cloth duster over his chest to conceal the ragged cuts on his chest and shirt and shifting his sword to the back of his belt so it didn't imprint against the coat, he slowly turned the door handle and slipped inside.

From across the vast space, he heard a voice. "Yeah, it might actually work out . . . No, I can't quite figure that out . . . Let me do some research before I say any more . . . No sir . . . Yes sir, I'm sure you'll be excited too."

A smile twisted the vampire's lips as he started forward. A young man in a gray business suit was speaking into a cell phone as he looked around the warehouse. When his eyes settled on Salem, though, he started, then added into the phone, "I have to go, somebody's here, maybe he can help me."

Hanging up, the young man strode forward with his right hand extended and a brilliant smile on his lips. "Hi!" he said in an assured tone, "Tyler Rowan, with United Textile Solutions."

Salem continued to smile, though he kept his hands clasped behind his back. Raising one eyebrow with a look of polite curiosity, he asked "May I help you, Mr. Rowan?"

Tyler Rowan seemed a bit startled by this greeting, but recovered his smile and asked, "You just might be able to. My company's looking to acquire a manufacturing and distribution center here in Chicago."

"And you're considering my warehouse?" Salem asked innocently.

Rowan adopted a more businesslike look. "Ah, you're the current owner?"

"I have . . . an interest in the property."

"Well, if you and your other holding partners are selling, I'm certain we could make you a very generous offer."

"Indeed?" Salem asked, looking intrigued. Careful to keep his hand out of sight, he placed it on Tyler's back and guided the man toward a ramshackle office in the corner. "Let's step into my office to discuss it."

Rowan fell into step, although his face clouded as he took in the "office." Acting as though he had not seen the look, Salem inquired, "You've been looking at different locations throughout the city, then?"

"What? Oh, yes. I'm here on behalf of United Textile, you know, scouting locations for the vice president of acquisitions," he said.

"They must have a lot of trust in you," Salem mused, "to assess locations on your own."

"The vice president knows who he can trust," Rowan said, "and this facility seems like it would suit our needs perfectly. Ample space for the fabrication systems. How much would—"

"And there's a basement complex," Salem interrupted in a thoughtful tone. "Plenty of storage space over two levels, if you have spare machinery. Did the vice president give you a list of locations, or did you find my warehouse yourself?"

"Hmm? No, no, I've just been checking local properties, getting a feel for them on the ground. I didn't want to waste his time until I had something really promising. Now, you and your partners—"

"That's smart," Salem complimented, ignoring the man's attempt at changing the conversational direction, "and it speaks highly of you, that you don't have someone haunting your every step. So I assume you haven't told everyone at United Textile about this place? My partners and I can be very particular about who we do business with, and if we can't come to some arrangement. . ."

"No worries," Tyler Rowan soothed. "If it doesn't work out, no one will ever know I was here but you and me. But I'm sure we—"

Exactly what he was sure of Salem could only guess, for he seized Tyler by his gelled hair and chin and snapped the man's neck with a single, effortless twist. Letting his corpse drop in a heap, Salem said ruefully, "I'm afraid I'm going to opt not to lease at this time."

Whistling to himself as he patted Tyler's pockets and withdrew a key, wallet, and cell phone, the vampire crushed the phone in his grip, then sauntered over to the loading docks and slid open the single door, which was level with the ground. He jogged over to Tyler's car and drove it inside before sliding the door back down. Hefting

Tyler's body into the trunk one-handed, he laid his hand on the lid, then reached inside and jerked Tyler's watch into view. Smiling faintly as he read the time, he closed the trunk, tore off the two license plates, and threw a tarp over the car. Salem admired his handiwork a moment and then, satisfied, started across the warehouse.

Unbuttoning his coat to keep his gladius within easy reach, he touched the cuts on his chest and gnarred. The pain was nothing; once he was asleep, the cuts would be a memory by nightfall. But it had been close this morning—had it really only been hours ago?—and Salem did not like close calls. Particularly not when they had anything to do with Shafax.

Diverting from the main work area, the vampire slipped into a side hallway, passing by stairs that led up to the administrative offices. Beside the staircase, heavy doors were chained and padlocked shut beneath a sign proclaiming: AUTHORIZED PERSONNEL ONLY. Riffling through his pockets, Salem eventually produced a key ring with half a dozen mismatched keys. Selecting one, he opened the padlock and tossed it and the chain aside, then opened the door and stepped into the darkness over a concrete staircase down.

"Why couldn't Shafax have chosen nighttime?" he complained aloud in the pitch black. "King of All Vampires, and he wants to duke it out at fucking dawn . . ."

Patting around by the door, his clawed hands found a small padlocked lockbox. This time, Salem simply ripped it apart and drew out a flashlight. Once it sputtered to life and illuminated the way, he slipped down the stairs, glancing without concern at the weird and twisting shadows his light cast over rotted furniture, rusted equipment, and stacks upon stacks of boxes. The dry pipes suspended a few inches below the ceiling were a mess of cobwebs, and unseen rodents squeaked in surprise, scampering away from the light. Taking the second staircase down to the subbasement, Salem picked his way through a mess of machines and control panels, shouldered open a corroded door, and shined his light inside.

Two long boxes sat side by side, mildewed and covered in dust, a half-decayed rat corpse lying beside one. Salem reached down and pulled on the lid of one of the boxes; the wood groaned in his hand as he pried the nails free. The box was half-filled with dirt, and Salem grinned. He took a handful in one hand and let it spill through his fingers.

"Home sweet home," he said, clicking off the flashlight and clambering into the box. Shafax would keep for the day. When the night came . . .

Noon arrived as Salem was musing over the possibilities, and absolute darkness took him.

ANITA GAVE Simon a head start, waiting in the doorway of her train until the speaker chimed and reproved, "*Doors closing.*" Darting out onto the platform, she tried to hide behind one of the wind shields insulating a bench, but it was wasted effort; Simon staggered off down the stairs without a backward glance. The wind was howling now, and the clouds overhead had darkened to ominous gray, but he seemed not to notice as he trudged away from the station.

Anita trailed after him, suppressing the urge to call Marion and tell her what was going on. What would she say? That Simon didn't look like he could manage another step, but had somehow dragged himself across half the city? It was starting to sound ridiculous even to Anita. And what was she going to do if he did make it home without incident? Just call a cab? She wasn't even sure where she was.

As they left the train station behind, Anita realized she had no idea where Simon lived. At first she kept a careful distance, afraid he might turn into any of the crowded-together houses they passed. But as he continued to plod straight ahead, pausing occasionally as if to catch his breath, Anita started to shorten the distance between them.

The houses they passed were becoming more run-down. More than one block had a pile of demolished rubble where a house should have been. A few had iron fences around their small lots, but most of these were rusted and bent, and one gate was secured to its post with barbed wire. Anita didn't like the looks she was getting through the windows of the bars they passed, or from the clerk at the dingy gas station Simon shambled past.

Clutching her coat closer around her, Anita picked up her pace a bit, getting as close to Simon as she dared. She was starting to regret the lurid purple coat and almost called to Simon, but caught herself. What explanation could she offer that wouldn't anger him?

The snowstorm broke as they crossed through a broken guard-rail into an unkempt baseball diamond with grass growing through the baselines. Anita's teeth chattered so loudly she started to wonder whether Simon might hear her, but the sudden and violent onset of snow had her tailing him more closely still. She did not want to lose sight of him here.

That became more challenging with every step, because in the time it took them to cross the field, the snowstorm approached blizzard status. Barely twenty feet separated Anita and Simon now, but she was squinting against the wind to see him at all, and she didn't notice the road until she took a step onto it.

The shrill honk of a horn had her leaping back, and she stumbled on the curb and fell back upon the sidewalk with a gasp. Rolling down his passenger window, the driver shouted, "What the hell's wrong with you, stupid bitch? You wanna die?"

"I'm sorry," Anita apologized, getting to her feet.

"Sorry my ass; you coulda been a hood ornament!"

Anita looked over the roof of the car for Simon, but she had lost sight of him.

"Hey! I'm talkin' to you!"

"It was an accident!" Anita snapped. Then, trying to keep the heat out of her tone, she added, "I'm really sorry I was in your way. I'll be more careful."

"Yeah, whatever." The driver shook his head as he drove away.

Anita looked both ways this time, then bolted across the road. She made it to the opposite sidewalk, but gasped as she nearly ran headlong into a brick wall. Pressing her hands against it, she looked to both sides. On the stoop to her right, a cluster of men eyed her with raised eyebrows. She went left instead, and took only a few steps before she heard the voices.

"Not so tough now, are you? Bastard!"

"Lenny Nelson was my friend, fucker!"

There were sounds of a scuffle, a gasp of pain, and the distinctive thud of something hitting the ground.

"Oh, you're gonna pay for that . . ."

Anita poked her head around the corner and the blood drained out of her face. Simon was backed up against the alley wall, hands raised, elbows tucked in to protect his rib cage. Four men were facing him, and a fifth was on the ground, holding his stomach and gasping for breath. Even as Anita watched, the group of four rushed Simon, two of them succeeding in pinning his arms back against the bricks. As Simon struggled in their grip, one of the others punched him across the face, and his head drooped.

The men laughed, and the one on the ground managed a raspy chuckle as he put one palm to the ground and started to lever himself up. Anita clapped her hands over her mouth in horror and lurched forward before she caught herself. What was she going to do? She'd only taken taekwondo for three months before quitting with her yellow belt; she wouldn't bet on herself against even one of Simon's attackers.

Then another of the gang grabbed Simon by the neck, forced his chin up, and punched him right between the eyes. Simon grunted, a little blood leaking from the cut above his left eye, but then cried out in pain as his attacker followed with a shot to the ribs. He cringed away from the blow as much as he could, and Anita wondered if his ribs were broken.

That sound of pain, however, kick-started her anger, and she gritted her teeth. Even if it was a lost cause, she couldn't stand by and do nothing. Glancing around desperately, she spotted a few boards lying on the sidewalk nearby; they seemed to have fallen or been pulled out from over a window on the first floor. Hefting one that didn't have any nails in it, Anita steeled herself and turned back to the alley.

All five of Simon's attackers were facing him now. Even as Anita crept forward, holding her board in shaking hands, one of them kicked Simon's shin as another hit him in the gut. The man in the center was drawing back a fist when Anita took a deep breath, darted forward, and brought the board down on the back of his head.

Her aim was a bit off; the board hit more of his shoulder, though it clipped his ear and the side of his neck. But he gave a pained cry of his own and toppled forward into Simon. There was a second of confusion as the two other men who weren't holding Simon's arms whirled around, eyes wide until they focused on Anita. Simon's gray eyes turned toward her, blankly incredulous. In the following second, when all of his attackers were shifting their attention to Anita, Simon reacted.

Drawing up one leg, he kicked out and connected with the knee of one of the men holding him. The man screamed, reaching down to clasp his leg as he toppled backward. Wrenching that arm free, Simon turned it into a palm strike on the man holding his other arm, sending him staggering down the alley. The man Anita hit had already sunk to the ground, clutching the back of his head. The two remaining men started toward Anita, but stopped when they realized the greater danger might be behind them.

They split up, one continuing toward Anita while the other turned back to Simon. Anita swung her board at her attacker, but he leaned back and the blow swiped through the air. Before Anita could cock it back for a second swing, the man charged her and caught her by the wrists. He grabbed her jaw with his free hand.

"Real bad idea, bitch," he breathed. Anita glared up at him, tugging fruitlessly against his grip. The man's blue-gray eyes bored into hers, and the chewing tobacco on his breath flooded her nostrils until she choked. She kicked him in the shin, but he was pressed up against her body and only snarled through his teeth. He let go of her jaw, and Anita wrenched her face away from his. She didn't see where his hand went until her stomach exploded in pain, all the air driven from her lungs as the blow collapsed her diaphragm. Her legs turning to water and the board slipping from her fingers, she sagged to her knees, retching and panicking as she tried and failed to suck in a breath.

Still holding her wrists, her attacker looked down at her on her knees. "Yeah, I think I like you right there," he sneered. "You can—"

He suddenly lurched forward, face smashing into the wall like he was trying to headbutt his way through it. Shrieking, he released Anita's wrists to clutch his nose; blood poured through his fingertips and dripped onto Anita's jeans. Then a pale hand landed on the man's shoulder and jerked him around. Simon punched him so hard that he stopped shrieking and collapsed to the ground.

Anita looked up at Simon's battered face. Even slightly out of focus, his gray eyes burned.

"Get out of here," he growled, teeth gritted, as if he would rather have taken his chances without her help.

Anita had half a second to register hurt before she had to wheeze, "Look out . . ."

He turned in time to raise his hands; one of his attackers had thrown a rusty iron chain at him. The chain bounced off Simon's arms, but he caught it as it started to fall. The attacker moved in, and Simon took a blow on the jaw as he tried to thread his fingers through the tangled chain. When he got a grip and swung his fist,

Anita heard the crack of the man's jaw from five feet away as the steel connected. He fell back face-first against the other wall, then Simon spun him around and gave him a ferocious backhand with his chain-wrapped fist.

Still winded, Anita had no breath to cry out when one of the men lying on the ground lurched toward her and grabbed her collar. He jerked her forward, pinning her to the ground and holding his forearm across her chest. The hateful look in his eyes and the flaring red on his right ear made her realize he was the one she had hit with the board. Evidently he realized it too; he spat in her face.

"Let's see how pretty you look with no fuckin' lips!" he hissed, and bent his face toward hers. Anita struggled to escape, clawing at his face with her blunt nails while his saliva dribbled down her cheek, but he snapped at her fingers and she pulled them back.

Then a length of rusty steel appeared around his neck, tightening like a noose. Eyes bugging out, he lurched up to his knees away from Anita, clawing at his throat. Simon stood over him, a coil of chain in each hand, tugging it tighter as her attacker's face flushed red and his gasps started to wheeze toward silence. His work boots scrabbled on the ground as he tried to force his way to his feet, but each movement was weaker than the last.

Even with the memory of his teeth coming toward her face vivid in her mind, even shuddering against the feeling of his spit slithering down her neck, Anita couldn't bear to watch it—he was dying in front of her eyes. "Simon," she wheezed, struggling up to her hands and knees. "Simon, let him go."

The chain clicked as one link tightened past another. Anita's attacker had fallen silent; his tongue lolled out and a blood vessel burst in his eye, the red seeping out to border the hazel.

"Simon, stop!"

Simon looked down at her, and Anita recoiled in shock. The look in his steel eyes was so violent, so filled with fury . . . but even as she stared at him, the fire left his gaze, and he relaxed his hands.

The chain loosened, and Anita's attacker slumped forward, collapsing to the cold alley floor. She watched him anxiously for a long moment before she saw the faint rise and fall of his chest.

Slumping back against the alley wall, Anita pulled her legs close to her body, then wrapped her arms around them and began shuddering. She ducked her face against her knees and almost screamed when someone's hand dropped on her shoulder.

"It's me," Simon said. His voice had no strength to be sharp, though there was an edge to it. Anita looked up at him, fearful of what she might see. That ruthless intensity had frightened her. But when she saw the lifeless sag of his features and the bruises on his pale face, her heart unfroze and she reached out to place her hands on his shoulders.

"Simon, are you all right?" she asked. Her voice was still a whisper, even though she could breathe again.

He looked back at her, eyes bleary and face slack, and Anita cringed; she had never seen anyone who looked less all right. But he took a deep breath and managed, "I'll be fine. I just need . . . to rest . . ."

"Simon, you need to go to a hospital," Anita said firmly. She wiped the spit off her cheek with the cuff of one sleeve, grimacing down at the man at her feet. She was sorely tempted to kick him—*Let's see how many people you bite with no teeth*—but forced herself to focus on Simon. "Come on, I'll call an ambulance."

Anita started digging in her pocket for her phone, but she couldn't get a grip on it with her trembling fingers. Simon struggled to his feet and caught her by the wrist.

"No," he said, his voice hardening a bit, though it was still faint. He blinked several times, struggling to focus on her. "No, Anita. I'll be fine."

"No, Simon!" Anita insisted. She wasn't sure why she was pressing him so hard—there was more light in his eyes now than when she'd found him on campus, and some strength in his hand—but it seemed important. Blinking, she realized tears were streaming down her cheeks. The sensation reminded her of the spit on her face, and she shuddered for a long moment before she half-screamed, "Why can't I find my phone?!"

"Anita?" Simon asked. His voice was sharper now, and his hand moved from her wrist to her shoulder to steady her. She looked up at him and saw his eyes widen; the gash on the left side of his face stretched with the movement. "Anita!"

"What?" she sobbed, seizing the lapels of his coat.

"I think maybe you should go to the hospital," he said, and even though he frowned, he wrapped an arm around her shoulders. She slumped against him, shivering as she nodded.

"M-maybe . . . w-we can both go," she offered, managing a weak smile.

Simon grimaced but nodded, and started to tow her down the alley.

"You're limping," Anita observed faintly. She blinked, frowning and rubbing her head, wondering why it was getting harder to focus.

Simon said something in reply, but Anita missed it as her legs gave out and she slipped into blackness toward the ground.

HOURS LATER, Simon sat slumped in an urgent care waiting room, his elbows resting on the wooden arms of an uncomfortable chair, its fabric scratchy on the back of his neck. Marion de Santos sat beside him, her arm around Nancy Rothard on her other side and Anita's purple coat folded in her lap.

He was more exhausted than he could ever remember being, half-conscious of his surroundings and still in a great deal of pain. But by the time they had gotten to the urgent care and the women had cajoled him into speaking to a doctor, the sun had set, and some measure of strength had come back to him. He had sat in the examination room until first the nurse, then the doctor walked in, met his gaze, and walked back out, filling out his charts and pronouncing his injuries superficial.

The police had arrived too, but Anita seemed confused about what had happened, leaving Simon the only credible witness. Like Anita, they weren't convinced by the story about falling, but luckily, they had interviewed him one at a time.

"This kind of thing happens all the time in that neighborhood," he had suggested to each officer, concentrating as hard as he could.

"Yeah. Dangerous place," the officer said, frowning like he wanted to look away, but not managing it.

"This doesn't bear investigation at all."

"It'd be a waste. We'd never find the two guys." With Anita vague on the details, Simon had changed a few of them.

"Especially since all you have to go on is Anita's statement."

"Especially . . ." The officer had struggled, face crumpling as his mind rebelled against swallowing such monstrous lies. The hand with the pen hesitated over the notepad, twitching like it wanted to take a note.

Simon gritted his teeth and focused harder, feeling his eyes glowing red in the examination room the officer was using for privacy. The cop's look of pain relaxed into docile obedience. "The man didn't have anything, so there's no point taking his info," he recited robotically. "And the kid's statement by itself is useless."

"Very good."

The two Chicago cops had left looking confused but displaying no inclination to come back and try again. But the effort had strained what little focus and power Simon had left. Even now, sitting and doing nothing, he felt a hollow lack of his usual strength. He wanted to feed, but he wasn't sure he'd even be able to overpower a strong human. He wanted to rest, but dawn was hours away. He stared at the impressionist paintings by nameless artists, the only features of the off-white walls of the urgent care aside from the emergency evacuation plan and a poster advising ways to avoid cold and flu.

With nothing to command his attention and his mind wandering, he thought back on the day's events and his appalling series of decisions. First, there was the foolish choice to meet Anita rather than resting; that was the cause of all the others. Had he slept instead, by now he'd be awake again, mostly recovered, and able to hunt; the new blood would go a long way to repairing what remained of his injuries from Salem.

That error was reckless enough by itself. But then he had allowed Lenny Nelson's crew to catch him, and only Anita's intervention had saved him. That, of course, was another failure—he had made it halfway across Chicago without realizing he was being followed. And to top it off, he had taken a taxi all the way north to Evanston and walked right up to the Rothards' door with Anita shivering in his arms.

He kept wondering what would have happened if it had not been the middle of December, if sunset did not come at four thirty in the afternoon, if he hadn't been able to hypnotize the police and the medical staff . . .

A few other patients had come and gone—several in various stages of what seemed like a nasty flu, a vomiting child and his parents, and a heavyset man whose three-day case of the sniffles had somehow become "urgent," among others—but fortunately, no one was bleeding. Bleary and unfocused as he was, Simon heard Marion and Nancy's heartbeats only faintly, and he didn't even notice Dr. Rothard's until the man was in the room and speaking.

"Nancy! Where is she? Is she all right?"

Simon focused his vision to find Nancy holding her husband's forearms, looking tired and careworn but not overly worried. She managed a smile and said, "I think she'll be okay, Rick. It sounds like she was more frightened than anything else."

"But your message made it sound like . . ." He trailed off into an anguished choke, and Simon frowned, focusing harder and sitting up. He hadn't imagined Dr. Rothard had such an emotional reaction in him.

The movement caught the heavy man's peripheral vision, and he turned to glower at Simon. "What happened?"

Simon opened his mouth to respond when a soft, tired voice came from the other side of the room. "Hi, guys."

Anita looked more sheepish than anything else. She was brushing her chestnut hair back and accompanied by a female doctor, who held a clipboard in one hand and the door for Anita with the other. The Rothards crossed the room to her side, leaving Simon to trail in their wake. Marion came up beside him, offering her arm with a small smile, but Simon just shook his head.

"Is she all right?" Dr. Rothard demanded again, though his voice had abandoned aggression and reverted to urgency.

"I'm fine, Dad," Anita reassured him, accepting a hug from her mother, but her father didn't even bat an eye; he was still focused on the doctor, who nodded.

"Acute stress reaction," she declared. "Nothing broken. She might have some bruising on her wrists, and her memories are a little fuzzy, but that'll be it."

"It all happened so fast," Anita said, frowning and rubbing her head.

Dr. Rothard relaxed a bit, placing a hand on Anita's shoulder as if he wasn't convinced she was real.

"But . . . what exactly happened? Your message said she got assaulted," he said to his wife, before his eyes turned to Simon again.

"I got off the train, and two men tried to grab me." Simon wanted to get his version of events out rather than let Anita piece things together. "Anita was following me, and she hit one of them from behind and distracted him so I could get free, and then I pulled them off her."

Anita blinked, seeming to struggle with that. "I remember he was standing over me," she said slowly, her bright eyes narrowed with concentration. "And then you hit him . . ."

Simon shrugged, saying nothing. Nancy put in gently, "He brought her home to us, and then we came here."

Dr. Rothard frowned. "Why didn't you call an ambulance directly? What about the police, what did they say?"

Nancy raised a hand before he could get any further. "The police have already been here and interviewed Simon and Anita. They said they'll contact us if they find anything."

She leaned in closer, and Simon's vampire ears just barely caught, "And maybe Anita's not the only one who was a little in shock. He did what he thought was best."

Dr. Rothard frowned again, but then looked back at Anita.

"Why were you following him in the first place?"

"I was worried about him . . . since he was hurt."

All eyes turned back to Simon, and Dr. Rothard's widened behind his glasses. Only now did he seem to notice the extent of Simon's own bruising. "Good Lord, what happened to you?"

"I fell down a staircase," Simon recited. Though the conversation was getting more tiring, he had repeated this lie so many times he was starting to envision tumbling down one of the staircases in his apartment building as if it had actually happened. "It looks worse than it is."

"Well, it looks pretty bad," Anita's father replied, unconvinced, but his wife shrugged.

"That's what I said, but the doctor says it's all superficial," Nancy replied.

The doctor herself looked uncertain, glancing beneath Anita's chart at Simon's, reading it over as if trying to reassure herself. But she nodded and conceded, "Exam results were all negative . . . but if you want a second opinion—"

"I'm fine," Simon said, his impatience starting to leak into his tone. The doctor raised her eyebrows, but just shrugged.

"They're both clear to go, then."

Simon nodded and turned, shuffling toward the door.

"Simon, wait," Nancy said. The vampire squeezed his eyes shut briefly, but pulled his expression together and turned around.

Glancing at her husband, Nancy said, "We'll cover both of you, Simon. It's the least we can do."

Simon blinked. He had not even thought about paying or any-thing as mundane as human needs; his only thought was escape. He was silent long enough that Dr. Rothard spoke as well.

"Yes . . . from the sounds of things, you saved my daughter from . . ." His words trailed off into silence, but Simon noticed his plump lips pressed together; he imagined the man gritting his teeth behind them. Taking a deep breath as he pulled out a handkerchief and patted his forehead, Dr. Rothard eyed Simon for a moment, his expression ambivalent. "I'm still not certain I understand what was going on, but the fact remains that you helped her. We'd be happy to cover your expenses today."

With no energy left to focus on eloquence, Simon settled for covering his tracks with the humans instead. "Thank you."

He trudged along with them toward the front counter. The Rothards stopped to pay and Simon kept going, but Marion said, "Hey, we'll give you a ride, Simon."

"I'm fine," he called without stopping.

"Are you sure?"

He just nodded, waving a hand vaguely over his shoulder. He was at the automatic door when he heard Anita say, "I'll be right back, I want to walk out with him."

"Sweetheart, why don't you stay here with us? I think he wants to go." Dr. Rothard's voice carried a mix of gentleness and lingering suspicion.

"It'll only be a minute." Anita's voice was soft too, but insistent, and Simon heard her footsteps in pursuit. He continued out into the night, breathing in the cold air and pausing until the door opened again behind him.

"Simon?"

Taking in a deep breath as if it would help him, Simon turned to face her. Though her color was weaker than usual, Anita's eyes were alert and full of concern.

"I swear, I'm going to be fine," he said exhaustedly, but she shook her head.

"That's not it. There . . ." Anita hesitated, looking down, then turned her eyes resolutely up to his and said, "There's more to the story, isn't there? I can't remember it all clearly, but there were more than two."

Simon looked at her for a long moment. They were alone, and he thought he might have enough left in him to hypnotize her, too . . . but the idea made him uncomfortable for a reason he couldn't name. "It doesn't matter. Two, three . . . we got away."

"Yeah . . ." Anita paused again, then stepped forward and tentatively took his hand. "Thank you."

Caught off guard by the contact, Simon stared at her. "For what? You saved me." Some of his annoyance leaked into his tone; he tried to suppress it as he added, "I should be thanking you."

"You pulled one of them off me," Anita countered, shaking her head and frowning. Her free hand touched her cheek where the man had spat on her, though she didn't seem to remember why.

Simon shrugged again. "It doesn't matter; we're even. But . . ."

It would have been easier to leave it alone and walk away, but he had to know. "But why were you there? Why did you follow me?"

"I was worried about you," Anita said. She looked up at him with nothing but that same worry in her puppy dog eyes. "I didn't think you were going to make it on your own. And I didn't think you had really fallen." She frowned, tilting her head to one side.

Her voice was a whisper as she asked, "That part wasn't true either, was it?"

Simon opened his mouth to insist on it yet again . . . and the words died on his lips. The way Anita was looking at him, combined with the fog in his head and the stabbing pain in his ribs, addled his mind until he found himself saying instead, "What happened today—and what happened last night—it doesn't matter, Anita, really. It will do me more harm than good if you don't let it go."

Anita frowned at that, trying to interpret his words, and Simon groaned internally. There was no way that could be taken well, and when she pressed it . . .

"Then I'll let it go," she said. "As long as you promise me you'll be okay."

For a moment, the vampire just blinked, stunned. Then he nodded and squeezed her hand. "I promise." After all, it had been years since he had seen Salem. How likely was it that he'd run into his former mentor again? "The next time you see me, I'll be back to . . . usual."

"When will I see you again?" she asked, smiling a little now, even as she shivered in the night air.

"You should get inside, it's cold," Simon replied.

"When?" she pressed. As Simon hesitated again, she said, "I have to pick up a paper tomorrow at five at the Behavioral Sciences Building. Will you be around campus?"

"Sure," the vampire agreed without thinking. Exhausted and battered and pained and thirsty as he was, he didn't register how the reflex failed to startle him this time.

"All right, I'll see you then."

Anita looked back toward the door, then to Simon, a conflicted expression on her face. Her heartbeat accelerated, and his dormant thirst for blood whispered in his throat in response. The hand still wrapped around Simon's was trembling, and the vampire was about to point out the cold again when Anita licked her lips with a bracing expression, reached up to grab the lapel of his coat with her free hand, pulled him forward, and kissed him.

Stunned, Simon could only respond, his lips as cold as hers, moving around hers, the taste of her breath lingering on his tongue. His free hand curved around the small of her back, pulling her body against his. His palm slid up her spine, the instinct to attack trying to twist his fingers into claws, goading him to grab her by the hair to jerk her head back and expose her throat . . .

Then she pulled away, gently pushing on his chest, and smiled up at him as she squeezed his hand again. Still dazed, Simon blinked down at her, trying and failing to decide on an expression.

"I'll see you tomorrow," Anita said. Her voice was even, but her heart thundered as she took a step back, letting their arms stretch out before releasing him. She gave him a smirk. "Be safe until then?"

"I will," the vampire managed. Smiling, Anita turned and walked back inside, her heart racing. Despite being free to drop his human charade at last, Simon had the strangest urge to follow her, but he managed to master that impulse, instead turning and shambling off through the parking lot toward the cover of darkness beyond.

ELEVEN

THE SKY was already dark and thick with storm clouds as Anita stepped out into the cold five o'clock air, grinning at the B+ on her paper one more time before she stuffed it in her backpack. Hoping that it wasn't going to start blizzarding again, she pulled on her knit hat, tugging its long flaps down to cover her ears. Stepping down the exterior stairs as she zipped up her thick winter jacket, she glanced down the sidewalk toward the street. A single light nearby threw the surrounding skeletal trees into hazy orange relief, and as she took a deep breath of frosty air through her nose, Anita caught a mix of warm, appetizing scents from the convenience store next door. She had just taken a step in that direction when a harsh voice behind her said, "Anita."

Jumping, she turned to find Simon facing her. "Whoa! Where did you come from?"

"I was waiting for you," he replied, looking down at her without expression.

"Oh, sorry," Anita replied, adjusting the strap of her bag. "I hope you weren't out here waiting too long?"

"It's no trouble. The cold doesn't bother me."

Anita nodded, then studied Simon. His pale face was exactly as she remembered it from their first meeting—the lines sharp, his hair and eyebrows dark against his flesh, his gray eyes bright even with the light coming from behind him. She saw no bruises anywhere, not even blotches of yellow or green.

"You look better," she observed incredulously.

Simon's lips twitched like his mouth couldn't decide whether to grimace or smile. "I told you it looked worse than it was."

"Right," Anita replied, though she frowned a moment more. When she noticed him looking her over, though, she took a deep breath. "I'm okay."

Simon's dark brows pulled together so they nearly touched, and Anita gripped one of his narrow, muscular arms. "Seriously. I had some bad dreams, but I'm a lot better today. Sorry I freaked out on you yesterday, I just . . ."

"I'm sure it must have been frightening for you."

Anita shivered, but she let go of Simon before the tremor reached her fingers. "Yeah, it was. My mom said my brain just needed a reset, though. What about you?"

"I'm fine."

"It wasn't scary for you?"

She didn't know what to make of Simon's smile. "Not my first close call—nor my closest."

There was a nauseating thought. Anita was bouncing back, but Simon sounded so blasé, the alley fight might have been routine. Then again, she had lived her life relatively sheltered from the worst Chicago had to offer; for Simon, maybe it was.

The urge to ask gnawed at her, but she remembered his words at the urgent care and forced herself to shrug instead. Catching her backpack strap as it started to fall off her shoulder, she asked, "So, what do you want to do? We could probably grab a pretzel in here," she offered, jerking the thumb of her free hand over her shoulder toward the convenience store, "or we could go get something from Student East?"

Simon hesitated, his mouth open an inch, but before he could say anything, a small voice asked, "Um . . . excuse me?"

Surprised again, Anita turned to find a girl facing her from a couple yards away, farther than Anita thought was comfortable for conversation. She was a few inches shorter than Anita and wore a black hoodie zipped up to her throat with a pink kitten design on the left breast; the kitten smiled, but had several long scars sewn on its limbs and forehead that made Anita think of Frankenstein's monster. The girl's hood was pulled up over her hair, but she had a layer of white makeup on that made her nearly as pale as Simon. Dark eyeliner drew the gaze to her blue eyes, which darted skittishly between them.

"Uh . . . hi," Anita replied, studying the girl curiously. She felt like she should recognize her, but couldn't place her. The girl hugged her arms around her chest, but said nothing. Anita glanced at Simon, who was frowning at the new arrival, then looked back. Tilting her head to one side, Anita suggested, "Can we help you with something?"

The girl hesitated a moment longer, then blurted out, "Miguel wants to talk to you. Both of you," she added with a nervous glance at Simon.

"That's where I know you!" Anita said, smiling now. "You were with Miguel yesterday."

Simon turned to stare at her, but the girl gave a weak smile back. "Y-y-yeah, that's me. So, will you come talk to Miguel?"

"Miguel remains as persistent as he is deaf." Simon had found his voice at last, and it was sharp and cold. Miguel's friend shuddered, and even Anita flinched at the hostility. "How many times do I have to tell him to leave me alone?"

"H-h-he . . . he just wanted . . ."

The girl lowered her eyes, and Anita frowned sympathetically. "Why don't you want to go talk to him?" she asked Simon.

Rolling his eyes, Simon replied, "Believe me, it isn't worth the effort. He won't have anything to say that's worth hearing."

"That's not true," the girl squeaked, but when Simon turned his eyes back to her, she cringed and went back to studying her black boots.

Anita stepped a bit closer to Simon and nudged him in the ribs with her elbow. "Hey, come on, you don't need to be mean to her. Besides, I kinda owe Miguel one for yesterday." When Simon stared at her uncomprehendingly, she added, "He saw you and told me where to find you."

Simon groaned behind his sealed lips and closed his eyes, massaging them with the fingers of one hand, as if this news pained him. Anita looked at him for a moment, then turned back. "So, did Miguel want to get lunch someday next week, or . . . ?"

The girl's head shot up so fast that her hood flipped back a few inches, revealing a lock of strawberry blonde hair until she tugged the hood back in place. "Uh, actually, we're all hanging out in the Lincoln Hall oasis. If you're not doing anything . . . ?"

Simon lowered his arm and opened his mouth, but Anita caught his hand and squeezed it. The girl didn't miss the gesture, and her eyes widened.

"Sure, why not?" Anita said.

Miguel's friend looked back at her and smiled. "Great! He'll be so glad to hear it. Do . . . d'you want me to walk over with you . . . ?"

"I know where it is." Simon's icy tone left no room for debate.

The girl took a half step back. "Okay. I'll just go ahead and tell him you're coming, then. I . . . I'll see you there, I guess."

She turned to go, but Anita said, "Hey, wait."

When the girl stopped, Anita let go of Simon's hand to walk up to her. The girl arched her shoulders forward, contracting in on herself, but Anita just extended her left hand. "I'm Anita. I know I saw you yesterday, but we weren't really introduced. What's your name?"

The girl looked at Anita's hand as if she wasn't sure what it was, then cautiously took it with her own left. A group of three rubber bracelets piled together as they slid down her thin arm. "I'm Heidi."

"Nice to meet you, Heidi. You know . . . again," Anita said with a teasing smirk.

Heidi managed a smile, then started backing up again. "I'll go tell Miguel you're coming."

She turned and jogged off down the sidewalk, wobbling on a patch of ice before she righted herself. Glancing back as if to see if Anita and Simon had seen her, Heidi continued on with her shoulders hunched until she was out of sight.

Once she was out of earshot, Anita frowned at Simon. "Okay, what was that about?"

His arms were crossed over his chest, and his eyes narrowed. "I told you, Miguel isn't—"

"Yeah, I heard that part," Anita said. "I mean with Heidi. Could you have been any meaner to her?"

Eyes widening again, Simon said, "I wasn't—"

"You really were, Simon," Anita cut him off. As he stared at her, though, Anita sighed and shook her head. "I think you don't know how you sound, sometimes. But you don't have a problem with her, do you? No matter what the deal is with Miguel?"

Simon paused for a moment, eyes searching her face, then sighed. "No, I suppose not," he conceded, looking the way Heidi had gone. "He just . . . rubs me the wrong way. Miguel. It's gotten to the point that I never associate anything good with him, or any of his people."

"'His people?'" Anita repeated. "You mean his friends?"

Simon shook his head. "You should see the way they relate to him. They're definitely more like followers than friends." Finally turning his face back to hers, he rolled his eyes. "I guess you will see, won't you?"

Despite her brief irritation, Anita couldn't help but smirk. "I guess I will."

Taking Simon's hand, she tugged him down the sidewalk as she started off toward the road. He rubbed her hand with his thumb, but his expression was so distracted she thought it must be unconscious. Squeezing his hand again, she said, "I really do owe him one for yesterday."

Simon made a face. "Yes, what happened?"

"He and his . . . friends saw you. He told me where you were."

Simon's jaw locked, but he said nothing.

"It's a good thing, right? That I found you?"

Giving her an incredulous look, he asked, "And wound up in the urgent care because of it."

"Better than you ending up in a coffin." Anita shivered at the idea.

To her surprise, Simon laughed. Anita stared for a moment, but she wasn't going to waste the change in his mood. "See? Everything worked out. Today will too, you'll see."

Simon gave her a martyred look and sighed. "I wait in ecstatic anticipation."

"GET OUTTA here, you bum! I catch you digging in my trash one more time, I'm calling the cops! You hear me?"

"Yeah, easy for you in your nice warm restaurant with your big fat ass to keep you warm," Jim Hayden grumbled, shuffling away from the dumpster and sticking his hands in his coat pockets.

"What'd you say to me?"

"Nothing," Jim called, not turning as he ambled off down the alley. He stopped at the street and looked back, but the owner still stood in the back doorway, crossed arms resting on his protruding belly, a sashimi knife in one hand. Swearing under his breath, Jim turned the corner.

The wind cutting through the air and whistling off the buildings on either side of the street was like a slap in the face, and Jim cussed again as he pulled his coat tighter around his body. The strands of gray hair in his beard flicked up into his face, but his baseball cap kept his bangs out of his eyes, which stung in the breeze. He turned his head down, letting the wind beat the bill of the cap instead.

It was going to be another hungry night if somebody didn't have something to scavenge. Worse, Jim still hadn't found a good place to sleep. Some nasty bug was going around the shelters and underpasses he frequented, and Jim didn't feel like hacking up his lungs for a week. The construction yard down the street used to be a pretty reliable spot—there, he could get down into what was supposed to be a basement, out of the wind, and wrap himself up in one of the tarps that covered the smaller machines. As long as he replaced the tarp in the morning, nobody was any the wiser. But yesterday he'd overheard people yelling about damaged machinery down in the site. They'd probably have the cops doing patrols now, and Jim . . . well, Jim and cops didn't go together so well.

He passed a woman on the sidewalk and looked up hopefully. "Hey lady, can you spare a dollar?"

She hurried past without a word, looking straight ahead, and he muttered, "Yeah, that's right bitch, just keep walking, I ain't even here."

"Cold night, isn't it?"

Blinking, Jim looked around until he found a guy standing right next to him. "The hell'd you come from?"

The man only smiled.

Jim studied the guy distrustfully. His skin was icy pale, and his black hair cut short, like one of those military types. He wore a long black coat that was worn down in places, but as thin as it was and for all his talk about the cold, he seemed at ease in the wind. He smiled a twisted smile, and his bright emerald eyes were piercing, captivating. Jim shuffled his feet.

"What d'you want? You got a dollar?"

The guy took one hand out of his pocket to gesture down the street—no dollar in it—then set off like he expected Jim to follow. For some reason, Jim did. "I'm looking for a . . . friend of mine."

"Does he have a dollar?" Jim hinted. He didn't like this guy's voice—the way it stuck in his ears and make him shiver. Or maybe that was just the wind.

Glancing at Jim from the corner of his eye, the guy smiled to himself, then looked straight ahead. Jim almost asked how he could stand the wind lashing his face, but before he could open his mouth, the wind died down. The air was cold, but the sting was finally gone from Jim's face.

"Jesus, I thought it was never gonna stop," Jim complained, rubbing his hands together and pressing them up against his mouth, breathing hot air on them. The pale guy flinched, but then his expression smoothed over. "So what d'you want?"

"Like I said," the stranger said, his voice calm but . . . different. Jim leaned away from him. "I'm looking for an old friend. You been around this neighborhood for a while now?"

"I get around the city," Jim replied carefully. He stopped walking under a streetlight. If this guy wanted to roll him, he'd have to do it right in plain view.

The guy stopped walking too, but didn't seem to be looking for a fight. He just put his hands back in his pockets and nodded. "You know this area pretty well?"

"Good enough."

The stranger studied Jim for a moment, then drew a hand out of his pocket. In it were two foil-wrapped burritos Jim could smell from five feet away. Fresh, like the guy had picked them up at the taco place down the street. He imagined the warmth in his gut, and it rumbled.

"I don't need these," the stranger mused. "I'll bet you do. But I do need to find my friend."

Jim took a step toward the guy, who shifted the burritos farther away. For a second, Jim studied him, wondering if he could take him. But something in the man's cold smile and his weird eyes told Jim that wouldn't go well at all.

"Man, I ain't even got my own friends," Jim moaned, looking at the burritos again. "How am I supposed to know who yours are?"

"He looks a lot like me. A little taller, ponytail, gray eyes. You'd know him if you saw him."

"Man, he looks anything like you, and I think I'd remember him," Jim complained. Whatever this guy might be, "easy to forget" wasn't it. "I never seen anybody like you."

"Hmm," the stranger said, tapping his index finger against the burritos. For the first time, Jim noticed his fingernails were long and sharp, almost like claws. The guy was getting weirder and weirder, and Jim was suddenly sure he didn't want to meet—or be—the guy's friend.

"What d'you need your friend for?"

"I need his help," the stranger said, and now there was some emotion in his clipped voice—annoyance, Jim thought. The guy's lip curled, then relaxed. "Well, if he's not around here, he's not around here. I'll keep looking."

He turned, and Jim said, "Hey! Hey, man, it's not my fault I don't know him!"

The guy stopped, looked back, then shrugged and handed over the burritos. Jim grabbed them both quickly, pressing them to his nose and inhaling the warmth and scent until his stomach twisted. "Thanks, man," he said emphatically. "Hey, if I see your friend, I'll tell him you're looking for him."

The guy frowned. "Hmm. Can't have that."

He looked at Jim, and Jim looked back. The bright green eyes brightened, like they were illuminated from behind. Then they weren't green at all, but glowing red, and that fire bored through Jim's eyes and into his mind, until everything was foggy and indistinct . . .

Jim started as the wind lashed at his face. He was alone under a streetlight, the wind howling, with two hot burritos in his hand. How the hell had that happened? He remembered the fat sushi guy kicking him out of the dumpster, and then . . . oh, yeah, the taco stand. He must have gotten them there, that was right. Had the guy been nice enough to donate them, or had he been nice enough to not notice Jim liberating them?

He thought for a moment, then shrugged and continued walking down the sidewalk. "Screw it. Burrito's a burrito."

"NOW REMEMBER, 'ecstatic anticipation,'" Anita reminded Simon as they passed into Lincoln Hall and out of the cold wind. She relaxed in the warmth, pulling off her bobble-topped knit hat to let her chestnut hair spill around her shoulders, but Simon gritted his teeth. He thought stony silence would serve better than any response to which he could give voice.

Anita led the way to the student oasis down the hall, where Simon was unsurprised to see most of Miguel's retinue spread out. Three of them were seated on a curving orange couch; two had laptops open, and a third leaned against the armrest, reading a massive book. Looking closer, Simon read *The Collected Short Stories and Poems of Edgar Allan Poe.*

On the floor between the couch and the wall were a tall, heavy boy and a girl who looked just as tall but much thinner. Her black tank top had no shoulders, but an array of straps, and transparent mesh sleeves covered her arms. Her companion wore a black turtleneck that looked a size too small; he kept pulling on his collar.

Cards were set up between them, and as Simon watched, the boy slid three cards forward, turned them sideways, and smirked. "I attack. Total of sixteen damage."

The girl looked at the lone card she had forward, glanced at the cards in her hand, then turned some of the cards closer to her sideways. "Let's see . . . I use Murder . . ." she noted coolly, setting down a card, then tossing it aside. She picked up one of her cards and tapped it to one of his. "This'll defend, so they both die . . ."

She tossed her card aside as well, then observed with a smug smile, "So . . . five damage?"

The boy swore.

A few more dark-clothed students sat in high chairs at the floor-to-ceiling windows, reading or conversing quietly, their various pieces of silver jewelry glimmering in the artificial light. But most of the attention was on the center of the lounge. At a wide ottoman, Miguel Vargos sat facing one of his friends, his tan face thoughtful, index and middle fingers resting against his temple while his ring and pinky fingers lay across his lips and his thumb followed the curve of his jaw. He and his opponent studied a board resting on the ottoman, which had several black and white marbles laid out in rows.

Two girls flanked Miguel. Heidi sat on the arm of his chair, watching the board anxiously. She had thrown back her hood, and her chin-length strawberry blond hair framed her face. Only the tips of her fingers extended past her sleeves, and she picked at one sleeve with the other hand, seeming unaware of the movement. The other girl, who looked closer to Miguel's age, stood behind him. Her arms were crossed over her chest, and she had leather gloves stretching up to her elbows with half a dozen buckles and snaps on each. One hand reached up to her throat, rotating the pentagram that hung from her choker necklace. She had the same artificial pale coloring as Heidi and several of her other colleagues, but her eye shadow extended from the corners of her eyes, giving her a look Simon found vaguely Egyptian. She glanced up at Simon and Anita, frowned distrustfully, then nudged Miguel.

Miguel looked up too, but he smiled when he saw his guests. Looking back down at the board, he moved a black marble. His opponent moved a white one, then took a black one off the board and chuckled. Miguel chuckled too, and began moving another of his black marbles, jumping it around the board. Every time, he took a white marble or two off, until he finally stopped, leaving a single white marble against his seven black ones.

"Damn," his partner said, taking the last white marble off the board and putting it in a bag. "I concede."

Miguel laughed good-naturedly. "One of these days, Frank."

"Yeah, that's what you said when you taught me to play three semesters ago," Frank complained. Then he looked behind him, saw Simon and Anita, and stepped away from the ottoman.

Miguel got to his feet. His T-shirt hugged his slight frame, but apart from a silver ankh on his black cord necklace and a leather bracelet around his wrist, he wore no jewelry. "Simon. Anita. I'm delighted you had the time to stop by. Please, have a seat."

Anita took the chair Frank had just vacated. Simon would rather have stood, but with so much light around, he feared someone might notice he wasn't casting a shadow, so he dragged over a chair and sat at Anita's side. He felt the eyes of Miguel's whole group on him; the girl on the couch put a raven-shaped bookmark in her Poe, and the two card players leaned around the orange sofa to see better. Simon grimaced, then glanced up at the girl still standing at Miguel's shoulder. She looked back at him with a slight curl to her lip, and Simon fixed his eyes on her harder. They grappled for a moment, then the girl swallowed and lowered her gaze to the ottoman.

As Simon took his seat, Miguel smiled at Heidi, still on the arm of his chair. "That can't be comfortable. Don't you want a chair?"

"You want me to move?" Heidi asked immediately, getting to her feet, but Miguel sighed.

"Of course not, but I don't want you to be uncomfortable. Tony, let her have your chair, huh?"

Heidi's heartbeat accelerated, and she put her hand on the back of Miguel's chair. "Really, it's okay—"

"No worries, Heidi," Tony said. He got up, dragged his chair over, and mock punched her on the arm with a broad grin.

She hesitated, but smiled weakly back. Miguel patted the chair with a patient smile, and Heidi sat beside him as Tony moved to stand behind her. Miguel nodded encouragingly, then turned back to Simon and Anita.

"What do you—" Simon started, not giving Miguel a chance to speak, but Anita reached over to rest a hand on his sleeve. He felt her pulse through the leather, but annoyance with Miguel did a good job distracting him.

"Thank you," she put in. "For yesterday, I mean."

Simon clamped his jaw shut behind his sealed lips; the last thing he wanted was Miguel Vargos thinking about yesterday. His fears were piqued when Miguel glanced at him with a knowing smile before looking back at Anita.

"Hey, happy to help. A lot of us know what it's like to have people ignore us just because we don't fit their mold. I wasn't going to let that happen to Simon."

He looked at Simon. "I'm glad to see you looking better," he noted mildly. "You looked pretty beat up yesterday."

Simon was tempted to scowl and say nothing, but he was aware of Anita's hand still on his forearm, so he recited, "It looked worse than it was."

"Clearly."

Miguel held Simon's gaze a moment longer, then looked back to Anita. "I'm sorry I haven't had a chance to talk to you before," he said, sounding sincere. "Semester's been busier than I'm used to."

Anita tilted her head to one side. "Why would you have?"

Miguel leaned back and smiled. "Well, you always seemed to need a friend." Anita shuffled, looking a bit uncomfortable, and Miguel continued smoothly, "Which is all the more surprising, given how cool you've turned out to be. And I like to think, for all our eccentricities, we have in common the desire to be friends to people who don't have many."

Seeming unconscious of the motion, he laid his hand on the arm of Heidi's chair.

"Well, you can never have too many friends," Anita hedged, "but it's not like I don't have any."

Miguel's eyes widened. "Oh, I didn't mean that at all."

"Really?" Simon asked pointedly. He remembered Miguel approaching him for that very reason some time in the spring semester past.

Miguel looked over at him and nodded. "Really. Obviously I don't know all of either of your friends, but I do know my friends, and we're a good bunch." He looked around the little group with an affectionate smile, then back to Simon. "Open minds. Open expression. We're not going to judge you for how you dress, or any superficial crap that every moron here will think is a reflection of who you really are."

"None of us are ever going to make vampire jokes about you," he added to Simon.

Simon managed not to twitch. "Fancy that."

Miguel turned his eyes back to Anita and smirked. "For the record, though, Heidi and I liked your purple coat."

Anita smiled. "Thanks."

Miguel glanced at Heidi, who looked nervous, but blurted out, "Did you make it yourself, or buy it somewhere?"

"I made it," Anita said, a bit of pride in her voice.

Heidi smiled. "That's really cool."

"Maybe I could make you one," she offered, and Heidi beamed. Simon was surprised at the strength in the expression.

Miguel looked at Heidi thoughtfully, and Simon thought he saw a hint of a smile on the other man's lips, too.

"It'll probably be easier to find black than purple," Anita went on. Then she flushed. "I'm sorry, I didn't mean that it would have to be black. I just—"

Miguel laughed at the same time Heidi said hurriedly, "No, black's fine."

Miguel smirked. "I know, we do have a dark look to us. But who we are isn't the clothes or the makeup or the jewelry. Those are just sidenotes—very stylish sidenotes—but an outward expression of the real point."

"Which is?" Simon asked.

"That you can be who you really are with us, and we won't judge you. I'm serious," he added, for Simon had smirked at that. "You look around at us, and we're a diverse bunch. We don't have much in common, except that we're not going to take 'because God says so' or 'because I said so' as the final statement on anything. We think for ourselves. We do what we want. We look out for each other."

Miguel narrowed his eyes, studying Simon for a moment. "I'm going to go out on a limb and guess you're not really the religious type?"

Simon had no response, but Miguel didn't seem to need one. Nodding, he looked at Anita. "And you?"

Anita opened her mouth, but said nothing, a conflicted expression on her face.

Miguel nodded again, his expression softening. "You look around us, you'll see atheists, agnostics, Christians, Jews, Buddhists, pagans, Wiccans. We talk about our beliefs—quite a lot, actually—but not with judgment, and that's something you won't find much anyplace else."

Simon sighed. "Is that why you summoned us, Miguel? To give the 'we're all brothers in the same darkness' recruitment speech?"

The girl behind Miguel narrowed her eyes, but Miguel laughed. "We all have our darknesses, Simon. I know I do. I think you do too."

If you only knew. But really, Simon was afraid that if Miguel did know, he might become more interested.

Miguel turned his eyes on Anita. "And you. I think you have a lot of strength, maybe more than you think. But a lot of sadness, too."

Anita flinched, her heartbeat stuttering, and Simon bared his teeth, leaning forward. "I've just about had enough of you."

Miguel recoiled, his composed expression flickering. A few of his friends by the windows left their chairs and clustered behind him. Anita pulled her own expression together and squeezed Simon's arm again. "No, it's okay," she said, a bit thickly. Then she took a deep breath and said, "You sounded a bit like my mom. She used to be a psychologist."

Recovering his smile, Miguel said, "Really? I'll take that as a compliment; psychology is my major."

"Yeah?"

"Yeah. I was considering theater at first. I've always had an interest in drama—"

"—but you decided not to waste your time studying something you've obviously mastered?" Simon put in.

Miguel rolled his eyes. "But I found I'm more interested in how the mind works," he corrected. From the lingering tightness around his eyes, Simon could tell that Miguel was warier than before, but still congenial. "'What a piece of work is a man, how noble in reason, how infinite in faculty.'"

"Shakespeare?" Anita guessed.

"*Hamlet,*" Frank offered. He gave Simon a look. "I did decide to stick with theater as a major."

Simon looked back coolly until Miguel spoke again.

"Anyway. You guys are always welcome to hang out with us," he said, leaning forward to rest his elbows on his knees, gesturing expressively with his hands. "I hope you will. Actually, if you're not busy on Christmas Eve, maybe you'll hang out with us then?"

The girl behind Miguel stirred, frowning down at him. No one else's reaction was as strong, but several others leaned forward with interest. Heidi looked from Miguel to Anita, and Tony rested his hands on the back of Heidi's chair.

"On Christmas Eve?" Anita asked, clearly surprised.

Miguel smirked. "Well, I've never been much of one for labels, but we do have kind of a 'goth' tradition. Started here before I got to UIC."

A few others were smiling too, although the girl behind Miguel was no longer the only one frowning. Tony said, "It's been cooler since you showed up, though."

Several people nodded appreciatively, and Miguel chuckled. "Anyway, we always have a Christmas Eve party in a graveyard somewhere."

"In a graveyard?" Anita said, her large eyes widening.

"You're judging," Miguel noted, studying her expression with a shake his head. "No, it's probably not what 'normal' people do on Christmas Eve, but that's kind of the point. It's fun. You should come out with us."

"They should?" the girl behind him said, eyes narrowed.

Miguel shifted to look up at her calmly. "Yes, Sarah, they should."

Sarah seemed about to argue, but just gritted her teeth and looked away. Miguel turned back to Anita and Simon. "So how about it? It'd be a good way of getting to know us."

"In your natural element?" Simon suggested, but Miguel just laughed.

"It sounds . . . interesting," Anita said gamely, "but my parents are hosting a Christmas Eve party, and then we're going to Midnight Mass. I kinda have to be there."

Miguel frowned, but it looked sympathetic. He glanced at Simon.

"I can not think of anything I would rather do less." As he said the cold words, Simon's mind went to Salem, but in that moment, having endured this conversation so far, Simon thought he might take a rematch with the other vampire instead.

Miguel sighed, but nodded. "Well, the offer's always open. Anita, I look forward to talking to you again. Simon . . ." He shook his head, looking aggrieved. "I hope you're willing to keep an open mind. But I'm glad you've finally let someone in."

Simon gritted his teeth and got to his feet. He was relieved that Anita did the same, though she worked up a smile for Miguel. "Thanks for the invitation, anyway. I'll see you guys around." She gave Heidi a smile, too. "I'll see if I still have that pattern for the coat."

Anita turned and walked back toward the exit. Heidi opened her mouth as if to call after her, but seemed to think better of it. Giving Miguel a parting glower, Simon followed after Anita.

Neither of them spoke until they were outside. Taking a breath of cold air, Simon asked, "You see what I mean now?"

Anita frowned thoughtfully. "Sort of. I think he meant well. It was just a little . . . off-putting, I guess is the best way to say it. I don't like feeling like I'm being analyzed."

"Nor do I," Simon grumbled, wishing gaze could burn a hole through the building to where Miguel still sat.

"And okay, the graveyard thing is a little weird. But he seemed nice enough. Heidi and Tony, too. Maybe they're an acquired taste."

"I'm not sure they're a taste I want to acquire," Simon replied. *In any sense.*

Anita rolled her eyes, but she was smiling as she pulled her hat on. "I won't make you come with me next time."

Even better. Miguel would be able to wheedle information out of Anita, and why would she think not to share little details that Miguel's clever mind could put together to solve the puzzle that was Simon? Simon was not sure which would be worse: suffering through Miguel's presence or wondering what Anita had let slip in his absence.

Anita pulled up the sleeve on her right wrist, and her eyes widened in surprise as she looked at her watch. "Wow, I didn't realize we were there so long." She gave Simon an apologetic look. "I'm sorry, I actually need to get going. My parents wanted me home early tonight. I think they're still a little edgy about yesterday."

Simon nodded. Her words had reminded him that he had plans to hunt down a very particular five-course dinner. "I understand."

"When do you want to get together again?"

Despite his lingering anger, Simon smiled slightly. He found that it pleased him she had said "when," treating it as a certainty. "Tomorrow night?"

Anita shook her head. "Can't. I'm going shopping with Christine tomorrow. How about next week?"

"Certainly."

"All right, I'll call you. What's your number?"

Simon frowned and admitted without thinking, "I don't have one."

"You don't have a phone? At all?" Anita asked.

Managing to hold on to his expression, the vampire improvised. "I mean, I don't have one now. I use those disposable cell phones." To preempt the inevitable follow-up, he added, "Why don't you give me your number?"

"Sure." She dug out a piece of paper and a pen from her bag. Pressing the sheet to his chest, she scrawled her number on it and handed it to him. Simon tucked the sheet in his pocket.

"I'll call you next week."

"Okay." Anita hesitated, leaning forward as if she wasn't sure what to do. Her heart quickened. She half-raised a hand, then withdrew it as she took a step back, looking awkward. "I, er . . . I'll talk to you next week, then."

"All right," Simon said, confused. Before he could make sense of her reaction, she had turned and walked away.

MIGUEL WATCHED them go, frowning in disappointment. As soon as they were out the door, though, Sarah started in on him.

"You invited them for Christmas Eve, Miguel? Both of them?"

"Yes, I did," he replied without looking.

Sarah stalked around him to take Anita's seat. "You only talked to her to get to him."

Very slowly, Miguel turned his eyes away from the door to meet Sarah's angry gaze. He held it for a moment, then said gently, "That was a very callous thing to say."

Sarah opened her mouth, but then sighed, leaning back in the chair and cracking her knuckles. "Sorry," she muttered, "I didn't mean that."

"I know you didn't," Miguel said in the same soft voice, as if no one was present but them. "And I know you're not really a 'new people' person, but if we don't have open arms, then we lose everything we believe in and become just another clique. Besides," he added, nudging Heidi with his elbow, "it worked out the last time."

A few people laughed, and Tony reached down one hand to muss Heidi's hair. A hint of a blush surfaced through her pale foundation, but she was smiling too, and that made Miguel happy.

"Did any of you have a problem with me inviting Simon and Anita?" he asked the group at large.

"I thought Anita was nice," Heidi ventured so softly that Philip, on the floor with his Magic deck, asked what she had said.

"That Anita was nice," Tony repeated, and there was no missing his voice. "I think so too."

There were general noises of agreement, but Frank pointed out, "Well, Simon can be kind of a dick."

Still smarting about the drama comment . . .

"Yeah, but so can Sarah," Cole said, grinning, and several people laughed. Sarah gave him a venomous look.

"He's definitely not the friendliest just yet," Miguel agreed, "but there's something about him."

He looked at Sarah. "Even you have to admit that."

"I never said there wasn't," she said coolly. "He's got a really strong aura, really dark. Didn't you think?" she asked a pair of girls wearing pentacles that matched her own. They nodded emphatically.

"And that's all well and good, but . . . honestly, Miguel, the way he looked at you—I thought he was going to hurt you," she went on. Miguel heard a few of the others agreeing, more subdued now.

"He wasn't going to hurt me," Miguel reassured them. He chuckled in the face of Sarah's open disbelief. "I'm not saying he doesn't have a temper, but he wouldn't be the first of us, would he? Like I said, we all have our darknesses. Maybe if we come to understand his better, it won't trouble us so."

Sarah had no reply, and Frank sighed and nodded, as if unable to keep thinking badly of Simon. Miguel went on in a thoughtful tone, "But whatever it is about him, I definitely want to know. And what brings them together? So different from each other, and yet so good together . . ."

He shrugged, then pulled out his pocketwatch and consulted the bone-shaped hands set on the skull face. "I'm up for dinner. You guys?"

With the general agreement, Miguel got to his feet, pulling on his cloth coat and fastening the military-style buttons in the front. He passed by the couch and nudged Philip with the toe of one shoe. "Come on," he chided. "Keep your hand in order and play in the cafeteria."

Philip nodded and started to pack up the cards with Arianna. Miguel put his hands in his pockets and walked toward the door, falling in step with Sarah. On their way out, someone passing them called, "Don't cry emo kids, finals are over!"

Sarah's lip curled back from her teeth, and one hand drifted toward the coat pocket where Miguel suspected she kept her grimoire.

Stepping closer to her and refusing to look back at the hecklers, he took her hand in his. She stiffened at his touch.

"No hexing," he said under his breath. "Aren't you not supposed to do that? The Law of Return, what you deal out coming back to you?"

"Yeah, but trash like that—"

"For them?" Miguel asked. "You want to deal with the blowback for *them*?"

His tone made Sarah laugh despite herself. "Not worth it."

"Not at all."

She sighed, and Miguel rerouted the conversation, letting the rest of their friends get farther ahead. "Have you found us a site for the party? I really don't want to have to run from cops, like last Christmas."

"Okay, it is not my fault that Peter thought firecrackers were a good idea, the idiot."

Miguel suppressed a grin. "I didn't say it was, I'm just saying . . ."

"No cops."

"Yeah."

"I've got a couple places in mind. I'll need to read their auras."

"Want me to go with you?"

"Nah, I can handle it," Sarah said proudly. "By next week I'll know for sure. I want to find the best place we can."

"Definitely," Miguel agreed. "I want this Christmas Eve to be one to remember."

TWELVE

RUNNING HER fingertips through the black marble waterfall that poured down alongside the main staircase, Anita smiled up at the blue icicle and snowflake Christmas lights hanging from the mall's ceiling. As the escalator she was standing on reached the landing between staircases, she drew her hand out of the water, shivered, and wiped her fingers on her jeans. "Brrr."

"Well, what do you expect?" Marion asked, shaking her head and smiling. "It's twenty degrees out. It's not really the season for water."

Grinning back sheepishly, Anita said, "But we're inside. Water should be warm here."

Marion rolled her eyes, and Anita turned to study the enormous Lego statue in the center of the top level of the waterfall, a model of the water tower across the street that gave Water Tower Place its name that was almost as tall Anita herself. "That's so cool. I used to love Legos when I was little."

"Want me to get you some for Christmas?" Marion asked.

Anita laughed. "Nah. I'd want too many, you'd go broke while I was putting together the Chicago skyline."

They headed up the second staircase, waterfall fountains now on both sides, and Anita watched the blue lights shimmering in the watery black marble until Marion caught her by the elbow to tug her out of the way of someone walking down. Smiling apologetically at the man, Anita muttered under her breath, "Thanks."

"No problem," Marion said. "Do you think you and Christine will be a couple hours, at least?"

"Yeah, probably," Anita said. "I'm really sorry about this. Mom and Dad are going way overboard."

"Oh, no, that's not what I meant," Marion replied. "You take as long as you want; it's no inconvenience for me to wait. I just wanted to make sure I'd have enough time to pick up something for you."

Anita's expression brightened, then turned sly. "What are you gonna get me?"

"Yeah, nice try," Marion said dryly. "You can wait for Christmas like every year."

Companionable silence fell between them as they walked toward the center of the mall. More lights hung in the cavernous space that stretched five stories high, and the bright Christmas colors twinkled like multicolor rain. The metal guardrails on each level reflected the light down, and Anita sighed contentedly.

"So," Marion said in Spanish, leaning against the rail beside Anita, "are you getting Simon something for Christmas?"

Anita's eyes widened and her expression shifted to something close to panic. She responded in the same language, "I hadn't even thought about it. Do you think I should?"

Marion continued to look up at the lights, suppressing a smile. "That's the trouble of getting a new boyfriend right before Christmas."

"He's not—" After a pause, Anita added in a hopeless tone, "I don't know what we are, honestly. It's all so confusing."

Marion patted her shoulder, then gestured to a pair of padded leather chairs by the main escalators. She sat down with Anita and said, "Well, he obviously likes you. And you like him, right?"

"Yeah," Anita conceded. "It's just . . . I feel awkward, you know? Like I'm not really sure what to do now. I mean, I felt really close to him after what happened, but then he seemed so mad that I brought it up . . ."

"Men are like that," Marion said wisely. "They want to do all the protecting, but they don't like being protected."

"Well, he had my back as much as I had his."

"Yeah, but you saved him first. And maybe . . ." Frowning, switching back to English now that Anita had had her chance to practice, Marion replied, "You said his parents are dead, and you weren't in the best neighborhood. Maybe he's embarrassed about being from there, especially having seen where you live."

"Geez, I hadn't even considered that," Anita said, wincing. "I hope not. But it's not like that for you, is it? You've talked to me about where you grew up and stuff."

"Yeah, but I've known you for ten years," Marion pointed out. "It was harder for me at first, right after I moved in with you guys. You probably don't remember. But Simon's only known you for a week or so, and he's a guy, so he wants to impress you."

"Maybe," Anita said glumly. "D'you think I should've kissed him last night?"

Marion smirked. "Nah, don't be too eager. Make him wait. It'll be good for him."

She laughed, and Anita couldn't help but laugh too. As the sound was still fading from her lips, the elevator drew her attention. As one car rose to their level, Anita spotted Christine through the glass and rolled her eyes. "We really need to get her a runway and be done with it."

Christine sauntered off the elevator and started making her way around toward Anita, seeming unconscious of the eyes darting her way. Her white khakis clung to her legs, and her pale, knee-high leather boots gleamed with fresh polish. Her beige turtleneck sweater hugged her body where it was visible beneath her cream-colored leather coat. Her matching purse hung from her left shoulder. The pale-on-pale scheme might have made her beautiful face blend in had she not styled her lustrous raven hair around it, framing it in a halo of black.

Her expression was cool and detached as she walked toward Anita, and she didn't meet the gazes turning her way. One boy walking past her turned his head to stare and walked right into a pair of elderly ladies speaking in front of a store. Christine didn't turn at the sound of his embarrassed apology, but her ruby lips curved into a smirk.

Anita and Marion got to their feet as Christine approached, and her smile warmed. "Hope you haven't been waiting long."

"Hey. No, just a couple minutes," Anita assured her.

"How you doing, Christine?"

Christine turned her blue eyes to Marion. "Fine, thank you."

Marion nodded with a smile, then looked at Anita. "You'll call me when you're done?"

"Yeah."

"All right. You two have fun."

She headed off toward the escalator while Anita turned to Christine. "Do you have anything in particular you need to get?"

Christine shook her head, her hair shimmering around her face like the black marble waterfall Anita had admired earlier. "I should probably pick up something for my mom and dad," she admitted unenthusiastically. "You?"

"I still have to get my parents' gifts," Anita agreed. "Marion's too, but it might be hard to sneak it by her. I might have to order her something online."

They browsed around the department stores for a while, stopping to try things on. Christine laughed as Anita wobbled on four-inch stiletto heels; Anita laughed in turn as Christine tried on a flower-bedecked derby hat with a brim so wide it threw all of her face and upper chest into shadow. When Christine emerged from the changing room in a form-fitting scarlet dress, though, Anita grinned and applauded.

"It looks awesome on you, Chris," she admitted. "Very *Breakfast at Tiffany's.*"

Christine twirled on the spot, and they both giggled. As if summoned by the sound, a man with a store nametag on his pinstriped vest approached with a frown. He looked at them both—doing a double take at Christine—then cleared his throat. "Were you looking for something in particular, ladies?"

"No, just browsing," Anita replied with a winning smile.

The clerk didn't smile back. "We do have quite a few customers today," he hinted. "Were you planning on buying something, or . . . ?"

Christine arched a thin eyebrow. "What do you think, Anita?" She looked at Anita's feet. "Are you going to pick those up, or spare your ankles?"

Anita wiggled her toes at the end of the strappy leather shoes she was still wearing, then laughed. "They're a bit much for an impulse purchase. I'll stick with my boots."

Christine laughed back, but the clerk said, "Well, if you're not going to buy anything, maybe you should—"

"I'll take this dress," Christine cut him off coolly.

It was the clerk's turn to raise an eyebrow. "That dress is three hundred and fifty dollars, miss."

Christine met his eyes with no hesitation at all. "And?" she asked, giving him a patronizing look. "Don't you take credit? Or will I have to write you a check?"

The clerk frowned as it started to dawn on him that she was serious. "Er . . . no, we take all major credit cards, but—"

"Good," Christine cut in. "We'll meet you at the register when we're done. If we need anything else, we'll let you know."

The man looked taken aback, but Christine pivoted on the spot and swept back into the changing room. Anita thought of adding something gentler, but she didn't want the clerk to consider her easier prey, so she just smiled at him and took off her heels. She was still tying the laces on her snow boot when Christine emerged, carrying the dress on a hanger and looking very pleased with herself.

"Well, that worked," she observed.

"Yeah," Anita agreed. "Do you wanna hang it back up where it goes, or just leave it here?"

Christine frowned. "What do you mean?"

"Wasn't that just to get rid of him?" Anita asked, feeling as confused as Christine looked. "I mean, you're not really going to buy that just because he was a snob, are you?"

"And let him tell all his coworkers that we were just a pair of ditzes he chased out? Not a chance."

Anita followed Christine through the jewelry section, where Christine gave a display a cursory look before picking out a leather and gold wristwatch for her father. Anita wondered when her friend would call off the bluff, but sure enough, Christine bought the dress and had the store hold it for her until later. Anita bought a tie for her father—a little cartoon doctor smiled on it, and Anita wondered if she could ever convince her father to wear it to work— and then followed her out.

"That was an expensive point to make," Anita observed as they stepped out into the bustle of the mall again.

Christine shrugged. "I'm sure I'll find something to wear it to at least once. Besides, we're not kids. Nobody talks down to me like that, and you shouldn't let them either."

They next stopped in a jewelry store, where Christine browsed the necklace selection. Anita zeroed in on a pair of earrings in the shape of the Greek letter psi and set with small gemstones.

"Do you have these in aquamarine?" she asked the counter attendant. As the woman searched through her stock, Anita added to Christine, "It's my mom's birthstone. She'll love them."

"Psi for psychology?" Christine guessed, and Anita grinned and nodded.

As Christine continued to browse, Anita asked, "So, what are you doing for Christmas?"

Christine rolled her eyes. "Well, my parents have a party on Christmas Eve. I guess I'll probably see them sometime Christmas Day."

"You're not going to the party?" Anita asked carefully.

"No. It's really more of a business affair," she added with a deeper inflection in her voice; Anita recognized her way of mimicking her father's tone and meter.

Anita patted Christine's shoulder, but Christine shied away from the gesture. Wincing, Anita offered, "My parents are hosting this Christmas Eve. Some of my dad's work friends, but family friends too, and my Uncle Tim's coming in from Spain. You could spend the night with us, if you want?"

"Yeah, maybe I will." She did not sound particularly eager, but noticed Anita's concerned look and managed a smile as she squeezed Anita's hand. Then she glanced at a display and picked off a golden bracelet. "This is nice; I'm sure my mom'll like this."

Once Anita had bought the earrings for her mother and Christine the bracelet for hers, the girls wandered at a more leisurely pace through the mall. At Anita's request, they ducked into a photo booth. Christine tried out a few seductive looks on their first shots, but Anita grinned and came up with increasingly ridiculous expressions to match her. When Anita puffed out her cheeks and stuck the tip of her tongue out between her pursed lips while staring cross-eyed at the tip of her nose, Christine's jaw trembled before she burst out laughing. They both giggled in the final shot.

Anita leaned on a railing, looking at the shoppers below. "Remember when we came here in seventh grade?"

"I remember thinking a shopping trip was a weird stop on our city day," Christine said dryly. "'Here's your field trip—buy stuff!' You'd have thought my parents were the chaperones."

She snorted but didn't laugh, and Anita took her cue not to laugh either. Instead, she pointed down at the waterfall fountain she'd dipped her fingers in earlier. "I remember I tried to get you to jump in with me."

Christine laughed once before she could stop herself. "I thought Mrs. McCoy was going to blow fire."

"One more minute and I'd have sold you on it . . ." Looking at the next level down, Anita pointed. "Hey, want to get our picture taken with Santa?"

Christine rolled her eyes. "More pictures?"

Anita sighed. "You didn't have many people to tell you to take a break once in a while after you left, did you?"

Christine crossed her arms and looked up at the hanging lights. "I liked Hong Kong. It was challenging at first, but I learned a lot, and I'm sure it helped my application to Northwestern."

Anita bumped her with her shoulder. "C'mon, indulge me; it'll be a fun memory."

She towed Christine toward the line, where several children were waiting with their parents. Christine insisted on waiting until the line cleared out a bit.

"I'm not standing in line behind a five-year-old to get my picture taken with a creepy old guy in a suit," she said flatly.

When the line freed up, Anita and Christine approached the elf standing at the photo counter. He smiled at them both and ushered them in. The girls squeezed into the space on either side of Santa's wide throne.

"So, what do you want for Christmas?" he asked Anita gravely, but with a small smile visible beneath the white of his beard.

"Some new books would be nice," Anita mused.

"One of those tablets?"

"Nah, I'm old school," Anita admitted. "I like the feel of pages, you know? And the smell of a new book. You don't get that with tablets."

Santa smiled again, then looked at Christine. "And you?"

"Mmmm . . . a Ferrari would be nice," Christine said innocently.

Santa's eyes widened behind his glasses. "That's quite a present. Have you been a good girl this year?"

Christine glanced at Anita, and a mischievous light entered her eyes. Looking back at the old man, she scooted a bit closer, eyes narrowing above the curve of her lips. "Well, I have to admit," she purred, "I usually end up on the naughty list . . ."

Santa's cheeks flushed, but he was saved from having to answer when one of the elves called their attention for the pictures. While waiting for them to print, Christine giggled and said to Anita, "Okay, you were right, that was fun."

Anita rolled her eyes as she laughed back. "I can't believe you hit on Santa Claus."

They made their way down to the food court, where Anita asked, "Want to get some pizza?"

Christine's smiled was a bit forced. "Er . . . I think I'll just get a salad. You go right ahead, though."

She turned off toward the salad bar. Anita hesitated, then followed, picking up a salad and soup for herself. Christine watched her ladle on ranch dressing with raised eyebrows that Anita ignored. After Anita got a soda and Christine a bottled water, they sat down in plastic orange chairs to people watch while they ate.

"Not saying grace this time?" Christine asked dryly as Anita spooned herself some soup.

Anita hesitated, spoon in the air and dripping drops back into the bowl, then determinedly took the swallow of soup. Christine nodded, speared some salad on her fork, and said, "Why do you bother keeping up the act at home?"

Anita sighed, stirring designs into the tomato soup with her spoon. "It's not an act, so much . . . I don't not believe, I just . . . don't know what I believe."

"I started the same way," Christine said sympathetically. Pausing to eat a bite of salad, she washed it down with some water, then added, "Things didn't add up, and I got sick of hearing that I was going to Hell because I slept in on Sunday or gave Jack Dissler a blowjob."

"Oookay, more information than I needed," Anita replied.

Christine laughed, then added more seriously, "I like being me, not who some old guys or a storybook think I should be." When silence fell, Anita toying with her soup again, Christine prodded, "Have you talked to them about it?"

Anita took some more soup before she responded. "It's hard. My dad's useless for it, obviously, and my mom . . . I know she had a period where she was questioning in high school, but she wound up being more committed, so when we have talked about it, it always feels like she thinks it's a phase that'll just pass. And maybe she's right, and in ten years I'll see it her way, but right now it isn't really helpful, y'know?"

Christine made a vague noise of agreement around her salad. A pair of businessmen walked by, and she glanced up at them, smiling slyly and winking one long-lashed eye. Anita watched, then whispered, "You just like messing with people, don't you?"

Laughing, Christine tried for an innocent look, but Anita laughed harder at that. When they had composed themselves, Christine managed, "It's good, clean, harmless fun. Well . . . good and harmless, anyway."

In a casual tone, she asked, "So, have you seen Simon since Wednesday?"

"Wednesday? Oh, dinner. Wow, it's weird to think it was only three days ago. So much happened since then . . ."

"Really?" Christine asked with interest. "What happened?"

Anita hesitated. For some reason, she wasn't comfortable telling even Christine about following Simon, or the fight. He seemed so anxious to put it out of his mind, and everyone else's. "We got together Thursday and Friday. I met him on campus so we could hang out."

It was technically the truth, but it still gave Anita's stomach a twist. Christine's sharp eyes narrowed; she seemed to sense that something was being left out. Feeling guilty, Anita almost admitted the truth before Christine asked, "Did you hook up with him?"

"Um . . ." Anita was relieved that Christine had misinterpreted her discomfort, but wasn't sure this subject was any easier. "Well . . . I did kiss him."

"That's something," Christine allowed. "Was it any good?"

"Er . . . well, it was just for a couple seconds. He had to go. It was a spur-of-the-moment thing."

"Hmm." Christine sipped from her water bottle, and Anita was sure her friend saw the heat in her cheeks. As she set her bottle back down, Christine asked, "So are you two together now, or what?"

"I don't really know," Anita confessed. "He's kinda hard to read. I never know what he's thinking, and even when I do, I don't know why."

Christine smirked. "You're so cute sometimes."

"Well, you're the mistress of seduction," Anita quipped back with a small grin. "Why don't you tell me?"

"Go for it," Christine advised with a shrug. "He's kinda hot. If you don't do something soon, maybe some other girl will snatch him up."

She smiled, half-teasing, half-challenging. Anita's responding smile felt wooden, and for a moment her eyes tightened, but Christine didn't seem to notice as she picked at her salad. "Ugh. I'm not sure I can finish this."

Anita rolled her eyes and scraped the bottom of her soup bowl with the spoon. "All you got is salad and water," she complained. She poised the spoon like a catapult. "Eat your sissy salad, or we'll see how well red goes with beige."

"You wouldn't d—" Christine started, wide-eyed, but she stopped mid-word and glowered. "Yeah, you probably would. You're terrible," she complained, but she went back to her salad with only a few muttered grumbles.

They finished lunch while watching shoppers walk past, giggling particularly hard at a harassed-looking father as his three girls dragged him toward the escalator, all begging for cupcakes. When they had finished, Anita texted Marion, then led Christine up a floor.

"You know, cupcakes don't sound so bad," she ventured, pointing to the little bakery. "They have all kinds here. Cookies and cream, and peanut butter cup, and s'mores . . ."

Christine stared through the display case at cupcakes bigger than her fist. "Yeah. And then, to burn it off, we could just run to . . . Milwaukee?"

Anita laughed. "I'll split one with you?"

"Not a prayer. You have fun."

Anita bought a bottle of milk and a cupcake overflowing with chocolate chips, laughing at Christine's appalled look. Eating it with a plastic knife and fork, she grinned after a moment. "It's really good," she tempted. "You should try a bite."

Christine hesitated.

Anita took her friend by the hands, slipping the knife and fork into them. "Come on, Chris. You can cheat a little."

Sighing, Christine cut herself a sliver of cupcake. Anita almost chided her, but held back; anything was a victory. Taking her slice in one bite, Christine swallowed, eyes widening. Wordlessly, she took

Anita's bottle of milk and swallowed while Anita laughed. "Good, isn't it?"

"Very sweet," Christine replied in a small voice as she returned the bottle, and Anita chuckled again.

When she was done, Anita looked around for Marion, then asked, "So . . . how are things at Northwestern?"

Christine shrugged. "Okay, I guess. Not much different." She frowned. "I still don't understand why you left, though."

Anita sighed and leaned back in her chair, drumming her fingers on the arms. "It just . . . didn't feel right," she said. "I don't know what I want to do, and everyone there was so focused, like they had everything planned out. It was a whole school of you."

Christine feigned an offended look. "You say that like it's a bad thing."

Anita grinned. "You're better in individual doses."

Christine rolled her eyes, and they both chuckled. After a moment, Anita asked, "I haven't heard from anybody but you since I left. Do . . . do they ever ask about me?"

Christine paused just long enough before her answer that Anita knew it would be a lie. "Yeah, sometimes."

"Mmm," Anita responded, looking at the elevator and the hanging lights for a long moment. Then she rallied and asked, "Do you still want me to come to your Christmas concert Monday?"

"Of course. I'm playing second chair," she said proudly. "First chair's a senior, so I think I'll get it next year. Besides, I want *somebody* to be there."

There was an edge to her voice, and Anita almost asked about her parents before realizing the answer suggested itself. She was searching for something to say when she heard Marion's voice.

"You girls get everything you wanted?"

"Yeah, I think so," Anita said. She realized that she hadn't gotten anything for Simon, but thought it might have been better not to have to explain that one to Christine, especially when she herself wasn't sure where things were going.

Christine nodded, face smooth again. "I should be all set."

"Don't forget to pick up your dress," Anita reminded her dryly.

Christine snorted delicately. "Not a chance. So I'll see you Monday at seven?"

"I'll be there," Anita promised, then grinned. "Want me to bring some roses to throw for you, or will you have enough boys in the front row to do that?"

Christine rolled her eyes, but gave Anita a hug and a kiss on the cheek before she strode off toward the elevators. Anita's weren't the only eyes following her, but she thought they might have been the only ones with worry.

"I invited her to Christmas Eve," she mused aloud.

"Her parents aren't around again?" Marion asked, brow scrunching up along with her frown.

Anita shook her head as they started off toward the escalator. "I don't think Dad will mind, do you?"

"Not at all," Marion reassured her. Then she smiled a sneaky smile. "He might not even mind if you invited Simon . . ."

"Okay, no more Simon nagging today!" Anita said, although the idea was tempting. Then again, she wasn't sure about having Simon and Christine together again so soon . . .

She chided herself for the thought at once. Christine had been her friend since they were eight. More to the point, Christine was probably right. Anita needed to sort things out with Simon and figure out what exactly was going on between them. Everything would make more sense after that.

"ANY AVAILABLE unit in Sixteenth District, for a missing person."

Hans Richtein rubbed his eyes with the heels of his palms and forced himself to concentrate.

"Go ahead."

"Missing person, elderly white male, five foot six, gray hair, believed to have wandered out of a senior care center, possibly suffering Alzheimer's. We're still getting details . . ."

Hans stood with a groan and tried to work some feeling back into his legs, raising his knees to his barrel chest one at a time and wincing at the cracking of joints. His police scanner, trying to catch chatter from the entire city of Chicago at once, was a constant hum of words and reports, each blending into the next until it all jumbled together. Since buying the device two days before, he had conditioned himself to listen for the right words—"missing person," "homicide," "assault," "unresponsive subject." But nothing continued to turn into more nothing, and every hour increased his dread at the Master's inevitable punishment of his repeated failures.

The Master had warned him not to interfere in the battle with Flavius, that his "help" would just get in the way. And so he had remained far off, watching in awe as the vampires dueled in the misty morning. When the Master had failed—*No.* Hans slapped himself across the face with one meaty hand and donned a self-castigating frown. The Master was incapable of failure. When the Master had not conquered Flavius at the time he wished, the vampire king had commanded Hans not to try to stop Flavius's flight, either.

That blood was to be the Master's, of course. It was the entire reason they were here. But the Master's kind words—"You would be unable to vanquish him, even in daylight, and I could not replace you quickly enough"—had also reassured Hans that he was needed. Valued. The Master needed his help and wanted to keep him safe from harm.

And so, at the Master's command, he had taken to scouring the city for traces of Flavius. He'd examined potential hunting grounds marked by unexplained disappearances and suspicious corpses, searching for any sign at all that might give them a starting point to track their elusive quarry. America, Hans knew, was not Flavius's native soil. He could not go to ground and sleep for a century to elude them just anywhere—he must have spread repositories of his precious earth around the city.

The fruits of Hans's search littered the floor of the caretaker's cabin, which was lit by two camping lanterns. It might have once been warm and comfortable, if a somewhat cramped fit. The single bedroom and its attached bath led into the front parlor, where a crumbling chimney moaned and wailed as the cold wind without seeped through the cracks. Having disposed of the rental truck, Hans had stashed his doubled-up sleeping bags in the bedroom, and though the floorboards had rotted in the century since anyone had lived here, the winter's freeze had dried the floor enough that Hans could leave his work scattered across it without fear.

Yesterday had been all newspapers—hours in the Chicago Public Library printing off obituaries and police blotters for the past half a year, then hours more analyzing them, looking for patterns and trends of suspicious deaths and unsolved disappearances. Last night, the Master had dragged him down into the Chicago sewers, ghosting along over the floor while Hans tried to keep his boots out of the refuse, to look for cadavers with telltale injuries and stories for their summoned souls to share.

They found nothing, and the Master grew colder and angrier as the night hours dwindled toward dawn; he had stopped twice to feed, and Hans thought he saw a look in the Master's eyes, aimed his way, not unlike the way he looked at prey. When they emerged from the manhole as the eastern sky turned gray, the Master had spared only two hissed words for his servant before vanishing to his resting place: "Find him."

He had tried. He had tried so very hard. But the leads were few, and Hans dared not investigate without the Master's approval. He knew—and had seen through experience—that he was a pale, insignificant shadow compared to even the least of vampires. How much more so to this one, the object of the Master's vengeful fury all these years?

"Well?"

A shiver chased itself from his tailbone to his skull at the sound of that harsh, funereal voice, and Hans scrambled around to find the Master towering over him, long-nailed fingers already half-curled into claws at his sides. His cowl threw his face into shadow, but Hans felt the eyes on him, ready to reach into his mind and tear out the answers they sought if he did not find his voice.

"M-M-Master," Hans stammered, falling to his hands and knees, lowering his head. His voice was hoarse from disuse and dragged from weariness. "I have searched, Master. I have only a few leads."

"Speak."

Sitting up onto his heels, Hans riffled through the piles of paper, desperate not to keep the Master waiting. As he struggled to get everything in order, unnatural chill crept over him, making his hands shake and his torso tremble despite three layers of clothing. Finally, he spread out a few stacks.

"Here, Master, is a man gone missing from his job at a factory three months ago. His car was found in the parking lot, but no one has found any trace of his body."

One veiny hand rose, and the pieces of paper drifted up into the Master's grasp. He read for a long moment, then levitated a Chicago city map into his other hand. "This is the spot?"

Hans stood to look at the map, not wanting to rely on his memory. "Yes, Master."

"In other words," the Master replied coldly, every word whistling as if hissed past sharp teeth, "not two kilometers away from where we are right now?"

As Hans looked down at the map, comparing one spot to the other, a searing pain flared behind his eyes, as if someone had stuck needles through them. Collapsing back to the ground and pulling on handfuls of his hair, he whimpered, "Mercy, Master!"

"Do you really believe he would be so stupid as to continue hunting so close to me? Or perhaps you think he is my equal, and has no need to fear me?"

"No!" Hans screamed, aghast as much at the idea as at the splitting agony seemingly tearing apart his face from the inside. "No, Master, never!"

Without warning, the pain disappeared and the Master stalked away. "My greatest servants spent, hounded through Europe by those infernal hunters, and now this is the best you have assembled."

He thrust a clawed hand at the stacks of papers, and Hans heard the sneer in his voice. "What else?"

"Several r-r-reports of young people who went missing three days ago, Master. B-but I think they are the ones he killed here. Isn't this the girl you . . ." He trailed off as he raised the newspaper, the horrifying memory of that dead voice speaking through dead lips overpowering him for a moment.

The cowl turned toward the picture in the headline. "Perhaps," the vampire seethed. "What else?"

Struggling to pull himself together, the German said, "A murder at a nightclub a month ago. A woman was stabbed in the neck, but police found little blood."

The news clippings drifted up into the vampire's withered hand. As he perused each and dropped it to the floor, Hans read the headlines again. STABBING DEATH AT LOCAL NIGHTCLUB. NO LEADS IN BIZARRE NIGHTCLUB SLAYING.

As the vampire lord discarded a clipping labeled: NIGHTCLUB "MURDER" A SUICIDE?, he conceded, "A possibility. 'No evidence of assault was found on security footage,'" he quoted. "Nor would there be, if it was Flavius's work."

Profound relief rushed on Hans. He had served the Master faithfully in hunts for lesser immortals; to fail now, in this greatest pursuit, was unthinkable.

The vampire king dropped the last newspaper clipping—BLOOD, SWEAT, AND TEARS CLUB REOPENS AS POLICE INVESTIGATION CONTINUES—and paced away, lifting a hand into the black shadows beneath his cowl as if rubbing his chin. "Perhaps . . ." the dead voice mused, but there was a spark of intensity in it now. "Perhaps he seeks the comfort of past successes to soothe the wounds of failure. Where he has succeeded before, he might succeed again."

Abruptly, he turned and stalked back into the parlor. "Come."

Getting to his feet with a thrill of excitement, Hans followed into the winter evening, donning his heavy jacket as he went. Pulled along in the Master's wake, he heard the hissing voice say, "We must go among the mortals again. We shall make the usual preparations."

"Of course, my lord," Hans replied. Then he thought to ask, "What will we do if he isn't there?"

"I will know it if he tries to flee the city," the vampire replied confidently, "and you will continue to search for evidence of his movements. But mine is the patience of immortality, and his is the desperation of the hunted. Tonight or tomorrow or a month from now, he will return. And I will be waiting."

THIRTEEN

"**K**ILL THE Bing Crosby, Dad!" Anita shouted down the hall as she wrapped a garland around the staircase banister, rolling her eyes. Marion shadowed her from two steps below, winding a cord of lights around the garland. Christmas warblings of the 1940s pursued them up the stairs.

"You're all dressed up already?" Marion inquired, looking over Anita's black slacks, purple flats, and almost-but-not-quite-matching purple blouse. She grinned. "Aren't you supposed to make your date wait?"

"And leave him to suffer with the King of Christmas?" Anita replied. Marion pressed her lips together, keeping her chuckle sealed behind her smile.

As if on cue, the soft tinkling of wind chime tones filled the foyer, and Anita darted past Marion to answer the door. She had left the porch lights on this time, but Simon's eyes still gleamed. At first, Anita thought he was wearing the same red shirt as before, but then she noticed the banded collar, buttoned all the way up under his jaw. He wore a black suit, just a little loose on his lithe frame. She wondered if he hadn't had time to get it tailored, and hoped he hadn't picked it up for this.

"Hey! Wow, you look nice."

"Thank you," he said, stepping in past her. His steel eyes flicked up to Marion, still on the staircase and winding a strand of lights around the newel post at the landing. "Good evening."

"Hi Simon, how you doin'?"

"Well enough."

"You didn't have to get so dressed up," Anita said, cocking her head to one side.

Simon shrugged and glanced down the hall toward the music. "I thought too much was better than not enough."

Sighing, Anita wished she could tell him he was overreacting. Instead, she just patted his arm. "Thanks." As the phone rang down the hall, she smiled up at Simon. "So, I know we were talking about a movie, but how would you feel about dinner first?"

To her surprise, Simon's eyes narrowed, and he looked un-comfortable. Anita's face fell, and started, "It was just an idea. If you don't—"

"Phone, Anita," Nancy Rothard said, coming into the hall. She gave Simon a warm smile, seeming not to notice his discomfort. "Hello, Simon."

Turning toward her, he smoothed out his face and nodded. "Good evening, Mrs. Rothard."

"Nancy," she corrected him firmly, then held the phone out to Anita. "It's Christine."

TAKING THE phone, Anita stepped into the parlor, tapping the fingertips of her free hand against the arm of the sofa. "Hey, Chris, what's up?"

"You look very handsome, Simon," Nancy said.

Simon wondered whether he would be able to hear Christine's side of the conversation in perfect silence, but it was hardly a request he could make. Instead, he forced a wooden smile. "Thank you."

"Simon and I were just going out," Anita was saying. Her expression clouded as she listened. "Oh. Uh, I don't know . . ."

"Ah, Simon." Anita's father turned the corner from the great room at the other end of the hall, walking up behind his wife. In contrast to Nancy's blue jeans and reindeer sweater, he looked to still be in his work clothes, khaki slacks and a pale blue dress shirt with perpendicular lines of brown and darker blue making little squares. His glasses framed his deep-set eyes.

"Dr. Rothard."

"Anita tells me you're going out to a movie?"

"I think so . . ." Simon took the opportunity to glance at Anita. She had turned her back on the foyer, but her heartbeat accelerated.

"Well . . ." she said. There was a pause in which Simon could almost hear Christine's voice, and Anita sighed, though the sound was much too soft for the receiver to pick up. "Okay, hang on, I'll ask."

When she turned to find an audience, her bright brown eyes bulged for a second before she controlled herself. Covering the receiver on the phone with her thumb, she asked, "Simon, Christine wants to know if we all want to go out dancing instead."

"Where would this be?" Dr. Rothard asked, frowning now.

Anita relayed the question, then reported, "She says she knows a club down in the Near North Side that's twenty-five and under only."

Dr. Rothard pursed his lips, but Nancy looked thoughtful. "That sounds all right, Rick. And they'd be going as a group."

Dr. Rothard looked at Simon in a measuring sort of way—Simon wondered if the man was debating whether his presence was likely to make matters better or worse—then sighed. "Yes, you're probably right. You'll leave the name and address of this place?"

"Of course," Anita replied, but her eyes were back on Simon. Her heart was racing, and he frowned curiously despite himself.

"But it's just her idea," she added. "If you don't want to, I can tell her another night."

Christine made Simon uncomfortable, but anything was better than trying to get through another dinner without eating. It would be even more obvious with just the two of them. "No, let's go out with her."

The heat that had crept into Anita's cheeks drained out; Simon watched the capillaries in her skin contracting. Then she turned, cleared her throat, and said, "Sure, Chris, that sounds great!" Simon was startled by the sudden enthusiasm in her voice; it didn't match her still-galloping heart. "Yeah, we'll be ready when you get here. Okay. Bye."

She hung up, took a deep breath, then turned around with a smile. Simon looked at her curiously; something was lacking in the expression. "She said she'll be here in just a few minutes. I guess I'd better go change . . ."

"I'll stick with what I'm wearing," Simon offered, testing a smile and a bit of humor.

Anita smiled again, but then looked away and raced up the stairs, calling, "Be right back."

Simon frowned after her, reflective eyes narrowed, until Dr. Rothard spoke.

"I don't mean to impose, but since you're here, Simon, perhaps you'd help me carry something up from the basement?"

"What? Oh . . . sure." Simon could hear Anita's heartbeat even from there, and part of him wanted to go after her, but Dr. Rothard was already opening a door under the staircase and disappearing from sight. With one last, frustrated glance up toward the second floor, Simon followed.

The stairway down was carpeted, but the basement below had cheaper vinyl flooring, though Simon judged after two steps that there was still supporting wood under it. He caught a glimpse of a laundry room across from the stairs before Dr. Rothard called to him from down the hall. Simon took in the storage shelves at a glance, but his eyes lingered on an easel and spots of dried paint on the floor. "Anita's studio?"

"When she paints and the weather's inclement, yes." Dr. Rothard levered out a heavy-looking wooden chest from a shelf, the decoratively carved box ornamented with shiny silver at each corner.

Simon swallowed, approaching warily. Trying to sound conversational, he asked, "Is that real silver?"

"Hmph?" Dr. Rothard grunted. "No, it's decoration. The real treasure is inside. Help me with this, will you?"

Simon took one end of the box and lifted, but as he walked backward out the door and toward the stairs, he frowned to himself. He had more than enough strength to lift Dr. Rothard himself over his head with one hand. But the chest . . . perhaps it was not so much heavy as weighty. The vampire felt as though it was pressing down on his hands, not by its weight or mass, but by some force it was generating.

He carried the box up the stairs and down the main hall, listening for Anita. He caught a hint of her heartbeat above him before he had to move on toward the great room, where Nancy and Marion waited. Simon and Dr. Rothard set the box down by the hearth. While the family clustered around it, Simon retreated a few steps, turning his head toward the door and concentrating. Anita's parents and Marion were so close that their heartbeats tapped insistently on his eardrums, but Anita's room was just above the kitchen ceiling . . .

"What do you think, Simon?"

The vampire turned back, annoyed, until his eyes focused on the gleam of gold on the hearth.

The lifeless eyes of the statue bored straight into his chest, and he felt like a giant hand had caught him around his heart and squeezed. Every part of him shuddered in a spasm radiating from his heart to the tips of his fingers and toes. He wanted nothing more than to smash his heel through the floor and escape into the basement, but the strength had drained from his limbs. He felt hollow, empty, and worthless, naked under a spotlight and unable to escape the gaze of those suffering eyes piercing him from beneath a crown of thorns.

Retreating toward the door, Simon raised his hands as if against attack. His mouth opened, fangs extended, and he let out a choking cough that was his best effort at strangling a frightened hiss.

Simon heard Anita's footsteps above him as she crossed the upstairs hallway. Too busy admiring the crucifix himself, Dr. Rothard had not turned to see Simon's reaction, but as Nancy glanced back, the vampire struggled to control himself.

"Simon?"

"Exquisite detail," he said from the door, half-leaning around it already. The distance helped, but even only looking from the corner of his eye, that golden gaze burned through him. As Nancy frowned and the others started to turn toward him as well, Simon spun toward the front door and called, "Ready to go?"

Some of his strength returned as he ducked around the wall and darted down the hallway, footfalls silent on the hardwood. Coming down the steps, Anita asked, "I'm sorry, did you say something?"

Simon opened his mouth to reply, but the sight of her took his breath. Snug blue pants hugged her legs, and her nearly backless black halter top accentuated her fit form. She had wrapped her long hair into a bun, and even though a few loose strands showed it had been a hasty job, she had a pair of black lacquered hair sticks with sapphires glistening on the ends stuck through.

"What?" Anita asked, though she managed a grin. "Sometimes I match."

Simon could only stare. The tight neck of her top curved around her collarbone and the base of her neck, highlighting her throat. Blood rushed through the arteries on either side, and every quick pump of her heart sounded like an invitation in the vampire's ears. Unable to help himself, he took a step toward her and laid one hand on her hip.

Her eyes widened at the intensity of his half-dazed expression, but she did not pull away. As his eyes gleamed, Anita laid a hand on Simon's chest, the other slipping under his jacket to curve around his side.

The doorbell rang.

Simon and Anita both jumped, and he stepped out of her reach to try to pull himself together. Blinking as if coming out of a trance, he watched Anita frown, then take a breath, fix a smile on her lips, and open the door. Still not recovered, Simon turned toward Christine and immediately wished he hadn't.

Anita's outfit hinted at her body in a way that made Simon squeeze his mouth closed to keep his fangs retracted; Christine's left so little to the vampire's imagination that it began to get away from him. Her black leather pants looked like they had been molded to her legs, and even though she wore a short black leather jacket, the pink choli top beneath cuddled her breasts together. The plunging neckline dipped halfway down her cleavage, and her gold choker necklace was woven into an intricate latticework with alternating pink and onyx stones. Her pink lipstick matched her top and her nails, visible on her creamy pale hands and the toes at the end of her three-inch heels. The extra inches put her nearly at Simon's height, and she smiled right at him.

"Hi again, Simon," she purred.

"Er . . ." The vampire struggled for words, trying to control his instincts. He knew he had never tasted anything as sweet as her blood would be just now. As both of theirs would be. The temptation to slap one into unconsciousness for dessert and drain the other as a main course was almost painful, and even though he had cut his nails short yet again, his fingers curved into claws.

Christine smirked, as if his inarticulate reply was enough for her. Anita frowned, and as Simon tried to find something to distract himself, he thought he caught an edge to her tone as she said, "Hi, Chris. We're ready to go."

"Great," she said, one long-nailed finger tucking a strand of her black hair behind her ear. She seemed almost unaware of the motion as her finger continued the sweep down, curving over her neck to the center of her choker before she drew it back. Simon imagined catching her neck with his own hand and drawing her flesh against his lips. His fangs would pierce right through that soft, silky skin, and if he was fast, she wouldn't have time to scream . . .

"Mind if I drive?" asked Christine.

"Nope." Anita's voice was bright, but brisk. "Let's get going."

Dr. Rothard tromped down the hall and said, "Well, you both look . . . nice."

He added nothing else, but his tone was almost disapproving, as if "nice" was the highest compliment he could bear to pay, and Simon grounded himself on that negativity.

"Thanks, Dad." Anita vanished into the closet, returning a moment later wearing a black leather jacket.

"Where is this place you're going?" the doctor asked.

"It's called Amici," Christine said, giving him a bright smile. She pulled a business card out of the inside pocket of her coat and extended it. "This is the info. I got it the last time I was there."

Dr. Rothard adjusted his glasses as he looked down at the card, and Christine looked from Anita to Simon and back, then gestured with her head toward the door.

"Well, have a good night, Doc," Christine said as she opened the door.

"Hmm? Oh . . . thank you." His jowls turned his frown almost into a scowl. "Not too late . . ."

"They'll be fine, Rick," Nancy soothed him, coming up from the other side. "Come on, we need your help with the tree."

As he turned, Nancy looked past him and winked. "Have fun, kids."

"Thanks, Mom," Anita called before Christine pulled the door closed.

Anita slid a bit on the icy walkway, and Simon offered her his arm. The cold air helped dissipate their body heat, and Simon took a deep breath of it to clear his head. Anita took the front passenger seat of Christine's red Infiniti Q60, and Simon slipped into the seat behind her. As Christine pulled out of the driveway, it began to snow, and she complained, "Looks like we're definitely having a white Christmas."

"That's good," Anita said. Simon envisioned the smile on her face.

"Is it?" Christine cranked up the heater, and it blew their scents back over their seats into Simon's face. Closing his eyes, he clamped his jaw shut and reminded himself that there was no way to stun or attack Christine without getting them into a car accident.

"Of course! It's not Christmas without snow!"

Christine made a noncommittal noise, then said, "I'm excited to check out this club we're going to."

Anita's voice echoed Simon's confusion. "I thought you told my dad that you've been there?"

"Amici? I have, but we're not actually going there," Christine replied with a disbelieving laugh. "The last time I was there, it was nothing but frat guys and desperate townies from the suburbs. No thanks."

"You mean we lied to them?"

"They'd have pulled the 'While you live under my roof . . .' card if we said we were going to a real club, and you know it," Christine said. Anita didn't reply, and Christine continued, "Besides, I really do want to check this new place out."

"I'm not twenty-one, Chris," Anita pointed out. "How are you planning to get in?"

"I haven't met the bouncer yet who I can't get past," Christine said confidently.

Anita fell silent, her heart stammering with what Simon assumed was nerves. To distract himself from that, he asked, "What is this place called?"

"Okay, it's not as emo or Winston Churchill as it sounds," she cautioned around a light laugh, "but I saw it on the news, and it looked pretty sweet. It's called Blood, Sweat, and Tears."

SIMON WAS living a nightmare from which he couldn't awaken, and he was almost certain he was going to kill one or both of them, and most of the bystanders, too.

In the wake of the unsolved, inexplicable murder (or even less comprehensible suicide) of a young woman at Blood, Sweat, and Tears, the club's management had responded swiftly and wholeheartedly by becoming gaudier. During the downtime while the police closed the club, the management replaced the dance floor with glass sensor plates. Stepping on one triggered dozens of LED lights embedded in the plate, and a shift of weight changed the color. The lights had just enough wattage to bathe the dancers in a rainbow of colors without being so bright as to distract. When the smoke machines produced their coils of fog, the light warped and twisted in the mist.

Of course, management had to at least pretend to address security. The artificial fog no longer reached head height, the space under the stairs had been filled in with black wall paneling, and the bouncers were stricter than Simon remembered. Even Christine's charm failed her, although a quiet word and a moment's gaze from Simon did the trick.

"What did you say to him?" Anita had asked as they slipped inside, while Christine stared in surprise.

Simon just smiled. "I have a way with people."

He hadn't smiled since.

Anita had started off at arm's length, her hands around his neck, his at her hips. They swayed with the music as Christine spun herself through a gaggle of admirers, pressing up against each in turn for a few seconds before moving on. Remembering what had happened the last time he saw a beautiful woman at the center of attention here, part of Simon ached for history to repeat itself.

Then Christine had made her way back to them after going off to drape her jacket over a chair at the bar. He caught the sharp scent of alcohol mixed in with her warm breath, and the flush of heat and exertion in her cheeks and neck was so tempting that Simon had to bite his lip to distract himself with the pain. As he swallowed his own blood, Christine shook her head.

"What is this, middle school?" she laughed over the thunder of bass. "We're at a club, guys, act like it!"

She took Simon's hand, and he was far beyond the ability to even think of resisting as she jerked him out of Anita's arms. Her back pressed up against his chest as she rolled her hips against his body, reaching over her shoulder to trace her nails on his cheekbone. Simon knew if he took her hand, there would be no stopping his instincts; he would press her wrist to his lips, his teeth would snap open the arteries in her arm, and he would drain her dry right there on the dance floor. So he pressed his palms to her sides, running them down to her hips, dragging his blunted nails along her flesh. Her heartbeat accelerated, and he heard the ragged intake of breath through her teeth. He leaned his lips toward her neck and breathed hot on her flesh, and she shivered.

Then Anita stepped back up, taking Simon by the shoulder and spinning him into her arms. Her jaw was hard with determination, and she slid her fingers up to the base of the vampire's skull, running them into his ponytail until the knot loosened. Her hand turned his face toward hers, away from Christine, and her eyes were wide as they met his. Straddling his leg, she pressed her body up against his. Simon saw every movement of her throat as she swallowed. "Got it, Chris, thanks."

Christine looked annoyed for a moment, then blinked, stepping back from Simon with a baffled look. Recovering after a second, she smiled seductively at a tall man with a crew cut wearing a Navy T-shirt who had been trying to catch her eye and crooned, "C'mere, sailor boy."

Then he could spare her no further attention. Anita's chest pressed against his, and her heartbeat sang through her flesh and into his as if he had a pulse too. One of his palms pressed against her bare back, and she shuddered but clung to him all the tighter. Every motion was enhanced with their bodies entwined; with his hands on her, Simon knew every movement she was going to make the instant she started to shift. He felt the flow of her blood in his fingertips, tasted her sweat on the air between them. The artificial mist reflected red and blue and green across her face, and he stared at her with desperation. He recognized the spellbound look in her eyes when they locked onto his—he could hypnotize it into exis-tence on command—but he had not turned his powers on her . . .

He did not notice the song change, but when Anita leaned in closer and all Simon could smell was her sweet breath, Christine re-appeared on his other side. Her blue eyes were almost electric with intensity, and when she caught the lapel of his jacket and tugged, he released Anita so he didn't drag her off balance and lurched into Christine's embrace. She pulled him into her arms and locked one hand behind his neck. The other caught his arm and slid his pale hand down her thigh. The leather was so thin there that her pulse throbbed from beneath the toned muscle as he revolved them both in a circle, Christine pivoting on the ball of her foot.

Still unaware of the music, the vampire only caught on to the next song change when Christine pulled her leg free, took Simon's hand, and spun herself out before whirling back into his arms. The sharp Latin rhythm, somewhere between salsa and tango, had only cleared a few dancers from the floor, but the pack gave Simon and Christine a wide berth. She spun around him expertly, Simon moving to complement her. But as she rolled out into another turn, Anita caught Simon's free hand and pulled him away.

She was not as talented as Christine, her footwork less nimble, but her expression was so alive that it startled Simon. She moved in perfect time with him, as if they were two halves of one whole. A sweat-slicked strand of hair had strayed into her face, but she made no move to bat it aside.

Christine stole him back on a turn, swinging one leg up to rest her heel on his shoulder. Someone gasped in the crowd, and several onlookers whistled. He dipped her and she reclined with it, arching her back so her breasts heaved with the breath that was coming in pants now. As he drew her back up, Simon gazed into her eyes, and he had never seen such a demanding look in a human.

Anita slipped back in then, evidently determined to keep up; they had Simon so unbalanced that he reeled from each to the other as they took him. Seizing Simon's hands, Anita pressed them to her sides and leaned sideways as if falling. Seeing her intention at the last second, Simon spun her in a cartwheel before depositing her on the floor. More gasps from the crowd brushed meaninglessly at his ears. A third young woman stepped forward and look at him hopefully, but Christine appeared in his peripheral view wearing an expression so ferocious that the woman stepped back again.

Anita pressed her back to Simon's chest, slid down into a crouch until she was almost sitting on the floor, then wormed her way back up the vampire's body. She reached without looking and took his hands again, setting one on her stomach and pulling the other to her neck. Her racing pulse sizzled through his fingertips, up his arm, and into his mind until everything faded but the haze of her body heat and the lust for her blood.

Unable to help himself, he pressed his lips to her neck, and she shuddered. He opened his mouth as the fog shifted the light away from his face, fangs descending.

With a sharp snare drum cascade, the song came to an abrupt end and the floor lights went out. The crowd cheered as the mist caressed their forms. Panting, Anita rocked back, and the back of her head smacked Simon in the side of his jaw. They both lurched away from the collision, Anita clapping a hand to her head, and in that moment, she looked so vulnerable that Simon reached for her neck.

Stop! he commanded himself.

Why? the rest of him demanded.

He couldn't put the thought into words, could find no articulation for the protective instinct so powerful it rivaled the thirst. But it was enough that he drew back his hand and pressed it to his mouth as the lights came on, willing his fangs to retract.

"Sorry! You okay?" she asked, rubbing her head.

Not trusting himself to words, the vampire only nodded.

Anita swayed on the spot. Her feet inched backward, but her upper body inclined like she wanted to fall into Simon's arms. Then Christine was there, face flushed.

"Let's go get a drink," she said in a husky voice, putting a hand on Anita's arm.

"Yeah . . ." Anita said, looking stupefied. "Yeah . . ."

Neither of them invited Simon to join them, though each looked back in turn. The vampire was grateful as he slunk into the shadows off the dance floor and squeezed his hands into fists. He glanced around to ensure no one was looking at him, then snapped one fist into the wall. His hand went straight through the acoustic fabric and cracked the concrete beneath. His breathing was ragged as the air whistled in and out past his fangs, stubbornly still extended.

Across the club, he saw Anita and Christine at the bar. Christine was batting her eyelashes at the bartender and licking her lips. Simon more imagined than really heard the bartender's heartbeat accelerate, and when he produced drinks for the girls, Simon noticed that no money changed hands. The current song was heavy metal—Simon saw heads bobbing arrhythmically like a churning sea—and even his hearing could not catch the girls' words through the din. Darting through the shadows at the edge of the club, he got close enough to pick out their voices with concentration.

"All right, I'm getting sick of watching this," Christine was saying. Her heartbeat was still faster than normal. "If you're not going for him, you've lost your mind."

"Hey, this club thing was your idea!" Anita returned with more fire than Simon would have expected. "I just wanted to do dinner and a movie."

"It was a good idea!" Christine retorted. "And you can't always take the 'twenty dates before I kiss his cheek' approach. When the opportunity is there, you have to grab it!"

"Look, it's my problem," Anita hissed back. Though his natural defensive instincts protested, Simon squeezed his eyes shut and stopped breathing so he could focus on listening. "And I have kissed him—"

"And you still don't know if you're going out? What the hell are you waiting for?"

"Why do you even care?"

"Because you always do this, Anita! You sit and you don't decide and you don't want to push or get let down and you wind up missing out because you're too afraid to just go for something!"

There was a moment of silence, then Christine demanded, "Is he yours or isn't he?"

"I don't know!"

"We're not eight anymore, Anita. If you don't do something, some other girl will."

Focused as he was, Simon heard the faint sound of a sizeable gulp, then the sharper sound of a glass being slammed onto the bar top.

"Where are you going?" Anita asked in a voice so quiet Simon had to strain to hear it, and so dark it almost didn't sound like her.

"I came here to have fun," Christine retorted. Then Simon heard her heartbeat approaching, and he opened his eyes in time to see Christine step to the edge of the dance floor. She looked around until a flash of a green spotlight illuminated Simon. Striding toward him, her blue eyes blazing, she caught him by his cold hand and didn't even wince. She grabbed his collar with her other hand and pulled him forward. "Come dance with me."

Her floral scent overpowered the traces of whiskey on her breath and erased every other thought from his mind, and she met his eyes without even a trace of hesitation. He offered no resistance as she dragged him onto the dance floor, pushing her way through other dancers. As the heavy metal died and switched awkwardly into hip hop, Christine whirled and clapped her hand to his cheek so hard it was almost a slap; her nails dug into his flesh.

"Come on," she urged, her body all but on top of his. The vampire's hands moved automatically, one encircling her waist, the other catching her by the back of her neck so roughly she gasped aloud. But the pain didn't dissuade her, and Christine's raven hair felt like feathers as she brushed her face against his.

Simon caught sight of Anita at the edge of the dance floor, staring at the pair of them with an expression somewhere between hurt and disbelief. Christine's scent was all around him, the taste of it on the tip of his tongue, and her pulse thrilled through his hands. The temptation to pull her neck to his lips burned, but the look in Anita's eyes broke Christine's power over him. Placing his hands on Christine's hips, he tried to lever her away without hurting her.

"Don't do that," she panted, her eyes wild and full of need. He pushed harder, but she grabbed his ponytail and pulled her mouth up to his.

Her breath was sweet, her lips fuller than Anita's, and her heartbeat pounded up her arteries and down through the vessels so hard he felt it in her kiss. Her tongue reached for his, brushing his lips and the points of his fangs, and he tasted the alcohol on her breath. The nails of her other hand clawed his cheek.

Opening his eyes, Simon saw Anita crossing the floor toward them, and he pushed Christine back with more force. She staggered away from him as he broke her grip, and had only a second to stare at him desperately before Anita stepped between them. She stared at Christine for a long second, face registering fury and betrayal, then slapped her so hard that Christine lurched a step sideways.

Christine's pale skin was on fire in the shape of Anita's hand. She goggled at Anita, looking angry and hurt and thunderstruck all at once. The people nearest stepped back, some looking eager for the show, others like they just wanted to get out of range.

Anita's voice was ferocious as she said, "He is mine."

Her heartbeat stuttered and Simon watched the color flood her cheeks. She turned to him, and the fire in her eyes withered as she took in his wide-eyed expression. Her jaw trembled, and so did her voice as she asked, "Y-you are, aren't you?"

The vampire looked between them. Anger was winning out on Christine face, but she turned demanding eyes on him too. Anita looked at Christine, and her face fell.

Bloodlust took second place as Simon's own fury at last erupted. He stepped between them, faced Christine, and bared his teeth. He said coldly, loud enough for Anita to hear, "Step off."

Blank shock covered Christine's face for a second before she recoiled from his ferocious expression. In the next second, a hand grabbed Simon by the shoulder of his suit coat. "All right pal, let's go."

He turned to find another bouncer holding Anita by the elbow. She pulled against his grip, and Simon snarled, "Let her go."

The bouncer holding his shoulder tried to jerk him sideways, but Simon refused to budge. As the one holding Anita looked back, Simon glared at him. He poured power into his gaze, and the man let go of Anita like she was electrified.

Reaching up to squeeze the bouncer's wrist in his hand—a wrist thicker than his own forearm—Simon heard the man's strangled sound of pain through his gritted teeth. For a split second, the vampire was tempted to crush down, to squeeze the bones in the wrist together until they crumbled to dust and the muscle was reduced to paste under the flesh . . .

Then Anita turned to look at him, and Simon released the bouncer. The big man lurched back, gasping and holding his wrist as Simon stepped to Anita's side. "Let's go."

Her expression had returned to anger, and she nodded without looking back. "Yeah."

The crowd parted for them as they stormed toward the door, side by side. Simon reached for her hand at the same time she took his, ignoring the eyes he felt on their backs as they left into the wintry night.

⁓

"HOW VERY intriguing indeed."

The harsh rasp of the Master's voice pulled Hans Richtein's attention away from the commotion below. Watching through the tinted window of the small, second-floor VIP room, wearing a black suit and shirt with a white tie, he looked every inch the imposing bodyguard he was supposed to be. He had seen the blaze in the young man's eyes, had watched him overpower a beast of a man who might outweigh Hans himself.

"A vampire, Master?"

"Of course he was," the Master replied, leaning forward from his spot on the leather sofa. "I could see his lust for their blood as he mingled with them, let alone this careless use of power where even a mortal could observe."

Hans frowned. He remembered them dancing, but his eyes had been on the pale girl with the shiny dark hair, on the way her body had writhed to the beat, the way the light had glistened off the sweat on her breasts . . . "I did not notice, Master," he said, the cringe in his voice as much as his face. "Should I punish myself?"

"Later, perhaps," the vampire mused. Rising, he ghosted to the glass, watching as the dark-haired girl below waved off the bouncers' attentions and stalked toward the bar, face flushed and eyes red-rimmed. She sat down and snapped her fingers.

"Another vampire . . ."

"It was not Flavius who killed here, my lord?" Hans risked.

"Very likely not," the vampire concurred. "But this little creature will be of use to me."

Hans stared down at the bar in confusion. He doubted the Master was interested in the girl's body, and if the vampire wasn't Flavius . . . but . . . but perhaps the Master meant her as a reward? A reward for his faithful service? Those soft lips, supple breasts, the curve of her body against his muscular frame . . . it had been so long, but worth the wait for a reward like—

"No vampire could pass through this city without Flavius knowing it," the Master interrupted Hans's spiraling thoughts, bringing them back to reality. "No one of our kind escapes his notice but I, to whom he will forever be inferior. This vampire is known to Flavius, I am sure of it. Likely knows him in turn. To know one will be to know the other. I catch this whelp, and he will lead me to Flavius. The girl knows him, and is enemy to him now. She will know everything I need. So I shall . . . persuade her to share it with me."

The vampire extended his arms, a long, snarling rasp escaping his lips. The veins on his hands smoothed into his flesh, and his hooked, talonlike nails shrank to human proportions.

He straightened the lapels of his tuxedo and smiled. "Come. Let us begin the seduction."

THE LIGHT wind blew snowflakes into swirling patterns around Anita as she stared over the side of the bascule bridge into the Chicago River below. A rusted red truss separated the sidewalk from the street, although some passing cars honked and a few kicked up slush in their wake. Anita seemed not to notice. Her arms were crossed on the iron guardrail overlooking the river, and her chin rested on her wrists.

Simon gazed nervously down at the waves, choppy in the breeze. He was safe on the bridge—movable or not, it was still permanently in place, so he could cross on it—but the instinctive fear of drowning was powerful anyway.

They had walked in silence from the club—walked for block after block, holding hands. Simon let Anita lead, using the silence to ensure he had a handle on his instinct to kill. Once they reached the bridge, Anita had sighed, released his hand, and taken up her spot. Simon leaned on a truss, watching the color fade from her fingertips and toes as her ears turned red. Snow was starting to accumulate in her hair.

"Anita," Simon finally said, though he was at a loss for where to go from there.

She shuddered from head to toe, then straightened. Snow slipped off her bun and down her neck, and she shivered again.

"There's snow on me," she said, baffled.

Simon rolled his eyes and took off his jacket, draping it over her shoulders.

"Don't," she said, squirming. "You'll get cold."

"I'm fine," he said. He tucked the coat over Anita's, and his hands lingered at her collarbone. She looked up at him, then squeezed her eyes shut and wrapped her arms around his waist. Her pulse was blessedly faint through the layers of clothing

"I shouldn't have done that," she whispered.

Simon hugged her carefully, rubbing her shoulder with one thumb. "What's done is done."

"I shouldn't have slapped her. I don't know why I was so angry."

"She *was* out of line."

Anita pulled back to look up at him. "I'm sorry about that," she said with a wince. "If I'd known she was going to . . . we shouldn't have come out tonight."

"It's done. Forget about it."

Anita hesitated, her big brown eyes searching Simon's face for a moment before she spoke. "Thank you for sticking up for me, but . . . look, I'm glad you had my back, but if you were just backing me up, you can tell me. I won't be mad."

She tried for a smile. "I promise I won't slap you."

Simon stared at her, eyes narrowed. He still was not sure what bound him to her, but he sensed it was moving beyond reason. "I wasn't. If you want me," he said, and he heard the bewilderment in his voice, "I'm yours."

Anita's smile expanded into the real thing, and she hugged him again. When she pulled back, she looked at him speculatively. Her teeth worked her lower lip from the inside, but it still startled him when she hissed and pulled her hands back.

"Mmmph!" she muttered, pressing her fingertips to her mouth. Simon took in a breath so he could ask, and all emotion slipped off his face.

He smelled her blood.

As Anita shook her head with a little laugh and started to turn, Simon caught her wrist and pulled her back. Her eyes widened as she saw his fierce expression and his mouth descending toward hers. His cold lips caught hers, parting them, and his tongue brushed along the smooth flesh until the tip of his tongue caught the wound. The taste of her blood electrified him. He had but to extend his fangs, snap through her lips to leave her mouth a gaping, bloody mess, drink every drop until his body was flooded with the ambrosial taste and its promised power . . .

Anita's eyes closed and she wrapped her arms around his neck, cupping the back of his head with one hand. Her heart beat faster, pumping just that little bit more blood through the wound and into her mouth as her tongue found his.

She had licked the cut, Simon knew, because he tasted her blood on her tongue as he kissed her. For weeks, he had been dreaming of the taste, and it did not disappoint. It promised strength and vitality that feeding on the usual gangbangers and drifters never delivered.

Anita brushed his cheek softly. Warm, and caring, and trusting.

With a gasp, Simon pulled away, panting from the effort. His hands, holding Anita, shook, and when she felt them trembling, she looked up into his face, surprised. Then her soft brown eyes warmed, she smiled, and she drew him back down into another kiss.

He kissed her back, drawing her body against his. He forced himself not to seek out her blood again, concentrating on the feeling of her lips instead, almost as cold as his and chapped from the wind but still thrilling in a way that had nothing to do with thirst. The taste of blood was fading from her tongue, and Simon was glad for that. He breathed in Anita's vanilla scent and enjoyed her warmth pressed against him.

When she pulled away, taking a deep breath through her mouth, she smiled up at Simon, kissed his lips once more, and took his hand. "I should probably get home," she admitted. "Let's see if we can find a cab; an Uber'll take forever."

As Simon walked off with her, Salem's voice nagged him in memory. *Open yourself to human emotions and you're inviting their weaknesses. Bond with them, make yourself close to them, and you might as well walk into the dawn and save them the trouble of staking you.*

Salem was older, wiser, more experienced, and vastly more powerful. Simon thought over the words as Anita's eyes hunted for a taxi light amid the headlights. When she looked up at him, she squeezed his hand and smiled.

Go to hell, Salem. Simon smiled back and let go of Anita's hand to wrap his arm around her shoulders as they walked on through the snow.

"Y'KNOW, Y'KNOW . . . if you were with me, I'd never slap you," the guy at the bar slurred with a sloppy smile. He winked one eye, and that whole side of his face lurched. "Unless you were into that."

Christine gave him a withering look, her eyes blazing. "Go find some dumb blonde you can puke on after your fifteen seconds of sex, jackass."

She turned back to the bar, snapping her fingers. The bartender frowned at her, and she struggled to compose her emotions as the jerk next to her stammered at her. Ignoring him, she said as sweetly as she could manage, "I seem to be all out."

"I think you've had enough," the bartender said, and Christine saw no compromise in his face. He even took her empty glass back.

As the bartender turned away, Christine grumbled, resting her forearms on the bar and her chin on her arms. Her cheek still stung, but the blow hadn't hurt as much as the whole situation. Anita had waffled and hesitated and done nothing, and then when Christine expressed some interest, she swooped in to take over with that air of wounded dignity. And Simon! He had wanted her too; the way he touched her, the feeling of his breath on her neck . . . even the memory made her shiver with desire. He had played her cold and kicked her to the curb the second Anita realized what she hadn't bothered to care about until then.

"Trust me baaaaaaaby, I'm like . . . like eight inches."

Christine wondered if she could pull the bottle of whiskey in front of her out from the bar and break it over the guy's head before the bartender caught her.

Before she had decided whether to try, there was a scuffle next to her. She hoped the guy had fallen off his stool, maybe cracked his head on the dance floor. If he was still lying there, she could step on him as she left the bar . . .

"May I purchase a drink for you, my dear?"

The voice was so different, so instantly captivating, that Christine looked up.

Sitting in the spot so recently occupied by the drunk and his supposed eight inches was a man whose appearance was as different as his voice. He wore a white tuxedo that contrasted with his black shirt and tie and accented his tan skin. His bald head shone in the lights from the dance floor, but his features were strong and handsome even without hair. His cheekbones were sharp, his jaw broad and strong. When he smiled, his white teeth gleamed. His eyebrows were so thin and flat Christine thought they looked penciled-on, and he wore a pair of designer sunglasses that completely obscured his eyes.

His voice was soft, but with a hint of timbre to it, a subtle baritone that gave it some strength; it sent a shiver down her spine. His thin lips curved into a smile again, and Christine had the strangest thought that his words could slip through the air as softly or powerfully as he wanted. She had met her father's Middle Eastern business friends in Hong Kong, even gone with him to Dubai, but she had never encountered an accent quite like his.

She blinked. "Um . . . sorry, what?"

The man made a small exhalation through his nose and smiled, as if he was laughing as subtly as he could. "Or perhaps you'd care to join me in my private room?" He gestured negligently toward a winding staircase that led to the second-floor gallery. "It gets so noisy down here. One can hardly hear oneself think."

Christine found her eyelids getting heavier, as if she were being hypnotized. But two could play at that game. Blinking her eyes back open, she gave her most alluring smile. "Do you think I'm the type to go off into dark corners with strange men?"

Rounds of vodka and whiskey tainted her voice, though she wasn't so far gone as not to recognize it. But her companion only smiled and got to his feet.

"If you'd rather try your fortunes down here, be my guest." His thin eyebrows rose over his sunglasses, and he turned away.

His voice beckoned her even as his body showed such a lack of interest. He turned, studying the club as if looking for someone else. Christine frowned, eyes narrowing. She wasn't getting brushed off twice in one night. Besides, something in that exotic voice made her think even Simon wouldn't compare to what she had found here.

Getting to her feet, swaying only slightly, Christine slid her arm through the man's elbow and ran her nails down the sleeve of his forearm, then across the back of his hand. As her fingertips brushed his skin, she was surprised by a chill colder than Simon's flesh.

Then the man turned his face to her and smiled, and Christine stopped worrying.

"I'll check out what you've got," Christine said breathily, missing the indifferent tone she was aiming for.

The man seemed to notice, and the corners of his mouth curled up. "Splendid." His sibilant, whispering voice dragged out each syllable. He laid his other hand over hers to tow her along. "Come."

They walked up the curving stairs and were nearly to the dark glass door of the VIP room when Christine felt someone behind them. She turned to find one of the most massive men she had ever seen towering over her, his suit doing nothing to disguise what she thought must be a bodybuilder's physique. His brown eyes met her blue ones, and Christine's widened. There was an intensity in the huge man's eyes that bordered on mania, and as he took in her body in a way she recognized, she clung a bit tighter to the arm of her escort. The giant man leered at her a moment longer, then stepped past them both to open the door.

"See that we're not disturbed by the riffraff," Christine's companion instructed.

"Yes, my lord."

He closed the glass door behind them, then took up a position facing away from her, hands clasped in front of him like a bodyguard. Christine frowned as she sat down on the plush leather couch.

"My lord?" she repeated.

Reaching for a bottle of champagne on the table before them, her host smiled to himself. He poured them each a tall flute. The tinted glass overlooking the dance floor muted the music; still audible, but a pleasant background that allowed for conversation rather than an overpowering racket.

Extending one glass to Christine, he waited until she took it, then reached out one long finger and laid it on her lips. "Can you keep a secret?"

Though his flesh was cold, Christine turned her head, eyes half-closing as she moved her face to brush that finger along her lips and onto her cheek. She had the strangest urge to extend her tongue, to taste that cold skin. Swallowing hard, she managed, "I can keep a secret."

He smiled, raising his glass in a toast. "Among my own people, I am king."

"King?" Christine repeated. She had been to half a dozen of the countries that still had monarchies, even met a prince or two, and she had heard of royals visiting other countries. But this particular nightclub? And with only the one bodyguard? She thought about the bodyguard again as she took a sip of champagne. The intensity, the almost worshipful tone . . . it was possible.

Christine smiled smugly to herself and tossed back the rest of her glass. "A pleasure, Your Majesty."

"Oh, my dear," the king said with a smile that made Christine lean toward him even as she shivered, "I'm sure the pleasure will be all mine."

"Maybe it will," she whispered, batting her eyelashes, but it was her breathing speeding up. What was it about him? He was still leaning back on his side of the couch, gently swishing his glass of champagne with a casual smile. She had resisted guys who had put on a lot more charm than this. "What makes me so special?"

One long-fingered hand gestured toward the window. "Such a pity to see a perfect blossom trampled underfoot. It broke my heart, my pet."

Christine's annoyance returned, hotter than it had been before. "That was such a bitch thing to do," she complained, aware that her voice sounded whiny but past caring. "She didn't even want him until she saw that I did."

Was that right? Hadn't Anita said—

"She's jealous of you," the king said silkily, and Christine found herself nodding. "And who wouldn't be?"

"And Simon," Christine ranted on. "If he really wanted her, he should've just told me. I'd have backed off. But instead, he just . . ."

"Led you on. Deceived you. Used you for his own purposes and cast you aside the moment something more useful came along."

The words cut to Christine's core, and she set her champagne glass down with shaking fingers. "Yeah." Her voice was very small. "Yeah."

"I understand, lovely one," the king reassured her. His voice was dry, but comforting. Christine felt stronger when she heard it, and she wanted to hear it again.

"I'm sorry," she said, clearing her throat and fanning her face as she felt a faint sting in her eyes. She blinked a few times, then fluttered her eyelashes at her understanding companion. "You probably don't want to talk about this."

"On the contrary," the king assured her, smiling. "I should like nothing more than to hear every word you have to say on the subject. Perhaps somewhere more private?"

He leaned in then, passing his glass from hand to hand and setting it on the table. Christine leaned back, then froze as those long, cold fingers traced her neck. Her breath came in quick pants, and a flash of heat spread over her skin as her legs trembled. The breath on the side of her neck made her whimper.

"I have a room in the city. Won't you join me there?"

"Yes!" Christine gasped, grabbing onto his collar, her eyes wide and frantic.

The king smiled and snapped his fingers, and the door opened. "Yes, Master?"

"The lady and I wish to retire for the evening. The whole evening," he added in a whisper in Christine's ear, and she wrapped a hand around his back as her whole body started to tremble. "Bring the car around."

"Immediately, my lord."

"Come, my vision of perfection," the king breathed.

She did.

"MAYBE IF we catch him—"

"Man, ain't shit we can do to him, and that's it."

Ryan grimaced at Tommy, who glared back over his broken leg, casted from thigh to toes. They were in the cluttered back room of Ryan's uncle's pawn shop. Tommy sat on a plastic case of car batteries with his broken leg propped up on a shorter cardboard box of Christmas ornaments. Ryan leaned against a metal shelf with his arms crossed and a hood pulled up over his ball cap. Steve, though he sat on a stool facing the open door to the front of the shop, wasn't really part of the conversation; instead, he was puffing on a joint and wandering from one song to another in an off-key tone, giggling occasionally.

"Every crew around here's gonna be movin' in on us after last week. What're we supposed to do? Nothing?"

"Hell no, we don't do nothing!" Tommy said. "I'm going up to my cousin's place in Kenosha for a while."

Ryan stared at him. "You're leaving Chi-city?"

"Man, I don't wanna die!"

"F'real," Steve commented absently.

"We're not gonna die," Ryan snapped. "There's three of us—"

"Last time there were five of us, and look how well that went!"

"Only because that bitch hit me with a board," Ryan grumbled. "If I ever see her again . . ."

"You'd better thank her." Tommy shifted on his box, grunting as his leg moved. "I saw that whole thing, man. If it weren't for her, Simon woulda popped your head right off with that chain."

Ryan winced, brushing his fingers over the still-raw skin of his neck. The bruising was starting to die down, but he kept flashing back to his vision fading as he gasped for air . . .

"And Carlos and Richie went to find him, didn't they?" Tommy pressed. "You seen them since?"

"No, but—"

"I don't think we're ever gonna see them again. Man, Lenny was my boy too, but we gotta put this thing to bed."

Ryan had no reply.

Spinning in slow circles on his tool, Steve glanced out the front window and stopped so suddenly that he fell off the stool and into a box of fishing tackle. Staggering to his feet, he stared out into the shop. "Man, ain't . . . ain't that him?"

"Who?" Ryan demanded.

"It is!" Steve shouted. Then he giggled and shambled out of view, muttering, "Mo'fucka be rollin' up in my block, all creepy and shit . . ."

Ryan and Tommy traded glances, then Ryan stepped into the shop; Steve was already shuffling toward the gated front door. And sure enough, out on the street was a dark-clothed man, his skin pale in the extreme, his hair as black as his long coat, though he looked like he had cut it.

Ryan stared at Tommy. "It's him. He's really right there."

Tommy stood on his good leg and looked nervously at the door past Ryan's shoulder. "Man, maybe we should leave it alone . . ."

"He's right there!" Ryan snapped, pulling the pistol from the front of his pants and press checking the chamber. "We're doing this, right now."

Steve struggled with the locked door, the bell on it jingling and dancing as Steve swore. Then the bell clanged as the door slammed open. Ryan led the way to the front of the shop, Tommy hobbling behind him, in time to hear Steve shout, "Yo, bitch, bring yo creepy ass on over here . . ."

Ryan saw Steve outside the door waving what looked like a five iron; a bag of golf clubs lay overturned on the other side of the counter. Then Steve stopped and let the hand holding the club drop to his side.

"Whoooooooooooa," they heard him say. "Yo, man, you ain't Simon . . ."

The next second, Steve was airborne, sailing back through the door and crashing into the counter so hard that the glass shattered and the steel framing bent. There was a hideous snap from the center of Steve's back, and when he slumped to the floor, his arms flailed like noodles. "What the fuck . . . man, my legs . . ."

Appalled, Ryan and Tommy spared a second to stare at the broken counter and their broken friend on the floor. By the time they looked up, their target was already inside. Crossing the room in the blink of an eye, he dug his toe under the club in Steve's hand, flipped it up, caught it in midair with one hand, and swung it back down so quickly the air whistled around it. The club connected with Steve's head; one eyeball went soaring across the room, and Steve stopped flailing.

Tommy screamed. The pale man hopped up onto the ruined display case and kicked him in the face. His head snapped backward with a shower of blood, and he made no sound as he collapsed to the floor.

Ryan backed up, but he was wedged into the corner of the counter and had nowhere to go. Simon's lookalike dropped the club and hopped down on the same side of the counter, one hand flashing out like a snake to catch Ryan by the throat. He panicked, kicking uselessly, all the memories of Simon strangling him flooding back until he gasped a weak moan through his closing throat. He leveled the pistol still in his hand and fired into the guy's gut.

The man winced, then rolled his emerald eyes. His free hand snatched Ryan's gun hand, pinning it to the wall with so much strength that Ryan couldn't even budge it. He squeezed, and Ryan whimpered as his wrist started to fracture. He dropped the gun and the pressure relaxed enough that the bone stopped breaking, then the man let go of Ryan's neck to brush open his coat—cloth, Ryan noticed now, not leather like Simon's—and examine the bullet hole.

"Dammit, I just replaced this shirt last week!" he complained. Glowering into Ryan's face so fiercely that Ryan cringed away as far as his trapped arm allowed, the guy said, "That's really irritating."

Sighing, the pale man held his open palm under the bullet wound, bleeding a little onto his stark white skin. Ryan watched in voiceless horror as the guy gritted his teeth, screwing up his face in concentration, and the bullet wormed its way out of the wound, dropping into his hand. The guy glared at him, then pressed the bullet against Ryan's abdomen. Ryan found his voice in a scream of pain and slapped with all his strength against that impossibly powerful hand. The guy ignored him and kept pushing the round—first through his hoodie, then his shirt and skin, until his thumb had dug an inch into Ryan's guts.

"See?" he chided, loud enough that Ryan heard him over his own wails of agony. "Not pleasant, is it?"

"Man, what do you want?" Ryan sobbed.

So quickly he wasn't sure how it happened, Ryan was on the ground. The stranger still held his wrist with one hand, and now had one combat boot pressed on his sternum. The guy raised one pale finger, the nail sharp like a claw and still dripping Ryan's blood, to his lips and sucked on it for a moment before shrugging. "Meh. I've had better."

Then he looked down at Ryan, his emerald eyes gleaming in the darkness, and Ryan's sobs died in his throat.

"You're going to tell me everything I want to know," the stranger snarled. "Every time you don't, I'm going to tear off one of your limbs. So you've really only got four chances to get this right, and experience tells me that people have trouble focusing after the first time. So I suggest you get it right on the first try."

"What do you wanna know?" Ryan squeaked.

"You know Simon."

"Man, everybody knows Simon!"

"Where is he?"

"I don't know where he is!"

The stranger pulled on his arm, and it popped as it sprang out of the shoulder joint. Ryan only managed a second of a piercing shriek before the foot on his chest slipped down to his solar plexus, stomped the breath out of his lungs, and dug the embedded bullet a little deeper. Wheezing as tears of pain streamed down his cheeks, Ryan tried to whisper, "P-please . . . p-please . . ."

"Simon?"

The pressure on his gut relaxed, and Ryan sucked in as deep a breath as he could. "Man . . . I don't know . . . where he is!" he gasped. "If I did . . . I'd have gone . . . after him! Don't nobody . . . wanna . . . talk about him! They're too . . . too afraid, man!"

"I'll bet they are," his tormentor sneered. "Take a guess."

"Last time I saw him was maybe ten blocks away!" Ryan wailed. His body wanted to writhe away from the pain in his arm, but the boot on his torso kept him pinned in place. He managed to sob the name of the street.

"Hmm," the stranger said, glancing out the door. "Getting warmer. Too late tonight, though. I guess I'll have to try tomorrow. This is inconvenient, you know?"

Twitching, Ryan looked past the guy to the other end of the counter. Tommy's feet stuck out from the back room, surrounded by shattered glass; they weren't moving at all.

"Please don't kill me," Ryan begged.

The guy looked back down and smirked. "Sorry," he said with a shrug, "but if I'm going to be catching up with Simon, I can't do it on an empty stomach, can I?"

CHRISTINE CAME back to consciousness slowly, tossing and turning in the grip of a nightmare to which she couldn't put a name. She remembered a hideous red light and suffocation and pain . . .

Then she awoke, blinking against the morning light streaming through a wide window. She shifted and found herself lying on the soft linens of a king-size bed, the sheets twisted around her legs. As she tried to untangle herself, she realized she was naked.

For a moment she looked around, wondering how this had all happened. Then it came back to her in a rush. She had met a king in the nightclub, and he had brought her here. The details were fuzzy, and the harder she focused, the less she remembered. She only remembered the feeling of flying inside her own body, raw ecstasy, every nerve singing with pleasure. There had been a bit of pain, too, but that only added to the pleasure . . .

Sighing, she leaned back against the pillows with a small smirk. All right, so she had gotten played a little bit. The guy wasn't a king. He'd taken her here—a hotel somewhere?—they'd done their thing, and now he was gone with another notch on his belt. She felt sore in all the right ways—and some unusual ones too—but Christine couldn't find it in herself to feel too irritated.

"Screw it," she said, and her smile widened as she closed her eyes. "Worth it."

Then there was a knock on the door.

Sitting up, Christine blinked again, frowning. The light seemed brighter than usual. Then again, the window faced directly east, and the heavy curtains were drawn, revealing Lake Michigan beyond, gleaming blue in the sun. "Housekeeping," she muttered to herself. Then, drawing the sheets up to cover her nakedness, she called louder, "Yeah, come in."

The door opened, and the heavy bodyguard walked in. Christine's mouth fell open in surprise, then her eyes narrowed. She understood the guy being part of the con, but it must have taken some nerve to stick around. Last night might have been excellent, but if this guy thought he was going to catch sloppy seconds just for that, he had another thing coming.

"Good morning, ma'am," he said with a faint accent Christine thought was German, although his English sounded very natural. The guy looked studiously at the window, although Christine saw him glancing at her now and then from the corner of his eyes. "My master the king instructed me to apologize on his behalf; he had to leave early this morning on state business, but commanded me to see to your every need and make sure you get home safely."

Christine stared so long that the guy finally turned to look at her. His eyes wandered only once before he caught himself.

"You mean . . ." Christine started, then stopped, unable to process his words. Shaking her head, which swished her long hair over her shoulders and tickled her bare flesh, she gave it another try. "You mean he really is a king?"

The bodyguard stared at her. "Of course he is."

Christine leaned back against the headboard, grappling with that. She reached one hand behind her to shift the pillows to support her back. The sheet slipped down her side, but she pinned it with her other elbow before it exposed much. The bodyguard's eyes widened, then he took a deep breath and looked back out the window. Christine giggled, the heady sense of euphoria starting to return.

"How about we talk in a minute, after I put something on?" Christine suggested. Then she smiled wickedly, winked, and added, "After all, I'm completely naked under here."

The guy trembled, swallowing hard, and Christine had to bite her tongue so she wouldn't laugh. With a deep breath, the bodyguard said, "As you wish, ma'am."

Bowing, he swept from the room and closed the door.

Leaning back into her pillows, Christine laughed for no reason she could think of. It was nice to know she hadn't been duped—or at least that these guys were going to bizarre lengths to keep up the ruse—but more than that, she felt invigorated. Even though her body was tired and sore, and part of her wanted to pass out for another dozen hours or so, her mind refused to be still. Blurry as her memories were, she could still see the king's face clearly, feel his breath on her neck, the scintillating chill of his touch . . .

She emerged from the bed and stepped into the bathroom, hunting for a robe. She found one hanging on the door, and as she swung it on, she glanced in the mirror.

"Holy crap!" she said, staring at herself.

Her hair was mussed and her eye makeup had run a bit, but it didn't look too bad; with a minor fix here or there, she could make it work. Her lips were smeared red, as if her pink lipstick had darkened, but that would only take a bit of cleaning as well. She could not say the same about the lines of red marks along both sides of her neck, along the curve of one breast, and even on the inside of her thigh. She brushed each in turn, and found the skin raw and sensitive. A faint trace of dried blood came away from the spots on her breast. As she grazed the marks on her thigh, though, she had a sudden and vivid recollection of the king's teeth there, his lips and tongue on her flesh, working their way up her body . . .

She leaned against the sink, arms trembling and gasping for breath, for a long moment before she managed to compose herself.

"King's a little kinky, isn't he?" she commented to the body-guard as she stepped into a little dining room where a full breakfast spread was set out for her. Taking the seat at the head of the table, she spooned herself some eggs and sausage and dug in. Part of her was aghast, but she was so hungry she couldn't be bothered to care.

Extra hour at the gym, so what?

Standing across the room respectfully, the bodyguard cleared his throat. "I'm sure he didn't mean to offend you, ma'am . . ."

Christine laughed, pressing her napkin to her mouth. She grinned across the room at him. The euphoria wasn't wearing off. "If it's going to be like that, he can bite me all he wants."

The bear of a man nodded to himself. Christine gestured to the food, feeling amiable. "Care to join me?"

"What? Oh, no, thank you. I've already eaten." But he stared at her almost nervously, as if he wanted to ask a question but was terrified to speak the words.

"What's your name?"

"Me?" the guard asked, as if the question confused him. "I . . . Hans. Hans Richtein, ma'am."

So he probably was German. But Germany didn't have a mon-archy . . .

"Penny for your thoughts, Hans?"

"I . . ." Hans hesitated, then whispered, "What was it like?"

Christine paused in the act of sipping water, the glass held to her lips, her thin eyebrows darting up her forehead.

"I mean . . ." The heavy face contorted in frustration, and then he took a step forward. His brown eyes took on some of the inten-sity Christine remembered from the night before—frenetic, almost manic. "What . . . what did it taste like?"

Inhaling the water in a rush, Christine coughed several times, spraying it on her plate. Then she set her glass down and chortled for a long minute, tears running down her eyes. When she could speak, she grinned up at him. "I'm hurt," she teased. "Here I thought you were checking me out. I didn't think you swung that way."

He stared a moment, then flushed bright red. He stammered, "I . . . not what I meant . . ."

Christine laughed again, leaning back in her chair and shaking her head. Then she sighed and pushed her plate away. "So, I guess you drive me home and tell me to keep my mouth shut about His Majesty getting it on with an American girl from a club?"

"His Majesty thought you'd want to see him again," Hans said, looking wary and baffled at the same time, as if he was translating her words into a language that made more sense. "Don't you?"

She hadn't expected that. She thought about the taste, the feeling, the sensation, the bliss to which she'd awoken—so pleasantly exhausted and yet so inexplicably powerful. She thought of saying no to that . . .

"Yes," she breathed, and there was no humor on her face. Her eyes widened, and her hands seized the folds of the tablecloth compulsively. "I want to. I need to. When can I see him again?"

Hans nodded, reassured. "He hoped he might see you tonight . . ."

"I have to wait that long?" Christine demanded. She winced—it sounded way too clingy, even to her—but the thought of waiting was almost physically painful now that she knew she could have him again.

"Unfortunately, yes," the bodyguard apologized, and the sympathy in his face told Christine he understood entirely. Maybe he really did have a thing for his boss. Well, too bad, the king had picked her. "But if you're free—"

"I am," Christine promised. "I will be. Can you pick me up, or should I meet him—"

"If you'd like to shower and dress, ma'am, I'll take you home," Hans cut in. "And then the Master will visit you tonight."

Christine got to her feet, and the mania in Hans's eyes reflected in her own. "I can't wait."

FOURTEEN

SALEM WAS getting close; he was certain of it.

He had not stopped to ask questions, and no one had volunteered to help his search since the trio in the pawn shop, but the signs were promising. The neighborhood was a good hiding spot: boarded up windows, quiet hand-to-hand transactions just out of the glow of streetlights, and a little bit more snow than the roads should still have, given that it hadn't snowed since Salem got his lead. It was a place where people wouldn't ask questions or pry into frightening things. A little too exposed, perhaps—a few too many humans in the general area for complete peace of mind—but then, Simon had always been a little off.

Those factors alone would have made the neighborhood a suitable resting place for any vampire, but Salem was becoming more and more convinced his particular quarry was at hand. He was used to humans cringing away from him, but this was different. Like the amateur golfer three days before, a second of mistaken recognition preceded discomfort; when they flinched and looked away, it was not from the automatic fear that accompanied him like an aura, but fear born from the knowledge of what someone who looked like him could do.

They knew Simon, and dreaded him. Salem laughed aloud at the idea; as he did, a man who had been advancing toward him rocked back on his heels as if he had thought better of it.

As Salem sauntered across a baseball diamond to the street beyond, he saw a couple people standing in the doorway of an apartment building. They glanced at him, did double takes, then moved across the concrete porch away from the door. The movement seemed so automatic, a routine to follow to ensure safety, that Salem smirked to himself and started toward the doorway.

He had laid one foot on the first step up to the porch when a distinctive, familiar sound registered in his pointed ears. Glancing upward into the dark sky, he saw the shape that went with the sound of flapping, leathery wings. The bat soared north, and Salem's bright green eyes narrowed as he followed its progress. There were none of the usual jinks and course corrections a real bat would employ, no dives for prey or sudden shifts. It flew in a doggedly straight line, as if following a homing beacon, and even as it soared out of hearing range, there was no hint of a tiny heartbeat.

"Really?" Salem complained, rolling his eyes. Turning north, he darted across the street, picking up the pace once he was out of sight of the mortals. Simon had a lead on him, but a leap put Salem on the second story wall of a dilapidated house. Climbing nimbly to the roof, Salem hoisted himself onto the shingles in time to see the dwindling shape winging its way northward, banking up toward cloud cover.

Sighing, Salem leapt off the roof, shifted in midair, and flew in pursuit.

BY THE third ring, Anita had already given up hope.

"C'mon, c'mon. Pick up!" she barked at her cell phone.

The line rang again indifferently.

"Please?"

"*This is Christine Stokely,*" her silky voice recited on the message. "*Leave me a message and I'll get back to you.*"

"Liar," Anita grumbled before the phone beeped. When it did, she opened and closed her mouth several times, then sighed and hung up.

"Anita?"

She looked up to find her mother at her bedroom door, wearing a white turtleneck on which Anita had embroidered gingerbread men three Christmases ago. "Your father's looking for you."

"Okay."

As she studied her daughter, Nancy's expression became inquisitive, tinged with concern. "Are you all right, honey?"

"Yeah. It's just . . . Christine," Anita said, waving her phone in one hand.

"She's not coming tonight?"

"No." Anita laughed mirthlessly. "No, I'm pretty sure she's not."

Nancy glanced over her shoulder toward the sounds of the party echoing up the stairs, then walked into the room, sitting on the foot of Anita's bed while Anita herself leaned back on her pillow. "Something you want to talk about?"

"We're just . . ." Anita hesitated, not sure what or how much to share. She hadn't gotten around to telling her parents about Simon yet, and this seemed like the wrong way to broach the topic. ". . . fighting."

"Did you two have an argument when you went out Friday?"

"Yeah . . ."

"Something about Simon?" Nancy asked knowingly.

Anita started. "How did you . . . ?"

"Sweetie," Nancy said with a gentle smile, reaching for her daughter's hand. Anita let her take it. "It's obvious he's important to you."

Sighing, Anita leaned back against her headboard, batting her dreamcatcher with her free hand. "Yeah."

The sound of a familiar, heavy tread on the stairs drew both their eyes toward Anita's door, and Nancy squeezed her hand before letting it go. "We'll take some time to talk after the party, all right?"

"Yeah. Sure."

They got to their feet and walked out into the hallway in time to see Richard Rothard ambling their way. For once, Anita thought her outfit might pass muster better than her father's black slacks and argyle sweater vest. Nancy kissed his cheek. "We're just on our way down, Rick."

Dr. Rothard seemed stymied by that, looking at Anita and then back at his wife. ". . . right. Well, let's get going, then, we have guests."

The sounds of conversation mingled with Christmas music grew louder as they approached the staircase, but Marion's voice was loudest and closest of all. "Hey Simon! Merry Christmas."

"And to you." Simon's distinctive, dry voice was quieter, but somehow still made its way up to the Rothards. Anita found herself facing her father's pursed lips and her mother's raised eyebrows.

"Um . . ." Anita had invited Simon on the taxi ride back following the disaster in the club. Apparently she had forgotten to relay the news.

"I wasn't aware we were expecting Simon," Dr. Rothard said coolly, his hazel eyes narrowed behind his glasses. The sweater vest made it hard to take him seriously, and Anita looked down; now would be the wrong time to laugh.

"You should have asked, Anita. But maybe it's for the best," Nancy suggested, "since Christine isn't coming."

Anita winced, and Dr. Rothard frowned. "We talked about Christine beforehand," he replied, his voice quiet so as not to echo down the staircase. He fixed Anita with a grimace. "These are work and family friends, Anita."

"So?" Anita hissed back. "Simon's my friend. And it looks like half your friends called in sick."

Dr. Rothard looked ready to retort, but Nancy squeezed his arm. "Now isn't the time," she pointed out. "Our guests are going to miss us."

Her husband met her eyes a moment, then nodded. "We'll discuss this later, Anita," he promised in a tone that made Anita sure she wasn't going to enjoy the discussion. "Let's go."

He led the way down to where Simon waited, wearing a bulky green sweater that disguised his rangy build. His ponytail was tucked in on itself into a small bun at the base of his neck, and his sharp gray eyes found Anita the moment she came into view. At the same moment, Marion returned from the closet wearing a Santa Claus hat and a broad smile. Her honey-colored eyes followed Simon's gaze to the staircase, her smile fading just a bit as she looked at Dr. Rothard's expression. Both of Anita's parents swept down the hall toward the kitchen without a word, though Nancy gave Simon a smile.

Anita wanted to kiss him, but three people she didn't recognize were admiring a painting in the parlor, so she just took his hands in hers. As always, they were cold to the touch. "Hi."

"Hey."

"You want some eggnog, Simon?" Marion asked on her way back to the kitchen.

"No, thank you."

Anita gave Marion a grateful look as she passed and, once she was out of earshot, turned back to Simon and smiled up at him. His restless eyes ranged over the people nearby and darted toward the louder commotion down the hall, but after a moment he looked down at Anita. "What?"

"Nothing," she replied, squeezing his cold hands. "I'm just glad you came."

His steel eyes tightened, shifting toward the staircase. "Even with the trouble it's going to cause you?"

"You heard that?" she asked, flushing with chagrin. "I was hoping they were quiet enough that no one would."

Simon shuffled, looking away from her again, and Anita felt a stab of anger at her father. After a second, Simon replied, "I got the gist . . ."

Blowing out her breath, Anita shook her head, closing her eyes and gritting her teeth for a moment. "Sorry. It's not you they're mad at, it's me."

Studying her for a long moment, Simon glanced at the people in the parlor, none of whom seemed to be paying them any attention. He looked hesitant for a moment, then raised one of her hands to his lips. They were as cold as the rest of him, but Anita half-smiled anyway and said, "Thanks."

Taking a deep breath, she put on a cheerier expression. "Come on, let's go get some cookies or something. And I want you to meet my Uncle Tim."

She towed him down the hall through a throng of her parents' friends and acquaintances, most of them wearing varying degrees of dress clothes, though she spotted denim here and there. One or two said hello, but most of them either looked past her or focused on Simon instead. She paused at the kitchen counter, gesturing to a plate filled with multicolored cookies.

"Want one?" she asked, picking out one for herself and taking a bite.

Simon patted his stomach; his sweater gave way quite a bit before his hand met his body. "I'm fine, thank you."

"You sure?" Anita tempted him. "I helped make them."

"I couldn't eat a thing," Simon replied with a small smirk.

Anita swallowed the rest of her cookie and grinned. "Oh, fine, don't try my cooking."

It felt more natural to tease him than she remembered; maybe things were going to be easier from now on, now that they were officially together. "Come see how the great room turned out."

Simon followed a few paces behind her as she wormed her way through the throng of guests collected in the doorway. She pointed out the strands of lit garland hung around the room's walls and chuckled with Simon at one of her father's doctor friends, who was picking out the melody of "Silent Night" on the piano and looking very pleased with himself.

"Stop it, Bert, they have a stereo!" his wife hissed.

"Don't listen to her, Berthoven!" someone else called, and a few people laughed.

Near the French doors that led to the deck was a robust Christmas tree, trimmed with soft blue lights and so weighed down with ornaments that several branches drooped toward the ground. Anita and Simon skirted the throng of people clustered around the buffet table set up in the middle of the room so she could show him the stockings hung on the fireplace mantle.

"I made my uncle's last week," Anita admitted. It hung on the far end of the fireplace, beside Marion's. She turned to see Simon's reaction, and his expression shocked her. His eyes were downcast, his jaw clamped so tight it trembled, and his usually cool expression looked frayed to the point of breaking. "Simon, what's wrong?"

He glanced back up, then retreated a step. Anita frowned, looking back at the mantle, and her eyes fell on the polished golden crucifix, gleaming in the light of the room. She turned back to Simon and steered him away, looking up at him. "Are you okay?"

"I'm fine."

She remembered him using the same words when she had found him at school, battered and bruised, and she pressed her lips together. "Let's go talk somewhere more private?"

"Sure."

They had barely wrangled their way back into the kitchen before she caught Simon's wrist. "Oh, wait, before we go . . ."

She led him across the kitchen to the dinette, where a tall, thin man was staring out the window, a full glass of eggnog in his left hand. He wore a tailored three-piece gray suit with a burgundy dress shirt and striped tie beneath. His sand-colored hair was combed neatly and his mustache trimmed. He turned as Anita approached, and his sea green eyes became alert and watchful.

"Uncle Tim!" She glanced at his glass and smirked. "Am I the only one who's going to enjoy the Christmas food?"

Timothy Rothard rolled his eyes and set the glass down. "I took it to be polite," he admitted. "Mustn't make waves at my brother's party, must I?"

Anita giggled, and the corners of her uncle's mouth turned up. Reaching a hand behind her to hook it around Simon's elbow, she ushered him forward and said, "Uncle Tim, this is Simon, my . . . friend."

She stumbled on the word, realizing just in time that she shouldn't tell her uncle anything she wasn't yet ready for her father to know. He didn't seem fooled though, and smiled dryly before looking at Simon and offering his hand. "Timothy Rothard."

Simon shook, pausing slightly before he replied, "Simon Melas."

As their hands met, Anita watched her uncle's smile fade just a bit. His eyes narrowed as he said, "A pleasure, I'm sure."

Simon studied him briefly, then offered, "Anita says you work in Madrid?"

Anita was a little surprised that he had remembered the detail. Her uncle nodded. "That's right."

"What do you do?"

"I work with an international service corporation. We deal in humanitarian aid." That was as far as Anita had ever gotten, either; discussions of international networking and the difficulties of non-governmental organizations made her eyes glaze over. Tim Rothard glanced at her, then looked back at Simon. "How do you know my niece?"

"We go to school together," Anita put in, her own smile fading. She didn't like the suspicious set of her uncle's mouth; it made him look like his brother. "Simon helped me study for my Western civ final—which I managed to scrape a B on, believe it or not," she added to Simon.

"I'm amazed." She elbowed him, and he added, "I mean impressed."

"Ha ha," Anita said, though her narrowed eyes lost most of their feigned ferocity when she grinned at him.

Watching their easy banter, her uncle opened his mouth to speak, but Anita's mother interrupted him, coming up from the other side.

"Enjoying the party, Tim?"

After a moment, he pulled his eyes away from Simon to his sister-in-law. Picking the eggnog up off the counter, he smiled unconvincingly. While Nancy laughed, Anita took one of Simon's cold hands.

"Hey, why don't I show you the lights we put up outside?" Anita suggested. Her tone was light, but she gave Simon a meaningful look, and he nodded slowly. "Wait here, I'll run and grab our coats."

"I don't need mine."

"It's no problem, I'll have to get mine anyway," Anita called over her shoulder.

"Really, I don't . . ." Simon said behind her, but his voice trailed off into silence as she headed down the hall.

Weaving through the throng of guests packing the main hallway, Anita made it to the front closet without incident. Though the Rothards had piled the majority of their own coats in her parents' bedroom to make space, Anita's vaguely dressy red wool coat was still there, along with Simon's distinctive leather duster. As she tucked both over her arm, she frowned; his coat was heavier than she remembered, as if he'd attached weights to it.

The return trip did not go as smoothly.

Marion stepped into the closet with a pair of coats as Anita was stepping out. She took one look at Simon's duster, grinned, and said in Spanish, "Stealing away for a rendezvous? Scandalous."

Anita rolled her eyes and passed by without a word, but she had no sooner made it to the foyer than she almost walked right into her father. Like Marion's, his eyes went to Simon's coat; unlike Marion's, his face slipped into a frown. "Where do you think you're going?"

Knowing she was already in hot water for inviting Simon at all, Anita kept her voice pleasant and agreeable. "I'm going to show Simon the Christmas lights we put up out back."

"I'm sure that can wait," Dr. Rothard said, eyes still narrow.

Anita's temper started to heat up again. "It can, but it isn't going to."

Jowls flushing, Dr. Rothard snapped back, "You're not going to go skulk around out of sight while we have guests, Anita. You can act like an adult for one night and help us entertain—"

"That's where I'm going," Anita cut across him. "To entertain my guest."

She turned her back and stormed off toward the kitchen. She didn't dare look back, but one of the people in the parlor called out to her father, and she knew he would be diverted, at least for the moment. She was nearly at the end of the hall when she heard her uncle's voice.

"—probably just a little worn out from work," he was saying. "I just had an off feeling about him, that's all."

"He's a little different, but he's been a good friend for Anita," Nancy Rothard replied. There was a pause, then, so faintly Anita had to strain to hear it, her mother said, "Remind me to talk to you after the party about that. This isn't really the time, but suffice it to say, he's definitely looked out for her."

"All right." Tim Rothard sounded reluctant, and Anita heard him sigh. "Like I said, maybe it's just work stress. Jumping at shadows."

"Has work been hard?"

"These last few years have been very difficult," he admitted. "Maybe it's getting to me. But he just rubbed me the wrong way."

Anita's eyes widened in disbelief. He had known Simon for all of thirty seconds, and already he was going to be on her father's side? Not trusting herself to even look at them, she stalked through the kitchen toward the dinette's doors. Her mother called after her in surprise—she imagined the looks of guilt on their faces at being overheard talking about her—but she went right through the doors onto the snowy porch, where she saw Simon waiting.

Whatever expression was on her face must really have been something, because no sooner had he turned at the sound of her approach than his steel eyes widened. "What—?"

"C'mon," Anita said, thrusting his heavy duster into one of his hands and donning her own coat. Without even looking at the Christmas lights, she dragged him toward the staircase down into the lawn. He came without complaint, and she relaxed a bit of the stiff set in her shoulders. Between the judging and suspicion from her family and Christine's persistent silence, she needed Simon to still be on her side. It was comforting to have him here, someone she could still count on.

Someone she could trust.

THE LONG, curled lashes framed her blue eyes, accented by the faint dusting of smoky color on their lids. Her soft lips glistened red, and shimmering black hair framed her face, styled up in elaborate curls. The gold chain of her necklace hugged her neck all the way around, and the ruby-studded, heart-shaped pendant rested in the hollow of her throat, just above the line of her new Hepburn dress. She knew that when she exhaled, her cool breath would smell of mint.

Christine still frowned. She did not often wear full makeup, but lately the cream in her skin had faded. She felt more washed-out and tired than she had in a long time, and some of the smoking around her eyes was to disguise the circles starting there. Her soft pale skin was starting to turn chalky, and she had added blush to keep it light and vital.

She sighed at the mirror, then glanced out the bathroom door, though of course the doorbell still hadn't rung. She wouldn't have missed it. He was coming again tonight, and when they were to-gether again . . . she shivered in anticipation.

Stepping into her bedroom, her scarlet stiletto heels clicking on the tile until they found the soft carpet of her room, Christine looked through her closet for something to go along with the dress, mostly to pass the time. It was uncomfortable waiting, uncomfort-able being away from him. She wondered if this was what love was like: the pining, the painful yearning to be with him when she wasn't, and the sense of belonging and protection when she was.

Her room was lit only by the lamp above her headboard—these past days, the dark felt more comfortable somehow—and so she eventually noticed the glow from her phone. She crossed the room and picked it up.

Anita again. She had stopped leaving messages, but she had called every day since that night. Christine looked at the simple words *ANITA CELL* for several long seconds, one side of her perfect mouth turning down.

There was really no point in feuding anymore. Yeah, Anita had been out of line in slapping her, but she had made Anita sweat for a few days now. She would probably even let Christine slap her back to even things out, if she asked.

But she hadn't called back. Whenever she brought up the con-tact in her phone, some quiet, insistent voice in the back of her mind suggested that she shouldn't go through with it. It wasn't being petty; Anita could just afford to wait for another couple days. Chris-tine was having to live with being patient, so why shouldn't Anita?

She had discussed Anita and Simon with him on more than one of their dates, and the king was an engaged listener. He had seemed interested in both of them, and showed no impatience at all when Christine spoke, sometimes rambled, about her childhood friendship with Anita, how it had been renewed last year, even if it hadn't been quite the same; she had even confessed how that sense of unwilling remove had troubled her, something she hadn't even been able to tell Anita. She had told him of Anita's decision to leave Northwestern and her own unhappiness with it, the introduction of Simon into their relationship, and how everything had become confused since then . . .

"Yes," the king had agreed, and Christine trembled at the memory of his soft, sibilant voice in her ear. "Yes, I imagine he had that effect."

The hand that wasn't holding her phone drifted up to her neck and the small, still-raw wounds there. It wasn't bad, really; Christine had done kinkier things, and her parents had been out of the house enough lately that she'd only needed to worry about a turtleneck one day since she'd first been marked. She had made no effort to cover the bite marks with makeup, not since the first night after she had met her lover and he had frowned at the change. She'd pouted at his disapproval theatrically, but his soothing voice had taken her worries away. What did it matter what other people thought, whether she met their standards of beauty, or even her own? What did the bites or even the growing pallor in her skin matter? *He* thought she was beautiful. And the marks were an outward sign of what she hoped for all the more every time they met—that it would work out. That they would stay together forever.

He would leave eventually, she knew. He couldn't very well be royalty and stay outside his own country, wherever it was. Whenever she asked, the conversation drifted off the subject, but she had vague memories of him speaking to Hans when they thought she was asleep, discussing Europe and Asia and Africa after their "business" in Chicago was done. She knew she would go with him anywhere he asked. She wouldn't miss the cold of Chicago, and she was more than old enough to quit living in her parents' house. The only person she might really miss . . .

Christine's fingers tightened on the phone in her hand. Part of her was still mad, but she was starting to miss Anita, and Anita obviously missed her. A quick conversation wouldn't hurt, would it? She pressed the call symbol, wondering if the inevitable back-and-forth of apologies would make the time pass more quickly . . .

The doorbell rang.

Dropping the phone onto her desk, Christine grabbed her black and red lace shawl, then wrapped it over her bare shoulders before hurrying down the two flights of stairs to the front door. The house was dark, with only the foyer lights on. Christine opened the door and was unsurprised to see Hans Richtein lit by the porch light. He wore a light gray suit today, but it was no more tailored to his muscular frame than the black one had been. Couldn't he afford to get the suit altered? It seemed like it would reflect badly on his boss.

"Good evening, my lady," Hans offered with a bow.

The words soothed Christine's annoyance; it was as if she was already royalty too. They gave her hope for the future, and she couldn't help but take some pride in the way the man's eyes tried and failed to be subtle as they took in the curves her snug dress highlighted.

"Hey," she said. "Where am I meeting him tonight?"

The burly man half-smiled. "He's waiting for you in the car. Once you're ready to leave—"

Christine knew that it would be best to make him wait just a little, to savor the anticipation so when she deigned to appear, he would be as eager for her as she was for him. She knew it, but the words still left her breathlessly, "I'm ready now. Let's go."

Toying with him was all well and good, but she felt the ache of his absence more intensely now, as if some part of her sensed his nearness. Hans stepped out of the doorway, gesturing down the walk to where the familiar black car idled in the driveway. Christine took the scraped, salted stairs carefully, containing her eagerness so she wouldn't slip on any lingering wetness. Hans opened the car's rear door for her, and she slipped inside.

It was little warmer in the car than it had been outside, but any worry about the temperature flitted out of Christine's mind when she saw his face. His thin lips curved into the dark, secretive smile that always thrilled her, promising mystery and adventure the more they were together. He still wore his sunglasses—Christine had never seen him without them—but she imagined the affectionate gleam in his eyes.

He took her hand in his own cold one and pressed it to his chilly lips. "I've missed you, lovely one."

"Me too," Christine breathed. She curled up into his side, not bothering about her seat belt as the car backed out of the driveway and onto the road.

"Home, Master?" Hans asked over the seat.

The sunglasses turned down to Christine's face as the quiet, commanding voice answered, "Home."

Christine had met him at the hotel, in a club, and in a private house he had said one of his people was renting, but he had never spoken of his home. Was he leaving? Uneasy, she asked, "Home?"

"Yes indeed." She started to frown, but his voice stopped her train of thought. "Would you like to come with me?"

She could not stop her eyes from widening. As much as she had hoped for this moment—dreamed of it, obsessed over it, seen it in her waking thoughts and the subconscious of her fitful sleep—it still made her tremble. "Can I?"

"Of course." His dry voice caressed her mind and brushed her fears away. "I think the time has come, my pet, for our relationship to change. To grow."

"What do you mean?"

She couldn't achieve more than a whisper, but he responded as calmly as if the conversation were idle and casual. "I have given you much these days we've been together, have I not?"

"Yes."

"Shown you much?"

"Definitely," Christine promised, her blue eyes wide, searching his face in vain for any clues to the thoughts in his unfathomable mind.

"And there is much more still," he promised in a tone that made Christine press a palm longingly to his chest. "I can show you a life of which you could never conceive, every one of your dreams fulfilled."

The car swerved for a second before it corrected itself. The king's face finally betrayed some emotion—a flicker of annoyance as he looked at the back of Hans Richtein's head. Christine thought she saw the bodyguard cringe down a bit in his seat, but her lover spoke again, and thoughts of Hans drifted away.

"I can share with you all that I am," he whispered in her ear. Falling silent a moment, he raked the bottom of her earlobe with his teeth, and she whimpered despite herself. "If you wish it."

"Yes," Christine said immediately, nodding into his shoulder. "What do I have to do?"

He pushed her shoulders back, and even through the sunglasses, the force of his gaze was magnetic.

"You must give yourself to me entirely." His voice was darker now, harsher. "I will give you everything, and I require everything in return."

Even as his voice reached that secret place in her heart that he seemed to have created just for himself, his words frightened her, and she frowned. She heard the edge in his voice, the hint of danger. She didn't know what he was planning, but she was suddenly sure that there would be no going back, and suddenly unsure she wanted to agree. She had known him only a few days, after all; she knew so little and had to guess so much. All the vague answers and shifting topics of conversation, all the secrecy and silence . . . she could order Hans to stop the car, get out on the sidewalk, and never see either of them again . . .

If they didn't stop me. The thought brought her a moment of terror. She had teased Hans, flirting and toying with his obvious desire. She glanced at him, wider and taller than the seat he was in, and knew she could never fight him off if he didn't want to be fought. And something inside her told her she would be better off going a dozen rounds with Hans Richtein than even one with his master.

What had she gotten herself into?

"Christine."

That voice, speaking her name, demanded her attention. Her eyes met the reflective lenses of his sunglasses, and she realized she had leaned away from him.

Could she leave him? There was something ominous about him, and she wasn't at all certain that unraveling the mystery would be a pleasant affair. But could she leave it unknown? She knew she would always wonder, would always be tormented by the "what ifs."

"What do you mean," she asked carefully, "by 'everything?'"

"You leave everything behind," he said. "Be mine. Forever."

Christine's stomach twisted at the same time her mind recoiled. There was an undercurrent to his words, a crocodile lurking just beneath the surface of the river, but she wanted him so desperately that she could not even form a response. He studied her for a moment, then let go of her hand, reached out his long index finger, and pressed it to her gown above her sternum.

Her heart warmed at his touch, the heat spreading through her body until she gasped. Her veins tingled, as if something in her blood had reacted to him.

"Christine."

She gazed at him helplessly. Every second, it became harder to remember why she was afraid.

"Come with me."

She nodded.

"Give yourself to me."

Her ruby lips framed the words and her throat gave them voice. "I'm yours."

"Belong to me. Forever."

There was no fighting it, and as that aching, desperate need flooded her veins, she lost the desire to. "Forever."

SIMON LET Anita drag him down the curving staircase from the deck to the snow-covered lawn, eyes narrowed in confusion. He had stepped out under the guise of looking at the Christmas lights on the house, but mostly to get out from under Timothy Rothard's eyes. Something about the sandy-haired man's expression had made him uneasy; that restlessness was becoming far too common with the Rothards.

However, in making his escape, he'd missed whatever was bothering Anita. Her face was flushed in a way that had nothing to do with the cold, and her heart pounded like she was Simon's own personal percussion section. It was distracting, but her unhappiness kept his mind off the flow of blood in her neck. A back corner of his mind marveled at that, with no little disquiet, but he ignored that as well.

The vampire heard the other guests outside remarking on Anita's sudden appearance, but she either missed the comments or ignored them as she led Simon toward the hedge maze on the north of their spacious lawn. The maze's pattern was not complicated— they reached the center with three turns—but the tall hedges shielded them from view, and the lights and music of the party faded.

Anita tore the antler headband out of her hair and threw it across the clearing, then brushed the snow off the stone bench with one sleeve. Simon glanced around the small enclave at the heart of the maze; aside from the bench, the only feature was a solid steel group of concentric rings, which Simon identified as an armillary sphere, sitting atop a concrete pillar.

"Wanna sit with me?" Anita asked as she plopped down on the bench.

Simon slung his leather coat on with practiced ease, his concealed kukri knife slapping against his leg. He had taken to carrying the weapon since his encounter with Salem and the debacle with the gang the next day. At first, he had worried Anita would notice the knife, hidden behind a Velcroed fold of cloth, but she looked beyond noticing much of anything.

He sat beside her, and she took one of his hands in both of hers. "Hey."

She didn't seem inclined to go on, and Simon studied her. Her jaw was set and her eyes hard, but she wasn't meeting his gaze. He found it bothered him, and after a moment he asked, "What did I miss?"

"I'm just so sick of it, Simon," she said, sounding weary as she leaned against him, head on his shoulder. "I feel like everything's coming at me all at once. My dad's mad and I don't know whose side my mom is on and Christine's ignoring me . . ."

Simon drew his hand out of hers and wrapped it around her shoulders. He grimaced to himself, at a loss; in the alley, her pain had acted on him like a stimulant—given him the strength to beat his enemies half to death—but there was no enemy to fight here.

"I'm sorry," was all he managed.

Anita nodded, nudging his head with hers as she leaned into him. "I'm just . . . so sick of all of it," she said again; Simon heard the tightness in her voice, envisioned the lines of stress on her face. "Sick of being treated like I'm not my own person, like I can't be trusted to choose how I dress or who I hang out with, like . . . like I'm a disappointment. Like I let him down by being who I am."

That stirred something much deeper than Simon expected, and as Anita's hands squeezed into fists, he rubbed her arm and pressed his lips to the top of her head. The scent of her shampoo mingled with the usual scent of her skin and the blood beneath sent a whisper of desire down his throat, but he ignored it.

"Has it always been this way?" he asked.

"A while," she admitted. "Since high school. I just . . . never really fit in, I guess. I made friends, and I lost friends. I like people, but I'm not a good little social butterfly hostess. A lot of the girls I went to school with were pretty catty, and once Christine wasn't there to keep them on a leash anymore . . ."

She trailed off. Simon squeezed her arm, and she sighed. "Sorry. I don't mean to whine. I'm just running out of people I can talk to."

"You can always talk to me," Simon found himself offering. His instinctive internal flinch at becoming ever more bound to a human was smothered by the smile Anita managed for him.

"Thanks." She kissed him, and the warmth of her lips and the blood behind them seeped down into him, but she pulled back before his mouth could drift to her neck, and after a moment she looked at him, curious, almost hesitant. "Can I ask you something?"

Anything was better than dwelling on the memory of what her blood had tasted like the last time they kissed. "Sure."

"You don't . . . I mean . . . do you have a prob—" Her face contorted in frustration and her big eyes narrowed. Then, as if measuring every word, she said, "Does it bother you that we're Catholic?"

It certainly isn't convenient. He frowned at her, wondering where he had let his control slip. "Why do you ask?"

"Does it?" she insisted.

"No. Why?"

Anita looked at him for a moment; Simon thought she was trying to read a lie in his expressionless face. "When you saw the crucifix in the great room, you looked really uncomfortable."

The vampire remembered then, and winced. "Er . . ."

"I mean, is it because they're so overt about it?" Anita sounded embarrassed now. "I told them I thought it was a bit much for a party, but they wouldn't hear of it. 'The reason for the season' and all that. I'm sorry if they made you uncomfortable. You're not really religious, are you?"

Shuffling uncomfortably, Simon pulled his arm back. Anita frowned and shifted so she was facing him.

"It's never been part of my life," he replied.

"And it makes you uncomfortable when other people are so open about it?" Anita pressed.

"You could say that." He suspected his frustration had reached his face, because Anita's brown eyes were soft with concern and she was opening her mouth to speak again. He headed her off. "What about you? Miguel seemed to think you weren't very religious either."

It annoyed him to have to even think of Miguel, let alone bring him up in conversation, but Simon was desperate to get Anita off the subject of his reaction to the crucifix before he let something damaging slip.

"Yeah . . . not really, I guess," Anita replied, sounding uncertain. She looked at the hedges in the direction of the house, as if she could see through them . . . or didn't want to meet Simon's eyes. He had successfully diverted her, but she frowned in a way that pained Simon to see.

"I don't really know what to believe. That's another thing that pisses my dad off," she added, and the hardness returned to her voice. "Gotta be the good little religious girl or there's something wrong with me . . ."

She dug into the pocket of her pants and pulled something out, cradling it in her palm. "I told them I'd wear this. My Uncle Tim got it for me a couple years ago, and I know it's beautiful, but it just feels . . . fake. Like I'm pretending. I don't want to be unfair to them by pretending I'm what I'm not . . ."

"Or unfair to yourself?" Simon suggested. He couldn't see what she was looking at.

Anita turned her face back to him and half-smiled. "That too."

"What is it?"

Anita closed her hand and held it out. Simon extended his open palm beneath it.

As she opened her hand, Anita started, "It's real Spanish silver, and the—"

Simon missed whatever else Anita said when scalding pain stabbed his palm and tore a shriek from his throat. He jerked to his feet, opening his hand and waving it as if to put out flames. The immediate pain disappeared, but the burning ache lingered, and he clutched his injured hand with the other, staring at Anita in disbelief. She was on her feet too, and her eyes were wide with unmistakable terror as she staggered back into the hedges on the other side of the bench. Still stunned by the pain, Simon looked down to where the object had fallen into the snow.

It was a glittering silver necklace, and from it hung a sapphire-studded silver cross.

In mounting horror, Simon looked down at his hand. The flesh had charred and blackened in the exact shape of the cross, with faint, thinner lines of burned flesh where the necklace's chain had touched him. Looking back up at Anita, feeling the echo of her dawning realization and fear on his own face, Simon didn't need the touch of his tongue to confirm that his long fangs had extended.

He reached his unburned hand toward Anita. He had no idea what he could say to calm her, but before he had even opened his mouth, she screamed.

FIFTEEN

SIMON CROSSED the heart of the maze before Anita could draw breath for a second cry. His burned hand caught her around the small of her back as the other clamped down on her mouth. "Don't scream!"

Her eyes filled her face, and she struggled instinctively in his grip. She tried to scream anyway, but his palm muffled her voice. Her heart hammered in her chest as she slapped Simon's arm. She had been surprised before by the tough muscle in his thin frame, but she had never imagined how strong he truly was; she might have been shoving against a wall.

And that surprising, unreal strength, mixed with his cold skin, his deathly pallor, his inexplicable recovery from horrific bruising, the frightening gleam in his bright gray eyes, and the long fangs where his canine teeth had been a moment before, created a mental image from which her entire rational being shied away. She couldn't force herself to think the word, to even entertain the idea . . .

"Anita, stop!" he hissed, but he didn't look angry—he looked desperate and frightened. "I'm not going to hurt you!"

Anita had not processed the voices on the deck getting louder, agitated, but now she heard one echoing over the yard. "Anita? ANITA!"

Simon looked that way, grimacing. His teeth were just as long and sharp in profile, and Anita shuddered so ferociously that it made Simon, still clutching her against his body, tremble too.

He turned back to her, his reflective eyes pleading. "Anita, please. Please don't tell them."

She stopped screaming into his hand and stared at him blankly. She wondered whether he had lost his mind, or she had.

He glanced toward the house again, as if he had heard something she hadn't, then fixed her with his gaze. They were almost nose to nose, but even with her body trapped in his iron grip and those long teeth inches from her, she didn't think she had ever seen him look so vulnerable. "Anita, listen," he said, the words chasing each other off his lips. "I'm not going to hurt you. Please don't scream."

Numb with shock, she nodded, and he drew his hand away.

"Please don't tell them."

"Simon . . ." Anita was not surprised that her voice was a whisper and on the edge of breaking. "Simon, what the hell are you?"

She had a horrifying presentiment that she didn't really want to know the answer.

Simon glanced away again, and even Anita could hear the hurried footsteps approaching now. "Listen, I swear I'll tell you anything you want to know. I'll answer any question you have," he promised. "But now is not the time. Please. Please trust me."

What could she say? How could she keep something like this to herself? Even as her mind rebelled against the truth, some deeper part of her knew. But even if he was . . . she refused to think the thought. But whatever the truth was, could she deny Simon this? Who would she have left?

The voices and footsteps were very close now.

Anita looked into Simon's eyes and whispered, "Okay."

He nodded and stepped back, digging in his pocket for a pair of black leather gloves that he put on. His mouth hung open, and as the long canine teeth shrank back to normal size, he gave a small rasping noise, as if in pain. Anita shivered, looking away, then stooped to pick up the silver cross where it had fallen with another shudder she couldn't repress. She wondered what would happen if she stuck it out in Simon's face . . .

"Anita!"

Both Rothard brothers came around the last corner of the hedge maze. Dr. Rothard's heavy face was flushed, his chest heaving; he must have run the whole way from the house. Tim Rothard's eyes settled on her briefly before moving to Simon. Anita noticed her uncle had a rosary around his wrist, the crucifix in his hand.

"We're okay, Dad, it's nothing."

"What happened? The guests thought you were being attacked!" Anita didn't miss how his suspicious, accusing eyes went to Simon. She found it harder to resent than before.

"I . . . dropped my cross," Anita said, holding it up so they could see. "Simon went to pick it up for me." He tensed at her side, but she was into the lie now and continued, "I-I stepped on his hand when he was down there, and he yelled. It . . . it scared me so much that I screamed."

She glanced at Simon, then looked away when he turned to look at her. "Sorry if I scared you."

"Scared us?" The worry on Dr. Rothard's face gave way to fury. "We had one night with our friends, and now they think my daughter's getting murdered in my backyard!"

"Well, go give them the good news that I survived, then!" Anita snapped. Her nerves frayed raw, she had nothing left to control her temper.

"Can't we have one event where you don't—"

"It was an accident!" Anita yelled, and she found herself taking a step toward him. "What's your problem?"

"Don't you take that tone with me, Anita Joy!" Before she could respond, Dr. Rothard turned to Simon. "We're going to Midnight Mass at Holy Name Cathedral. Were you planning to show up for that, too?"

Simon looked uncomfortable. "I'm sorry, Doctor, but I can't—"

"I don't care, I just needed an answer. It's about time that you headed home, isn't it?"

"Dad!" Anita said, aghast at his rudeness. At Dr. Rothard's side, Tim pulled his suspicious eyes away from Simon to stare at his brother.

"Anita, get in the house now and get dressed for church. We're sending the guests home; the party's over."

"Dad, you can't just—"

"Get inside!" he roared.

Anita, Simon, and Tim Rothard all jumped. Anita's jaw trembled, and her eyes stung. She felt humiliated in front of Simon, and that embarrassment mixed with her fear of Simon himself into an emotional jumble that she thought was going to tear her apart. She locked her arms around her chest to hold it in one piece.

In the following silence, Dr. Rothard's chest heaved and his face almost seemed to glow red. In a flat, overcontrolled voice, he said through his teeth, "Simon, I think it would be best if you went home right now."

Simon glanced at Anita, and she stared at the ground, shivering. After a second, he looked away and slipped between the Rothard brothers without a word. Anita followed after him, wanting to say something, but the words caught in her throat. He did not reenter the house, but strode around the side and out of sight toward the front lawn. He never looked back.

FROM HIS vantage point behind the chimney on the neighbor's roof, Salem watched Simon trudge toward the front yard, his former protégé's shoulders stiff. Once the younger vampire was out on the street, Simon glanced around, slipped into a deep enough shadow that human eyes would be unable to pick out details, and shifted. The bat took two skittering hops before it was airborne, winging away south.

Salem's emerald eyes turned back to the yard. The girl was crossing the deck, arms still around her chest and head lowered as she stalked into the house. Salem could not pick out many of the quiet words as the two men in the hedge maze conversed. The thinner one put a hand on the fat one's shoulder for a moment, then they both started back toward the house.

"Still playing a fool's game, Simon," Salem breathed to himself.

He needed Simon's help, which meant he had to keep Simon alive for a while, but he hadn't anticipated anything like this debacle. The girl knew; the quiver in her voice and the machine gun rate of her heartbeat left no room for doubt. It was only a matter of time before she told someone, or tried to tangle with Simon on her own. And with Shafax in town, time was a commodity of which Salem was running short.

He watched as the party guests finished mingling and trickled from the house, glancing around the sky now and then to make sure Simon wasn't lingering. Once the yard was clear, Salem crossed to the girl's roof, prowling across the snow. Kneeling to listen, he heard the hustle and bustle of people moving inside, all speaking with the familiarity of family and sounding impatient. They were never going to leave the girl alone at this rate.

Sure enough, the next time the door opened, they were all funneling out into the family SUV. The same man who had bellowed at the girl in the maze opened his window and yelled for her twice before she emerged from the house, heart still racing. Salem sighed as he watched them drive away. He might have gone for the kill on all of them, but on the off chance one of them managed to get back over the threshold . . . well, that would have made things more complicated. And slashing them all to death would leave puzzle pieces even Simon could put together.

Salem needed his erstwhile student focused, and the boy had gotten a little temperamental last time . . .

As the SUV passed its mailbox, Salem saw the ROTHARD emblazoned on it and started. He stared for a moment, then shook his head, putting the disturbing thought out of his mind. "Even I'm not that unlucky."

Then his thoughts went back to Simon's new vulnerability.

"A fool's game," he repeated aloud, massaging his closed eyes with his thumb and middle finger. Midnight Mass at Holy Name Cathedral, the father had said. They would be untouchable inside, but if the girl liked to dawdle and Salem was very, very lucky . . .

He snapped his eyes open. With the greater danger at hand, now was not the time for adding needless risks.

"Game's over."

"I HAVE to hand it to you, Sarah," Philip complimented, "you've outdone yourself."

Sarah said nothing, but Miguel saw her smug smile. The hood of her black satin cloak framed her face, and she carried a leather-bound book in one hand and a purple candle in the other. Philip wore a black cloth jacket adorned with enough tightening straps and zippers that Peter had asked him if it was bondage gear. Rachel was wearing rubber elf ears and a Santa hat that clashed magnificently with her deliberately ripped black denim jacket and teardrop makeup; Cole, walking at her side, kept blinking and looking at her as if he was sure he would see something different if he tried hard enough.

"I'll say," Adrienne agreed, shivering in the cold wind. "Leah and Caroline are going to be so pissed that they missed this."

"Well, Leah lives in Nebraska and Caroline lives in Pennsylvania, so it's a bit of a commute, don't you think?" Frank mocked.

Adrienne snickered. "Shoulda stuck around for the holidays."

"Easy for you to say, you live in Orland Park! I had to come down from Milwaukee!"

"Hey, you didn't have to come—"

Miguel didn't bother to keep track of their bickering, but he had to agree with Philip's and Adrienne's assessments. From the moment they passed through the rusted, wrought iron gates, it had been obvious why Sarah chose this place. A blanket of mist lay over the ground, and while the nearer headstones stuck out, those across the graveyard warped and played tricks on the eyes. It wasn't hard to imagine the round curve of a distant headstone as a hunched-over figure waiting to rise, or the angel atop a decadent memorial as a bat-winged demon about to take flight . . .

Miguel smiled. It was perfect.

"It's called Saint Brigid's," Sarah replied, looking around proudly like she had built it herself. "There's a ruined chapel in the center that'll be perfect."

The group walked along the decaying path toward what Sarah assured them was the heart of the cemetery, and as he surveyed them Miguel was reminded of a caterpillar. They weren't the type to huddle together, so they kept expanding outward to check out interesting headstones and monuments, but something more than the chill made them drift back to the group not long after.

After a while, he noticed that one length of the caterpillar wasn't expanding outward.

"Hey, Peter," he called, and the whole group stopped, Philip and Arianna turning away from a smashed headstone that had once been a miniature stone cathedral. "Didn't you say you wanted to do some gravestone rubbings?"

"I did," Peter replied in an appreciative voice, looking around as several of the others made noises of interest.

"Why not now? Preliminaries before the main event, if you will." Miguel smiled at Sarah, who smirked back.

There was general agreement, and they went off in groups of two and three. Miguel waited a moment, then turned around. Tony wandered off in Peter's direction, and just behind the spot he vacated, Heidi looked as if she had been holding a shield that had just disintegrated in her hands.

"Hey," Miguel said, walking over to her with his hands in the pockets of his black military coat. "What's wrong?"

Heidi's thumbs stuck through the holes she had worn through the cuffs of her usual hoodie. She smiled for an instant, then looked down, leaving Miguel to look at the black hood covering the top of her head. "Nothing."

Miguel took a deep, patient breath, then laid one hand on her arm. She started, but he said, "Heidi."

"What?" she asked, still looking down, her defensive tone shot through with holes. "It's nothing."

"Brittany's home from UPenn?" Miguel asked.

Heidi sighed, and she leaned forward to rest her hooded head against Miguel's shoulder. "Yeah."

Miguel said nothing and just patted Heidi on the back. After a moment, she picked her head up, but still looked away. "Sounds like she's got *summa cum laude* sewn up, unless she bombs something in the spring, which she won't," Heidi reported. "Her internship people from last summer offered her a job, so of course she has to decide between getting right into work experience or picking up her master's to have stronger credentials right away. Mom and Dad are . . . are really proud."

Her voice cracked, and she sniffled. Rubbing her nose, she smiled far too brightly and said in a quavering voice, "B-boy, it's really c-c-cold, isn't it? Gets my nose all runny. Hope I'm not getting sick too."

"Heidi . . ."

"Not that they shouldn't be proud," Heidi continued, her words running together. "It's really great. I'm really glad everything's coming together for her. It has to be nice, lots of peace of mind and stuff, and she—"

"Heidi."

She stopped and looked at Miguel. He saw her picking at the hole around one thumb with the other and took her hands to still them.

"Heidi, they love you, too."

"Of course," Heidi replied, smiling her fake smile that never reached her eyes.

Miguel held her gaze, his eyes narrowed but lips arranged in a gentle, wistful smile, and it took only a moment for Heidi's expression to disintegrate. She leaned against him again, clutching his fingers so hard they hurt.

"Mom and Dad asked me about my grades once," she whispered. "Brittany hasn't asked about UIC at all. 'Oh, Heidi, it's so great to see you! I've missed you so much! I can't wait to tell you what I did this semester!'"

The bitterness in her voice was suddenly so intense that Miguel winced. Reassembling his expression before she got a look at his face, he asked, "You don't think she missed you?"

"I think she misses a little sister she can tell stories to and give the sucky Barbies to and get to play the cat when she makes dorky movies with her friends," Heidi said. "She doesn't miss *me*. Not the me I am. She doesn't even know who I am anymore, Miguel. None of them do. The only grade I've gotten so far is a C+ in astronomy, so obviously I'm not gonna be Brittany in college any more than I was Brittany in high school."

Miguel didn't bother with reassurances he knew she would find empty. Instead, he let go of her hands and gently took her shoulders, guiding her back a step. He waited until she met his eyes. "We care. We're here for you, Heidi—the you that you are. That's what friends are for."

Her blue eyes were watery, but she managed the most genuine smile he'd seen yet. "Thanks, Miguel."

"Any time."

"Miguel."

He looked up and saw Sarah's eyes on him just before they went back to her watch. Squeezing Heidi's arms and giving her one more smile, he jogged over. "What's up?"

Sarah held up her watch the wrong way. Before Miguel could turn the digital numbers around in his head, she said, "It's almost midnight. I wanted to start right on the hour."

"Think they've got clocks on the other side?" Miguel asked dryly.

Sarah didn't smile back. "This isn't a joke, Miguel. I've got a really strong feeling about this place. It's like the dead are . . . restless here. Can't you hear them whispering? It's not just going to be me talking to them this time. I have a real sense they're going to talk back."

Miguel studied her for a moment, then nodded. "Then we should probably move along. You said the chapel's—"

Both of them jumped as a shriek pierced the silence of the graveyard, and several of their friends cried out too. Miguel cast about in time to see Heidi smacking Philip hard in his chest and walking away, arms tightly crossed, head down. Behind her, Philip wiggled his fingers and said, "Boooooooooo!"

A few people laughed as they realized what had happened. Miguel's eyes followed Heidi's progress until she leaned against a dead tree, rubbing her eyes. "Let's bring it together, guys," he called. "Sarah says it's time."

"Well, if the Mistress of Murky says game on, then on the game is!" Cole proclaimed grandly, strutting forward into the fog.

Sarah and Adrienne started quibbling with him, but Miguel wasn't paying attention. He let most of them pass by, then caught

Tony's eye and nodded toward Heidi. Tony nodded back, then moved to Heidi's side, striking up a conversation with her in his deep voice. Miguel waited while the rest caught up, then put a hand on Philip's shoulder at the end of the pack.

Philip smiled sheepishly. "Yeah, I know, but it was funny."

"She screamed pretty loudly," Miguel observed. "Probably could've heard her from the street."

"I know, right? I just came out of the fog and poked her, and it was like—"

"Philip, how long has your dad been out of rehab?" Miguel cut across him.

Philip's eyes widened as if Miguel had slapped him. After a moment, he answered slowly, "Two months."

"Depression, right? That's why he got into that stuff in the first place?"

"Yeah . . ."

"Because of your mom?"

Philip looked somewhere between uncomfortable and resentful. "Yeah."

Miguel fixed him with his emotionless gaze. "How well do you think he's going to do resisting that if he gets woken up Christmas morning to bail out the one kid his ex-wife didn't take with her?"

Resentment won out in Philip's eyes, but Miguel stared him down, and after a few seconds, Philip's face flushed. He swallowed, took off his glasses, and wiped them on his sleeve. "Not . . . not too well."

"Yeah, I thought that too."

Philip brushed at his eyes as he put the glasses back on, and Miguel pretended not to see. In a humiliated voice, he said, "I'm sorry, Miguel. It was just a joke. I didn't mean to . . ."

"I know."

"Sorry."

Miguel nodded, then patted Philip's arm. "Maybe tell her that too."

"Yeah."

They caught up quickly; Sarah and Cole were sniping at each other so loudly that Miguel rolled his eyes. "I could swear I told her I didn't want to run from cops this year," he muttered. Philip laughed, still a bit awkward.

"Sarah," Miguel interrupted whatever she was beginning to say. "Didn't you say we're on a deadline?"

Sarah grimaced, but looked at her watch again. "Yeah. Let's go."

As she led the way forward and Philip shuffled toward Heidi and started speaking to her quietly, Miguel nudged Cole. "Maybe pick your battles a bit there, *agent provocateur*?"

Cole snickered. "Anarchy is the spice of life, Miguel."

Miguel sighed. "I really can't say often enough how I don't want to run from cops . . ."

Cole raised his hands in mock surrender. "Okay, okay. I'll let the Wicked Witch do her thing."

"Thank you."

They caught up again, and now the chapel Sarah had mentioned was a hazy smear of white rising from the distant fog. As they passed beneath a skeletal yew tree, Heidi looked up and shivered. "That's creepy."

Miguel followed her gaze and raised an eyebrow. In every branch of every bough, glistening black eyes gleamed back at him. Someone raised a phone, and in the light from the touchscreen Miguel saw that the dark shapes attached to the eyes were birds.

"That's a loooooooot of crows," Rachel observed; the bobble of her Santa hat had fallen over one of her eyes.

"Ravens," Philip corrected.

Everyone looked at him, and he adjusted his glasses. "What? I did a bio project on animals used in the symbolism of death. 'The

Boogeyman's Bestiary: Cultural and Biological Connections in . . .' I posted it on my blog, guys. Didn't you read it?"

No one replied, although a few people chuckled. Rachel smothered her grin and asked, "The symbolism of death?"

"Er . . . yeah," Philip rallied. "Yeah, the Swedish considered them the ghosts of murdered persons. A lot of cultures associate them with the dead and lost souls. Omens of bad fortune. I could go on and on . . ."

"Don't," Adrienne suggested.

Philip flushed, then stammered, "But y-yeah, they're ravens. Which is unusual, actually; crows are more common in urban environments. But you can see the distinct glossy sheen on their feathers, as opposed to the duller coats of crows. And the slight curvature to their beaks. And that one there, see? The signature wedge shape to the tail, as opposed to the fan shape common to—"

"You are such a bird nerd," Peter said.

Miguel gave Sarah a look, and she announced loudly enough to draw everyone's attention, "Omens of ill fortune are good omens for us. Come on, we're almost there."

They followed her toward the white shape, but Miguel noticed Heidi glancing more than once at the ravens. Stepping to her side, he said, "They're just birds."

"Y-yeah, I know . . ."

"Nothing to be afraid of."

"Yeah . . ."

"If you don't want to be part of Sarah's séance, you don't have to."

"I know."

They almost walked into Tony. Frowning, Miguel touched Tony's back. He just stepped aside, and Miguel worked his way forward until he was side by side with Sarah. "What is it?" he breathed.

Her eyes were narrowed and fixed straight ahead. "I think somebody beat us to it."

Miguel looked forward and noticed the dim light leaking from the chapel's doorway and windows. It was faint and flickering, and he wondered if someone had set a fire.

"Maybe some homeless people went in to get out of the cold?" Jared suggested.

"Maybe . . ." Miguel replied, eyes narrowed. Maybe it was just the atmosphere of the graveyard, the way the raven-filled tree branches had seemed like hands groping in the fog for human prey, but something about the broken stone chapel suddenly felt wrong.

"Maybe we should go," Heidi suggested. Miguel wasn't surprised to hear her voice at his shoulder.

Sarah made a scathing sound. "We've come all this way. We should at least check it out."

They fell silent, and Miguel realized they were all looking at him. He frowned, but even if somebody inside took objection to them, there were twelve of them. "It can't hurt to look. But be quiet."

They crept forward, most of them filing toward the windows. But Sarah and Tony went right for the open door, and Miguel kept pace with them. The shuffling of feet in the snow as close as his shadow told him Heidi had tagged along. He managed a proud smile for her, then slipped to Sarah's side by the door and peered inside.

His eyes widened and his mouth fell open in blank shock. Sarah's nails dug into his forearm through his coat sleeve, but he couldn't tear his eyes away to check on the others.

Four stone pillars held up the ceiling, and a torch had been tied to each one with barbed wire. In the center of the room, a flat slab of new concrete was laid out like an altar, bigger than a king-size bed. Four iron spikes were driven into the corners of the slab, and a cord of steel wire was tied to each one. And all four cords were tied to a young woman.

She was spread-eagled on the slab, bound at the wrists and ankles and completely naked. A red dress and a pair of red heels were discarded nearby; the dress was torn, and Miguel thought it might have been ripped off. The woman was shivering, and her pale skin was turning red and yellow in spots on her fingers and toes. Silky black hair spilled around her head as if she had smashed her skull and her blood was seeping out black. Her perfect breasts heaved with her shuddering breaths, and even as he felt compelled to help her, struck by her obvious discomfort, Miguel found himself aroused. Shifting, uncomfortable and embarrassed, he almost advanced when movement caught his eye.

He had been so intent on the woman, her naked flesh bathed in torchlight, that he did not see either man until they moved. Near the girl's head was a man so gigantic he made Tony look small. His shaggy blond hair was disheveled, but Miguel didn't pay it much attention; the hungry, almost predatory gleam on his wild face was too terrifying. Miguel began to rethink his plan to go in and help the girl; there would be no getting past this guy unless they all rushed him together. But if he was going to hurt the girl, who looked like his prisoner . . .

Then the other man moved, and Miguel forgot any plan at all.

His black robe concealed all of him but his hands, which were gnarled and laced with bulging veins. His long, curving, glassy nails glimmered in the torchlight as he flexed his fingers, one by one. He was several inches shorter than the bigger guy and noticeably slimmer, but Miguel had no thought of fighting him, not even the faintest passing notion.

The hooded figure drifted forward, and the woman spoke.

"P-p-please," she said. Her face turned to look into the hood, lower lip managing an attractive pout even as it quivered. She didn't sound afraid, but the freezing cold was strangling her words. "M-m-my lord, p-p-please . . ."

"Shh." It wasn't a shush like any Miguel had ever heard; it was the hiss of an anaconda in the jungle foliage, a mocking exhalation as its prey shivered among the ferns below. Heidi trembled against his back. "A moment more, precious one, and it will all be over."

"M-m-my lord . . ." There was a hint of fear in the girl's voice now, and her face was uncertain.

"You leave everything behind," that maddening voice said. It was dry and breathy as a whisper, but it carried nonetheless. Miguel felt more powerless, more rooted to the spot, with every syllable. He knew that if he stood there long enough, listening to that voice, he would sink down to the ground and curl into a ball, lost in the horror.

He tugged on Sarah's shoulder, but before she could even start to turn, the hooded figure sank to its knees at the girl's side. It bent over her bound right wrist, and Miguel hesitated. Was he going to untie her after all? Was this some overdone BDSM game that even the dom had decided had gone too far?

His nails stroked the steel wire and brushed along the girl's forearm, tracing the lines of vessels that worked toward her elbow. The hood dipped into her elbow, then drifted toward her wrist. Perversely fascinated, still frozen in place, Miguel thought he must be kissing her.

Then the girl lurched, her back arching as much as the cords permitted. Her eyes stared straight upward, her mouth wide open and working soundlessly. Her expression could have been agony or ecstasy. But when the hood drew away, blood poured from the woman's wrist, and even as they watched, a droplet slipped from the darkness of the hood to splatter on the floor.

Heidi dragged in one breath, then another, each getting faster and harder. Miguel knew that if she screamed, they were all going to die. Turning, he clapped a hand over her mouth at the same time Tony wrapped his muscular arms around her tiny chest and squeezed, forcing the breath out of her. With her lips pressed to Miguel's hand, she made only a small huff. Her face was so stricken with terror that Miguel wasn't sure she had even noticed them holding her. Philip slumped to the ground from his window in a faint. Everywhere Miguel could see, his friends were glued to their windows with identical expressions of transfixed horror.

Still holding Heidi to him, Miguel looked back in time to see the robed man—no, no human had a voice like that, the *thing*—kneel down at the girl's leg. She looked dazed as the creature traced a hooked nail along the inside of her thigh. "Everything you are."

And he plunged the nail into her leg.

Someone lurched away from a window and vomited, but Miguel couldn't tear his eyes away to see who. His own stomach churned as he saw the finger dig down to the first knuckle, then withdraw with a spray of scarlet blood. The hood lowered to the wound, and the spatter of blood squirting onto the concrete was replaced with greedy slurping and swallowing.

Heidi tried to pull her head away from Miguel's hands, but he was so frozen that he locked her in place without trying. Tony leaned on the door at Sarah's side, his arm shaking, and Sarah's rapt expression was starting to decay. Her eyes were wide, manic in a way that frightened Miguel almost as much as what was happening in the chapel.

He looked back in time to see the figure lurch away from the girl. Her skin was turning waxy, and the front of the robe was splattered with blood. The creature ghosted to her head, and the hood tilted to gaze down on her. "You are in me," the hateful voice intoned, "as I am in you."

It began to chant in a language Miguel had never heard. The chant was dry and monotonous, but the shadows cast by the torchlight warped and shifted as if they had minds of their own. Miguel watched a wavering shadow turned into a dragon, which turned into a leering snake, which turned into a glaring eye, which turned into a fluttering locust, which became again a simple shadow.

In his arms, Heidi whimpered. She pressed against Miguel, and one of his feet slid in the snow to brace himself. Her hand rose, thumb still stuck through the hole in the cuff, and pointed. Miguel followed the gesture and his heart stopped.

Across the chapel was an old, weathered statue covered in spots with dead moss and the dark stains of age. Her face was in a nun's hood, and identical cracks stretched down from her eyes. Blood flowed into those cracks, dripping down her face and sliding onto her chiseled robe. Even as Miguel watched, the blood around one of the stone eyes surged and streamed down the cheek.

The chanting stopped, and Miguel saw Heidi's, Sarah's, and Tony's faces turn with his own back to the creature. It knelt at the woman's head and brushed a lock of her raven hair back with such gentleness that Miguel's heart twisted at the outrageousness of the lie. The gnarled hands brushed down her cheeks to cup her face, lifting her head up as if he meant to kiss her.

"Belong to me." The voice picked at the insides of Miguel's eyes and gnawed every vertebra in his spine. "Forever."

Then the long fingers tightened around her neck and the thumbs jabbed into her throat. Blood gushed around the wounds as the hands withdrew, and the young woman's naked body thrashed and writhed against her bonds. Her struggles were pitiful, and each convulsion was weaker than the last, each spurt of blood from her throat more of a gurgle. Her quivering body slumped to the concrete, and her raspy gasps faded into silence.

Miguel was dimly conscious of pain in his hand; Heidi's teeth had closed on his palm as she struggled to keep the scream locked behind them. Sarah stared still, but there was no rapture on her face now; her eyes were wide, as if she had just come out of a nightmare and discovered that what she had woken to was worse than what she had woken from. Tony staggered away from the door, heaving and trying to control his stomach. Miguel only gaped.

The big man stepped forward. "Master . . ."

One of the figure's bloodstained hands rose, two fingers elevated casually, and the blond man fell silent at once. "It is done. We will wait until she awakens," the voice announced. "And until then . . ."

And with a horror that clawed its way down his spine and chilled every nerve in his body to ice, Miguel watched the cowled face turn to the door.

"My rites are not yours to witness," the figure declared as it rose.

Miguel lurched back, dragging Heidi with him, a second before the doors burst open. One of them caught Sarah, still frozen on the threshold, in the forehead. She collapsed to the snow, and Miguel's brain struggled to process her suddenly deformed face and the sunken depression where the curve of her skull had been. Blood leaked from her ears as her lifeless eyes stared upward.

Tony turned, and one of the long-fingered hands caught him around the neck and jerked forward. There was a loud crack; Tony's entire body went limp, then slipped through the opening fingers to the ground.

The suddenness of it pinned Miguel in place, but his friends on both sides screamed and started to flee. The cowled figure turned to the large man. "Stop them!"

Then the figure was gone. Miguel's muscles unlocked, control returning to his paralyzed limbs, and he turned in response to new screaming on his left to see Jared's head lying on the ground, staring at Miguel; the rest of him was several feet away. The creature caught Philip as he was still getting to his feet and flung him back at the chapel. Philip hit the wall so hard that he left a trail of blood as he slid down it.

Rachel was running, but she tripped over a headstone and went down with a cry of pain. The hooded figure was on her in an instant, catching her by the neck and jerking her to her feet. She screamed, "Oh, God! Save me!"

The creature flinched back and gave a bestial snarl as if Rachel had slapped him. His fingers opened, and she slipped out of his grasp and ran. The doors banged open again, and Miguel looked in time to see the blond man barreling toward him, a knife in his enormous hand.

Then the hideous voice snarled, "Here, fool! Stop her!"

The heavily muscled killer changed course midstep, as if he had been pulled by the shirt front. Breaking into a flat-out run, sure-footed and faster than his bulk would have suggested, he caught Rachel in only a few seconds as she stumbled among the graves, the mist rising like a wall in front of her. The first stab came down between her neck and shoulder. The second went right into the side of her neck, and as she twitched, the man reached around and stabbed through the front of her chest so hard that Miguel saw the point of the knife burst out her back.

Pain flared in his foot as Heidi stomped on it. His arms sprang open and she bolted, running aimlessly. Her panic jolted Miguel into action, and he caught up to her in seconds.

"Heidi!" he said. She screamed and lurched away from him, and he grabbed her, turning her around and forcing her to look at him. He knew he had to get her out, and it stabilized his voice and broke through the fog of horror. "Heidi! We have to run. We have to get to the road."

She stared at him for a moment, then nodded, terrified beyond words. Taking her hand, Miguel dragged her away from the chapel. Screams echoed in the distance, each loud and frightened and very quickly silenced. He couldn't bear to put names and faces to those sounds, or the sheer terror of it would rip apart his thoughts and leave him helpless until the creature got around to them. He had to save Heidi. He had to keep Heidi safe. He was going to get her home to her parents and Brittany. He, Miguel, was going to get home to his mother and Diego and Xavier.

He recognized the bare yew a few yards away and ran that way, pulling Heidi along in his wake. The tree, the broken church monument . . . his mind raced through the landmarks backward, plotting the course, navigating to safety. They made it to the shadows under the tree with no sounds of pursuit.

Without warning, the branches seemed to come alive, bobbing and writhing in midair. Miguel cried out in panic, sure for one wild moment that they were going to grab him. But then it became obvious what had happened: the ravens had all taken flight at once, and the sudden absence of their weight had rattled the branches.

Then the ravens turned as a cloud of black and banked back down.

Miguel cried out again, this time in pain. Beaks snapped at his cheeks and his neck, gouging into his hands and digging through his jeans into his legs. He squeezed his hands into fists and shielded his eyes with his forearms. Beside him, Heidi shrieked in agony, then collapsed to her knees and sobbed as she hugged Miguel's leg.

"Make it stop!" she pleaded. "I want to go home!"

The wings buffeted him, slapping his face. Heidi shrieked again; one of the ravens had landed on her hood and was pecking at the back of her skull, flapping its wings. Past fear, numbed to anything but his desperation to escape, Miguel punched the bird, and it toppled off her. The flock swooped away, and Miguel wrenched Heidi to her feet before they came around for another pass.

"Come on!"

He tugged her across the snow, and every step ached. He felt the warm ooze of blood on his thighs, and his vision swam. The foggy shapes in the mist blurred, and his grip on Heidi's hand loosened. She, however, seized his fingers with desperate strength, and Miguel forced himself to struggle on. As they wound through the headstones, it occurred to him that only silence followed them now. No flapping wings, no pursuing footsteps, no screams, no pleas. Only his feet and Heidi's slipping and crushing through the snow, his breath and Heidi's in panicked, aching gasps.

Pulling Heidi past a mausoleum, he saw the towering iron gates of the cemetery. The fog swirled around them, but the street beyond looked clear. They burst into a sprint and Heidi pulled ahead, tugging on Miguel's hand as they raced for the road.

Ten feet away, the gates crashed closed with an echoing bang. Miguel ground to a despairing halt, but Heidi slipped through his fingers and smashed into the bars headfirst. She collapsed to the ground in a heap.

Miguel knelt at her side and shook her urgently, ignoring the blazing stitch in his lungs. "Heidi, wake up! Heidi, we have to go, you have to wake up!" Her hood slipped back, but her eyes stayed closed, and panic seized him. "Heidi, WAKE UP!"

Touching.

Miguel lurched to his feet, staring around him, trying to find the source of the sound in the still, silent graveyard. Then he sank back to his knees, clasped his head, and opened his mouth in a soundless scream as the voice spoke into his thoughts.

You weaken yourself, slow yourself, to save another from a terrible fate. Miguel clawed at his head and his fingernails widened the cuts left by the ravens as images flooded his mind. It was *his* strong, sure hands that caught Jared by the jaw and tore his head from his neck. His fist smashed Arianna so hard in the chest that it went straight through, showering shards of spine onto the ground. His face closed toward Cole's battered neck, toward the warm spot on Cole's throat . . .

"STOP!" he screamed.

Perhaps you might have escaped me, alone. Miguel saw this, too. He sat beneath the Christmas tree at home, hugging his little brothers, the three of them up in the morning to open presents with Mom right away so she could get to bed after a long shift. Helping his brothers put together the 3D puzzle he had bought for them. Going to sleep with the knowledge that his friends were dead, that everyone was dead, and—

"Please," he choked. "Please stop."

You might have escaped me, but you stayed for that little wretch, and now you will both be ours. How . . .

". . . pathetic."

Miguel forced his eyes open.

It towered over him, mist draping over its shoulders like the clasps of a cape. The long fingers were steepled, the curved nails clicking against one another. Fresh blood dripped from the cuffs and collar of the robe. No light penetrated the hood, but Miguel could imagine the sadistic smile.

Something bumped Miguel's foot. Behind him, Heidi was stirring, groaning in pain.

The sound acted on Miguel like a stimulant. Somewhere in his chest, his heart burned, and he said through gritted teeth, "You can't have her."

The cowl tilted to one side, and Miguel sensed the thing's amusement.

"You can't have her!" he roared, and threw himself at it, the muscles in his thin arms straining, fully prepared to rip the thing into pieces with his bare hands.

One clawed hand shot out to catch him by the face, and the darkness claimed him.

SIXTEEN

T HE CATHEDRAL'S bright lights gleamed on the gilded wooden beams of the ceiling, and the resinous smell of incense lingered in the air. The layered chords soaring from the Dutch organ above the main entrance reached out to every ear. With every pew filled and worshippers lining the walls, body heat warmed the packed space. Pine trees and poinsettias decorated the sanctuary, and blooms of red and white set off the granite and bronze of the altar.

Anita processed none of it.

At her side, Marion had the Gospel open in one hand, and was referencing it as the cardinal's homily went on. Her other hand held Anita's, though she could have stabbed Anita in the thigh with no more effect. Nancy Rothard sat on Marion's other side, holding her husband's hand with one of her own and patting it with her other, occasionally glancing down the pew at her daughter. The doctor himself never took his eyes off the red-capped figure at the pulpit, but the set of his jaw and the tightness in his eyes betrayed him.

On his other side, Tim Rothard looked absorbed, still holding the crucifix of his rosary in one hand.

Anita didn't notice any of that, either. She didn't see the white-and-gold-robed cardinal some twenty yards ahead, or the mass of people around her, or the lights or the decorations or the beauty of the architecture. When her eyes were open, she could only see the crucifix suspended above the altar. Carved from a single piece of wood, the figure of Christ hollowed out from the center of the cruciform shape, it dominated Anita's mind. She saw the shape in black, seared into pale flesh as if by a branding iron.

And when her eyes closed, she saw only reflective gray staring back at her, and long white fangs.

She was unaware of the sweat on her forehead and the flush in her neck and cheeks; despite the warmth of Marion on her one side and a stranger on her other, she hadn't taken off her winter coat. She stood a few seconds after everyone else, sat again when Marion pulled on her hand, and stared without seeing.

Every moment she dwelled on the memory, and every moment it seemed harder to believe than the last. The smoke curling off Simon's hand, the fangs where Simon's canine teeth should have been, the desperate plea in his eyes for her silence, for her complicity in the secret of what he really was . . .

Anita jumped and lurched away from a sudden pressure on her arm, a strangled sort of gasp in her throat.

Marion stared at her, drawing her hand back in surprise. It dawned on Anita that the rest of her family members were on their feet, and the rows ahead of her were already empty as everyone filed toward the front of the church.

"Time for Communion, Anita," Marion whispered in a worried tone as she took in Anita's vacant expression.

Anita got to her feet, hands clasped in front of her, and trailed behind Marion. She tried to focus so she wouldn't walk into anyone, but the crucifix suspended in midair over the altar kept intruding into her thoughts.

"The Body of Christ."

With a start, Anita realized she had made it to the head of the line. The priest held the little circle up. Anita started to extend her hands, then looked back up at the wafer and shivered. She had been taking Communion since she was a little girl, even after she had ceased to believe it was anything more than a piece of bread. It had always made her a little uncomfortable, like she was disrespecting actual Catholics by playing along. But it had never been worth the fight with her parents when she got home.

But as she looked past the priest's confused stare, past the wafer, to the crucifix overhead, she saw again the black burn in Simon's hand and wondered. If Simon could really be what Anita was dreading, then the little circle in the priest's hand . . .

"The Body of Christ," the priest repeated, and despite the heat of the cathedral, Anita trembled. To one side, the cardinal had paused in the act of distributing his own Hosts to stare at her, and someone behind her in line cleared his throat. Anita pulled her hands back, crossed them over her chest, and walked shakily away before the priest could respond. She wondered again what would happen if she held her little cross out in Simon's face. She wondered how his pale skin would react to touching the Host. Would it burn a black circle instead of a cross? Shambling back into the pew, she stumbled over a kneeler someone had left down, but managed to catch herself on the back of the bench in front of her before half-falling into a kneeling position beside Marion.

She tried to distract herself with people watching as parishioners filed back to their seats, but she saw the wrong things. A heavy woman wore a cross between her breasts; it was simple wood, but it still reminded Anita of the cross in her own pocket. A girl who looked to be fifteen or sixteen had hair the same flat black as Simon's. A toddler gave a sudden, loud squeal that made Anita think of her own scream of horror, and when the father pressed his hand over the boy's mouth and whispered something, Anita felt Simon's icy flesh against her lips and his harsh, desperate voice in her ear.

"Let us pray."

Anita got to her feet and tried to focus on the cardinal's voice, but the words went in one ear and out the other. Before she knew it, the choir erupted into "Joy to the World." Anita had always liked the carol, but she was having trouble making her mouth frame the words. She sang a few bars tunelessly, then gave up and just bowed her head and stared at the wood of the pew in front of her.

Eventually, the last notes of the carol faded and the attendees broke into applause. As the others pulled on their coats and started into the aisle, Anita looked back toward the front of the church, then blurted out, "Do you mind if I stay for a minute?"

Both of her parents looked at her, then each other. Her mother asked, "What's wrong, sweetheart?"

"Nothing. I just wanna . . . um . . . pray for a minute."

Their surprise was obvious, but Anita knew they would not object.

"You want me to wait with you?" Marion asked.

Anita shook her head and tried for a smile; her lips mangled the expression. "No, it's okay, I remember where we parked. I'll be right there."

Marion still looked hesitant, but Dr. Rothard said in a gentle voice she hadn't expected, "It'll be a while before we can pull out anyway. Take your time."

Anita watched them go, then worked her way down the center aisle against the flow of traffic. She stood under the hanging crucifix, trying to find the words for her dilemma. She couldn't find it in herself to wonder if it had really happened; though every thought of it made her shiver, she was sure that the incident was real. Was Simon a monster? He definitely wasn't normal, not human. And the cross had burned his hand, but Anita didn't know whether it had been the cross itself or the sterling silver it was made of. Neither really struck her as than the other.

A sudden and vivid memory fought its way to the surface, an image she had suppressed—Simon standing over a gasping, dying man, strangling him to death with a metal chain. Anita remembered her own pleas for Simon to stop, and the animal rage in his eyes before he had obeyed. It hadn't been adrenaline or even hate, she realized, but a slip in the illusion of humanity.

Who could she tell, though? How could she ever prove this? She doubted Simon was going to hold the cross again in front of other people to confirm her story.

Anita wandered to one side of the cathedral, to a small shrine set into the wall. If there was no way to prove it . . . what if she didn't tell anyone? Would Simon hurt her? He'd been alone with her half a dozen times before and never harmed her; he'd even interceded to protect her against others. The way he had held her, the way he had kissed her . . . the horror in the hedge maze tainted her memories, but Anita couldn't forget them. Simon had passed on every chance to hurt her when she'd had no reason to suspect him; would her knowing the truth change that?

He had promised to explain, to answer her questions. Was that just buying time, trying to shut her up long enough to make an escape? Or was he going to tell her the truth?

And if he did, did she want to hear it?

"Excuse me."

Anita jumped, and when she whirled around with wide eyes, the young priest jumped too. He raised one hand, palm out. "I'm sorry, miss, I didn't mean to startle you. We'll be closing the cathedral in just a few minutes . . ."

With a shock, Anita noticed the church was almost empty. Her family would be looking for her soon. "Oh, sorry."

"No, it's all right," the priest replied with a kind smile. "I'm sorry if I disturbed you while you were praying . . ."

"No. No, I'm good," Anita said. She glanced around and head-ed toward the nearest door. "Bye."

"Merry Christmas!" he called after her.

"Yeah, you too," Anita said, though she wasn't sure he heard her. She stepped out into the cold night, the frigid air stinging her warm cheeks, and found herself in the little alley between streets. Before her was a small, snow-covered garden with a white statue that seemed to blend into the ground. To her left, she saw the glow of light from the front of the cathedral and the parking lot beyond. Starting that way, she stuck her gloved hands in her pockets.

After a few steps, the ground swirled in front of her. At first, she thought a gust of wind had caught the snow piled on both sides of the icy alley, but as it billowed, she realized it was fog. As she looked around for a manhole that might be emitting hot air, the fog thickened, coalescing into a wall in front of her that blocked out the light from the street and muffled the sounds of the cardinal greeting his flock.

Anita came to an uneasy stop. It would take a long time to go all the way back through the cathedral, but something about the fog made her uncomfortable.

Stop it. She gritted her chattering teeth. Her nerves were frayed almost to their breaking points, and she was jumping at shadows. The new reality she was trying to wrap her mind around was bad enough without adding in the environment. She closed her eyes and took two deep breaths, trying not to see the burned cross shape in her mind's eye.

When she opened her eyes again, the mist was giving birth to a man, Anita was suddenly far beyond fear. White tendrils of mist peeled back off the man's shoulders, as if he was still pulling free of trailing vines. As Anita stared, speechless with shock, the man turned his eyes on her—emerald eyes, far too bright in the alley's gloom—and smiled a wicked smile.

Anita turned and ran. She had no thought of direction or destination; she just bolted back the way she had come, arms and legs pumping as she sprinted. One foot slid on the ice, and she toppled to her knees. Pain registered through her thin dress pants, and there was a rush of cold air over her head. Struggling to her feet, Anita launched herself toward the opposite end of the alley even as fog rose that way too, obscuring the lights of the parking garage across the street.

The green-eyed man strolled nonchalantly out of a side alley in front of her.

"H-How . . ." Anita stammered, looking behind her into the thick fog. When she looked back a split second later, the man was only a few yards away, now leaning on the wall opposite the cathedral. "You were just . . . how did you . . ."

"The dead travel fast." His voice had an air of amusement, but she still shuddered when he spoke. He smiled at her as he shifted his weight off the wall, and for the first time she saw his long fangs.

Every horrifying thought and dark reflection Anita had endured in the last two hours flooded her mind, and she backed away into the garden, bouncing off the statue. Her pursuer kept pace, but as her back pressed up against the bricks of the school building behind her, he closed the distance.

"Are you going to drink my blood?" Anita blurted out. It was the only thing she could think to say, and her hands clapped down on the scarf on her neck.

He stopped barely more than an arm's length away, his expression somewhere between amusement and annoyance. "You did connect the dots, then." His voice sounded peeved, and he shook his head. "'Don't expose yourself to humans,' I said. 'They'll figure you out,' I said. Does he listen to me? Of course not. Idiot."

As he grumbled aloud, Anita remembered the silver cross still in her pocket. She scrambled for it, but her gloves slipped on her pants, and his sharp emerald eyes caught the movement. He took the last step and, faster than she could see, his right hand had her by the neck.

"No, I'm not here because I'm thirsty," he told her. Terrified, she looked up into his reflective green eyes. His rank breath filled her nose and turned her stomach. His face was handsome, in a rough way, but the gleam of those eyes and the sharp fangs consumed every other thought. "You just happen to know too much for my peace of mind."

He gestured back toward the alley with his free hand and clicked his tongue at her. "You should've been more careful," he whispered. "Icy out here. You could fall and break your neck."

He started to squeeze her throat. Anita struck his arm, but she could already feel the pressure building in her face and her head getting light as his grip crushed on her throat and the arteries in her neck . . .

He paused, eyes narrowed, mouth open slightly and head tilted away from her. Anita continued to slap ineffectually at his arm, but the man paid her no attention at all. His expression was one of intense concentration, as if he was listening hard. Suddenly, his eyes widened, and in another flash of movement Anita's eyes couldn't follow, his right hand vanished under his long cloth coat while his left pinned her against the wall. His right hand started back out of his coat, clenched around the hilt of what looked like a sword. An instant later, the dull scrape of metal from the half-drawn blade registered in her ears.

But by then he had frozen, staring straight ahead at Anita's forehead. There was a glimmer of metal at his neck, and Anita slowly realized it was the blade of what looked like a crooked machete that ended in a handle clenched in a pale hand.

"Let her go, Salem, or so help me I will kill you right here."

Since the terrifying moment in the garden, Anita had remembered Simon's voice with shudders and instinctive fear. His harsh whispers had plagued her thoughts during Mass and poisoned every memory she had of him with double meanings and unspeakable alternate interpretations. But now, pinned by this thing that meant to kill her, Anita felt a surge of comfort and safety that left her stunned. She didn't dare to speak.

The man holding her continued to stare straight ahead, and only his lips moved. "Hello, Simon," he said, annoyed again, as if he was reciting lines. "How are you?"

Simon's voice came back cold and hard. "Better than you're going to be if you don't let her go."

Salem rolled his eyes, but kept his head still. Looking at the gleaming blade at his throat, Anita didn't blame him. "She knows, Simon."

Anita could see the top of Simon's head behind Salem's. "It's my problem to deal with."

She was a *problem*. The idea of Simon *dealing with* her made Anita shiver in Salem's grip. He glanced at her, then sideways, trying to see over his shoulder without turning his head. "You could've dealt with her in the maze, but you didn't."

Anita's eyes widened. "You were spying on us?"

Salem's hand closed on her neck, constricting her windpipe. As she gasped, he reproved, "Quiet, Breakfast. The immortals are talking."

Anita choked for just a moment before Simon's blade moved, pressing against the side of Salem's neck. Salem grimaced and leaned away from the blade, but he relaxed his grip on Anita's neck to what it had been. She dragged in a quick, grateful breath.

"Let her go," Simon repeated.

Salem growled. "Humans don't get to know about us, Simon. Do you not remember me telling you that?"

Anita shuddered as Salem's sharp thumbnail brushed her neck, but Simon pressed his blade so hard Salem leaned away from it, and said in a tone of frightening hatred, "Not this time."

Summoning all her courage, Anita volunteered, "I'm not going to tell anyone."

Her voice came out as a whisper, but it was obvious they had both heard her. Salem gave her a scathing look. "How very believable."

Simon edged sideways so he could peer around the back of Salem's head. Anita could only see one steel gray eye, but saw a mix of emotions in what was visible of his expression. With a sudden rush of confidence, she said more forcefully, "I don't care about you, but I don't want to get Simon hurt."

She was still afraid of him, and still afraid to hear him answer all her questions. But with him here, his presence keeping her safe and giving her strength, she found the words were true.

"Other than burning a cross into his hand," Salem put in dryly. "And how is this in any way good for me? I release her, and off she goes, and here I still am with a knife at my throat."

"If you let her go, then I'll let you go," Simon promised.

Salem laughed, smiling with his teeth and showing his fangs. "Her lie was more convincing."

"Call it a fair trade," Simon said. "You let me go two weeks ago. We'll be even."

While Salem considered this with a frown, Anita thought over Simon's words. "That was you?" she snapped at Salem. "You're the one who hurt him?"

"Anita," Simon cautioned her.

Salem raised an eyebrow. "Protective, aren't we?" Then his eyes narrowed, and he searched her face for a moment before glancing down at Simon's hand and the knife handle in it. Anita saw the slight dimple in the side of his neck widen against the knife edge with his sharp intake of breath. "Simon!"

"Salem . . ."

"You did it again, didn't you? I thought you would've learned your lesson—"

He fell silent as Simon drew the knife tighter, and a thin trail of blood leaked from the side of Salem's neck. The look on what Anita could see of Simon's face was ferocious, but Salem just bared his teeth and squeezed Anita's throat again. She choked, pulling uselessly on Salem's hand. After a second, Simon's moved the knife, and Salem relaxed his grip again.

"Let her go." Simon's voice was a dangerous growl, and Anita shivered.

"Even if I let your little pet human go," Salem spat back, "that still leaves me with a knife at my throat!"

"You aren't really in a position to negotiate," Simon snapped.

Salem grimaced in frustration. "If you're wrong about her, we'll both be in incredible danger."

"If you don't have a head, you won't have to worry about it."

Salem sneered, but his eyes tightened thoughtfully. He studied Anita in an interminable silence, and she tried to meet his eyes without fear. She wanted to say something to reassure Salem or stand up for Simon, but the words wouldn't come.

Salem sighed, shaking his head.

"Mark my words, boy, this won't end well," he promised. But he opened his hand, and the pressure on Anita's neck disappeared. Her legs were jelly, and she slid down the wall.

"Anita, run!" Simon snapped. He hadn't moved an inch, still keeping Salem at bay with the knife.

Leaning on the wall for support, Anita pushed herself back up to a standing position. Salem lowered his arm slowly until it was out of her way. She saw his other hand clenching his sword hilt so tightly that his pale knuckles had turned almost pure white. A very different kind of panic gripped her; what was she leaving Simon to face? He had a tiger by the tail, and when he let go . . .

What could she do? She still had the cross in her pocket. Could she keep one of them at bay, but not the other? Could she help Simon at all, or would he just be forced to rescue her again?

"Anita!"

His voice cut through her indecision. "Simon . . . I . . ."

"Run! Now!"

She staggered away a few steps, galvanized by the undisguised desperation in his voice. From the side, she saw him behind Salem, holding the shorter man by the back of his collar. Simon turned his face toward hers, and Anita was sure the grim, brutal, hopeless determination in his expression was going to haunt her as much as the memory of the burn on his hand. As she gazed at him, he nodded once, then looked toward the alleyway.

Swallowing hard, Anita turned and ran into the mist, fighting back a sob.

SIMON LISTENED to her footfalls fade away, following her heartbeat until it was lost amid the others near the cathedral entrance. He tried to focus on the sound—a pleasant last thought. Then he took a deep breath, pulled the knife away from Salem's throat, and stepped back.

Salem turned, and there was no mistaking the fury on his face. His hand was still on his gladius; Simon looked at it, then sighed and slid his kukri knife into its sheath, now fastened to his belt.

Salem raised his eyebrows. "After all that, you just give up?"

Simon looked back at him. "You beat me two weeks ago and you didn't have the sword. What would be the point? You let her go, and I let you go. Now you're going to kill me, or you're not. What's it going to be?"

Salem appraised him, as if contemplating that very question, then took his hand off the sword to point skyward. Strafing so he could look while keeping Salem in his peripheral vision, Simon saw a high-rise a block away, towering over Holy Name's roof.

"Let's talk somewhere more . . . comfortable, shall we?" Salem glanced at the cathedral next to them with distaste.

Simon frowned, but nodded. Seizing the ready-made excuse to put space between himself and Salem, Simon took a running jump onto the roof of the school building, then shifted and flapped his leathery bat wings until he was airborne. He considered fleeing before Salem realized he was gone, but the elder vampire obviously knew where Anita lived; if Simon didn't placate him now, she would still be in danger.

Giving the cathedral a wide berth, he circled around the block and came at the high-rise from the north. Rather than exhaust himself against the wind, he landed on the lowest of the building's tiered roofs and reverted to human form. Taking a moment to spot the few lights that were still on, Simon picked a piece of wall surrounded by dark windows and climbed up by hand.

Salem was waiting for him on the highest roof, looking out toward Lake Michigan with his sword in his hand. Simon hesitated by the edge of the building, but Salem turned to smirk at him and sheathed the weapon again. "Not for you," he promised. "I just got bored waiting."

Approaching slowly, Simon asked, "What do you want?"

"Many things," Salem said cheerfully, "and not all of them are healthy for you. Fortunately for you, there's only one thing I need."

"And that is?"

Salem sneered, though Simon didn't think Salem was sneering at him. "An old acquaintance of mine has dropped into town for a visit. We're having an . . . unpleasant difference of opinion."

Simon frowned. "What's the difference?"

"His opinion is that I should be dead. As you might expect, I disagree."

Simon glowered. "So far I'm on his side."

"That's because you haven't met him, and you're an ungrateful simpleton with no appreciation of the context. But that's beside the point."

"And what is the context?"

"Eh, don't worry about it," Salem said with a dismissive wave Simon distrusted at once. "One of us is going to die, and I've decided it needs to be him. I want you to contribute to the cause."

Simon rolled his eyes. "Why don't you just kill him?" When Salem hesitated uncharacteristically, the younger vampire's gray eyes widened. "You can't beat him alone? *You* can't beat him?"

"It's not so much—"

"You need my help?"

Salem gritted his teeth and forced out, "Something like that."

Simon stared for a moment. "What am I going to do that you can't?"

"Oh, I'm sure I'll find a use for you."

Simon didn't doubt that, and he was sure he wouldn't like whatever plan Salem came up with. "Why should I help you? What are you to me now?"

Even as he spat the words, part of him flinched inside. But he thought of Anita in Salem's powerful hand, and his eyes hardened.

Salem looked incensed. "I let you live!"

"As I did you."

"Because I didn't kill your little girlfriend!" Salem snarled. He winced, apparently at his own word choice, then glared at Simon. "Tell me you're not, Simon. Tell me I misread you both and she's just a long, unreasonably drawn-out dinner plan."

Simon bared his fangs. "We're not talking about her. Why should I help you?"

"Because of your pet human," Salem said coldly. When Simon narrowed his eyes, the other vampire added, "Because you don't want me to stray across her path some night you aren't around."

Simon snarled, the sound ripping up his throat. His hand twitched toward the kukri knife on his belt, but Salem just smiled. "Give it a try, if you want."

Slowly, Simon mastered his temper, though he looked at Salem with loathing. "If I help you, you have to leave Anita alone."

"Yes, yes."

"Not just until I do whatever it is you want me to do," Simon insisted. Summoning his courage, he took a step forward. "Forever. You never lay a hand on her, no matter what she knows."

Salem rolled his eyes. "And if she decides she can't abide there being vampires in the world? Are you going to deal with it?"

"I'm not going to lie down and die for anyone," Simon responded, choosing his words carefully. "But you leave her alone. That's the price of my help, take it or leave it."

He put as much iron into his words as he could manage, even though he knew his position was pitifully weak. He had spent the element of surprise, and no power he now possessed would stop Salem if his former teacher wanted Anita to die. Nor was he at all convinced that Salem really needed his help. But under the circumstances, bravado was better than nothing.

Salem grimaced, but nodded. "Agreed. You do what I need you to do, and I leave your pet human to you. You have my word."

"All right. What do you want?"

Salem frowned, striding to the edge of the roof. Controlling a sudden urge to push him off, Simon joined him instead, though he left several feet between them.

"I still need to come up with the best plan of attack," Salem admitted in a thoughtful tone. "I'll let you know when I've figured it out."

"How?" Simon asked. "Including tonight, I've seen you twice in five years."

Salem smirked. "I'll drop by your apartment and knock on your door; how does that sound?"

Simon's eyes widened, and Salem laughed. It explained how Salem had tracked him to Anita's house, although that did not make it any more comfortable. "Maybe I'll move."

Salem shrugged. "Maybe you will. I'll look you up at your girlfriend's place instead."

Simon stiffened, and Salem snickered again. Sauntering over, ignoring Simon's tension at his approach, he clapped the taller vampire on the shoulder. "Isn't it wonderful being together again?"

"Delightful," Simon said through gritted teeth.

Salem grinned. Simon had just enough time to register the sudden force against his arm before he was falling through the air, plummeting toward the ground forty-nine stories below. Forcing himself to focus, he shifted, and his leathery bat wings caught a breeze. Riding it back up, he fixed his tiny eyes on the rooftop, but Salem was already gone.

THE HEADLESS torso dribbled blood down the back of Hans's shirt; draped over his shoulder, gravity was draining it like a fowl hung to dry. The ravens had pecked at the decapitated head before he had picked it up, and he thought his thumb might be brushing up against a hole they had started to bore in the flesh of the scalp. But Hans's face was calm and collected. He vaguely recalled a time when the grisly task might have unsettled him, but that seemed far away, like remembering something he had seen in a movie—not the foggy shadows of *before*, but a weaker, lesser time in his service.

The mausoleum door hung open, still loose on its hinges after the Master and Flavius had nearly battered it to splinters. Hans ducked into the cramped space and shrugged his shoulder to pitch the headless corpse onto the pile of its dead friends. Tossing the head into the corner, he turned and fitted the door back into its frame. The lock was shattered, but he managed to wedge the latch into the jamb.

The graveyard was quiet as Hans headed back toward the chapel. The ravens still flapped from spot to spot, snatching up entrails he had missed or discarded, and a coyote had found its way in too, investigating a smear of red in the disturbed snow. Watching it feed for a moment, Hans slowed his pace, and one hand drifted to the back of his belt. Drawing out the knife, he saw with disappointment that the blood on it had frozen already. What would it taste like when he was like the Master? When it warmed his throat and sang through his veins, giving him so much strength, so much life . . .

He cringed away from the blade, stuffing it out of sight. That kind of thinking never pleased the Master—focusing as it did on himself instead of his duty. The day of eternal reward would come; he must be patient. He hurried into the chapel.

The hooded figure stood over its dark altar, hands palm to palm. The torches still burned in their barbed wire brackets, and blood still dripped from the Master's sleeves. The Master's arms were no more visible than his face; the shadows in the sleeves seemed woven of the same darkness as the cowl. The hooded figure did not stir as Hans entered and gazed down at the slab.

Christine's eyes had fluttered closed in her last seconds, and the blood was frozen around her throat where it had pooled. Hans slunk to the Master's side, head bowed so low that it was beneath the vampire's. However, he could not take his eyes from Christine's naked form, and he swallowed roughly. Death had not warped her beauty the way it had on those bodies he had just concealed, even though they were still warm. They bore horror in their faces and mutilating wounds on their corpses, while every inch of Christine's porcelain skin seemed more inviting than ever.

At last, nothing was hidden from him; she could hide behind none of her coy secrecy now. Hans remembered her deliberate flirtations, her intentional taunting every night he had attended to her needs. His face contorted with vindictive pleasure as his eyes plundered her. But as he relished the soft curves of her legs, his palms chafing against his thighs, his mind was brought up short.

Frosted blood on the concrete left no doubt where the Master had pierced her thigh, but her creamy flesh was undamaged and almost snow white. Curious, Hans looked past the Master and saw the young woman's arm, unblemished as well. Her elegant throat was intact, and every second he watched, her face grew lovelier.

His breath quickened, and his enormous body trembled. Her beauty was painful, her voluptuous perfection too much. He knew she was dead, but she was still so desirable . . . perhaps the Master wouldn't mind, if he was quick and—

"The rites were as they should be," the Master's voice mused into the silence. Hans's eyes shifted to the cowl. "The time draws near."

Hans welcomed the chance to look back down at her. Struggling to keep his voice purely deferential, he asked, "How long will it be, Master?"

Whispery and guttural at once, the voice hissed back, "Let us find out."

Hans registered the rush of wind across his face and the pain in his knees as they hit the ground beside the altar at the same time he found his forearm in the vampire's long-fingered grip. The Master jerked him forward, and Hans threw out his other hand to catch himself. It slid across Christine's cold flesh before he planted it on the slab. The touch of her skin was electric, and Hans could not stifle the moan of desire that broke through his lips. Held out over her, every part of her so close he could reach it with his lips or tongue if he but bent his face down, it didn't even register in him that her body was barely warmer than the slab.

"Wake, little one," the Master's voice oozed, and his free hand curled down to brush a lock of Christine's shiny black hair out of her face. "Wake, and take the first offering of what will be yours. Wake."

The hand drifted up to Han's forearm and tore his lower sleeve off with an effortless tug of three fingers. The hooked nails brushed the inside of his wrist, and, with a casual flick, split the skin.

Richtein winced and grunted against the pain, pulling instinctively against the icy grip before he calmed himself. He watched his own blood drip onto the dead girl's ruby lips, splattering on her chin; one drop slid up her canted lip into her nose. The sight of his own blood spilling had become so routine that it did not hold his interest, so his eyes began to drift, exploring her body, and his planted hand slid closer to deepen his exploration.

But even his absorption in this most desirable of prizes could not deafen him to the twin metallic snaps, as loud as gunfire. The restraining grip on his arm was suddenly crushing, and the pain in his wrist flared. Gasping, he twisted and found her clamping his bleeding arm to her lips, her teeth cutting into his skin, working the blood free. The broken steel wires trailed from her wrists.

The Master freed him, stepping back to observe, and Hans lurched forward, tugging on his own arm. With nothing to lean on, he sprawled across her, but the collapse of his bulk on her svelte frame did not seem to bother her at all. The greedy slurping rang in his ears, and Hans had no room in his mind to be aware of being pressed up against her; the fear was too great.

"Master!" he pleaded, but the Master did not stir, features hidden in his hood as he gazed down.

Hans threw himself face-to-face with Christine, intending to muscle himself free, but her eyes paralyzed him. They were wild with hunger, ferocious in their savagery, reflective and cruel. The gleaming blue was still the most beautiful thing he had ever seen; lust and loathing warred in him, but her eyes swallowed him whole. He dared not even blink, lest this vision of perfection be taken from him. He gazed at her, enraptured, even as the chill seeped through his body and a gentle, comforting fatigue settled on his powerful limbs.

"Enough, Christine," the Master's papery voice commanded.

Her fangs sank into his wrist deeper, locking him in place.

"Enough!" the Master repeated, and he moved in a blur. One hand clapped onto her forehead at the same time the other tore Hans's arm from her grip. Her nails dug furrows into his flesh as it was ripped away from her. Her arms stretched out for him as she snapped her teeth at the Master, and Hans felt an urge to go to her. More than an urge; a need, a yearning. Those arms were reaching for him, and the Master was denying her! What kind of monster was he?

Hans leaned toward her, desperate compassion on every line of his face, but the Master made a flicking gesture and Hans soared across the room, landing hard against one pillar. Cradling his aching arm and pressing hard on the wound to stanch the blood flow, Hans watched as Christine bucked her legs and ripped herself free from the other wires.

She twisted out from under the Master's hand; it had been holding her down with so much force that his palm smashed into the stone and gouged a chunk out of it. Christine sprang to her bare feet, lips smeared with blood, open murder on her livid face. She launched herself forward at Hans, but the Master caught her by the hair and hurled her into the opposite wall. She smashed into the stone so hard it cracked into shards behind her.

Dropping to her hands and the balls of her feet, stunned but still alert, Christine hissed. Blood sprayed in a mist from her lips. The Master towered over her, and his voice echoed in the enclosed space as he snarled, "Stop."

Christine hesitated, her jaw clenched, her entire body trembling.

"Not yet, precious one," the Master crooned, even as he raised a clawed hand toward her. "Its life still has use to us."

Christine snarled at him.

"Yes," the sibilant voice agreed. "But other blood is prepared for you."

The smooth, pale face turned to one side, the reflective blue eyes studying the Master skeptically from their corners. The vampire lord ghosted back to Hans's side.

"Awakened in so little time, and already her mind begins to return." The fiendish pleasure was obvious in his rasping voice.

Cold was stealing through Hans's body, and his teeth chattered, but he managed to force out, "W-w-well done, M-M-Master."

"Of course it was," the voice replied. One veiny hand gestured toward Hans, though the cowl did not turn his way. "Bind that before it becomes problematic."

As Hans took gauze wrap from his pocket and started to wrap his bleeding wrist, the Master crossed the room to Christine. He extended one hand, and she cautiously placed one of hers in it and stood. Hans stopped in mid-wrap, ogling her glorious perfection before remembering that the Master had commanded him to tend to his wound. He focused on the already bloodstained bandage to keep his eyes away from temptation.

"Soon you will be everything you were and more, child," the Master's voice reassured her. "Perfection. And then we shall go visit Anita."

Christine hissed.

"And Simon."

She snarled, and Hans shivered.

"Are you not finished?" the voice demanded, and its abrupt chill told Hans the Master was speaking to him again. He looked up, and the two figures loomed over him. Christine's chest heaved with her panting breaths as she gazed at his injured hand, and that sight kept Hans's eyes for a second. But the stare within the hooded cowl bored down into him, and he wrenched his eyes away.

"Finishing, my lord," he promised, tucking the end of the gauze wrap into its folds.

"Then come," the Master commanded, turning away. Christine hissed down at him, but reluctantly followed. "You must prepare my perfect one's bed while she takes her first meal. They are restrained?"

"Yes, Master."

The cowl dipped in a nod, and the two vampires disappeared across the chapel. Hans winced as he flexed his injured hand, then stood, leaning against the pillar as disorientation churned his stomach and fogged his mind. As he fought for control, his eyes fell on the statue of Saint Brigid. He studied the bloody tear tracks with growing unease, some nameless discomfort writhing within him. The sight stirred forgotten memories: whispered bedtime prayers, the German words of a chaplain in a desert encampment, the sound of bells . . . memories of *before* . . .

What was he doing? What had he done? He touched his un-injured hand to his forehead, and then to his heart, and his fingers drifted toward one shoulder . . .

"Come!" the voice insisted.

Hans blinked away the distracting thoughts, gave the statue a last glance, and hurried to attend the Master.

SEVENTEEN

CHRISTMAS MORNING was a subdued affair in the Rothard house. Exhaustion dragged at Anita; she had a distinct memory of the eastern sky pinkening out her window before she drifted off to an uneasy sleep. They pried her out of bed a few hours later for presents, but even sleep-deprived, Anita saw the lingering concern in their eyes. She picked at her French toast, spearing a bite with her fork and drawing shapes in the syrup.

Had someone asked her during Mass whether she could have been more afraid, she would have given a shaky, unstable laugh. Now, as much as she was still afraid of Simon, she was also afraid *for* Simon. That hopeless look on his face terrified her. The cowardice of leaving him to fend for himself after he had saved her life gnawed at her heart. But what could she have done? Then again, wasn't doing something better than doing nothing? The arguments fenced back and forth in her head.

She tried to focus when they moved into the great room for gifts. Marion's brothers were out of town, so she had joined the Rothards for Christmas morning, too. Continuing a ten-year tradition, Anita had bought Marion a novel in English and Marion had bought her one in Spanish—along with a box of Legos. Anita managed a laugh at that. Clothes and new books from her parents, a new silver and ruby rosary and a violet and cyan top from her uncle . . .

"It's a Spanish design, from one of the best marketplaces in Toledo," Tim Rothard said when Anita's father balked at the ruffled sleeves, the low-cut neckline, and the dozens of tassels dangling over the midriff. There were also a few gift cards and some pieces of candy in her stocking. She tried to smile when they liked her gifts, and curled up in their midst without complaint for a family picture.

"Smile, Anita," her mother reminded her.

Stealing away at the first opportunity, Anita lay down on her bed and tried to think. As much as it pained her, she could do nothing for Simon now. She had to believe he'd made it out, that he was just overreacting, that his nerves had been so frayed by concern for her that his face hadn't gotten over that worry . . . that his fear wasn't for himself . . .

But if Simon had survived—no, *since* Simon had survived—he would probably be coming to see her. Rolling onto her side to stare out the window at the lake, Anita tried to reassure herself that this was good; he had promised her an explanation, after all. And if he came with explanations, he probably wasn't coming to hurt her.

It's my problem to deal with. Were they just words to get her out of the taunting vampire's grip, or was there a real threat in Simon, too? She remembered the cold hand pressed against her mouth to smother her scream . . .

Well, at least I've got until sunset to think . . . At that, she let out a giggle that sounded hysterical even to her ears. Or did she? She had seen him in the daylight . . .

"Anita?"

She rolled over to face the door at the sound of her mother's voice. Nancy Rothard leaned on the doorframe. "Are you feeling okay, sweetheart?"

"Not really," Anita admitted.

"Is it about last night?"

Anita's eyes widened before she realized what her mother was talking about. Nancy nodded while Anita was still grasping for a response and took a seat at the foot of the bed, patting her daughter's leg. "I know your father embarrassed you last night, and I think he feels bad about it."

"I . . ." Anita struggled to focus. "It's fine. He doesn't need to worry about it. If Simon hadn't come . . ."

I wouldn't have found out he was a monster. A monster wouldn't have tried to snap my neck in an alley. I wouldn't have left Simon to die for me . . .

She shivered, her breath hitching in her throat, and before she could control it she was leaning on her mother's shoulder and crying. Nancy stroked her hair and patted her shoulder.

"It's okay, sweetie," she said. "Ask next time, but don't worry about it now."

"It's not that," Anita managed to get out.

"Your father?" Nancy guessed, and Anita didn't know how to deny it while keeping the secret. "We'll talk. But I hope you'll talk to him too. If you both hear each other out, maybe—"

"Yeah," Anita interrupted, sitting up and wiping her eyes. "Yeah, I'll see what . . . I'll talk to him. Do you mind if I take a nap now?"

"Are you feeling sick, honey? You look tired."

"Exhausted, nauseous . . ." She didn't even have to lie.

"Do you want me to have your dad come look at you?"

Anita forced herself to grin. "I don't think I need brain surgery, Mom. It's probably just a twenty-four hour thing."

Nancy stood, frowning. "Well, see if a nap helps. I'll check on you later."

When she was gone, Anita closed the door, dropped the curtains, and lay in the dark for hours. Sleep didn't come, though she rolled onto her side and feigned it when Marion checked on her for a late lunch. Her breathing gradually slowed, and she forced some measure of calm on herself. Much as the idea of hearing the truth frightened her, she knew she needed to pass that hurdle if she was ever to recover any peace of mind.

As the curtains darkened and threw the room into shadow, Anita sat up. She looked through her jewelry box until she found a simple white rosary, a gift for her First Communion. The silver cross from her uncle was prettier, but Anita couldn't stand the memory of burning Simon. Then again, why take out the rosary at all unless she didn't trust Simon not to . . .

She winced. Simon had saved her, even put himself in danger to do it. Simon, who had fangs and incredible strength and the ability to bring down five grown men. After a moment of indecision, Anita put the rosary around her neck and tucked the crucifix into her shirt. *Just in case.* She tried not think about what it was in case of.

There was a knock on the balcony door.

MIGUEL LISTENED a moment more to the sound of metal scraping on stone in the darkness, to the hisses and moans sliding through gritted teeth, before he said in a low voice of forced calm, "Frank, stop before you hurt yourself."

"We can't stop!" Frank snapped back, his voice bordering on hysteria. "We have to get away, Miguel! We can't stay here until those . . . those things . . ."

A sob strangled the rest of the sentence. Something shook against Miguel's right leg—Heidi, her leg extended to touch his, quivering in the blackness. Or maybe just shivering; the room was as frigid as it was pitch black. Miguel wasn't sure how long it had been since he woke up to frantic, prodding kicks in his leg, but his eyes hadn't adapted to the darkness since. He hesitated to voice his suspicions aloud, fearing that one or both of the others would become even more hysterical at the thought that they were buried alive, but Miguel was certain they were underground.

Their hands were bound with barbed wire to what felt like stone, tight enough that even tiny Heidi could not slip free. Miguel's arms were suspended over his head, just low enough that he could kneel without pulling on the barbed wire; sitting all the way down dug the sharp metal into his wrists. His arms had passed the pins and needles tingling phase and were completely numb, and his knees ached as he shifted back and forth from kneeling to crouching. Heidi had already slipped once on the loamy ground and been cut.

The musty air reeked of rot and mildew, and Miguel fought the urge to vomit. Remembering how they had gotten here didn't help. Miguel refused to mention the other scent he'd detected, hoping Frank and Heidi had missed it—the faint combination of lavender and seaweed, like the lotion Adrienne always put on her hands.

The room was confined enough that, among the three of them, they could stretch their legs out to hit all four walls. Adrienne was not with them.

Miguel took a deep breath of fetid air, and his stomach churned. "Calm down," he said, keeping his voice low so Frank would have to stop scuffling to hear it. When the sounds of struggle ceased, Miguel continued, "It's already cold; we'll be in more trouble if we're bleeding, too."

On his other side, Heidi's breathing accelerated, and Miguel cursed himself for the slip. The icy air, fear, and physical discomfort were clouding his ability to think. "It's going to be all right," he said, struggling to keep his teeth from chattering so his voice would stay soothing. "We'll get out."

"What if we don't?" she whispered back.

"We will," Miguel said forcefully. "Just stay calm."

Frank tried to laugh, but it turned into dry, choking gasps. "How?" he demanded. "Those . . . those things killed everybody, Miguel. I s-s-saw Peter's f-f-face . . . he didn't have any EYES!"

"Quiet!" Miguel hissed as Frank's scream echoed around them. Heidi started to cry, and he groped blindly with his leg until he found hers, nudging her gently.

"He didn't have any eyes, Miguel! Where were his *eyes*?"

Miguel sought the words that would keep them both calm and help them think, but found a hollow inside. He knew how Frank felt; the image of Jared's head lying in the snow was seared into his memory, along with the knife tip sticking out of Rachel's back. And those horrible visions, the haunting knowledge that he could be home right now . . .

Stop it. Heidi and Frank needed him, and if he fell to pieces, they would have no hope at all.

As he was still searching for words, he heard heavy, shuffling footsteps; Heidi tensed, and Frank's fractured whimpering quieted to wheezing pants through his nose. A faint light appeared in the gloom; it was not directed their way, but Miguel still had to blink against the change in the perfect darkness. His eyes adjusted in time to catch the outline of a door before the light moved away.

"There's the way out," he breathed before Frank or Heidi could make any noise. "Once we get free, there's a way out."

The surge of hopefulness was enough to keep the horrible memories at bay. His mind wanted to panic, to sink into those hideous images of Sarah's smashed face and that robed figure looming over him, but he was the closest thing to a level head left. His friends needed his help.

"How do we get free?" Frank asked. Desperate hope emerged in his quavering voice; the light in the darkness seemed to have been a stimulant for him. Even Heidi's breathing slowed.

Relieved, Miguel tried to think. "If one of us can get out, he can untie the others."

"Or she," Frank whispered back. "Heidi, you're the smallest. So get out and help us!"

Miguel grimaced, but he heard a dull scraping as Heidi struggled against her bonds. The whimpers that cut through the darkness pierced Miguel's heart. "I can't," she choked. "It hurts . . ."

"Well, suck it up!" Frank hissed, the desperation winning out over the hope now. "You're the smallest, you have to help us!"

"She'll hurt herself!" Miguel snapped. "Why don't you try to get out?"

"Oh, don't make excuses, Miguel!" Frank snarled. "If she doesn't get us out, we're all gonna die!"

"Don't put that on her!"

"Well then, you get out!"

Gritting his teeth, Miguel tried to shimmy his hands free, but the barbed wire lanced the soft flesh of his wrists and hands no matter which way he moved. He wasn't sure what it was tied to, or if they had jammed it through the wall itself, but it was layered on itself several times over. As blood started to leak onto the cuffs of his coat and slither down his arms, Miguel conceded defeat.

"Okay," he said, trying to be kind. "Heidi, maybe if you work your way down slowly, you can—"

"I can't!" she wailed.

"Heidi, it's okay . . ."

"No! Miguel, they killed everybody! They're going to kill us! I don't wanna die like this!"

"Heidi, calm down . . ."

"You have to help us or we're gonna die, Heidi!" Frank hissed.

"Guys . . ." Miguel started, panic building in his chest and shortening his breath. Before he could get out another word, light silhouetted the doorway again. Heidi and Frank struggled against their bonds as the space beyond brightened. Then the doorway was obstructed by a shadow.

The figure there seemed made of darkness, and the light behind it dimmed, unable to pass its umbral aura. Miguel froze in place, his limbs immobilized by the eyes he could not see, an invisible narcotic of the spirit. Frank and Heidi grew still on either side of him.

"All for me?" a seductive voice purred. Miguel's heart beat faster. He had never heard anything so alluring or more terrifying.

"Just one for now, I think," a deeper, raspier voice replied. Heidi quaked next to him, and his own arms twitched in his bonds.

The shadow flowed forward, blocking out everything. Miguel looked up at it, mouth open but unable to speak. The darkness stretched around him, smothering him, until he could see nothing, smell only decay, and hear only the hammering of his heart in his chest . . .

The shadow turned to one side.

"No!" Frank shrieked; barbed wire scraped and feet scrabbling on the ground. "Not me! Please! Please, not me!"

There was a crunch of stone breaking, and then shuffling as Frank was dragged across the floor. "Let me go!" he sobbed, wailing and screaming. One of his flailing legs kicked Miguel, and Miguel cringed away from the contact. "Please, not me! Please! PLEASE!"

His screams echoed as he was pulled from the room, and Heidi started to cry. The scrape of steel on stone and pained gasps broke into her sobs; Miguel knew she was jerking on her own bonds, but the words to comfort her would not come.

Frank's screams peaked, then choked off, replaced by animal snarls and the all-too-familiar sound of tearing flesh. Heidi screamed too.

Sudden, blinding light speared Miguel's eyes, and he closed them, turning his face away. Footsteps approached, but he was still on his knees; as he tried to reposition, hoping at least to get a kick in, a cloth was pressed against his mouth and nose. Afraid of being smothered, he gasped without thinking, and a sweet, chemical smell raced into his lungs. The sounds of screaming, struggles, and feeding quieted, then faded to nothing.

FOR A moment, they faced each other, the cold evening wind slipping past Simon's shoulders into the warm bedroom. Anita looked up into his unreadable gray eyes.

"Hi."

"Hi."

"So . . . I guess we have a lot to talk about," Anita ventured.

Simon grimaced, as if he would rather do anything else, but nodded.

Shuffling uneasily, Anita stepped back and gestured to her room. "Come on in."

Simon stepped inside, closing the balcony door behind him. He looked around, his eyes lingering on the closed bedroom door, then leaned against Anita's desk. He was back to all black and wearing gloves, which drew Anita's eyes to his pale face. He studied her silently, arms crossed, waiting for her to speak.

"So . . . I guess you didn't need me to invite you in, did you?" Anita asked. Her flimsy smile didn't last long.

Frowning, Simon shook his head. "No, I guess I didn't."

Anita didn't know how to ask what she needed to, how she could possibly begin this impossible discussion. Simon studied her a moment longer, then sighed, closing his eyes and lowering his head. He took two deep breaths, steeled himself, then looked up at her. "Anita, I'm a vampire."

Anita's knees gave way and she fell back onto the edge of her bed, staring forward sightlessly. She knew it was true—it was the word her mind had been rebelling against for a day now—but hearing him state it so baldly made her realize some piece of her had been holding out hope, clinging to denial. His words stomped down on that mental grip and sent her plummeting.

Simon shifted like he meant to go to her, but thought better of it and waited. After a moment, Anita managed to pick up her head, though she still couldn't look at him. "Okay. You're a . . . a vampire." She shivered. "Okay."

His gaze was so incredulous Anita felt it before she turned to see it. "That's it?" he asked. "'Okay?'"

"Well, what do you want me to say?" Anita snapped.

"I'd think you would—" Simon started, but he caught himself and took another breath. His voice was more controlled when he said, "I figured you would have questions."

"I . . . Simon, I don't even know where to start," Anita admitted hopelessly. But she knew that was a lie, and that this would never get anywhere until she forced it out. As Simon was opening his mouth, she managed, "Are you going to kill me?"

His eyes widened, and whatever he had been planning to say went unspoken. "Of course not!" He looked offended. "How can you ask me that?"

"You just said you're a . . . vampire!" The word still wasn't coming naturally. "What am I supposed to think?"

"If I wanted to kill you, why would I have saved you last night?" he demanded.

Anita hesitated. It was like he was speaking the same thoughts she'd been wrestling with all day. "How did you know? Why were you there?"

Now Simon looked uncomfortable. "I went there. Your father said you'd be there, and I . . . I don't know!" he admitted, waving one hand. "I don't know what I was thinking. I knew I'd have to talk to you. It was the wrong place, but I wasn't thinking clearly. But I saw you come out, and I saw Salem . . ."

He trailed off, teeth bared and gritted. Anita was still for a moment before she realized she had been looking for the fangs. "You got away?"

"He let me go."

"Just like that?"

Simon frowned. "I talked to him. He promised he won't give you any more trouble."

The vampire's body was rigid with tension, his eyes downcast as if he was deep in thought. Anita was sure there was more to the story, but she got to her feet and took his hands. "Thank you," she whispered. She stared at his chest to avoid meeting his eyes. "I'm glad he didn't hurt you."

"Yeah, me too," Simon said dryly. But he tugged on her hands, and she stepped forward into his embrace, resting her head on his shoulder. It felt comfortable and right and disconcerting and wrong all at once.

Before she could make sense of her feelings, he shifted his weight uncomfortably and steered her back. She forced herself to look up and saw him rubbing his neck as if he had a cramp and studying her with narrowed eyes. Then his expression hardened. "Why are you wearing a rosary?"

Anita's hand went to the beads around her neck, and she took a step back. "I didn't know . . ."

"I'm not going to kill you!" Simon snapped. "If I wanted to kill you, you'd already be dead!"

Eyes wide, Anita retreated a few more steps. Simon winced and looked out the window, pressing his gloved hands to the white trim. "I'm sorry." His voice was strained, but the acid had gone out of it. "I'm sure this is hard for you too. Keep it on, if you want."

Staring at his back, Anita felt a surge of guilt. She waffled in her mind before she reached up and took the rosary off her neck, slipping it into the pocket of her pajama pants. Crossing the room, she touched Simon's back.

"Okay," she said, taking deep breaths. "Let's talk."

He turned around, and his face was expressionless again.

"Have . . . Simon, have you ever killed anyone?" Anita asked in a small voice.

His pause was short. "Yes."

"A lot of people?"

He shrugged, and his indifference stung Anita. "I don't really keep count."

The horrible possibilities flooded her mind, turning Simon into every kind of monster her imagination could produce. "Why?"

"I don't even keep track of—"

"No," she interrupted. "I mean, why do you kill people?"

"Sometimes in self-defense," Simon hedged. Then he sighed and added, "But usually because I have to."

"Have to?"

"I need blood to stay strong."

Anita was grappling for a way out. "Can you . . . I don't know, can you drink animal blood? Or get donated blood?"

"Been reading up, have you?" he asked coolly. Then he shook his head. "No, it's only human blood. And only live human blood. I guess what we take isn't the blood so much as it is life. The blood people donate is separated from the life it sustains. It isn't the same."

"Life . . ." Anita repeated. She didn't realize she had sat back down on the bed until the hand that wasn't on her forehead fell on her comforter. "I . . ."

"That's where the 'psychic vampire' fiction comes from, I suppose," Simon said distastefully. "The idea of stealing life directly. But it doesn't work that way either. Blood is the only medium."

"And you have to . . . kill people?" Revulsion saturated her voice, and her stomach twisted.

"Have to?" Simon repeated. Anita looked up with strange, sudden hope and found him frowning. "I guess technically we don't have to, but we have to feed more often if we don't take a full blood supply. It's more easily noticed."

"'We?'" Anita repeated, trying not to entertain the mental image of him *feeding*. The memory of his fangs made that difficult.

"Vampires."

"Yeah, I figured that," Anita said tersely. "I meant, how many are there? Is it just you and . . ."

"Salem? No." Simon shook his head. "He told me once. Something like more than five hundred, but fewer than a thousand?"

Anita wrapped her arms around herself. "A thousand vampires . . ."

"In the whole world, I mean."

"Still . . ." A thousand vampires. Her mind couldn't even see the lesser nightmare of a thousand Simons. She was picturing a thousand creatures like Salem, cold, mocking, and pitiless, lurking in the dark, feeding the world over . . .

She didn't notice Simon moving until he sat beside her and wrapped an arm around her shoulders. She leaned into him, still shaking. "You're okay with one," he asked, "but not a thousand?"

Anita leaned away to look up at him, feeling guilty but unwilling to lie. Her face was apologetic as she said, "Honestly, Simon . . . I don't know if I'm okay with one."

His expression hardened, but he looked away as he drew his arm back. "Yeah," he said, voice tight and tense. "Yeah, I didn't think so."

"Well, what do you want me to say?" she demanded. She grabbed his coat with one hand. "You just told me you're a murderer! How am I supposed to feel about that?"

"I don't kill for fun!" he snapped. "I do it because it's what I am."

"That's kind of the problem, Simon," she replied. "It's not you, it's . . ."

She trailed off, and Simon's heavy brows pulled together. "What, you're okay with who I am, but not what I am?"

Anita searched for the words. It seemed like a strange hair to split. She couldn't put the two images together in her mind—Simon the hunter, preying on innocent people and drinking their blood, and Simon her boyfriend, protective and gentle and risking his life to defend her. She had to be missing something.

"Do you . . ." She heard the vacancy in her voice and tried to pull herself together. "Do you kill good people, or just . . . ?"

"Human concepts of good and evil don't mean much to us," Simon admitted. "I've watched your kind for a long time. None of you are completely innocent or completely not."

"Well . . . what about kids?"

"Of course not!"

Simon's tone was so offended, his face so incensed, that Anita's voice was equally sharp as she replied, "Well, how am I supposed to know? You said good and evil don't mean anything to you."

Simon bit back whatever his instinctive reply was going to be. "There are lines even I don't cross. I'm a monster, not an animal."

Anita took some comfort in that, but she had no idea what to say. Simon gauged her for a long moment before he sighed.

"If you want me to go, I will. I'll walk out that window and you'll never see me again. Or Salem," he added. She wondered if he could hear her heartbeat picking up. "You can try to forget us, or whatever you need to do."

Anita wasn't sure why that thought hurt; it sounded like the sane option. She trusted Simon enough to have faith in his word, in his assurance that he would keep Salem away. The thought of the other vampire made her shiver, and the reassuring squeeze of Simon's hand on her shoulder comforted her even as she knew it shouldn't.

"I . . . I don't know what to say, Simon," she admitted. "None of this even seems real."

"Tell me about it," Simon grumbled.

"What's that supposed to mean?"

He sighed and gave her a look. "Salem wasn't just mocking me, Anita. Humans aren't supposed to know about us. I've never . . ." He stopped mid-sentence, wincing, then said, "I've never told a human what I am before."

She suspected that wasn't what he had been planning to say. After a moment, she asked, "So why me?"

"Well, after last night, I thought you'd figured out most of it anyway," Simon observed pointedly.

"But . . ." Something niggled at her, and she thought for a moment before realizing what it was. "You said you aren't going to kill me."

"I'm not!" Simon said, exasperated.

"Why not?"

He stared at her. "What?"

"I mean, that's good," Anita clarified. "Don't. But, if you have to drink blood, why don't you want mine?"

He rolled his eyes. "Trust me, I do."

Anita checked herself before she shivered this time. "So . . ."

She couldn't force the question out, afraid of the answer, but Simon sighed and got to his feet. "So if I'm going to be killing and feeding on humans anyway, why someone else and not you?"

Past words, Anita just nodded.

Simon leaned against the window again. "I don't know. I was going to at first. That first night we met, I . . ."

He stopped abruptly, face guarded. Anita forced some saliva down her dry throat, but her voice still came out hoarse. "You what?"

"I came here," he admitted. "I followed you and Marion here to . . . well, you can imagine what I came here to do."

Anita shuddered, drawing her knees up to her chest and wrapping her arms around them. "I had a nightmare that night," she remembered, looking down at the baseball bat still leaning against her headboard. "Was that . . . ?"

"Me? Yes," Simon confirmed, and this time it was he who did not meet her eyes. "I was very close, but I decided not to. And then when we met at the library, I could've had you afterward in the parking lot, but I didn't then, either. And the more I kept putting it off, the less I wanted to do it."

"Wait," Anita said. "You said the first night . . . but I hadn't invited you in. How could you have—or is that even a thing?"

"It is, and I'd have hypnotized you," he said bluntly. "You saw me, for a second. That's why you don't remember anything, why it just seems like a nightmare."

"You . . . what, messed with my mind?" Anita's voice sounded somewhere between annoyed and appalled.

"Well, I couldn't exactly let you remember what you saw!" Simon snapped.

Anita took two deep breaths, trying to fight down her discomfort. In a quieter voice, she asked, "You can do that?"

"What, hypnotize people?" Simon seemed to be struggling more to keep his calm. "Yes."

"That's how you talked us into the club," Anita realized. Simon looked startled, so she added, "Remember? When you and Christine and I . . ."

She trailed off. In the shadow of the revelations about Simon, she had almost forgotten about Christine. Now she felt guilty for that, too, even under Simon's gaze.

"Er . . . yeah." When she didn't look at him, he asked, "What is it?"

"Christine," Anita confessed, and she laughed weakly. "I know it's stupid to be worrying about it with . . . with all this, but I haven't heard from her since that night."

"Do you really want to?" Simon inquired.

Anita saw the distaste on his sharp features. "You two are really my only close friends," she said. "Now she's ignoring me, and you're . . ."

"A monster."

Lying back across her bed, Anita didn't know what to say. She couldn't stand to think about Christine now, so she asked, "What else can you do? Aside from hypnosis."

She looked up at her ceiling for a long time before Simon replied, "I can hear your heartbeat."

Anita craned her neck until her chin rested on her sternum. He was frowning at her. "That's it?"

"No, but it's distracting," he replied. He waved one hand at her phone. "Why don't you call her?"

"She doesn't pick up. I left her messages." But Anita looked at the phone sitting on her desk. Maybe tonight would be the night . . .

Simon followed her gaze, then shrugged. "Go ahead. I'm not going anywhere."

Anita picked up the phone and found Christine at the top of her recent contacts. "Come on," she complained as it rang. "Come on, pick up . . ."

And then the phone cut off in mid-ring.

"Anita."

It wasn't a question, and there was a sharp edge in Christine's tone that Anita didn't recognize. She hadn't realized how angry Christine was at her. "Hey, Chris . . ."

"Hey."

"Look, Chris . . ." Anita sighed. Simon's reflective gray eyes probed hers, but he did not speak. "I know we ended things on a bad note the other day . . ."

"Yeah."

"I feel really bad, Chris," Anita said plaintively. The silence on the other end of the line stretched on until she added, "Can we talk?"

Christine breathed into the phone; it sounded like a sigh, but a little harsher. "Could you come over?" she asked in a smooth voice. "Now would be a good time; I just got rid of my parents."

She laughed, and Anita knew she should be comforted—if Christine was in a good mood, they might be able to patch things up—but that laugh made her shiver. "Y-Yeah. Yeah, sure, I'll be right over."

"See you then."

Anita looked up at Simon as the call ended. "I'm sorry . . ."

He shook his head. "No, it's fine. I'll meet you down there."

Anita squirmed. "I don't know if that's a good idea. I mean, our fight was kind of about you," she added. "You being there might cause more problems than it solves."

The look in Simon's eyes chilled her. "I wasn't coming with for Christine."

She stared a moment before another cold shudder clawed her spine. "You said he was going to leave me alone."

"And he said the same thing to me. I'd rather not take chances."

Anita put her face in her hands, trying to slow her breathing. Simon knelt in front of her, laying one gloved hand on her shoulder. "I'm not going to let anyone hurt you."

Nodding, Anita fanned her face with both hands for a second against the sudden heat in her cheeks. "Okay. Right. Downstairs. I'll get changed and meet you there."

Simon nodded, and his hand moved to brush her cheek, cupping her face. He leaned toward her, and she couldn't stop the instinctive cringe, thinking of his fangs and wondering if his lips would taste like blood . . .

He grimaced and pulled back, getting to his feet. "Downstairs."

He pulled open the door and leapt off the balcony without waiting for an answer. Anita sighed as she got to her feet, closing the door and pulling the curtains back in place. She ran over the conversation in her head as she got dressed, and was so distracted that she put her sweater on backward. As she traded her pajama pants for jeans, her hand closed on the rosary and she stuffed it in the jeans' pocket. Lacing on her combat boots over the mismatched toe socks she had been wearing with her pajamas, she grabbed a pink and blue striped knit winter hat and stepped out into the hall.

As she reached the bottom of the stairs, she met her father coming from the living room. "Ah, Anita. Er . . . I was just coming to check on . . ." He trailed off, eyes narrowing as he appraised her more carefully. "Are you going somewhere?"

Cursing internally, Anita said, "Yeah. I'm just going over to Christine's."

"Anita, it's Christmas. I'm sure Christine's parents want to spend time with her."

"Actually, she said they just left," Anita replied. "She's there all by herself."

Dr. Rothard frowned. He seemed to want to say something, but held himself back. Thinking of Simon lurking somewhere around the house waiting for her, Anita took a deep breath and said, "Dad, Christine and I had a fight, and we haven't been talking. I need to clear things up with her. I'll come right home, okay?"

"What did you fight about?" His tone was unusually kind, and Anita was so startled that she replied truthfully.

"Er . . . well, Simon."

Her father looked uncomfortable, and took his glasses off, wiping their lenses with the end of his polo shirt. He made a show of inspecting them before he put them back on and sighed. "Anita . . ." he said. "Look. I'm still not—you should've asked your mother or me before you invited him last night."

"Yeah," she replied, trying not to sound impatient. "Yeah, I know."

"But . . . I'm sorry I yelled at you in front of your friend. That was inappropriate."

"Yeah, it was," Anita agreed, a bit sharply. But as he grimaced, she realized this was the least of her problems. "But I forgive you. Just don't do it again, okay?"

He nodded, scowling, but said only, "Not too late tonight, Anita. Your uncle's flying back in the morning."

"Right."

Grabbing a coat and the keys to the SUV, Anita stepped out into the cold night.

"WHOA! I didn't see you there."

"I'm sorry if I startled you."

Simon didn't sound particularly sorry, but then, Salem couldn't blame him. Not only because the girl had reacted exactly as he expected her to, but . . . really, what was the point of apologizing to a human anyway?

He lay flat on the Rothards' roof, listening to the girl's footsteps as they grew muffled with the garage roof over them. The engine rumbled to life, and the SUV swung out of the driveway and down the road.

Salem shook his head. Domesticated vampires—the idea was repulsive. But he leapt off the roof, shifted forms, and flew after them anyway.

He had spoken of coming here to needle Simon, to keep him from neglecting his end of the bargain. He had never imagined the boy would come back here the very next night. But Simon's apartment had been deserted, and Salem had stopped only for a quick snack with slow reflexes before trying his luck up here. And sure enough, Simon was at the girl's cozy little home.

The SUV went a few blocks away before it pulled into the driveway of a three-story house even more opulent than the one it had left, vaguely Mediterranean with its curving walls and Roman tile roof. Perching on a telephone pole, Salem watched as the human and Simon got out, listening hard to hear their voices.

"Look, just wait here, okay? I won't be long."

"Right."

"Simon . . ."

"It's fine, Anita."

Salem rolled his tiny bat eyes, then watched as the girl stepped onto the wraparound porch.

"Weird. Why would she have all the lights off?" The girl tried the doorbell several times. "Huh. I wonder . . . hey, door's unlocked. Christine?" she called, and the echo of her voice carried through the open door.

"I don't like this, Anita. Something feels wrong."

"It's just Christine, Simon. Just wait for me."

"Yeah . . ."

Salem gave it a moment, listening to the girl's voice growing fainter as she wandered into the house, still calling her friend's name. Then he hopped off the telephone pole, spread his wings to catch a breeze, and glided down behind the SUV. Shifting precisely, he morphed so that his boots came down on the ground in a brisk walk, and he crossed silently to the front stairs.

Simon had been pacing back and forth out of sight, but his head turned at the movement. His eyes widened, but while his hand was still reaching for his kukri knife, Salem flashed up the staircase. One hand pinned Simon's knife hand while the other leveled the point of his gladius against the younger vampire's throat.

"I'm surprised you didn't offer to hold her purse," he noted, smirking.

Simon leaned away from him, and Salem let him pull free. The taller vampire hissed and whispered, "What are you doing here? You gave me your word—"

"And you trusted it so much that you felt the need to dog her every step," Salem cut him off. "Is she your pet human, or are you her pet vampire?"

Simon's eyes glowed. "Salem . . ."

"I came here for you, not her," the elder vampire interrupted again. He heard the girl's voice inside, but ignored it. "I told you I'd come find you if you weren't home."

Simon gritted his teeth, but the hellfire faded from his eyes, leaving them shining steel again. "You came up with a plan?"

"We're going to do reconnaissance," Salem confirmed. "I've got a theory and I want to test it."

Simon paced away again, looking through the still-open door wistfully, though it might as well have been ten feet of steel to them. "What's the theory?"

Salem's eyes followed his pacing. "My acquaintance has a very conquest-oriented mind. He's the type to consider ground he's taken to be his, and stick around to gloat about it."

Simon paused to look through the doorway again, then asked, "And how does that help you?"

"Because I think I know where he's resting."

Leaning on the doorframe, Simon eyed him distrustfully. "And how does that . . ." He fell silent, frowning, and then his eyes widened. "He kicked you out of your own resting place, didn't he?"

Salem snarled. "Why is it that when it's annoying for you to put the pieces together, you do, but when it comes to food, you're totally clueless?"

Salem glared at the house, envisioning the girl inside. Simon extended his fangs and stretched his arms out. "Look . . ."

But he fell silent at once, gawking at the doorway again. Salem was staring too, emerald eyes wide with surprise. Simon's arm had passed right over the threshold.

"Have you been here before?" Salem asked slowly, eyes narrowing again, looking around him and raising the sword.

"No," Simon replied. As if afraid it was going to burn him, he edged the toe of his boot over the threshold. It met no resistance, and Simon planted his foot inside. He looked back at Salem as if seeking an answer, but Salem had none to give.

While he was still trying to force the impossible to make sense in his head, a piercing shriek of terror ripped through the house. Simon turned toward it like a scented hound, fangs bared, and before Salem could grab him, Simon was gone.

EIGHTEEN

LEAVING SIMON on the porch, Anita ventured into the dark house. She was used to the vast open space of the foyer, which stretched all the way from the marble floor to the ceiling of the third story, but without the usual light from the chandelier and the rooms that flowed off in all directions, it seemed large and lonely. She remembered sneaking out of Christine's third floor room when they were kids, giggling and squealing at shadows until Mr. or Mrs. Stokely caught them and sent them back to bed. But they had been together, safe in each other's company.

"Christine?" she called, listening to her voice echo up to the third floor and back down. She was tempted to turn on some lights herself, but she beat the urge down. It wasn't her house, and with things strained between the two of them, she didn't want to rock the boat any more.

"Chris?" she called again, laying one hand on the elaborate iron-work railing that swept up the carpeted marble stairs. "Mrs. Stokely? Mr. Stokely?"

She remembered that Christine had said they were gone, but Anita wished they weren't. She felt desperate for some company—some human company. Part of her felt bad leaving Simon outside—not that she could have invited him in herself; he had explained on the way that only someone who actually lived here could do that—but another part of her appreciated the brief respite. She had no idea how she was going to handle *that* situation, and even sorting things out with Christine seemed preferable.

Her steps echoed on the marble, loud and oppressive against the silent house. Cold sweat dewed on the nape of her neck, and Anita started to wonder whether dealing with Simon might not be the easier task. She took out her phone and called Christine again, and the sound of Christine's tango ringtone echoed from somewhere above. She didn't pick up.

"Hey, Chris!" Anita yelled as she reached the second-floor landing. "Where are you? This is creepy!"

As if in response, a light turned on above. Relieved, Anita was up the second staircase to the landing on the third floor—an oval observation point looking down on the foyer below—before she realized the light wasn't coming from Christine's room, but her parents'.

"Christine?" Anita called. It didn't feel right walking into the Stokelys' bedroom, but in the gloom, she felt drawn to the light like a moth. She was far beyond her tolerance point for the abnormal.

"Chris? Anybody in here?" she asked, sticking her head around the corner. The overhead lights bathed the Stokelys' king-size canopy bed in a muted amber glow, but there was no movement and no response. Anita crept in, peeking around at the corners of the room. The little sitting room adjacent to the bay windows was empty. The oriental wall hangings draped down undisturbed; one waved, but it was above a heating vent. "Christine, if you're in here, this really isn't the night . . ."

She made it to the center of the room, eyeing the closed hangings around the bed as she moved. The house was as warm as ever, but Anita shivered. She slunk toward the bed, face screwed up against a sudden, awful apprehension. By the time her hand caught the gold hangings, it was shaking. Taking a deep breath, Anita wrenched them open.

The bed was made neatly, throw blankets and pillows in place.

Gritting her teeth, embarrassed by her fear and pushed to the breaking point, she roared, "CHRISTINE!"

"No need to shout."

Christine's smooth purr came from the doorway, and Anita whirled around, eyes wide. Christine herself leaned against the door, wearing black flats along with her leggings and a form-fitting silk paisley blouse. Her black hair gleamed, and her skin shone snow white against the darkness of the hall behind her. Her lips glistened with what looked like ruby lip gloss, and they pulled into her alluring smile.

"Where the hell have you been?" Anita snapped, forgetting that she had come on a peacekeeping mission. She stormed across the room. "I'm really not in the mood for this crap! I'm having the worst day of my life and I—"

She cut off, lurching to a halt five feet from Christine. Her sable-haired friend had turned her face from where she was still leaning on the door, but her smile twisted, turning mocking and cruel, and her eyes reflected the light in a way that was horrifyingly familiar.

And standing this close, Anita saw the white points of sharp fangs extending down onto Christine's bottom lip.

"No . . ." she whispered. Her mind reeled, unwilling to accept it. "No, no you're not. You're not!"

"Worst day of your life," Christine mused, shifting her weight onto her feet and moving closer as Anita retreated. Her silky voice sent chills from Anita's neck to her heels. "Would you believe me if I told you it could still get worse?"

Anita's breaking voice was nearly a sob. "You can't be. This isn't real." The denial sounded pathetic in her ears, but she couldn't force herself to believe. "Chris stop. Stop. Just stop it . . ."

"Awww," Christine cooed even as her lips pulled back to expose her fangs, longer than any of her pure white teeth. She mocked, "Wittle Anita doesn't bewieve it?"

Drumming her nails against the floor-to-ceiling armoire—nails that ended in glassy claws—Christine grinned beneath her narrowed eyes. "Want me to prove it?"

Horror latched onto Anita's heart, and she went cold. Whatever was in the armoire, she knew she didn't want to see. "Don't . . . Chris don't . . . please, stop . . ."

Christine winked one long-lashed eye and pulled the door open anyway, and the scream that had been building in Anita's panting lungs tore past her lips.

Bob Stokely tumbled out first, and his lifeless head bobbed on what little of his neck remained. His dress shirt was clawed to shreds, exposing the deep cuts on his chest. The cracked end of his spine stuck out through his neck. Julia Stokely toppled onto him. Her throat was torn wide open, as if something had taken a bite out of the center, and her body folded backward at the sternum where her back had been broken. They wore almost matching expressions of terror.

"Guess we're not going to do presents together," Christine sighed.

Anita continued to scream, but Christine crossed the room before Anita could do more than stagger into the post of the bed, and one white hand caught Anita's neck and strangled her scream into a gasp.

"Oh, don't get it all out of your system yet, Anita." Her lips curled into a horrible, contemptuous grimace on Anita's name. "You'll need some screams for later."

She leaned in close, and her proximity paralyzed Anita as surely as if her neck had been broken too. "You know, I'm still a little thirsty after Dad," she whispered in Anita's ear. Anita cringed as two points brushed the side of her neck. "You don't mind if I have a sip before we start, do you?"

Christine drew back suddenly, making a sound like she was gargling in the back of her throat, an animal snarl that didn't suit the almost overpowering beauty of her face, and then they were crashing to the floor.

Christine was on top of her for an instant before Simon grabbed her by the hair and ripped her off. She snarled bestially, but Simon hurled her across the room. The drywall cracked at the impact, and as Christine was still bouncing off, Simon snapped a kick into her head that put her on the ground.

"Run!" he barked over his shoulder.

Anita staggered to her feet and promptly crashed into the table in the sitting room area. Crying out as she put a hand to her throbbing hip, she leaned against one of the plush leather chairs and looked back in time to see Christine swing a haymaker punch that Simon caught. He pulled it over his shoulder like he meant to throw her, but she wrapped both arms around him, squeezing like an anaconda and digging her claws through his shirt and into his chest. Snarling in pain, he launched them both backward, and the corner post of the bed broke against Christine's back.

Her grip slackened, and Simon burst out of her hold. Spinning, he backhanded her and her head snapped sideways, leading the way as she crashed into the wall separating the bedroom from the master bath. Simon ripped a piece off of the broken bed—a three-foot-long chunk of wood ending in a jagged tip—and rammed it toward Christine's chest, but her hand shot out and caught his wrist. Snapping her teeth at him, she began to force his arm back. Even from an angle Anita could see the shock on Simon's face, but his free hand went under his coat and came out with the curved machete he had held to Salem's throat the night before. It slashed toward Christine's restraining hand, but she let him go and ghosted back with unbelievable speed. As Simon was still pulling the slash back, Christine kicked him so hard that he soared across the room, pulverizing the table next to Anita.

Simon spared her a single glance as Christine ripped two stakes of her own off the bed. "Go!"

Anita forced herself to turn and run. She heard the crunch of splintering wood and glanced back from the doorway. Simon was backing up toward her, wood shards at his feet, and even as she watched, Christine hurled the second stake; Simon slashed that one out of midair too. Terrified of getting between them, Anita bolted down the hall.

Careless with fear, she slipped on the rug covering the smooth marble floor and caught herself on the wrought iron railing before she hit the ground. Behind her, Simon roared in pain, and she looked back to see Christine striding out of the bedroom, her eyes glowing red. Anita ran for the staircase, but a single leap carried Christine to the railing of the overlook. Balancing on it with catlike grace, she gave a manic cackle.

The kick to Anita's chest was like getting hit by a car, and she landed on her back ten feet away, gasping for breath, arms curling around her aching ribs. In a flash, Christine was on top of her, jerking her arms away and pinning them to the ground. She snarled, fangs bared beneath an insane grin. Then she released one of Anita's hands, her own snapping up to catch a whirling silver arc. It froze as she snagged it out of the air, and Anita saw it was Simon's long knife. Flipping it in her grip, Christine raised it overhead and brought it down on Anita's chest.

Tucking her free arm to her body, Anita curled in against Christine's arm, trying to avoid the knife, but there wasn't enough space, and she gasped in pain as the knife cleaved through her jacket and shirt and nicked her back. It made a splintering crunch as Christine drove it all the way through the marble floor. She ripped it free and raised it again, but a black blur smashed into her and threw her off Anita.

Anita struggled to her feet and saw Christine and Simon wrestling for the knife, snapping at each other with their teeth. Simon turned in, throwing his back against Christine's chest as she tried to impale him. Caught off-balance, she lurched forward, and he pitched her over his shoulder and onto the ground hard enough that the floor cracked. Christine cried out in pain, but as Simon wrenched the knife out of her hand, she kicked at him. The blow caught him in the chest and knocked him to the ground as well, the machete slipping out of his grip.

Snarling like an animal, Christine launched herself at Anita, but Simon caught her ankle and she landed a few inches short. Hissing, Christine kicked him in the face with her free foot, and Simon bellowed. Christine pulled free and got to her feet, but Simon grabbed her from behind as her claws whistled toward Anita's face. When Simon got her into a headlock, Christine kicked out; the blow caught Anita in the stomach, and she folded like a piece of paper, all the air forced from her lungs.

Gasping as her legs turned to cloth, she slipped on the top step and fell. She registered several impacts on carpeted marble with cries of pain before her head struck a stair and she blacked out.

WHILE CHRISTINE was still on one leg and Anita was starting her plunge down the stairs, Simon snarled in rage and jerked them both sideways. They crashed straight through the wrought iron railing and plummeted toward the foyer floor two stories below. Christine managed to rotate in midair so she was facing him, and clawed him down to bone across the face. He hissed in pain, but before she could capitalize on the moment of vulnerability, she hit the ground.

Simon grunted as he smashed into her, but the floor had broken into shards beneath her body, and her face was dazed as she whimpered. Forcing himself to sit up on top of her, Simon punched her face hard enough that the wood base beneath the marble broke under the back of her skull. He had left the kukri on the third floor, but was prepared to tear off her head with his bare hands.

He seized her around the throat, but was struck by something so powerful that it hurled him off the vampiress. Spinning through the air, he crashed into the staircase, and two of the individual marble steps broke under him. Flipping out of the wreckage, he saw Anita lying dazed halfway down what remained of the staircase, having tumbled all the way from the third floor. Snarling and baring his extended fangs, he turned back to Christine.

She wasn't alone.

Looming over her as she groaned and rolled onto her hands and knees, taller even than Simon himself, was a robed and hooded figure. Every detail of the house was plain to the young vampire, but his night vision couldn't penetrate the shadow around the figure's face. The hooked talons on the ends of his fingers and the silence where his heartbeat should have been marked him for what he was, however, and Simon snarled, pulling off his gloves and raising his claws.

The shadow jerked Christine to her feet with one hand and pointed the other at Simon.

At once, the weight of the world seemed to land on his shoulders, and his knees buckled. An invisible force wrapped around his chest and squeezed until he groaned, feeling hairline fractures starting in his ribs. His arms glued themselves to his sides, and his fingers started to bend toward the backs of his hands.

"Where is Flavius?" a rasp from within the cowl demanded.

Gritting his teeth against the pain, Simon managed to hiss through them, "Who?"

His smallest finger wrenched itself backward, pressing flat to the back of his hand as it cracked between the first and second knuckles. Simon bellowed, then snapped his jaws shut so hard that his fangs cut the inside of his lower lip.

"Where is Flavius?" the voice repeated. Christine stood at his side, and her blue eyes shifted over Simon's shoulder to where Anita lay. Furious at her obvious intent, Simon tried to stand, but the unseen force was impossible to resist.

Without any warning Simon could see, the figure turned and the pressure vanished. Simon pitched forward, catching himself on his hands, but his eyes never left the other vampire. One gnarled hand shot out to catch Christine by the arm, then spun her in a half circle before hurling her through the air. She skidded across the floor, bowling over a couch and crashing through a glass coffee table twenty feet away. Simon had to trust his ears to follow her progress, because his eyes were stuck on the melee in front of him.

A flash of steel cleaved through the space Christine's neck had occupied an instant before, then whistled back toward the hooded vampire just after he had thrown the girl away. The shadowy figure twisted away from the sword blow, ghosting a few feet back to give itself space. "Ah, Flavius." It savored the name. "There you are."

"Here I am," Salem agreed, gladius raised to guard in front of his body. The fingers of his free hand were curled into claws, and he spared Simon no attention at all. Growling, Simon wrenched his broken finger back into position and held it there until it started to heal.

Salem and the tall vampire shifted from side to side, each seeking an opening. Salem tried a lunge, then skipped away from a slash of claws Simon was sure would have taken his head off. Glancing behind him, Simon saw Anita watching the contest with wide eyes, holding her head and clearly wondering whether she was still unconscious. A whisper of movement drew Simon's attention back a second too late to help.

Christine lunged at Salem's back. He pivoted and hit her with a back kick that sent her flying, but his enemy capitalized on the instant of distraction. Off-balance, Salem slashed at one of the claws coming toward him, but the hooded vampire drew it back and drove the fingers of his other hand down into Salem's shoulder. Salem screamed, forced to his knees, and slashed at the hand, but the vampire ripped it free. Salem flew back, and Simon lurched out of the way as the other vampire hit the iron balustrade hard enough to dent it. Blood poured from the jagged gouge in his shoulder. Salem rotated his arm with his jaws clenched, obviously trying to will the injury closed faster, while the hooded figure raised its blood-soaked hand into the shadow of its cowl.

A hiss like steam escaping from a pipe came from the darkness. "A first taste of what is to be mine."

"Don't bet on it," Salem snarled, but blood leaked out of the corner of his mouth. Simon helped him to his feet. He heard Anita stepping down the stairs behind them, but he didn't dare take his eyes away from the hooded figure.

"I knew the suffering of this worthless whelp would draw you out, Flavius," the cold voice mocked. One long finger pointed at Simon, and the opposite railing came alive, the metal groaning as it wrapped around him. Simon tried to get a grip on it and tear it apart.

Salem stared. "Hurt Simon to get to me? That was your plan? That's the best you could come up with?"

"Here you are," the vampire pointed out.

"That is pure, dumb luck," Salem complained. Unable to get a grip on the railing, Simon settled for flexing his arms to break it apart instead, but it resisted him. He wondered why Salem was bothering with taunts in the middle of a battle until he noticed that the wound on the elder vampire's shoulder was still closing, and realized Salem was buying time.

Their enemy seemed to come to the same conclusion and started forward. As he advanced, flexing his claws, Christine darted back to his side. Salem managed a nasty laugh. "All this effort to find me, and you're sharing your blood with another?"

The mangled, snarling sound from within the hood was less like a laugh than any growl Simon could have produced, but when it spoke, the voice seemed amused. "A tool, Flavius. A means to an end. She brought you to me."

Anita came to Simon's side, leaning from the last unbroken stair to pull on the iron railing wrapped around him without effect. She looked at him despairingly, and he felt the jumbled emotions on his face. Then her eyes widened, and she started patting her pockets.

Christine narrowed her eyes, but her companion went on, "All lives will serve me, Flavius. I have told you this before. But you are too troublesome to leave undead any longer."

"I'll endeavor to see the compliment in there."

The two enemy vampires surged forward as one, and as Salem rose to meet them, an invisible force slapped him back down. Anita dove past them both and threw herself into the path of the oncoming force. Simon's eyes widened in horror.

He cringed down away from the sight, trying to hide himself. The railing stopped squeezing him, but he didn't have the strength to break it. Anita stood in the center of the tumult, the crucifix of her rosary in her outstretched left hand.

Both of their enemies jerked to a halt as suddenly as if they had walked into a wall. Christine whimpered and cringed back, raising her hands over her face, and the taller vampire snarled. His clawed hands rose like he wanted to rip Anita limb from limb, but the closer his hands got, the more they shook. He hissed in frustration.

"Leave them alone!" she screamed, frenzy and rage mixed in her voice. She took a step forward, thrusting the little crucifix out, and the tall vampire gave ground, shielding himself with his hands. His face twisted away, and the motion was so jerky that his hood slipped off and pooled around his neck.

Anita screamed, and Simon felt like joining her.

The pale face had the remnants of a darker complexion, but the flesh was scabbed black and red in places. His brows were hairless and cracked. Other spots had strange deformities, bone spurs beneath the surface jutting out like small spikes of flesh. Protruding varicose veins slithered up his neck and over his bald head like worms beneath the scalp. His teeth were bared, and though his canine fangs were longest, every tooth was just as sharp. His maw stretched wide enough in its snarl that Simon could see the molars in the back, like jagged rock faces at the bottom of a thundering mountain.

But the eyes were what held Simon in place almost as much as the crucifix. The slit pupils were dilated, and the irises were the yellow of putrid pus. His sclerae were not white; they almost glowed blood red, and the centers of his eyes were islands of yellow and darkness in a sea of scarlet. Purple veins bulged out of the sea of red like surfacing serpents, like tiny moles had been digging toward the center of his eyes.

Anita screamed again and lurched back a step on reflex. The vampire's hideous eyes narrowed, and he took a slow, cautious step forward.

"Do not hold that little thing out like it is anything you believe, wretch!" he spat. "Do you think yourself a priest of your infant religion, to hold the image of your God like a standard before you? Do you think He cares about you? You, who have forsaken Him!"

Looking horrified, Anita staggered back again. The vampire's answering advance was quite deliberate this time.

"Yes," the voice that matched the face hissed. "I know you well, Anita Rothard. Christine has told me all about you. You pretend to the faith of your fathers and speak empty words you do not believe."

Simon watched as Anita looked at Christine. The vampiress wasn't cringing anymore, and Anita's arm was shaking. Simon felt his strength coming back to him, and he was torn between which feeling was worse—the abasement and frailty the crucifix inflicted upon him, or the knowledge of what it meant for Anita if that power gave out.

"Do you think your secrets are secret to me?" the vampire mocked, and he laughed that revolting laugh. "How you know you are unworthy of your parents' love? How they regard you with shame and disappointment—and who could blame them? How you watch the eyes of those you desire turn to your friend instead of you, and know you are beneath her? How every friend has abandoned you like the worthless nothing you are?"

"Chris!" Anita gasped, staring in anguish at Christine's cold face. The arm with the crucifix was sagging. "You were . . . Chris, how could you?"

Christine laughed this time, but it was the tall vampire who spoke as he closed on Anita. "She belongs to me. There is nothing she knows that I do not know, nothing she has that is not mine."

Anita gritted her teeth, but her voice was just a whimper as she looked at the thing looming over her. "Let her go."

"She will always be mine," the vampire taunted. "Is that justice? Would a God who loves you make your superior better still and leave you as this sniveling nobody? Turn your life into the nightmare it has become? There is no deity, no force in existence who can save you from me, and you know it."

Anita's arm curled inward, holding the crucifix close to her heart. Simon knew he could break the iron railing to shreds if he wished. He tried to find the words to encourage Anita, but they choked in his throat, and he knew he would never be allowed to say them. On the floor at his side, Salem was as taut as a piano wire.

"Yes, little failure," the vampire's rasping voice commanded as he loomed over her. "Lay down your cross and die at my feet. I will show you power you can believe in."

Christine smiled a cruel, anticipatory smile, closing in on Anita's other side. Anita's arm shook, and tears ran down her cheeks. "You. You did this to her."

"I did." One talon stroked Anita's arm, and Simon gritted his teeth in rage. He would have burst out from his cage and ripped that hand off at the wrist if he didn't know the thing could snap Anita's neck before he got close.

"She was my friend!"

"She was your better. She pitied you with her affection, nothing more."

"That isn't true!" Anita snarled. "We were friends before you did this to her!"

"I have given her power."

"You made her a monster!"

Christine hissed, baring her teeth as if to confirm the point. She tried to lunge past her master, but he elbowed her back hard enough that she staggered away several steps.

Anita's face lit up with fury, and she thrust the cross out. "Don't touch her!"

The hand on her arm released her as if she had caught fire, and the deformed vampire retreated with a savage snarl. His eyes bulged. "You dare wave that empty plastic idol at me as if—"

Anita took another step forward and struck Shafax dumb. Simon cowered down from the power radiating out of Anita like a heat wave. Salem hissed at his side, and Christine tripped over herself backing away.

Anita looked down at her, pity and loathing and misery on her face. "Chris . . ."

She took a step toward Christine, but the crucifix was still extended, and Christine screamed and backed up to the door, cowering and shielding herself with her arms. Her face turned away as if she could not bear to look at Anita. Anita froze in place.

"Lay down the cross and I will kill you mercifully," the robed vampire promised, but his harsh voice sounded flatter than before. The look on Anita's face was murderous as she thrust the crucifix at him in reply, and he pressed himself against the door, his shark teeth gritted.

"You cringe under the aegis of your enemy, Flavius!" he spat at Salem, looking over Anita's head even as his eyes kept darting to the crucifix and away—desperate to keep track of it, unable to endure its gaze. Watching the movement of his red and yellow eyes nauseated Simon. "You hide behind the standard of one whom your own people destroyed! You think this—"

Anita took another step, an arm's length away from their enemies, and the vampire cringed, seized Christine by the wrist, and snapped, "You escape me on borrowed time!"

With that, he smashed his way through the glass front door, dragging Christine along with him. Salem got to his feet and roared at Anita, "MOVE!"

Anita collapsed to the floor, hugging the rosary to her chest and sobbing. Salem was out the door in an instant, a throwing knife in his free hand. In the yard, the hooded vampire flung Christine away from him; she took a few running bounds before leaping into the air and shifting into a bat. Salem hurled his knife, but just before it struck home, the tall vampire burst into a shower of black-speckled insects the same yellow color as his eyes. The knife sliced one in half, but the rest buzzed their wings angrily and flew off, surrounding the bat in a swarm. The drone of their wings died off into the distance.

Finally snapping the iron railing, Simon strode to Salem's side. "Grasshoppers?"

"Locusts," Salem corrected, sneering after them. He sheathed his gladius under his coat, then looked at his shoulder. The pale flesh was fully healed, but Salem pulled at the ripped shreds of his T-shirt. "Son of a bitch!"

Anita was heaving on the ground, her weight on her shaking hands, and even as he approached her, she vomited on the marble. When she was done, she curled up in a fetal position, shaking. Simon knelt at her side and touched her shoulder. "Anita . . ."

She screamed and turned toward him, thrusting the rosary out. Simon threw himself back, tripping over the broken stairs, hands raised in front of his face. Anything to take those eyes off him, small but staring through him like he wasn't even present, like he was beneath their notice, powerless and shameful . . .

"Why is this happening?!" Anita demanded.

Salem cringed at the door, one foot out like he was going to flee too. Trying and failing to look at Anita without cowering, Simon said, "Please put it away. You're with friends now."

Salem snarled, and Simon hissed at him before amending, "Neither of us will hurt you."

"And Shafax is gone," Salem added in a tight voice.

Anita sat up, pressing her back to the wall and holding the crucifix in trembling hands. Her eyes were red, and she looked from Simon to Salem and back with naked distrust. Her heart was racing.

"Anita, please . . ."

Her brown eyes fixed on him, saw him shaking and shivering against the fragments of marble, and she took a deep breath. It hitched several times, and more tears slid down her cheeks as she squeezed her eyes shut, but she draped the rosary around her neck and tucked the cross under her shirt.

Simon figured it was the best he could hope for, and he got to his feet. Anita's sniffling echoed in the hallway as he went to her and offered his hands. She started to reach for him, then gasped and drew her hands back. He grimaced, realizing he hadn't put the gloves back on to hide his claws.

Going to retrieve them from the stairs, he turned to find Anita back on her feet and looking warily at Salem; his answering glower was a sight to behold. Simon stepped to Anita's side, then returned Salem's look. "Want to explain yourself?"

Salem's lip pulled back from his teeth. "I'm not sure I owe you an explanation."

"You brought this on us," Simon snarled back. "That thing was here for you, not us. You want my help, I want some answers."

"Help?" Anita choked out at his side, looking at him in confusion.

"Simon didn't tell you how he saved your neck last night?" Salem asked, smirking. "How very noble."

Snickering to himself, he crossed the cracked hallway and took a seat on the lowest stair still intact. Giving the torn shoulder of his T-shirt one more castigating grimace, he looked back at the pair of them. "Well?"

One look at Anita told Simon that staying on her feet was enough of a challenge, and speech was going to be beyond her for the moment. He demanded, "Who was that?"

Salem leaned back, stretching his arms out over a higher step. "His name is Shafax." Contempt dripped from his voice. "Shafax the Ancient One, King of Vampires."

Though he knew it was all in his mind, Simon felt cold. "He's the king? You want me to help you assassinate the King of Vampires?"

"A little regicide's healthy now and then," Salem offered with a grin.

"King?" Anita asked.

They both looked at her. She swallowed and leaned on Simon for support, but took a deep breath and said, "You have kings? Why?"

Simon looked at Salem, who rolled his eyes. Taking that as a refusal to answer, Simon said, "A long time ago, vampires fought each other. More often," he added, glancing at Salem. The elder vampire was ignoring them, tossing a broken piece of marble to himself, each toss higher than the last. "The position of king was created to arbitrate disputes between vampires before it got out of hand and humans discovered us. Right?"

Salem's eyes were on the chunk of marble falling from between the second and third stories. His pale hand snatched it from the air, but then he regarded Simon and sighed. "Yes, more or less.

That was the original theory, anyway. Some kings have been more forceful than others, but they aren't really supposed to rule. Shafax is taking 'king' a lot more literally than any of the rest of us ever meant it."

Anita struggled with this for a moment, then asked, "Why bother hiding?"

"What?"

"If you're so powerful, why bother hiding from people?"

A slow smirk twisted Salem's lips. "Imagine if sheep and ranchers didn't believe in wolves."

Anita shivered, and Salem laughed.

"Every so often," Simon went on, throwing Salem a glare, "vampires get together to elect a new king. The meeting's called a Corona, and—"

"Wait!" Anita said, and her large eyes flashed with anger. "You deliberately put that thing in charge?"

Simon raised his hands. "Don't look me at me. I've never been to a Corona. The last one was long before my time."

After a moment of silence, they both looked at Salem.

"I was there," he admitted. "The 1504 Corona, in Rome. It was a very close vote, but Shafax managed to pull the wool over enough of our eyes . . ."

He trailed off into a snarl, then shrugged. "For what it's worth, I didn't vote for him. He was a megalomaniac long before he turned himself into an animal."

Simon frowned. "Why is he like that? Is that . . . normal at some point?"

The idea was deeply uninviting, and Salem laughed coldly. "No, not quite. Didn't you notice the eyes?" When Simon frowned, trying to make something out of the hint, Salem rolled his own emerald eyes and said, "He's a blood glutton, Simon."

Simon snarled with revulsion. Anita looked at them both and asked, "What's a blood glutton?"

"A vampire who feeds on the blood of other vampires," Simon forced out. Just saying it aloud disgusted him.

"I thought you said you needed human blood to . . . to . . ."

"We do," Simon spared her.

Confusion was written on her face. "Then . . ."

"Human blood sustains us," Salem interrupted impatiently. He sat forward, resting his elbows on his knees. "But drinking the blood of another vampire makes us more powerful."

Salem raised his clawed hands. "Age makes us stronger; the older the vampire, the more powerful he is. But by drinking the blood of vampires, it's like adding to that total for free. Say I drank the blood of a hundred-year-old vampire." He paused to sneer. "It would be like adding another decade or two to my lifespan, and all the power that goes with it. Instantly."

"So he . . . he drank another vampire?" Anita asked.

Salem laughed without humor. "No one vampire can do *that*. Even as old as Shafax is, there's no chance. He must have consumed dozens of vampires by now, if not hundreds. And some of them were old enough that it made a difference, even to him."

Salem's lip curled, but Anita asked, "Why don't you do it?" They stared at her, so she went on, "You're vampires, right? What do you care?"

The harshness in her tone struck Simon, and he winced. Her answering expression was ambivalent, but it was Salem who answered.

"Any other vampire can kill a blood glutton. No consequences, no vendettas, no problem. Even if the blood glutton is the king. Maybe especially then."

"But why?"

"First," Salem answered, testy now, "the more vampires you drink, the thirstier you get. Simon, what are you down to now, one a week or so?"

It was Anita's turn to cringe, and Simon glowered. But Salem just waited with a patient grin, and so Simon spat, "More or less."

his cloth duster behind it. "Why do you carry that sword? There are better designs."

"I like this sword!" Salem spat, his teeth exposed.

Anita's hand went to her chest, to the imprint of the crucifix under her shirt. "'One whom your own people destroyed,'" she quoted Shafax, shivering. Simon met her gaze, and they both looked at Salem. In a small, almost awed voice, Anita asked, ". . . Rome?"

"The past isn't important!" Salem snapped at them both. "You need to focus on how we're going to kill Shafax."

"I'm not feeling particularly generous just now," Simon hurled back. "You brought this on us. I get the feeling if I just sit it out, I won't have to worry about you coming after Anita before long."

Salem hissed, but then calmed himself, and he smiled daggers at Simon. "Me? No, probably not. But you're deeper in this now than you were last night."

"How?" Anita demanded.

Turning his eyes and his cruel smirk on her, Salem laughed, and Anita shivered against Simon. "Because of you," he chuckled. "Simon's nothing to him, a passing irritation. No more annoying than a fly, and forgotten as quickly. But you? A pitiful little human forcing King Shafax out of a place he wants to be? A child with a plastic cross and some beads making the almighty Shafax cower like a beaten slave?"

Salem beamed, apparently relishing the memory. Then he fixed Anita with a piercing look. "I've known Shafax a long, long time. He will never, ever forgive that insult. He'll hound you to the ends of the Earth. He'd burn the whole world and everything in it just to get to you, and kill everyone you love for the pleasure of making you suffer. If he kills me, you two have no chance against him. None at all."

He glanced at Simon mockingly. "You could probably go to sleep, try to dodge him that way. You're old enough that you could go down for a century or so. But that leaves your poor little woobie with no one to protect her. And if he gets me, Shafax will probably be around in a century anyway—and you won't like the world you wake up to."

Anita shook at the menace in Salem's promise, and Simon found no words to comfort her. The older vampire seemed to enjoy her fear, but Simon heard no lie anywhere in his voice.

Salem watched them lean on each other for support and smirked. "That's what I thought. Meet you tomorrow night?"

"If he's that powerful, how are we supposed to kill him?" Simon demanded.

"Same way we kill any of us," Salem shrugged. "He's immortal, not invincible."

"And . . . and how . . ." Anita tried to ask. She looked at Simon furtively.

"Save it," Salem cut her off. "Simon's a big boy; you aren't going to hurt his feelings. Decapitation. Dawn's light. Fire. Cut out his heart and destroy it."

Anita swallowed. "Couldn't we just put a stake through his heart?"

Salem laughed. "You want to try to put a stake through him when he doesn't want one? You go right ahead."

Simon scowled at him. "That will kill vampires," he told Anita, "it just wouldn't be helpful here."

"Silver bullets through the heart would work too," Salem mused. He appraised Anita unenthusiastically. "Don't suppose you have some at home to go along with the necklace, child?"

"My parents don't even own a gun," Anita retorted. Her heartbeat accelerated as her face flushed. "And my name is Anita."

"Yes, yes."

"We're all on the same side here, aren't we?"

Salem fixed her with a cold look. "Let's get something straight. I'm on my own side. Simon and I are allies of necessity, for now. I'm just indulging his human fetish because I need his help."

Simon grimaced, but said nothing. Anita looked at him, and her expression hardened before she turned back to Salem. "What is your problem?"

Salem took a step closer, and Anita flinched, but she didn't move behind Simon. The elder vampire gauged them both, then sneered. "Ask your boyfriend."

His eyes were full of malice, and Simon glared back. Sweeping past them toward the broken front door, Salem called over his shoulder, "Tomorrow night."

"When?" Simon asked.

"Ten o'clock should be late enough. Gives us time to get in position, and most of the humans will be asleep."

"Where?" Anita added.

Salem froze in the doorway hissed under his breath. He spun around, bright eyes narrowed. "What does it matter to you?"

"I'm going with you," Anita said, crossing her arms.

"The hell you are. You'll be worse than useless, and I need Simon to be able to focus."

"I can do things you can't do," Anita reminded him, touching the rosary beads around her neck.

Salem winced, then said acidly, "And make us just as powerless as them. Not a chance."

"I have to go!" Anita insisted; the resolution in her voice was giving way to frenzy. "Christine's my friend! I have to . . . I . . ."

Salem's face smoothed over. "There is nothing you or anyone else can do for her. She belongs to Shafax now. She is lost."

"I don't believe that," Anita whispered, but she leaned back against Simon's chest. He put his hands on her shoulders.

"Believe what you want," Salem said. "It doesn't change the facts. And you'll just be a distraction if you're there."

"I need to see . . ." She twisted to look up at Simon. "Let me come with you."

"Anita . . ." Simon started, but Salem had woven the picture in his mind—trying to fight Shafax and Christine while protecting Anita from them. Then again, they hadn't done very well fighting the two vampires earlier even with Anita out of the picture.

"Please!" Anita grabbed the lapels of his leather coat and shook him. "Simon, please!"

Her hands trembled, and the quiver of her jaw coupled with the feverish light in her brown eyes showed him she was on the border of losing control. Taking her hands in his, Simon looked at Salem. "It could give us an edge? Three of us, two of them?"

His suggestion came off half-hearted, so he was surprised to see Salem's eyes tighten.

"Three of them," the shorter vampire corrected, rubbing a hand on his close-cropped hair. "Shafax has some human slave working for him too. Or at least, he was human the last time I saw him."

Salem's face twisted as some new thought occurred to him, and he threw up his hands with a growl. "Fine! Drag your pet human along too. Maybe Shafax will rid me of her before we kill him."

He stormed out the door, snapping, "Ninety-Fifth and Dan Ryan on the Red Line," over his shoulder.

The silence that followed his departure pressed on Simon's ears. Anita shivered in his arms while her heart jackhammered, though from anger or fear he could not tell. He wrapped his arms around her waist, and after a second, she rested her hands on his.

"There's nothing I can do for her?" she whispered.

"No."

She pulled out of his arms so she could face him. "There's no way for a vampire to become human again?"

Simon read the longing in her face, and he wondered if it was all for Christine. For the first time he could remember, the answer to that question bothered him, and that made him grimace too. "No."

She sighed, crossing her arms and looking at the broken floor. Simon searched for something to say, but finally observed, "We need to get out of here before someone sees the damage and calls the police."

Anita started, her eyes widening. "My car! It's in the driveway."

Simon nodded. "Go get it started; I'll just grab my knife."

He said the words, but his steel eyes flicked to the doorway and he hesitated. Anita seemed to have the same thought. "Do you mind if . . . ?"

"No, you're right," he agreed. Hopping to the first marble step that hadn't shattered, he offered Anita his hand and hoisted her up. They jogged to the third floor, and Simon found his knife on the tile. He frowned as he examined the blade, scuffed from chopping apart wooden missiles and piercing marble. It would need to be sharpened if it was going to slice through vampire flesh. There was blood on the blade too . . .

He looked at Anita, inhaled deeply, and took a moment to control the thirst that followed. "How bad is your injury?"

"My . . . oh." She reached over her shoulder, patted her back, and flinched. "It hurts, but I don't think it did much damage."

As Simon slid the knife into the sheath on his belt, making a mental note to return and bleach the bloodstains and vomit, Anita said, "Thanks."

He raised a dark eyebrow. "For what?"

"Protecting me. I didn't get a chance to talk to her, she just attacked me . . ." She trailed off, pressing her palms to her temples and digging her fingertips into her hair.

Simon's eyes narrowed. "Anita, you don't need to tell me what a bastard Salem is, but that doesn't make him wrong."

She turned away, leaning on what remained of the railing beside the gaping hole where Simon and Christine had smashed through. "You don't know that! There has to be something we can do."

"Anita," he said, "we're vampires too. We know how this—"

"Stop! Just . . . I can't . . ." She breathed out in a huff, blinking to keep the tears in her eyes and off her cheeks. She took several breaths, then said, in a tone of forced calm, "Anyway. Thank you for being there for me."

He took her hands and nodded. She leaned up toward him, her lips parting, but then seemed to change her mind and kissed his cheek instead. Her lips were warm on his cold skin.

Trying not to think about the change, Simon said, "We should go."

The drive back was silent, Anita staring straight out the windshield as Simon's restless eyes searched the skyline. He glanced at her occasionally, but her wooden expression gave nothing away. As they pulled into the driveway, he ducked down to avoid any eyes that might be watching from the house's curtains.

"Is it safe?" Anita asked in an empty voice, finally turning her eyes to him as the engine fell silent in the garage.

Simon studied her for a moment, but her expression was still lifeless. "Yes—no one here who shouldn't be."

Anita nodded listlessly. "Do you want to meet me upstairs?"

The vampire nodded back. "I'll wait for you on the balcony."

"Okay."

She got out without another word and trudged toward the house. Simon climbed up the wall, walked across the roof, and stood over Anita's balcony. The heartbeats of those in the house mingled together—Anita, her parents, Marion, and the uncle with the distrustful expression. Anita's heartbeat picked up and slowed down, and after a while, Simon went to lean on the chimney and wait, its smoke curling around him. It didn't bother him, even as he breathed it in; it smelled of cinnamon and pine along with the usual scent of fire.

Something was fracturing between himself and Anita even as circumstance conspired to force them closer together, and he wondered if Salem was right; perhaps his overexposure to humans was opening him to their weaknesses. He reeled internally, unable to make sense of his thoughts; he knew he could go down into the house and kill Anita's parents or Marion or the uncle with no guilt at all. But then he imagined Anita's reaction, and it pained him. The feeling was nauseating and powerful and not at all comfortable.

Maybe it would be better to be rid of her when Shafax was destroyed—if they managed the feat at all. But the idea of abandoning her to her own devices and returning to the familiarity of his own hunting was uncomfortable too. Safer? Certainly. The sane decision? Definitely; her revulsion at his diet made him skeptical this could continue forever.

Would he do it? He doubted it.

Realizing he had fallen into his thoughts, Simon started and sprang to the top of the roof, disturbing no snow with his light steps. He swept the yard with his gaze, but saw no darting figures or reflective eyes or swarm of locusts, and no fog but the smoke billowing up from the chimney. It was snowing, and the flakes landed on his black clothing, clinging rather than melting.

The balcony door opened, and Simon realized Anita's heartbeat had gotten much closer. When she whispered his name, he climbed to the edge of the roof and hopped down onto the balcony.

Her heart rate spiked, but she had controlled her expression by the time he turned around. There was little more life in it now, and she just stepped out of his way, holding the door open. Only her night-light, a miniature lava lamp, was on in the bedroom, and even with his night vision, Simon registered the way the soft glow lit her features.

She closed the door, slipped past him, and sat down on her bed, already back in her pajamas, the rosary gone from around her neck. "Sorry it took so long."

"It's fine."

She patted the spot on the bed beside her, and Simon sat, his back on the headboard and one foot on the floor. He left a little space between them, and Anita drew her knees up to her chest.

"You think we'll have to kill her," she said, still not looking at him.

Simon hesitated, but he didn't want to give her false hope that she'd carry into the fight. "Yes. If tonight's any indication, she'll fight for Shafax."

"What if she didn't? If you killed him first?"

"I don't know . . ." Would she be freed of his influence, or just thirsty for revenge? "I don't think it will work out that way. It's not the—"

She turned her head, looking at him from the corner of her eye. "Not the what?"

Simon grimaced, but he was caught. "It's not the tactical thing to do. Salem taught me how to fight vampires, principles of combat . . . everything, really." Wistfulness crept, unbidden, into his voice, and he checked the disgust on his face with effort; he didn't want to give Anita the wrong idea. "It's the better approach to take out weaker enemies first. Shafax is so powerful . . ."

He twitched, remembering that invisible grip squeezing him. "It's going to be a hard fight even with both of us together, two on one. If we got into it and she came at us by surprise, we'd be even worse off."

"Can you beat him? Even together?" There was a hint of concern in Anita's voice, but Simon didn't know whether she worried for him or just their chances of taking down the vampire king and leaving Christine undead.

"I don't know," Simon admitted. "Salem's an incredible warrior—much better than me. And we know each other's moves well. But I've never even heard of anything like what we saw tonight."

Anita nodded, rubbing her upper arms with her hands. Simon tentatively rested a hand on her back. She stiffened, then sighed and scooted over, leaning her head on his shoulder.

"I hate this," she whispered. He found nothing to say, and just held her. After a moment, she asked, "Who is he?"

"Shafax? I know as much as you do."

"No," she corrected. She shifted to curl up against his side, laying a hand on his chest. "The other one . . . Salem. Flavius. Whatever."

The way she pronounced the name made it clear Salem's distaste for her was reciprocated in abundance, though Simon could hardly blame her.

"He was my . . . I don't know . . . mentor?" He tried to find a perfect word to describe their relationship and found his vocabulary lacking. "Teacher. 'Friend' would probably be a stretch."

"Is he the one who made you a vampire?" Anita asked, sounding resentful.

"No," Simon replied. "He found me not long after I was turned."

"Who did it, then?"

"I don't know."

Anita shifted a bit, looking up at him. "Is that normal?"

"No. Not according to Salem, anyway. I have no memory of being human—which also isn't normal; Salem's never talked to me about his life, but I know he does remember it." Christine obviously remembered Anita, but Simon thought it best not to lead her thoughts back that way. Instead, he frowned, thinking about what Anita had deduced. "Now I'm more curious. Roman . . ."

Anita didn't share that curiosity. "What did he teach you?"

Simon sighed. "Everything," he admitted. "How to avoid detection, how to use my powers, some languages, all of my fighting techniques. Hunting techniques, survival skills . . ."

"It sounds like you two were close." There was no judgment in Anita's voice now, and her brown eyes softened.

"Yes. Don't get me wrong, he can be hard to get along with. His idea of teaching me how to shapeshift quickly was making me climb to the top of the Sears Tower and then throwing me off." Simon rolled his eyes at the memory. "But aside from you, he's the only . . . well, I guess 'friend' that I've ever had. We were together for a long time."

"How long?"

"Fifteen years? Twenty? Dates and time don't really mean much to us. If you don't count the human time, I'm probably not that much older than you."

In a careful voice, Anita suggested, "It seems like you and Salem hate each other."

Simon squeezed his jaw shut, keeping his lips closed to avoid baring his teeth in front of her. When he could speak, he said, "We do."

Simon watched the undulating blobs in the lava lamp. After a while, Anita whispered, "What happened?"

"It's a long story," Simon hedged.

Anita chuckled, and the sound was harsh and frail at once. "Somehow, I don't think I'm going to be getting much sleep to-night," she observed bitterly. She took a deep breath and added, "I've got time."

Sighing, Simon thought back over it, eyes narrowing. But Anita waited, and so he finally told her.

NINETEEN

Five years before
Chicago, IL, USA

CRAWLING AWAY on his hands and knees, Randall Wilkinson tried to suck in a breath, but the pain in his diaphragm wouldn't allow it. Each time he gasped, he barely got any air past his lips before his spasming lungs forced it out again. It felt like he was suffocating, but he dragged himself on, away from the taunting laughter, until a kick in his ribs put him on his back with a cry of pain.

He pulled his arms in around his chest and covered his face. A sudden, sharper pain erupted in his ribs as one of them stomped down on him. Without enough breath for a scream, he rolled onto one side, curling into a ball. The same foot kicked him in the kidney, sending a spear of agony through his back and pelvis. He'd had to piss before they found him, and he let loose in his boxers as the pain overwhelmed him.

"Fuckin' bum!" one of them said.

"I'm so uploading this later, man," another one chuckled.

"You want the cops involved, dumbass?"

"Yeah, like they're going to care about this bum."

Randall squeezed his eyes shut, teeth gritted, but tears leaked out of them anyway.

"He's fucking crying!" one of them mocked, and one of them spat on him.

He wanted to scream for help, but he saw no one who could help him; they had forced him deeper into the unkempt, waist-high grass where he had been dozing. The foul water he had landed in was still in his mouth, tasting of oil and runoff. The interstate was twenty feet above them, and the little avenue running under it was deserted for fifty yards in either direction. He had barely gotten out of his sleeping bag in response to the glare of their headlights before they had descended on him.

Two of them pulled him to his feet, grunting as they held him up; he didn't have the strength in his legs to stand. As they pushed him up against one of the concrete pillars that supported the over-pass, a hand pulled off his ball cap and a fist smashed across his jaw. He coughed, apparently on one of his captors—he heard someone say, "Eugh!" and felt a kick in his shin. He fell back to the ground. The gravel amidst the grass stung his hands and the side of his face, and he looked up at his tormentors. Even as one of them threw a rock that grazed his thigh, he was able to feel surprise.

They looked to be young college students, maybe even old high schoolers. He had expected some of the other guys; not everybody at the shelter he sometimes visited liked him. But these kids were all dressed clean, in nice jeans or khaki shorts. One of them held up a pricey-looking cell phone; Randall squinted away from the flash-light. All of them looked excited, almost scared, but they were all grinning, too. The youngest one picked up another rock and threw it. This one hit home, and Randall finally managed the scream as three of his fingers cracked.

"Stop!" he cried. "Dammit, stupid kids! Stop!"

The only response was a kick in the balls behind his curled-up legs. His whole body went limp as he tried to suck in breath through his puckered lips. They all laughed.

"Fuck you!" said the voice that went with the kick.

"Stupid, dirty, homeless . . ." This voice trailed off, as if "homeless" was the worst word he could think of and wanted to end the condemnation on a high note.

Someone grabbed Randall's shaggy hair, pulled his face up, and spat on him again; it ran over his eye. The guy dropped him back into the gravel, and Randall brushed at his face with his unbroken hand.

"And the humans call us monsters."

This voice was the deepest so far, and Randall shuddered again; mocking and snide, it barely sounded human. Then Randall heard gasps, and he forced his teary eyes open.

Two other people were looking down on them from the top of a grassy hill nearby, so similar that Randall thought they might've been . . . well, probably not father and son, but older and younger brother, maybe. They had matching pale skin and black dusters, though one had a ponytail and the other something close to a buzz cut. The tall one with the ponytail stood with his hands at his sides, gloved fingers trembling as if he were itching to grab someone. He didn't look much older than the guys surrounding Randall. The shorter guy leaned against a shrub, arms crossed, one eyebrow raised sardonically. Randall saw the wash of headlights on their faces, but even when the distant car turned away, their eyes still glimmered in the dark.

"Whoa!" one of the young guys said, backing up into another of his friends. All four of them drew closer together.

The taller of the newcomers snickered. "Allow me."

The shorter one smirked and gestured grandly. "Go for it. Save some for me, though."

Nodding, the taller guy advanced, and the four kids braced themselves. Stepping to meet them, the tall guy pushed one.

"Hey! Back off—" the kid started, pushing back.

The guy with the ponytail slapped both of the kid's hands sideways and struck him in the gut. The kid doubled over with a wheeze, and the ponytail guy grabbed his hair and kneed him in the face. The kid went down with blood pouring out of both nostrils.

Ponytail glowered, as if the sight of the blood angered him. From his spot against the shrub, Buzz Cut called, "Focus."

Ponytail hissed over his shoulder, and two of the kids rushed him at once. Turning back, he just stepped right between them and caught each by the wrist as they tried to grab him. He kicked one of them in the thigh—the kid screamed as his leg gave out—and snapped that same kicking leg around to roundhouse the other boy in the ribs. The second one went flying—Randall thought it must've been ten feet, easy—and landed a yard from Buzz Cut. The kid struggled to his feet and grabbed another rock, but in a blur of movement so fast Randall missed it, Buzz Cut had him by the wrist.

"He doesn't get weapons; neither do you," Buzz Cut reproved. He squeezed, and the kid dropped the rock, screaming. He pulled at the hand holding him without effect.

Randall worked up enough strength to scramble back a few feet as Ponytail turned to backhand the kid whose thigh he had stomped. The kid stopped shrieking and collapsed without another sound.

The kid with the cell phone looked at the scene for a split second more and bolted. Holding the now-unconscious rock thrower with one hand, Buzz Cut pointed with the other. His tone was needling as he smiled and said, "No escapees, Simon."

"I'm on it!" Ponytail—Simon, apparently—spat, and he ran after the cameraman. After a few steps he crouched and sprang. The leap carried him far—impossibly far. Randall blinked, rubbing his eyes with the heels of his palms as he sat up. By the time he looked back, Simon had the kid by the collar beside another of the bridge's supports. He threw the kid out of sight behind the pillar and followed.

The kid's scream was as terrified as it was brief.

Randall shuddered. As the insides dumped the adrenaline rush, pain took its place; his hand had already started swelling, his pants were soggy, his back was on fire, and he tasted blood in his mouth. Sitting was taking up most of his strength. He looked back at Simon's companion, who was dropping the limp rock thrower to the ground and brushing his lips.

"Th-Tha . . . th-th-th . . ." he stammered, coughing and then crying out in pain as his lungs pressed against his cracked ribs.

The guy glanced in his direction, then turned to watch Simon approaching. As he came into view, Randall noticed blood around Simon's mouth. He hoped Simon hadn't gotten hurt too badly.

Buzz Cut gave Simon an appraising look, then walked over toward Randall. "Sorry, didn't catch that."

"Th . . . thank you," Randall forced out.

The guy stopped, raising his eyebrows over a small smile. The expression seemed harmless, but the hardness in his bright green eyes made it mocking.

"For?" the guy prompted.

"Y-You saved me."

The two exchanged looks and chuckled. Simon grinned; the blood around his lips made his face a nightmare. He asked, "Saved you?"

"Y-Yeah," Randall said uncertainly. Simon and his friend both took a matching step forward as Randall gestured to the kids on the ground. "F-From them."

The guy with the buzz cut smiled, and Randall finally noticed the long canine fangs. "Ah," he asked as he closed in, "but who will save you from us?"

⌒⌒⌒

"CARELESS TEENAGE drivers," Salem observed, crossing his

arms and shaking his head. "Think they're invincible until they run through a guard fence and crash into an interstate pillar."

"And run over a homeless man," Simon added.

"That too."

They watched from the cover of the trees two hundred yards away as the fire spread through the Jeep's interior. Simon doubted it would explode, but it should burn fast enough that the lack of blood among the dead would go unnoticed. Cars were starting to slow on the highway as smoke poured up from beneath it, but there were no approaching sirens yet.

Salem studied the scene. "A little more cleanup effort than I usually like to put in, but . . ."

"You didn't do anything," Simon pointed out.

The older undead snickered. "The advantage of being the teacher. Now let's go."

"You go ahead," Simon replied. "I'll meet you back at home."

Salem narrowed his eyes. "You can't possibly still be thirsty. You ought to be good for a couple weeks after that."

Waving a hand with affected casualness, Simon shook his head. "No, I just want to stretch my wings. It's not even midnight yet; there's still plenty of time."

The emerald eyes stayed narrow and searched Simon's face for a long moment. Simon kept his expression impassive until Salem shrugged. "Try not to get toasted at dawn."

Simon rolled his eyes and smirked. "If you're going to get lonely without me, I could come back early . . ."

"Go, go! Away with you!" Salem snapped over his shoulder. He waved a hand, and thick fog rose around them. A thousand long grass fingers waved for his attention out of the mist as he strode forward and melted into it. The light May breeze seemed to blow it away.

Simon watched the fog fade into the trees, then turned the other way. Getting a running start, he launched himself into the air, shifting just as he reached the peak of his jump. His body shrank as the folds of his coat melded to his flesh and became wings. He began to plummet toward the grass and gravel, but had enough wing to flap just before impact, buying himself a few more seconds of airtime. That was all it took for him to complete the change, and the next flourish of his fully grown wings sent him soaring skyward.

It was only a few miles' flight, but that still gave Simon time to think. It was strangely thrilling to defy Salem, and he found no guilt anywhere within himself, though his search was admittedly cursory. His teacher's constant remonstrances about caution and discretion were getting old, and his vexing habit of accompanying Simon on hunts these past months bordered on offensive. Surely after all this time, Salem could trust him to hunt without leaving traces? It was Simon who had come up with the car accident ruse tonight, after all.

Salem had taught Simon how to mingle with humans—when necessary—without arousing their suspicion. But that was the difference between them; Salem seemed to consider interaction with humans something to be tolerated, but they made Simon curious.

Simon knew a moment of amusement as he imagined the look on Salem's face if the other vampire knew he had given Simon this idea. For all he apparently detested humanity, Salem had more than once dragged his protégé to some disused warehouse or old barn five cities away, where he had uncovered another bare-knuckle fighting ring. Though Salem didn't bother with it himself—unless someone challenged him—he always threw Simon into the fray and watched critically as his student tried out various techniques on the humans. Simon's supernatural strength ensured that he never lost, but Salem had a knack for finding techniques to criticize anyway.

The underground fights held no appeal for Simon; he appreciated the chance to practice on people he could beat, but they were never more than targets. As Simon tucked his wings and dropped out of the sky toward the corner gym, he felt the vindictive excitement of doing what he wanted to do, regardless of Salem's rules.

He had at last found a venue where he could mingle with the unsuspecting and slake his curiosity.

Jeff looked up as he walked in, giving him a half-smile. "Missed you the last couple nights, Simon."

"Sorry about that," Simon said, trying to smile back.

As usual, Jeff wore only sandals, a pair of old sweat pants, and a faded, baggy, sleeveless top that had started to fray around the hems. His heavy, rough face stretched like leather when he smiled, and Simon caught the distinctive odor of aftershave camouflaging tobacco. He was shorter than Simon, his close-cropped hair was whitening from its current gray, and his stomach rounded the bottom of his tank top, but his arms were still toned and almost as big as Simon's thighs.

"No problem, kid," Jeff assured him. He brushed at his cauliflowered left ear, then gestured across the gym with a twinkle in his pale green eyes. "Maya's been waiting for you, though."

Heading that way, Simon took in the gym, alert for danger. Most of the fluorescent overhead lights were off, although a couple illuminated the old boxing ring and the last two of the row of ten hanging bags. The lights gleamed off a row of dusty trophies sitting on a shelf. Fortunately, there were no mirrors—"This ain't a ballet studio," Jeff had said when Simon had asked—and the front windows were too far away to carry the interior light. The place smelled as it always did, of leather, sweat, and sawdust.

Raúl worked one of the bags, smashing at it so furiously that it might have insulted his mother. Matt lay on one of the weight benches in the dark on the other side of the ring, doing dumbbell presses. Maya and Jordan sparred in the ring; as Simon watched, Jordan trapped Maya's roundhouse to his side, but Maya dropped, hooked her other leg behind his knees, and swept him so forcefully that he bounced on the canvas.

"Hey, Simon's here!" she told Jordan, who groaned.

While Simon was still stripping off his duster, subtly slipping his kukri knife off his belt and into the pile of coat, Maya slipped through the ropes and jogged to his side. She wore a sports bra, shorts, and sparring gloves, although Raúl and Jordan were both wearing jeans like Simon's and Matt was still in his fast food uniform pants; the shirt with his nametag was draped over the rack of weights. Maya grinned up at Simon and punched him on the shoulder. The ease of the contact unsettled him, though none of the humans gave it so much as a glance, and her still-quick heartbeat whispered to him.

"Missed you," she said. "I've just been sparring with these losers the last few."

"I heard that," Matt called. Maya stuck her tongue out at him.

"You've been here every night?" Simon asked, taking a pair of loaner gloves down off a peg on the wall.

"Better than being at home," Maya said more quietly, and her smile was replaced by a look of loathing. "Listening to that fat *cabrao* tell me the only thing I'll ever be is a ring girl. He probably thinks I'm out running with a gang like every other *puda* on the block."

Simon felt an odd, inexplicable surge of protective ferocity. He wondered whether she would even mind if he walked her home, got her to invite him into her apartment, and went to meet this guardian of hers . . .

"What about you?" she asked as Simon slipped padded foam boots on over his black shoes. "Your uncle giving you crap too?"

Simon gritted his teeth, glad that keeping his fangs retracted no longer required concentration. "I'm losing patience with him. I don't need him looking out for me, but he clings to me like . . ."

He caught himself. A human would have said "my shadow," but for a vampire, that would have been a very dangerous comparison to make.

Maya's commiserating nod erased some of the tension from her face as she pulled herself up into the ring. "Come on, let's go a couple."

They sparred back and forth, Simon trying to match her speed while keeping his strength in check; even wearing the gloves, he could crush her skull with a single blow if he wanted to. He tried to stick to body shots instead, and she grunted and swore now and then when he connected, but she also slipped in a few jabs to his head, too. It wasn't unprecedented—Salem thrashed him regularly—but the sensation of being hit by a human and not retaliating with overwhelming force made him feel awkward and vulnerable.

They took a break after a few rounds. Maya sipped on her water bottle while Simon made a show of going to the drinking fountain and running the water against his lips. Jordan gave up jumping rope and walked over as Simon was straightening up.

"How's it going, Simon?" he asked, holding up one fist. Simon looked at it until Jordan smirked, shook his head, and lowered it.

"All right . . ."

"Little worried about Raúl," Jordan muttered.

Simon looked across the gym. Raúl was still hammering on the bag, sweat pouring down his face. His white undershirt was turning transparent where it stuck to his flesh. "What's wrong with him?"

"Some professor at Wilbur Wright thinks he's slacking," Jordan confided. "Jeff made him study for an hour before he let him work out tonight."

The vampire processed this, watching Raúl slam his wrapped fists into the leather and wondering if he was going to rip through it. Finally, he asked, "How's your mother?"

Jordan laughed mirthlessly, glancing at the yellowed, elementary school style clock on the wall. "What is it, eleven fifteen? My guess is . . . stoned, probably."

Simon wasn't sure how to respond to that, and his indecision must have showed on his face, because Jordan smiled. "Don't worry about it, man. Come on, let's see if I can do any better with you than I did with Maya."

He didn't, but Maya and Matt sparred first, so Simon had only knocked Jordan down twice when Jeff clapped his weathered hands. "All right, guys, let's clean it up."

It was surreal to Simon, running a push broom over the gym floor like Matt while Maya and Raúl wiped up the sweat from the ring and Jordan put the weights back on the bench. The fan blew their scents around the gym, more potent from the hours of exercise, and Simon shivered just a bit. He was full from the evening's feeding, but their scents were still tempting.

He realized he had been sweeping the same spot for ten seconds and hurried to move on. Maya was coming his way with a roll of paper towels, looking as if she had something to say, when Jeff's voice drew their attention. It was deeper, a bit more authoritative, the way Simon had heard him speak to the others when they weren't pulling their weight or putting in enough effort.

"Gym's closed right now, sir." His tone was courteous, but firm. "We'll open tomorrow at eight."

"No," a colder baritone returned. "I don't think you will."

The sound of that voice stunned Simon into immobility, his gray eyes widening in shock. He was dimly aware of Jordan frowning at him and Maya's eyes narrowing, but all he could force himself to do was face the entranceway.

"Sir, you need to leave, or I'm gonna call the cops," said Jeff, his voice less friendly now.

Standing on Jeff's other side, Salem was glaring right at Simon, and even from halfway across the gym Simon could see the fury in his emerald eyes. Every line of his face was hard, and his usual sarcastic edge was absent. His clawed hands were bare, but Simon figured Jeff hadn't noticed yet because they were balled into fists. Without looking away from Simon, he said, "They'd never get here in time to save you."

Stricken with horror, Simon turned to Maya. "Get out of here!" he whispered, knowing it wouldn't be enough even as he said it. "Take the others out the back way."

Maya looked between Salem and Simon for a second, and awareness dawned on her face. "That's your—"

"Yes!" Simon hissed. "Go! Now!"

"The hell I will," Maya said, looking as insulted as she sounded. "We're not going anywhere."

"Yeah," Matt said from behind him. Simon spared a glance to see Matt unscrewing the broom's shaft from the head before taking it in both hands like a staff. "He wants one of us, he has to come through all of us."

"You don't understand!" Simon half-snarled. "You—"

"You need to get your ass out of my gym now, pal," Jeff said, and there was no longer any pretense of civility. Simon turned in time to see him grab the lapel of Salem's coat with one thick, scarred hand.

Salem tore his eyes away from Simon to look into Jeff's face, and Simon watched as they shifted from green to red.

The palm strike snapped Jeff's head back with a burst of blood. His sharp eyes were squashed under his collapsed brow, and his heart fell silent before his body even hit the ground.

In the following second, while Simon and the humans stared in mute shock, Salem flashed across the gym and onto one of the corner posts of the ring. He balanced without effort, glaring down at them all.

Simon found his voice and roared, "What are you doing?"

"Cleaning up your mistake, you little fool," Salem spat back, and his eyes flicked to Jordan.

With a snarl of rage, Simon launched himself forward, smashing both hands into the post. The blow tore it free from the ring ropes, but Salem flipped off and landed behind him. A ferocious blow hit the back of Simon's head, and he pitched forward onto the post he had just torn free. Salem knelt over him, grabbed him by the knot of his ponytail, and smashed his face into the post again. Simon's nose broke and the front of his skull cracked.

"Get off him!" Raúl bellowed.

There were sounds of a scuffle, but it took Simon a moment to turn around, hissing in pain as he squeezed his eyes shut, trying to make his skull heal faster. He forced them open in time to see Matt choking Salem from behind with the staff while Raúl charged him from the front. Salem's kick sent Raúl flying back into Jordan. The vampire caught the staff on either side of his neck, ripped it apart, and turned to swat Matt into the rack of cast iron weights. He landed straight on his back with a scream, and the rack collapsed.

"Why?!" Simon demanded, struggling to his feet.

"Because you would've had to!" Salem roared back. Maya came up behind him and kicked toward his knee, but he slipped behind her and swept her planted leg out. She landed hard, the wind driven from her.

"They didn't know!" Simon screamed. He snatched up one of the broken halves of the broom handle. "They wouldn't have known!"

"No?" Salem asked. He had lifted one boot to stomp Maya's face, but he lowered it again, his eyes fading back to cold emerald as he returned Simon's glare. Grabbing Maya by the bun of dark brown hair at the back of her head, he dragged her up to a standing position. "You could've kept it secret?"

"Yes!"

"Fine," Salem said, and the finality in his voice was more terrifying than the rage. He pressed one nail to Maya's neck, drew a long scratch down her throat, and pitched her forward. "Keep it secret, then."

Simon dropped the broom handle and caught Maya automatically. The cut was bad, and blood splashed onto his shirt and neck as she collapsed against him. The warm drops burned on his skin, and the scent invaded his mind.

"Simon!" she gasped. She looked up at him, and pain turned to terror in her face. "Si—"

His teeth found her throat and silenced his name from her lips.

There was no resisting it. The taste of her blood was electric, intoxicating. He ached to stop, and could not imagine why. Every swallow made him stronger, and that strength was irresistible. Every taste was a new high, and he couldn't let himself come down.

And then his lips pulled at empty veins, and he looked down to realize she was gone.

"My legs!" Matt's scream registered in his ears. "I can't feel my legs!"

There was a grotesque crunch and the sound of splattering fluid before Salem said, "Now you don't need to worry about it."

Simon turned in time to see him throw the bloody dumbbell away from Matt's smashed head. He heard no heartbeats, and looked around. Raúl was slumped against the bathroom door, his chest sunken. Jordan had tried to crawl into the ring, and his upper body was still draped across the canvas, but his neck bulged unnaturally and his sightless eyes stared at Simon.

For a moment it was silent.

Then Salem was looming over him, fangs gleaming in the fluorescent lights. "Good job keeping the secret," he spat. "You aren't one of them, Simon!"

He kicked, and Simon was too frozen to block. The impact on his chest was light for a vampire's blow, but still put him flat on his back. Salem stalked away, snarling, "And now we have to cover this, too."

Simon lay there for a moment, trying to process it all, until the familiar, frightening crackle of fire commanded his attention. He saw the front desk in flames, and even as he watched, Salem tossed a smoking pack of cigarettes into the ring, which started to smolder.

"Get up," Salem sneered, kicking Simon in the ribs on his way over to the weight wall, where he lit another pack of cigarettes. Simon got to his feet, reeling from what Salem had done and had forced him to do. He put on his coat mechanically, catching his kukri knife as it spilled out and replacing it on his belt.

His hand lingered on the handle. Raúl. Jordan. Maya. Matt. Jeff.

"Let's go!" Salem snarled, grabbing him by the back of his collar. "Or are you going to stand here and burn with them?"

Their faces filled his mind as the roar of fire grew in his ears, and the power of Maya's blood spread. His share of the homeless man's assailants, too. The rush of energy, of those abilities beyond his grasp coming just within reach . . .

"Simon!" Salem demanded. "Let's—"

Simon spun so fast the world blurred to his own eyes, but Salem's hand on his collar was a guiding beacon. His hand flashed as he spun, jerking the kukri knife free and burying it in Salem's ribs.

"Agh!" Salem cried, shocked by the suddenness of the attack. He let Simon go and reached for his hip. Simon saw his intent and stabbed again, pinioning Salem in the shoulder of his sword arm.

The elder vampire flinched, but he caught Simon's right wrist with his other hand. Simon's left shot down, snatching the hilt of Salem's gladius and pulling it from its scabbard. He stabbed it through Salem's side, and as the other undead roared in pain, Simon screamed too, pushing him back until he pinned Salem to the burning boxing ring with his own sword.

A concussive blow to the chest lifted Simon off his feet, and he smashed into a vending machine, energy drinks bouncing off his head and shoulders as he landed. Springing to his feet, Simon saw Salem clenching his jaws as he slowly pulled the short sword out of his side. Somehow, Simon had held on to the kukri knife, but the wounds on Salem's ribs and shoulder were already closing. Salem's glowing red eyes fixated on him as blood poured out of his mouth through his teeth, and there was no mistaking the intention in that face.

Simon ran.

He heard Salem's gasp as he finished ripping the gladius out, but didn't stop to check. He threw himself at the wire mesh covering the opaque windows with enough force that he crashed through onto the sidewalk. Sheathing the kukri as glass shards dropped off his shoulders, he bolted down the street, already starting to change. By the time Salem leapt through the shattered window, Simon was airborne, his leathery wings propelling him away as Salem's screams pursued him.

Present

ANITA WATCHED the snow drifting down outside the window, waiting for more, but Simon didn't seem inclined to go on. She picked her head up off his shoulder to read his face, but it was devoid of expression as he gazed straight ahead at her closet. His eyes gleamed in the lava lamp's light.

"And then?" Anita prompted.

Simon blinked, but he didn't look down at her. His shoulders rose fractionally. "Then nothing. I rested as far from the place we'd been staying as I could get, and kept moving around until I found that apartment building. I've been there since."

He fell silent, and Anita tried to get a grip on her feelings. His story had frightened her, and not just the end; the way he had described the deaths of the four teenagers and their victim had been so chillingly matter-of-fact. But the regret in his voice as he spoke of Salem's massacre at the gym—and his part in it—had been real, she was sure of it. She tried to imagine herself in that situation, fighting against the only person she had ever considered a friend. She wondered if he understood her fear of facing Christine again better than he was letting on.

"You didn't try to kill him?" Anita asked.

Simon's eyes tightened a bit. "He's a much better fighter. I only got him at all because I caught him off guard. I'd never have been able to kill him."

"But you stabbed him in the body and the shoulder," Anita pressed. Exsanguination hadn't been on Salem's uncomfortably short list of ways to kill a vampire. "You didn't try, did you?"

He studied her a moment more before sighing and looking away. "I don't know. Maybe not. I suppose I should've . . ."

He trailed off, and Anita reached for one of his gloved hands. "I don't know if I can, either," she confessed. Just thinking of it hurt, even as the memory of those glassy claws and gleaming blue eyes made her shiver. "Kill Christine, I mean."

Simon looked at her. "You don't have to come. It would be safer for you if you didn't."

The idea was so tempting; she could curl up in bed, let Simon and Salem do what they had to do, and wait for Simon to come back to report that they had won. But what if they didn't? What if it was Christine and that horrible monster controlling her who appeared at her window?

And even if Simon and Salem triumphed, Anita knew the memory of the animal rage on Christine's face would torment her until she died.

"No," she said. "No, I have to. She's my friend. I have to . . . do something."

Simon looked like he wanted to argue with her, but let it go. "Do you want me to come get you, or . . . ?"

"Ninety-Fifth and Dan Ryan?"

"Apparently."

Anita wasn't sure whether she'd be able to take the whole ride that far south alone; aside from wondering whether her enemies would descend on the cars, it would be too much time to talk herself out of what had to be done. "How about you meet me at the Davis Street stop down the road at eight? We'll ride down together."

"All right."

He untangled himself from her, getting to his feet and stepping to the balcony door. His eyes searched the yard for a moment before he turned back. His face was ambivalent, but Anita thought he looked frustrated, even wary. He forced out, "You'd better keep that rosary around your neck until we're together again."

The concern in his eerie gray eyes looked genuine, so she nodded. "Okay."

"We need to be prepared for tomorrow. Get some rest."

She touched the rosary in her pocket as Simon turned to go, and it stirred the memories of the awful things she had experienced. The loathsome, captivating eyes, the color of blood; Christine's fangs as she snarled; the acid in Salem's dead voice. They were going to battle tomorrow, and if Simon was going to "prepare" . . .

"Simon!" she said impulsively, getting to her feet. He paused with his hand on the balcony door. Anita bit her lip, wondering how to say it, afraid of his reaction. But if she could make a difference and remained silent just out of discomfort, how could she live with that? And if they were going to be together, there had to be a middle ground. She knew she would never be able to endure the thoughts of those faces, those lost lives, coupled with the knowledge that their number was growing.

She debated long enough that Simon turned around. "What?"

"Please don't kill anyone tonight," she begged, the words spilling out of her as she rushed to say them before he could cut her off. "I know you need blood for strength, and if you have to . . . drink tonight,"—she couldn't force "feed" out of her mouth—"then . . . look, just please don't kill anyone for it."

He frowned at her. "Why not?"

The blank, almost critical incomprehension in his tone gnawed at her. "I couldn't . . . I can't be with . . . please. Please, for me."

She forced herself to meet his gaze as his narrowed eyes probed hers. His mouth twitched, but whatever expression was coming died stillborn, and he nodded. "Fine."

Sighing with relief that reached down into her core, Anita hugged him, slipping her arms under his leather coat to be closer to him and resting her head on his chest. "Thank you."

He didn't respond, and her momentary rush of elation waned. By the time he embraced her back, her face had fallen with worry, and his touch was perfunctory and brief. He drew away from her, his lips set in a hard line, and said, "Get some sleep."

She leaned away from the frost in his voice and just nodded, concern and hurt and confusion mingling on her face. He looked as if he might say something else, but then his eyes tightened and he turned. With a flourish of his leather coat, he leapt from the balcony to the roof. Anita heard a faint shuffle of dislodged snow just before the flakes drifted past the door, but by the time she stuck her head out into the cold night, the only movement was the crashing of waves against the lakeshore.

THE BUZZING shroud of locusts at last withdrew as Christine circled over the tombstones of Saint Brigid's Cemetery and swept down through the open chapel door on her leathery wings. The instant her tiny, clawed feet touched down, she was changing, growing as the wings melded into her arms and torso and disappeared. She gave a hissing sigh as the coarse hair covering her body shrank and vanished, her flesh becoming smooth and pale once more. Only the sable in her hair and her sharp fangs remained.

She looked down on the near perfection of her immortality. Fantastic, almost endless power thrilled through her, and she knew all that she could do with it—it was like his voice was there in her mind, answering every question the second she considered it. She had strength that had stymied even an older vampire. If she wished it, she could lift that worthless fool Richtein in one hand and strangle him in midair, and that her body would be safe from whatever blows he might profane her with.

But she also knew her limits. She couldn't fly and retain the unearthly beauty her transformation had given her. To take to the skies, she had to reduce herself to a mere animal, to veil her true self with hideous fur and repulsive webbing. And as she had flown to the home that had once been hers, she had been unable to pass the winding Chicago River and was forced to fly exactly over a bridge of human construction.

She scowled. Power like hers shouldn't have weaknesses.

Worse still, she was forced to take their word for the increase in her beauty. True, she had watched Richtein stumble over himself, unable to manage a coherent sentence as he gazed upon her, but she'd had almost that effect on him before. Anita's paralysis had been borne of fear, not awe, and who cared what she thought now, anyway? Christine snarled at the thought, but comforted herself with the knowledge that even if Anita was seeking this gift from Simon, as Christine was sure she was, blood as young as Simon's wouldn't endow Anita with the manifold glories the King of Vampires himself had given Christine.

Obviously, her beauty had had no particular effect on Simon; she rubbed her nose where he had punched her, ruby lips curling back from her fangs. But perhaps he was still so obsessed with Anita that he hadn't *really* looked at her. That had to be it. What other explanation was there?

The King of All Vampires, with his measureless wisdom and eons of knowledge, had told her she was the most beautiful thing he had ever seen. The words reassured her, and she immersed herself in them, as she had every sound that had passed his lips since they met. She was sure she could never forget anything said by that voice.

Nothing. Not one word . . . and as she thought back, a frown marred the perfection of her face.

The insectoid drone approached the door, and she attempted to control her expression. In a swirling rush of carapaces and gossamer wings, the locusts poured in, more and more until they formed a funnel cloud over the bare central space of the ruined chapel. The compulsion of respect and homage seized Christine, and she knelt as the tornado touched down.

The locusts piled on one another, tiny limbs scraping against exoskeletons and wings. The mound grew, swaying and writhing as each component fought for space. As the last circling insects landed on the heap, the yellow in their spotted bodies darkened, turning black as if they were being crisped. They squished themselves together, but no insect innards spilled forth; they melded, one into the next, legs and wings and bodies becoming indistinct.

At first Christine thought they had caught fire, as wisps of smoke coiled out of the mass. Then the black stopped twitching and became the sweeping folds of a bloodstained ebony robe. The sooty smoke coiled around the space for a head and solidified into the hood, raised again. Then glowing red eyes flared to life within that darkness, and Christine bowed her head.

For a second, anyway. She smelled blood—not the appetizing scent of life, but a sweeter, more powerful flavor that called to her all the more. It promised her secrets and power, knowledge long forgotten, ancient mysteries unraveled. Two black drops splattered on the ground before her knees, and she raised her eyes.

Her lord was examining the back of one gnarled hand, where a shallow cut healed before her eyes. Christine remembered the flash of a throwing knife in the dark and the squirt of bisected locust insides on the snow.

"Twice he has blasphemed me with the touch of his blades," said the only voice that could captivate her now, rigid with anger and laden with menace.

"It'll make the taste of his blood all the sweeter when you destroy him, my lord," Christine purred, arranging her features into a smile.

The cowl regarded her for a moment as the cut sealed itself. "Yes. Long have I pursued him, and he has frustrated me as many times. The failures of those who came before you to enact my will have cheated me of my victory for far too long. It is well that I shall at last end him myself."

Christine kept her smile seductive and enthralling, but her mind fixated on his words with something close to fear, a fear she had never imagined an all-powerful immortal should or could experience. *Those who came before you.* Surely there had never been one like her before. Of course not; a king must have servants, or what kind of king would he be? And had he not said she was perfect? The very ideal of the beauty of eternity?

She would have dismissed her fears without a further thought, but for the words he had spoken to Flavius.

"And when you've defeated him, my lord?" she asked, silk and sweetness in her voice. She listened to the sound, imagining it in his ears, and was pleased to hear a smooth purr instead of the dead, dry menace of Simon's and Flavius's voices.

"With Flavius annihilated, I will have the rest of them with ease," he returned. "And then my reign will truly begin."

Christine heard the certainty of victory and the anticipation of its rewards, but distantly; her thoughts fixated on the words themselves. *I*, he had said. *My reign.* Would he rule, then, without a Queen of Vampires at his side?

A hiss interrupted her thoughts, and that most precious voice said, "I thirst."

Christine got to her feet. "I'll come with you."

"Have you not glutted yourself enough for one night?" he snapped at her.

"To attend you, my lord?" she offered.

"Spend your time in my absence improving your powers," the voice suggested ruthlessly. "So when we find them, you will not fail me again."

Stung by the chastisement, Christine bowed her head, remaining silent as the black robes in front of her turned to black smoke and vanished out the door. When he was gone, she raised her eyes, and her face was set and hard as she crossed the chapel. She hefted the flagstone in one hand, lowered herself into the crypt, and replaced the cover, restoring the darkness that did not impede her eyes.

She heard three heartbeats, two strained and one healthy. Richtein's was slow and measured; Christine pictured him asleep between his master's resting place and her own, and rolled her eyes. But she directed herself to the other lives, the ones that would serve her needs.

A tool, Flavius. A means to an end.

The words haunted her, and she knew that if her sleep was not the silence of death, they would give her nightmares. Was that all she was destined to be? She couldn't believe it, but she would make sure. Her master would never doubt her value. She would ensure that his kingdom would have room for a queen.

She looked down on the young man and the girl, unconscious and shivering in the subterranean cold. Their frailty was pitiful, and it reassured her of her own value. He had saved her from that wretched existence; had he wanted a slave, he already had Richtein for that.

But it was best to be certain.

Her lord had given her power. Now she would give him perfection.

TWENTY

PAIN WRENCHED Miguel back to consciousness. The barbed wire rubbed into the raw flesh inside his lacerated wrists, and even as he tried to shift away from the pain, he became conscious of the agony in his knees. He had fallen asleep kneeling, and his joints felt like someone had struck them with a hammer. It came on so suddenly that he couldn't stop himself before he cried out.

"Miguel?" Heidi asked in a whisper.

The lifeless, hopeless defeat in her quavering voice pierced the fog of his torment. "Heidi?"

She did not respond right away, and Miguel took stock of himself. The pain in his wrists and knees was excruciating, and he squeezed his teeth together to keep his outcry to a hiss as he shifted to a crouch, extending one leg, then the other. Both knees cracked, then stung as blood flowed back into them. The balls of his feet barely had the strength to keep him balanced, and he almost pitched forward before catching himself. Even the simple act of rising to the crouch scraped the barbed wire against his already raw flesh, and his eyes stung as he squeezed them shut, though no tears came. He needed to rub them, to work up fluid, but the best he could manage was blinking.

The salty taste of blood was in his mouth, and his dry tongue brushed his chapped and cracked lips with little effect. His stomach twisted with hunger, though the charnel reek of the confined space made him want to vomit, and the thirst in his desiccated throat made even breathing arduous. A skull-splitting headache was setting in, and coupled with the cold, he found it hard to think. He was also conscious of pain in his neck, too; it throbbed, but it was lost under the deluge of harsher pains.

"Heidi!" he snapped, wincing as the edge in his voice chafed his throat.

"What?" she asked faintly.

"Don't just . . . don't just get . . . quiet like that," he told her, irritated by it. "You made me think . . ."

It hurt too much to say any more.

A long, hushed wail came from the spot in the blackness where Heidi was imprisoned. Miguel heard her trying to cry, but without water for tears or breath to sob. "I'm sorry . . ."

Working to focus through his irrational anger even as he nails of torture drove through the backs of his eyes, Miguel rasped, "It's . . . it's okay . . . we gotta . . . get . . . out . . ."

"Caaaan't . . ."

Thinking was becoming difficult; plans drifted out of his mind as quickly as they came in. It all came back to his hands; if he got free, he could get Heidi out too. If he couldn't, they were going to die. They would starve or exparch, and that was if they were lucky. Memories were blurring together, but the knowledge of Frank's miserable death stood out distinct and clear.

Even as he shuddered, Miguel found another memory drifting to mind. It was vague, more impression than memory. But that hypnotic, intoxicating voice couldn't be his imagination.

Tool, am I? it crooned from his subconscious. *A means to an end? I'll show him what I can do. He can't send me away . . .*

The longing in the voice tortured Miguel like the wire wrapped around his hands, but some deeper part of him associated horror with the memory. His neck twinged in time with the whispers of recollection, but he refused to dwell on it. He had to escape. He had to help Heidi escape. They weren't going to be means to anyone else's ends either.

Miguel pulled on his barbed wire bonds, and even as pain raced through his wrists and down his arms, he realized the makeshift shackles were looser. Had he slumped in sleep and drawn them out, or had his dried-out husk of a body gotten so thin that the bonds meant for a healthy human weren't tight enough anymore?

He pulled experimentally and the prongs dug into his flesh. He couldn't feel his fingers, even to rub them against each other, but his wrists registered the bite of steel. He shifted positions, trying to drag the blades of his hands down instead, but they wedged and got stuck. He couldn't turn them enough to put the palms of his hands to the wall.

"Can you . . . get out?" he whispered to Heidi.

She moaned, but gave no other response.

The hopelessness in Heidi's voice was settling upon him, too. He began to think of death with longing; surely nothing in any afterlife could be worse than this. Anything to get away from this abject misery, able only to listen to the one friend he had left dying while wondering which of his tortures would step forth to claim him in the end.

Heidi whimpered again, and Miguel felt her reach out to feebly tap his leg with her foot. She breathed something so quiet Miguel couldn't hear it.

"What?" he croaked back.

"Thank you," she managed.

"For what?"

"Being my . . . friend." Her voice was papery and frail. A strange gasping sound came from her spot on the wall, and she just repeated, "My friend."

Miguel knew she had given up, but instead of sinking along with her into the cold and dark and begging the end to come for them, her words lit a fire in him. He should have protected his friends, and they had been butchered. He should have come up with a plan in time to escape with Frank, but Frank had been dragged off in terror to a horrible end. And now Heidi was going to die because he was too afraid of pain to protect her. She had trusted him, and she was going to die knowing he had let her down.

The fire grew into an inferno, and Miguel shifted his feet to brace himself against the wall. He knew he could only stand to try once, and he took several deep breaths, each one sending razor blades up and down his throat. Then he drew a breath in, gritted his teeth, thrust his legs out, and dropped all his weight to the floor.

His wrists and hands were shrunken just enough. The barbed wire gouged furrows into his palms, and only the lack of energy for a scream kept Miguel quiet as he landed on his back on the cold dirt and stone. He choked and cringed and clenched his hands to his chest, a rush of blood flowing back into his aching limbs and pouring onto his shirt. He lay on the floor, curled into a ball, every part of him hurting.

Heidi's voice kept him from passing out into calm and peace and silence. "Miguel? Whaswrong? Areyoukay?"

Her words ran together, sleepy and disoriented, but they brought Miguel to his throbbing knees. He searched his pockets for his gloves, but they had been taken, as had his phone. Slow as an old man, he got to his feet, leaning heavily on the wall that had been his cell for support. His legs shook under him as he slid along it, and he almost tripped over Heidi when he bumped into her.

"Miguel?" she asked without surprise or any other discernible emotion, voice still hazy. "Yerlooose?"

"It's gonna be okay," he promised. Groping until he found her hands, he squeezed her fingers. His own were so icy that he could barely feel hers. "Hang on."

He slipped the cuffs of his coat down onto his bleeding palms, then wrapped the fabric around the barbed wire holding Heidi. Just shuffling over to her had sapped much of his strength, but he pulled for all he was worth. "Pull your hands out!"

At first, she didn't react, and Miguel groaned as his arms started to tremble. But then her hands fluttered against his like animals startled away, and he heard her gasp as she dragged her arms free. Collapsing to a seated position, Miguel reached for her in the darkness. He caught her shoulders just as she was starting to topple sideways and drew her against him. She shuddered, pressing her frozen cheek against his.

"We gotta go," he said. There was something they should rub to keep warm, but he couldn't think of what. All he remembered was that they couldn't stay. "Come on, Heidi, we . . . we have to . . . go."

He struggled to his feet, pulling on her arms. She clung to his neck, seeming welded into position there, but her weight dragged on Miguel as her legs refused to support her. As carefully as possible, he shifted her so she hung from one side. Patting the wall with one raw hand, he tried to find the door.

Some of Heidi's weight relaxed as he discovered the opening, and she took two small, tentative steps at his side. Keeping an arm around her waist, Miguel led her out into the space beyond, keeping a hand to the wall so he wouldn't lose his way. The air was still dank and musty, but the lingering traces of Adrienne's lotion were stronger here, though the omnipresent stench tried its best to smother them. Pressed to the wall, Miguel tripped on something cold and stiff, dragging Heidi down with him as he collapsed to his knees.

"Whaswrong?" she mumbled.

His fingers found cold flesh on the floor, brushing over eyes and a nose before he wrenched his hand back. His heart pounded, but he said, "Nothing."

Leaning on the wall, he stood again, pulling Heidi up with him. His hand stayed pressed to the bricks, but now he led with his feet, sliding the toes of his shoes forward. They made a ninety degree turn before his foot tapped something much more solid. Pausing, he reached beyond with his hand, and where the obstruction started, the wall stopped. Resting his shoulder against the wall so he wouldn't fall, Miguel lifted one foot and set it down on the obstruction.

It was a step. And beyond, another step.

Hope exploded in him, so fierce he gasped aloud. "Heidi," he rasped. "It's the . . . the way . . . out."

Her numb hands flapped against his chest, but she made no sound, and Miguel was careful to guide her onto the step behind him. Holding her hand, he led her forward, but the ceiling shrank; two steps up, he was hunched over. Pawing ahead, he found that the steps led right into the ceiling. He tried to straighten, and the stone above him scraped a little.

"It's a tile," he reported. "We gotta . . . lift it. Then we can . . . we can . . . we can go home."

"Home?" Heidi asked feebly.

"Come here . . . help me . . ." He helped her up the stairs, clenching his jaw so he wouldn't berate her for her slowness. When they were side by side, he made sure she was in place, then said, "One . . . two . . . three . . . push!"

He shoved, but he was alone in the effort. His legs trembled under him and his knees throbbed. Hunching down with a ragged exhalation, he said, "Heidi . . . you have to help me. Please?"

"Help," she repeated robotically.

"We can get out," he said, taking her shoulders and shaking her. "We can go home."

"Home," she said, but there was a little more life in her small voice this time. "WhatIgottado?"

He showed her again, and they both levered. Heidi whimpered beside him, and pain shot down Miguel's spine to his knees, but he forced words of encouragement past his ruined lips. Finally, a shove put the tile past the lip of the floor above, and as they rested, a ray of light shone down into the darkness and a hint of cold, fresher air forced its way through the foulness.

"Good!" Miguel whispered, patting Heidi's shoulder as she leaned against the other side of the stairwell, panting. "Now we . . . we just push."

Tucking his raw hands into his sleeves again, Miguel pushed on the edge of the tile, and Heidi shoved weakly with him. The light beyond was painful to his eyes, and Heidi's strength dropped off the effort as she covered her face with one hand. Keeping his own eyes closed, Miguel continued to shove, gaining by half-inches at a time. The square tile was three feet on each side, and Miguel thought it probably weighed a hundred pounds. His arms were limp, screaming with pain as he dragged effort out of them.

When a foot of space was cleared above, Miguel knew he could do no more. He slowly opened his eyes, letting the light sting in stages as his pupils contracted to adjust. When they had acclimated enough to see, he took in the arches and pillars of the chapel above them. The sacrificial altar where the girl had been murdered was gone.

"Come on!" Miguel encouraged Heidi, tugging on her. She toppled his way. "I'll pull you up."

Using the stairs, he got half his body out of the hole before he had to use his arms. Unable to lift, he settled for dragging himself out, clawing at other tiles, his hands scraping trash on the floor. Then he tumbled onto the cold stone.

He looked through one broken window and saw orange in the sky. Night was coming, and a deep, instinctive part of him knew what night would bring. The two voices would speak—one ancient in its evil, the other mesmerizing in its power—and he would obey. He would crawl back into the hole to die, and that would be the end of him. And Heidi.

He turned to find her slumped against the tile, her head sticking out of the hole, eyes closed. "Heidi!"

Lurching back to her, Miguel shook her several times before he finally slapped her. She blinked awake, then cried out in pain, wrapping her arms around her stomach. "It hurts . . ."

"I know," Miguel replied, "but we have . . . to go. Come on."

"Water?"

"Water," he promised. "And warm. And food."

Heidi nodded, her sunken, dark-circled eyes peering up at him as she offered him her hands. Her lips were bloody too, her hair disheveled, and her fingers were swollen and blue; the tips were turning black. As he took her hands, Miguel saw his own fingers were similarly deformed. There was blood on Heidi's neck, too, surrounding a pair of raw, angry wounds. He refused to think about what that meant and focused on Heidi's face as he pulled her free.

"WHAT HAVE YOU DONE?!"

The deep voice echoed from below as if the hole itself was bellowing. Heidi started, bumping her back against the stone wall of the chapel and crying out in pain. Then Miguel was being dragged back toward the hole as a vice-tight grip closed on his ankles.

"You can not leave! He does not will it!" roared a frantic bass voice from down in the dark. A light below silhouetted an enormous figure tugging on his legs. Heidi screamed too, eyes wide and frantic as she scrambled away from the hole. Miguel felt himself sliding back into the darkness.

"No!" Miguel sobbed, pulling uselessly at the flagstones. Heidi caught his wrists, but she was so small she was dragged along too. They would both be dragged down into that horrible place to die. They were so close; the free air mocked him . . .

Miguel caught hold of the tile that had covered the hole, and it slowed his progress toward death. Heidi let him go, picking up anything within reach and throwing it at their attacker, sobbing out a long, unbroken, whispery wail of fear. Her throws were pitiful, and an empty burger wrapper, a beer can, and a soiled newspaper all hit the floor beside their enemy. She was lifting a beer bottle when Miguel's hands slipped off the tile and his cheek scraped the concrete. A powerful hand closed on the back of his jeans for a better grip. Miguel looked back and saw rage and madness in that tough, brutal face.

Heidi shrieked, her eyes lighting up with fury as she threw herself past Miguel and slashed with the bottle. Her first swing missed entirely, and the second smacked on the enormous man's hands without effect. The third broke the bottle against the chapel wall, and shards of glass clattered into the blackness below. But as the man grabbed her by her collar to pull her down too, Heidi gouged the jagged end of what was left of her bottle into his eye.

"Agh!" Wailing in agony, he let her go, both hands flying to his face. Blood poured through his fingers, and as he staggered back, one of his feet slipped on the stairs. He slid down the steps with thunks that were all but inaudible under his screeching and toppled out of sight.

"Hurry!" Miguel said, pulling himself free from the hole as Heidi grabbed his arm to help. He pushed on the stone, then lay down on the floor to push with his heels instead. Heidi seemed possessed as she lay down beside him and began kicking too. The tile gave way inch by inch, and there was no sign of their blond attacker rallying. A final kick put the tile back in place and muffled the howling.

Miguel collapsed back onto the floor, never wanting to move again. Everything hurt. But Heidi knelt over him, tugging on the lapels of his coat and rasping. Every movement was torture as he leaned on her to get up.

They staggered to the chapel doors, open to the twilit grave-yard. The icy wind slashed him, and he gasped and staggered back a step, wondering for a moment if it might not be better to die in the chapel than to face the cold. Miguel remembered the unkindness of ravens descending on them, but the skeletal trees guarding the path were bare. They slipped and slid in the snow, banging their aching knees as they bounced off headstones. Heidi's weight dragged on Miguel again, slowing him down until every step was like slogging through molasses.

His eyes went wide as he gazed at her empty face. Her eyes were half-closed, her mouth hanging open, and her grip on his collar was loosening. The fight in the chapel had robbed what little strength she had left.

"Stay with . . . with me, Heidi," he begged. He wanted to stop and swallow some of the snow, and the moment he thought of it, his sere throat cried out with need. But he was sure that if he set Heidi down, even for a moment, she would never get up again. "Alm-almost . . . there . . ."

She blinked, but did not reply.

"Heidi!" he sobbed as the gates of the cemetery came into view. If they could only get out, they would be safe.

Heidi blinked again and her head lolled to the side, but she stared up at him. "Huh?"

"Stay w-w-with me!" he insisted, the cold wind clawing him. They were feet from the gates now. "It'll be a-a-all r-r-right . . ."

They were through. The street beyond the cemetery was de-serted, but the frigid air smelled fresher. Hope trickled past the screaming protest of every nerve ending in his body. Heidi licked her lips with her dry tongue and blinked again. The world spun as he looked around for the way to go.

"I th-th-think it's this w-w-way," he said, towing Heidi away from the cemetery. "C-C-Come on. Just a little f-f-farther . . ."

"WE'RE NEARLY there," Simon said over his shoulder as the train started rolling south from Seventy-Ninth Street. He stood with his back to the divider between the seats and the door, and Anita sat in the first seat of the long bench. She still had the rosary around her neck, but it was covered by her snug-fitting leather coat and the black turtleneck under that. Her blue jeans and black combat boots, combined with the tight bun into which she had bound her hair, gave her an uncharacteristically businesslike look.

She nodded at his words, lost in thought, and Simon turned his eyes back to watching the car, his head swiveling one way and then the other like an oscillating fan. He heard the heartbeats of the six other people spread throughout the car, along with Anita's inches away, but looking away from her allowed him to conceal his frustrated expression. Aside from a quick greeting at Davis Street and a discussion of directions as they changed train lines, neither of them had said a word to the other.

The train rolled into Eighty-Seventh Street, and half the car departed, most of them coughing and hacking as they went. One man boarded and gave Anita a roguish smile, then sauntered in their direction as if he meant to sit beside her. Simon met the man's eyes, and after a moment the guy shambled off in the other direction, bumping into the far divider as he went.

The train pulled out of the station and rumbled along for a moment before Anita said, "Sit with me?"

Simon hesitated. Their conversation last night, and her disconcerting reactions to his words, had started to convince him that Salem might be right. Not about killing her—certainly not that. But perhaps it would be better to cut ties when this was over, assuming they survived. Take another, longer break from UIC and observing humans, leaving the human to her world and returning to the routine of his.

"Please?" she asked when he didn't reply. Simon sighed, but the strange effect of her voice and her eyes worked on him the way it always seemed to, and he sat beside her. She took one of his gloved hands in both of hers.

Several seconds passed as Anita drew a few slow breaths, steeling herself for whatever she planned to say. She looked to make sure no one else was within earshot, then whispered, "You didn't kill anyone last night, did you?"

Simon's lips peeled back from his teeth in annoyance as he worked to stay calm. "No!" he hissed back, tugging against her grip. She refused to let him go, and she had an obstinate set to the soft lines of her face. "I told you I wouldn't, and I didn't. How long is it going to take you to realize—"

She took a firmer grip on his fingers with one hand as she pressed the other one to his lips. "I had to ask."

He tried to speak against her hand, but she shook her head. "Please, just listen," she asked. When he nodded, she said, "There are things about you that scare me, Simon. And I don't know what's going to happen to us, if we survive tonight. But if we can meet in the middle . . . I'm willing to try to make this work."

Simon stared at her. He couldn't articulate what he had been expecting her to say, but it was not this. He searched her brown eyes for indecision or deceit, but he saw only resolution. The fear was there behind it, as she had said, but he could not find a lie anywhere.

When she at last pulled her hand away, he was still searching for words. She tilted her head to one side, waited for a moment, then continued with an air of forced calm, "If you want to, anyway. If you don't, I get it. But I'll try if you will."

He didn't know what she meant by "meeting in the middle." He also had no idea whether they would survive the night—Salem's request for help had eroded much of his confidence in their chances even before he had encountered Shafax. And even if they all survived, this last month had been the most trying of his existence; even with Anita in the know now, he would still be walking on eggshells all the time around her parents and Marion, not to mention the constant temptation to bite Anita herself. He was starting to understand what Salem had meant about not belonging in their world.

It was safer to be done with her when the battle was over. If he committed himself to it now, saw her as just another meaningless human, then her life or death in the looming fight might not even distract him. His existence would be much simpler without her.

Simon looked into Anita's soft brown eyes and made the only decision that made any sense anymore. "Yes. I'll try too."

Words sufficient to the emotional maelstrom in his head failed him, but the look in her eyes took away the need for them.

Her tentative smile was far from the radiant expression he knew her to be capable of, but it was something. Lacing her fingers through the hair at the base of his ponytail, she pulled his face down to hers and she pressed her soft, warm lips against his. He kissed her until the train slowed.

"This is Ninety-Fifth Street, Dan Ryan."

Simon pulled away from her and got to his feet, feeling curiously light. He offered her one gloved hand, and she took it. They exited the train hand in hand, heading up the escalator and through the enclosed bridge that passed over the Dan Ryan Expressway. As they worked their way through a crowd milling around the buses outside, Simon caught sight of a familiar, sarcastic face in the shadows of a little taxi shack across the street.

"He's here," Simon whispered to Anita, and he thought it best to release her hand, anticipating Salem's reaction. They crossed the street and stepped into the shadows of the square brick building.

Salem looked them over and sighed, complaining, "You're sure the human has to come?"

"I'm going to see this through," Anita vowed.

Salem rolled his eyes and waved a dismissive hand. "Come along, I got our ride."

Behind the cab depot was a taxi, engine running and lights off. The cabbie stood beside it, his face vacant. Salem gestured to the back seat, and as Simon held the door for Anita, Salem said, "Turn the camera off."

They both looked at him, but it was the cabbie who responded. "I'm turnin' the camera off," he declared in a flat voice, reaching in through the window and toggling a switch. He straightened back up and announced, "The camera's off."

"Would you show up in the camera?" Anita asked in a whisper.

"No, but you would," Salem replied at full volume.

"He's being . . . controlled?" she breathed more quietly still as she slid in, looking at the driver, who hadn't reacted to Salem's words. He had returned to his original position, gazing forward with no expression whatsoever.

"I assume so," Simon said back.

"Will he be okay?"

"Assuming Salem doesn't kill him, yes."

Anita looked toward the driver with concern. "Can you do that?"

"Mind control? Not as long."

"Or as well," Salem added, slipping into the front passenger seat. "Let's hope your fighting skills are better than your hypnosis."

A snarl started in the back of Simon's throat, but Anita squeezed his hand and he swallowed his retort. She looked at the back of Salem's headrest and said coolly, "Maybe Simon can just sneak up on him instead."

It was Salem's turn to growl, and Anita gave Simon a brief smile that he returned with a smirk. The cabbie got in and flicked on the headlights, pulling out of the lot as Salem gave him an address. His hand drifted toward the meter, but Salem said casually, "No fare."

"No charge for this one," the cabbie agreed.

They rode in silence for miles, and Anita laced her fingers through Simon's after a while. He held her hand, watching Salem even though the elder vampire never took his eyes off the road. The buildings they passed grew older and less well cared for, and they were on a dark street of factories with only a few streetlights when Salem said, "Stop."

The cab came to a halt, and Salem gestured for Simon and Anita to get out. As he followed Anita onto the curb, Salem commanded, "Drive a couple miles and then forget you ever saw us."

"Ugh?"

"Very good."

The cab drove off; before the ensuing quiet turned awkward, Salem set off down the cracked sidewalk.

"Tell us about where we're going," Simon said. "It was your resting place, right?"

Before Salem could answer, Anita asked, "Wait—it was your place, but now he's there?"

"Evidently Salem's first clash with him went even worse than last night's," Simon said dryly.

Anita ignored Salem's growl. "But that doesn't make sense. Chicago's huge; why would he stay the one place Salem knows? If he's really thousands of years old, shouldn't he be smarter than that?"

Salem stopped and looked back. Simon had expected fury, so it took him a moment to recognize in Salem's furrowed brow a glimmer of respect—begrudging, and veiled behind generalized misanthropy, but the real thing nonetheless. "He should be. Once, he would have been. Now . . . you remember what I said about the effects of blood gluttony?"

"Going insane from too many memories?"

"Yes. For Simon—even for me—consuming all those memories would probably end in delusion, hallucinations, mixed recollections. Shafax is old enough to sort through them for a while, but that means the effects would settle in more subtly. The stronger he gets, the more arrogant he becomes—the more he thinks he's invincible." Salem's teeth gleamed in a streetlight as he smiled. "Let's go prove him wrong, shall we?"

As they resumed their trek, Salem called, "If you get an open shot on Shafax, take it."

Simon traded a surprised look with Anita. "Do you think I can kill him?"

"No," Salem continued in the same casual voice, and Simon's shoulders slumped. Anita nudged him supportively. "But I know him, and he'll think the same thing. He'll focus on me, see me as the only threat."

He smirked over his shoulder. "And I am—as long as he's smart. If he's not, if he makes a mistake, you might have an opening."

"Can you kill him?" Simon asked.

"Not likely," Salem answered without breaking stride; he sounded unconcerned.

Simon frowned and slowed. "Forgive me if I'm missing something obvious, but then why are we charging off to meet him?"

Salem paused also, rolling his eyes. "Neither of us is a match for him alone. But together . . ." Uncharacteristic sobriety drove even the mockery from his face. "Together, I think we have a better chance than anyone else to bring him down. The odds aren't great, but they'll never be better, and they will get worse if we delay. Mad or not, he grows stronger with every vampire he consumes. Sooner or later, with my blood or without it, he really may become invincible. And then we're all dead anyway."

Following in Salem's wake as he set off again, Simon examined the dilapidated buildings looming over them and asked, "This is it?"

"A few blocks away," Salem replied. He glanced back at Anita and rolled his eyes, adding, "It would be easier to just fly in, of course . . ."

Anita didn't rise to the bait, but at the end of the block Salem stopped, eyeing his surroundings. Simon did the same, but he saw no sign of movement. Aside from Anita's, the only heartbeats he heard were muffled and faint.

"You have your knife?" Salem asked, and Simon nodded, pulling back his coat to reveal the handle of his kukri. Salem nodded back, then looked at Anita. "What about you, Elevenses?"

"What about me what?" Anita asked, eyes widening.

"Did you think you'd face down the King of Vampires and his little bitchling with a happy smile and a can-do attitude?" Salem returned. "Or are you just here as our moral support?"

Anita flinched, but she reached beneath her turtleneck collar and pulled out her rosary. Salem eyed it warily for a second, then shook his head. "Not enough. Here."

He reached under his coat, and Simon saw a second sword hilt behind his gladius before Salem offered Anita a black semiautomatic pistol. She took it with surprise, not noticing Salem handing her a pair of spare magazines until he rapped her on the knuckles with them.

"Do you know how to use this?" Salem demanded.

"Uh . . . point and pull the trigger?" Anita asked, shifting the gun into an awkward grip. Salem pinched the bridge of his nose, and she added defensively, "I'm not really a violence person."

"Great . . ." Salem said, turning away and shaking his head as he led them on.

"What is this going to do against vampires?" Anita asked.

"Nothing," came the reply. "But if we come across Shafax's human minion, do me a favor and put a round through his head."

Anita swallowed, studying the pistol with undisguised trepidation. Walking at her side, Simon silently guided her hands into a better position, and when he demonstrated how to load the magazine and operate the slide, she smiled up at him weakly. They both nearly walked into Salem, who had stopped again in the middle of an empty street. Simon saw the side of Salem's coat bulge as the other vampire got a grip on one of his sword hilts, and he stepped in front of Anita, reaching for his kukri. "What is it?"

"Death," Salem replied, closing his eyes and taking a deep breath through his nose. "There's blood on the wind. Can't you smell it?"

Breathing in, Simon thought he caught a faint trace of it. "Shafax?"

"No, I don't think so," Salem answered, emerald eyes opening into a thoughtful expression. "Come, let's find out."

"If it isn't . . . him, why are we going?" Anita asked as Simon fell into step and drew out his curved knife.

"Always best to be sure. Besides," he added, glancing over his shoulder to give Anita a malicious smile, "maybe I'll have a snack before we start."

She shuddered, and Simon wrapped his free arm around her shoulders.

As they crept down the dark streets, a faint, high-pitched yowl wailed from down an alleyway, followed by an answering howl and a few yips. Anita jumped and looked at Simon. "Wolves?"

"No, too high-pitched," he replied. "Coyotes, probably."

"Oh," Anita said, relaxing a little. "I read something about that a few years ago. There's something like two thousand urban coyotes in Chicago; one of them walked into a restaurant once. I didn't know if you could . . . you know, wolves and vampires . . ."

She trailed off, and Simon said, "We . . . well, Salem probably could control them," he corrected himself, trying not to look frustrated, "but they aren't around to be controlled."

Anita nodded and tried a smile, joking nervously, "For all I knew, they might be werewolves."

"That's ridiculous," Salem snapped back. Anita started; Simon suspected she had forgotten he could hear her. "There aren't werewolves anywhere."

Anita stiffened at his tone, but her face relaxed. Salem allowed a second of silence before he went on cheerfully, "The last werewolf was killed in 1873. Everyone knows that."

Anita shuddered again. Simon bit back his defense of her, because the smell of blood was growing stronger. Without thinking, he advanced to Salem's side, twisting his kukri in slow, anticipatory infinity arcs. If it was either of their enemies, he would have to be fast.

Salem stopped at the mouth of an alley, pressing his back to the brick and peering past the edge of the wall. Then he relaxed, and there was bemusement in his voice as he said, in a volume far too loud for an ambush, "Well. This is unusual."

Simon slipped past him, knife raised, but paused at the alley entrance, where his eyes widened in recognition. "Miguel?"

Miguel Vargos stood next to a dumpster and a pile of trash cans and bags, looking frozen in place. Simon expected it was because he was almost naked; his coat and shirt lay in a pile at his feet, and even as he watched, Miguel pulled off his blue jeans with jerky, uncoordinated motions, then stood barefoot in his boxer shorts. His normally tan flesh had paled almost to Simon's own color, except for his fingers and toes, which were swollen and shades of purple and blue. His once-clever eyes were vacant and sunken deep in his wasted face, and his hair dangled limply across his forehead. He looked as if he had been tortured, and Simon saw the blood he had smelled oozing from Miguel's wrists. His heartbeat was very faint.

"Miguel? You don't have another pet human, do you?" Salem demanded, exasperated. As Simon shook his head, Anita approached behind him.

"Miguel!" she cried, darting past them both to Miguel's side. Stuffing the gun into a coat pocket, she laid a hand on Miguel's chest, but drew it back immediately with a gasp. "You're so cold! Miguel, what happened to you? Why did you take your clothes off?"

Miguel tried to respond, but only wheezed. Anita looked back with fear on her face, but Simon just shook his head, baffled. It was Salem who said, "He has hypothermia."

Strolling past Simon, the older vampire studied Miguel like a statue in a museum, two fingers of one hand brushing his chin even as the other still rested on his sword hilt. His voice was stoic and indifferent as he observed, "He's dying."

"Oh my God!" Anita replied, aghast, turning pale herself. She dug in her pockets and said, "We have to call 9-1-1."

In a heartbeat, Salem was at her side, gripping her wrist. Simon started forward, but Salem ignored him, fixing Anita with a stern look. "We can't afford more humans poking around here, and they won't help."

Anita glared at him. "We can't just—"

"You can't help him," Salem cut her off. "He has minutes left, if that, and nothing can save him now. You can hear it, can't you?"

This last was to Simon, and Salem turned to look at him. Simon hesitated, but listening to the faint, strained beats from Miguel's chest and remembering the many times he had heard a heartbeat drift toward silence, he couldn't dispute the verdict. Stepping to Anita's other side, he tried to keep his voice gentle as he said, "He's right, Anita, it's too late."

"No," Anita answered, but it was a whisper now. She turned back to Miguel, who was watching them all, his mouth framing the stuttered words that would not come out. There were tears in Anita's eyes as she reached out to him again, looking like she wanted to help but was afraid of breaking him. "Miguel, what *happened* to you?"

"H-H-H . . . H-H-H," Miguel choked out. Salem walked past him down the alley as Simon laid a hand reluctantly on Miguel's arm. Resting his thumb on the human's elbow, he felt the pulse slowing toward the impending stop. "H-H-H . . ."

"What?" Anita asked.

Miguel struggled to focus on her. His eyes squinted, like he was trying to blink but couldn't. He rasped a few times, then finally managed, "H-Hei . . . di . . ."

"There's a girl here," Salem called to them, nudging aside a few piled garbage bags with the toe of one boot. The ghost of hope flitted across Anita's face, but Simon heard the silence from the spot and knew the truth before Salem spoke the words. "She's dead."

What little life had come back to Miguel's face drained away, and he gave a soft, whispering moan. He toppled sideways, and Simon caught him, lowering him to the ground in a pile of garbage bags. Anita knelt in front of him, crying in earnest now, looking down the alley to Salem and then back to Miguel. Then she gasped.

Simon slipped his knife free and raised the blade, looking in all directions. "What?"

"They invited us to a party on Christmas Eve," she whispered in horror. "A party in a graveyard . . ."

Simon's eyes widened as he caught up to her intuition. Salem had taken up a position leaning against an alley wall, but he flashed back to them when Anita spoke, face abruptly intense. Kneeling between them, he took Miguel's face in both of his hands. "Look at me."

Miguel's brown eyes lurched to meet to Salem's, and Simon saw the emeralds glow red. "Who did this to you?"

Miguel's heartbeat faltered; the command in Salem's eyes did not touch him, and Salem frowned. But the dying man managed to gasp, "He killed them. All of them. It's my fault . . ."

"No, Miguel," Anita said, but Salem didn't even glance at her.

"Where is he?" he demanded.

"Gravey-y-yard."

"Where specifically?"

"The . . . the ch-ch-chapel . . . undern-n-n-n-neath . . ."

"Underneath?" Salem asked, but no magic was going to force anything else from Miguel. His heart was beating once every few seconds. Salem stood, turning away, and Anita took one of Miguel's hands. The fingers of his other hand squeezed vacantly at the air, and Simon felt compelled to grip it.

"Heidi," Miguel whispered. Then his grip loosened, his breathing stopped, and his heart fell silent. His empty eyes stared toward the dark sky.

Anita shook him twice, then wrapped her arms around Simon's neck, crying into his shoulder as she took ragged breaths, trying to control herself. Simon held her awkwardly with his knife hand, keeping the blade away from her body, as he reached his other hand out to close Miguel's eyes.

"Let's go," Salem said impatiently.

Simon helped Anita up, and she pulled her tearstained face away. "We have to call someone . . . we can't just leave them like this."

She looked down the alley, and her heart accelerated as she peered at the spot where Heidi's body was hidden.

Salem sighed and asked, "What would you say? How would you explain finding their bodies here?"

Anita struggled for an answer, and Salem stepped up to her. Reading her face for a moment, he frowned, but then said, "They're dead. Nothing can help them now. If you want to put this right, focus and help me destroy Shafax. It's weakness to mourn the slain when you can punish the murderer instead."

His voice was smoother than Simon expected, calm and persuasive, and Anita responded to it. She brushed the tears off her cheeks, swallowed hard, and met his gaze. "Right. Let's go."

Salem nodded and led the way out the other end of the alley. Simon took Anita's hand and followed, keeping himself between her and Heidi's body. She kept her eyes forward, taking slow breaths through her nose, but Simon glanced down. Heidi was curled into a ball among the garbage, tiny and pathetic in death. But she looked pretty too, in a way that Simon had never noticed before.

They traversed back alleys and smaller, snowy side streets. Occasionally, Salem guided them into deeper shadows as a car went by, kicking up slush, but they passed no humans on the way. Concerned for Anita, Simon thought that was best; if they passed some unwary mortal and Salem decided he did want a snack, Simon didn't think she could hold it together. Her face was set, but she had taken his free hand again, and now he didn't care what Salem might say.

They had been sneaking along so stealthily that Simon and Anita both started when Salem strode right up to the reinforced double doors of an extinct factory and kicked them open. He went in like he owned the place, leaving his confused companions to follow. Simon couldn't begin to guess what had been made here, although the thick layer of dust stirred up by their steps told him it hadn't been any time recently. Anita sneezed.

Salem crossed the warehouse and looked out the opposite door, edging it open a crack. As Simon and Anita came up behind him, Anita still rubbing her nose as her eyes watered, Salem opened the door farther for them to see. Across the street, the wrought iron bars of the cemetery fence stretched for blocks, with a slight indentation for the main entrance.

"That's our way in," Salem said, and his voice was dark with anticipation.

"Right through the main gate?" Simon asked. "Isn't that a little obvious?"

"Ordinarily yes, but Shafax isn't ordinary," Salem replied. "I don't want to get caught with some of us on one side of the fence and some on the other. He'll be able to sense my presence, if he hasn't already."

Simon looked at Anita. "What about us?"

"Unlikely. Mortals are beneath his notice and you're not much better. But I wouldn't wander too far. If he catches you alone, you're done."

The words did little to boost Simon's confidence in Salem's semblance of a plan, but the elder vampire didn't even look at him. Stepping away from the door, he stripped off his cloth coat and set it in the dust, then took the two swords off his hip. One was his usual gladius, and the other was a longer, curved Japanese katana that Simon also recognized. He remembered the feel of the venerable weapon in his hands when Salem had allowed him to practice with it, ages ago.

After leaning the blades against the door within reach, Salem pulled at his black T-shirt with the fingertips of both hands, then shook his head. Stripping it off and tossing it onto the coat, he muttered, "Not again."

Anita looked at him with a rush of indrawn breath. Simon glanced at Salem, then frowned back at Anita. Salem was well-muscled like a soldier, with powerful arms, a broad chest, and a tight core, but his pale flesh was no more unnatural than the rest of him. Apart from the twisted and pinkened scar flesh just above his heart in the shape of a circle no larger than a half dollar coin, there was nothing unusual about him at all. Anita caught Simon's look, took a deep breath, and shook her head.

Salem either missed her reaction or ignored it. "Better drop your coat too," he advised Simon. "You'll want complete freedom of movement."

Nodding, Simon threw his coat and shirt on the floor. He hesitated, wondering about Anita's reaction, but then peeled off his gloves as well, flexing his claws. Anita's heartbeat stuttered, but she came to his side and took one of his hands in hers, carefully running her fingertips down his fingers and sharp nails. Her face was hard to read, but her touch was reassuring. At least she didn't shiver.

"If you two are ready . . ." Salem hinted. He had the katana in his right hand and the gladius in his left.

Anita dropped Simon's hand, then clutched the collar of her jacket closed. "I hope you don't expect me to—"

"No," Salem interrupted dryly. He looked her up and down and cocked an eyebrow. "You don't really do anything for me, Entrée, and I need you to not be shivering while you're trying to aim."

Anita drew the handgun out of her coat pocket, grabbing it automatically before she remembered and shifted her grip to the way Simon had shown her. Her eyes flicked up to Simon's, and he nodded. "Good."

Salem sighed. "Just try not to shoot me; it's distracting. Now come, children," he added as he kicked open the door and strode out into the snow. "Let's not keep His Majesty waiting."

"YOU HAVE failed."

Hans Richtein cowered on the floor, the Master's voice pressing him into the dirt. The shame of his failure haunted him, but the physical pain kept intruding on his groveling. He had wrapped bandages and gauze over his mutilated eye, but of course it moved in time with his good one, and every glance stung.

The pain suddenly amplified, becoming acid eating away at the nerves behind the eye. Screaming, Hans understood too late that he had not responded to the Master. "Mercy, Master!" he begged, one hand pressed to his injured face an instant before he realized the mistake; the touch sent another sizzle of agony through him. "Please, Master, I'm sorry!"

"Two children," the gravelly rasp spat. "Injured. Ill. Dying. And yet you could not contain them."

Past words, Hans only sobbed.

"How could you fail us like this?" Christine shrieked at him. Her voice lost its husky seduction as it pitched high with stress. "You had one job to do!"

A sudden flash of pain exploded in his abdomen, and Hans slid across the mossy, dirty stone before impacting a wall with another cascade of pain in the small of his back. She snarled, and Hans dared not open his good eye to see the expression on her face.

"Perhaps tomorrow you will fail to protect us?" the Master suggested coldly. "Perhaps you will allow others to descend on us as we sleep and try to make an end of us?"

"No, Master," Hans whimpered, forcing his eye open so the Master could see the contrition in his mind. The hooded and robed vampire loomed over him, almost as tall as the ceiling in this cramped place, and two pinpoints of hellfire burned from the shadows of his cowl. Christine stood at his side, her radiant face twisting into something horrible in her fury.

"Maybe that's what you want!" she hissed, and her blue eyes erupted into glowing flame too. "Maybe you want to destroy everything we've done!"

"No!" Hans screamed. "Never!"

She kicked him again; one of his ribs broke. "I needed them!"

The pain behind his eyes vanished, and Hans was left to sob into the frozen stone floor. The salt in his tears burned his blinded eye as the Master turned to Christine. "Needed them?" he repeated scathingly. "They are mortals. They are nothing. We need none of them."

"I . . ." Christine said, her tone abruptly wary, almost frightened. "I just meant . . ."

"There are other lives to sate you," the Master cut her off. "Do not degrade yourself to the petty emotions of mortals."

"Yes, my lord," Christine said. "But—"

"Silence!"

She flinched back, the red glow fading from her eyes. Clutching his burning chest, Hans whispered, "Master . . . Master please, I need a doctor."

The cowl rounded back on him. "I offered you the chance to have the mark of your failure mended," the vampire said with awful indifference. "And did you bring them back?"

"I couldn't find them!" Hans cried. He had wandered the streets for hours in the cold, his eye throbbing, trying and failing to track the two escapees. His despair had compounded at every alley they weren't hiding in, every doorway in which they weren't taking shelter. If he didn't see a doctor soon, he would never see from his left eye again. That fear had gripped him as he groped and staggered, unused to the lack of depth perception.

Part of him had dared to consider going to the hospital against the Master's wishes. Even when the day finally came, when the Master made him great and strong and immortal too, he would still be half-blind if he didn't see a doctor soon. How could the Master let that be? His servants needed to be flawless, an imitation of their lord's perfection.

"I have no need for a servant who can not perform his duties to me," the vampire declared. "Perhaps your deformity will remind you not to fail again."

Again? There would be another chance! The Master was not going to cast him away! The hint of hope struggled to smolder away his pain and fear, and failed. He knew he should thank the Master for his abundant mercy, but he was so very vulnerable, so afraid of this weakness and what it might mean for him.

"M-Master," he said, carefully shifting up to a seated position. "If . . . if I were healed, I could—"

"Consider yourself blessed with my generosity," the Master cut across him, "that I do not take your other eye as well."

Blindness. Darkness forever. Groping in the emptiness, lost and vulnerable, deserted by the Master and abandoned to the cruelties of a world that was meaningless in his absence . . . Hans shuddered as he crawled forward on hands and knees, then pressed the hem of the Master's robe to his lips with a quivering hand. "Thank you, Master."

"I can find them," Christine volunteered; Hans shrank away from her contemptuous look. "I'll hunt them down and have them back in—"

"You will stay here until I command you to do otherwise," the Master spat at her, and she grimaced, looking frustrated and wary at once. For a moment, the vampire lord stood, flexing his talons.

Then his cowled face turned upward to the ceiling, as if the arches of weather stone had called to him. A low, serpentine hiss slithered from the shadows beneath his hood as his hands curled into claws. "He comes here? He returns *here*—he dares to challenge *me*?"

Hans cringed in on himself, the pain in his rib swallowed whole by instinctive dread at that baleful snarl. But the Master's long fingers flexed, and when he spoke next, fiendish glee replaced the fury. "But still . . . he has come."

"Flavius?" Christine asked. Before there was time for an answer, her ruby lips twisted into a sneer. "And Simon?"

"The wretches with which Flavius surrounds himself are of no interest to me," the Master answered with frigid disdain. "Only Flavius himself matters now. And he has come to me here to present himself for slaughter. Or perhaps he fantasizes of reclaiming the ground he lost. No matter. He is here."

The voice promised wrath and punishment, and Hans's mind welled up with images of vampires gargling on their own stolen blood as it was drained from their throats, of bodies staked and burned at rest in their coffins and tombs, and of cities burning as buildings collapsed upon themselves and terrified humans fled the inevitable doom. And over it all, the King of Vampires sat on a throne of skulls, some human, some with the longer canine fangs of vampires, all pouring blood from their bleached white eye sockets.

A vision of the future, the Master's long ages of work rewarded, the promise of Flavius's blood fulfilled. Hans blinked, and the vision was gone.

"Let me kill Simon," Christine pleaded, and the sudden intensity in her bright blue eyes was more unnerving to Hans than the rage had been.

"Why, have you learned something since I was forced to deliver you from him yesterday?" the Master hissed without looking at her.

Christine retreated a step from the contempt, but she rallied and said, "I can do it, my lord, I know it." In an attempt at her usual purr, she added, "It would be beneath a king to trouble himself with a peasant."

The hooded face turned to her, and the tension thickened in the air. But when the dead voice spoke, the smoothness of its whispery rasp recalled the Master's voice in the nightclub. "True. Kill him then, precious one. But ensure that you leave Flavius to me, and to me alone."

"I will," Christine promised, her eyes shining above the smile twisting her lips. She reached for one of his hands, but he flicked his fingers at her and she stumbled back a few steps before catching her balance. The wounded look that flashed across her face vanished in a second, replaced by resolution. "I won't fail you."

"See that you do not."

She disappeared down the corridor. Hans stared resentfully after her until the Master moved. Cringing on instinct, it took him a second to notice the vampire lord had walked away, not closer. Stepping up to the sarcophagus on which his own casket rested, the Master dipped one withered hand inside, then brought it up again before letting the sand trickle through his long fingers.

"She . . . she has the power to defeat Flavius, Master?" Hans inquired.

The vampire made a scathing noise. "Of course not. I shall be greatly surprised if she can even slay his underling."

"Then . . ." Hans felt the confusion on his face. "Then why . . . ?"

"She has served her purpose," the Master replied. "Had Flavius continued to flee, she was my link to him through the underling Simon and that accursed human."

The naked malevolence at the mention of the girl made the voice itself a weapon; Hans imagined that his Master could speak in that voice to the girl and the very sound of it would slay her.

"But Flavius has come to me," the Master continued, his voice under better control, "and so Christine has become superfluous."

"And . . . and if she does triumph over the younger vampire, Master?" Hans dared to ask.

"If she does, Flavius will surely destroy her," the vampire replied. "And if he can not be bothered with her, then I will reclaim what is mine, once I have Flavius's blood."

"Queen," he added with disgust. "A god needs no consort."

Something about that was wrong, Hans was sure of it. He had no love for Christine; she had denied him again and again, in every way available to her. But she had such trust on her face, a commitment Hans thought might approach the depth of his own. He frowned, staring at the ground with his remaining eye, and almost didn't notice as the Master laced his fingers together in front of his hidden face.

"But the death of the underling would be convenient," the sinister voice conceded. "Let us send aid to the would-be queen."

His harsh laugh picked at Hans's brain, the sound unsettling him in an unfamiliar, unpleasant way. Then the ancient voice began to chant, monotone words and phrases rebounding off the stone walls and echoing on themselves. The air tingled with magic, stretching out through the ground and into the sky beyond.

In the darkness down the hall, something stirred.

TWENTY-ONE

SALEM LED the way across the street with Simon and Anita side by side a few steps behind. Though they walked through uncleared snow on the sidewalks and slush on the road, Anita noticed that only her steps made any sound. She tried not to think much about that, and the looming gates of Saint Brigid's Cemetery did a good job diverting her attention. The wrought iron fence soared to twice her height, and the bare trees beyond glowered down on her. Clouds blotted out the moon above.

Salem walked right up to the closed gates and peered through. Anita stepped closer to Simon, who was tossing his kukri knife from hand to hand. The stiff set to his face contrasted starkly with the glimpses Anita had caught of Salem's casual expression.

"Nervous?" she asked him quietly. She was sure Salem could hear her, but he seemed absorbed.

Simon was trying to see past Salem into the cemetery, but he glanced down at her when she spoke. He caught his kukri in his right hand and kept it there. Studying her face for a moment, he opened his mouth, then decided against whatever he had been about to say. Ignoring the question, he said instead, "Stay close to me when we're inside."

Anita nodded, then had a thought and stuck the gun Salem had given her in her left pocket. Reaching up to her neck, she pulled off the rosary, draped it over her right wrist, dropped the crucifix through the loop on the other end, and pulled it tight. The beads caught against each other securely, and the little crucifix dangled until she caught it in her hand.

"My Uncle Tim taught me this," she said, smiling up at Simon. She tried not to let it bother her that he seemed too uncomfortable to smile back. "He said it's a good way to keep it within reach when you're not praying with it. And I can let it go to use both hands."

She dropped the cross, letting it dangle again, and used her right hand to support her left's grip on the pistol. Simon adjusted two of her fingers, careful not to touch the rosary.

". . . right," he said.

"We're clear," Salem announced, sticking his swords into the snowy dirt beneath a faded bronze plaque Anita couldn't read. She jumped when, without any warning, Salem simply grabbed one of the gates and ripped it right off its rusted green hinges, then leaned it against the wall. The swords were back in his hands before the metallic shriek's echo had died away.

"Subtle," Simon commented.

Salem snorted. "He knows we're here, there's no point in stealth now."

"You're sure he's here?" Anita asked, and the idea brought back all her fear and unease. She had focused on Christine, spent long hours wondering how she could pry her friend away from whatever the thing had done to her. What spare thoughts she did manage were devoted to how to make things right with Simon. The dilemmas had dominated her so completely that she had been able—in the sunlight or the bright lights of the train—to put thoughts of the ultimate enemy from her mind.

But now, under the watching trees and the arch of the gate, those fiendish eyes were all she could think of. Mutated eyes, animal's teeth, and inhuman, insane rage, all fixated on her with the unstoppable force of a volcano. *He'd burn the whole world and everything in it just to get to you, and kill everyone you love for the pleasure of making you suffer.* She shuddered; Salem's uncaring, taunting assessment had carved out a permanent niche in her mind.

Salem didn't seem to care much now, either. "Oh yes."

"Can you feel his presence?" Simon asked.

The other vampire smirked mockingly. "You can't?"

Simon frowned, narrowing his eyes as if he were concentrating, but Salem just snickered and jerked his head toward the open gate. "Let's go," he said. "Time to put an end to this."

He slipped into the graveyard first. Anita swallowed, leaned up on her tiptoes to kiss Simon, and found him rigid with tension; his cold lips moved stiffly against hers even as his free hand brushed her cheek. Then he pulled away and followed Salem, and Anita brought up the rear.

The second she stepped past the gate, she understood what Salem was talking about. The cold air grew heavier, as if the bite of winter's chill had coupled with the oppression of summer's humidity. Even the breeze smelled unhealthy, like a gust over a sewer grate; the graveyard smelled earthier, but no less rotten. Something was off, too, like the air was pressing on her eardrums. Then she realized it was silent.

Not the "silence" of the back streets and alleys through which Salem had taken them, with the background clamor of the city in the distance. Anita had lived in and around Chicago all her life, and its native soundtrack was so much a part of her experience that she no longer even noticed it . . . until it was gone. But the cemetery was so perfectly silent, so devoid of sound, that every uncomfortable shuffle of her boots was deafening and every ragged breath thundered in her ears. As Simon and Salem moved ahead of her like wraiths, she felt horribly exposed.

Without warning, the snow on the ground seemed to swell upward before it turned into fog, thick and white and obscuring everything. It hovered around them at waist height, and Anita's imagination kicked into overdrive, picturing every slimy and awful thing that could catch her legs unseen. She tried not to run to Simon's side.

"This is freaky," she whispered, and try as she might she couldn't keep the fear from her voice. She had the oddest notion the mist was watching them.

"This isn't you, is it?" Simon asked Salem, and the older vampire shook his head, peering around the misty graveyard with narrowed eyes.

"No." He raised one sword, face taut for a moment with effort before it relaxed into a grimace. "And I can't overpower it. Shafax."

The name made Anita shuffle closer to Simon. A second later, a high-pitched howl cut the silence like a knife. Anita whirled toward it, but another answered from the other direction. She glanced back at the gate, but as if responding to her thoughts, a third howl came from the opening. Then they were coming from all directions, yips and canine barks mixed in.

Simon stepped in front of her protectively as he looked around for the source of the sounds. She was surprised when Salem mirrored him, pressing his back against hers and raising both swords to guard. Tremors rattled her body; she took her finger off the trigger of her pistol.

Something growled in the fog, and both vampires turned toward it, edging Anita behind them. Through the space between their pale bodies, she saw a pair of amber eyes glaring at her. They came closer, piercing the fog to reveal a narrow canine muzzle. Smaller than a wolf, but shaped the same way . . .

"Urban coyotes, huh?" Salem asked.

There was another growl, and a second coyote crept forward, its sharp teeth bared. More slipped forth from the fog, some perching on the long, sarcophagus-shaped monuments around the graveyard, others slinking toward them through the undulating blanket of white.

"I didn't think coyotes preyed on humans," Anita observed in a small voice as the canines started to circle, eyes never leaving her.

"Coyotes don't travel in packs of"—Simon glanced around—"seventeen, either. He must be summoning them."

Salem snarled then, and Anita cringed up against Simon's back until he flinched away from the touch of the rosary around her wrist. The sound was as bestial as anything coming from the coyotes, and several of them retreated, baring their teeth even as their ears flattened back along their heads. Salem snarled again, but this time it sounded more annoyed.

Then one coyote darted at Anita's side; the scrabble against snow was her only warning. As she was still turning, there was a flash of pale flesh and shining steel, and the coyote's body fell to the ground even as its severed head rolled forward, bumping Anita's leg before it came to rest. She gasped, choking back vomit as blood poured from the stump of its neck and its exposed muscles steamed in the cold air. Simon flicked his kukri, and a line of blood splattered onto the snow.

The impromptu pack backed up, still snarling, and Salem spun both his swords. "Maybe they'll react better to their natural predators. Simon?"

Anita couldn't make any sense of that, but Simon asked, "You'll cover Anita?"

"Yes, yes."

Simon slipped the kukri into its sheath and flexed his clawed hands. He snarled at the coyotes, but the sound twisted, deepening and becoming more guttural. He convulsed forward as if something had struck him in the gut, then dropped onto his hands and feet, still making that horrible gargling noise. Anita reached out a hand to him, frightened, but Salem cautioned her, "I wouldn't."

Simon's pale flesh darkened. She thought for an instant he was turning gray until she realized thick, coarse fur was erupting through his flesh. He bared his teeth, and they were all sharpening into points, reminding Anita horribly of Shafax's shark teeth. Simon's black pants turned gray and morphed into fur, and a shiver rolled from his neck to his tailbone before the back of his pants stretched out into a tail. His face elongated, ears coming to sharper points as they traveled to the top of his head. He growled again, and it was more menacing than anything the coyotes could produce.

As Anita stared in shock at the wolf that had just been Simon, head and shoulders taller than any of the animals facing him, he sprang forward, catching the closest coyote around the neck and tearing out its throat with a quick twist of his powerful jaws. Anita backed up until she bumped into Salem as Simon skipped away from the snap of another coyote's teeth, then reared up to bring his claws down on the animal's snout. The attack missed its eyes, but the coyote yipped and scrambled back, four long cuts bleeding across its muzzle.

Then the pressure on her back was gone, and Anita whirled around to find Salem in the midst of three coyotes. As she watched, he spun in a lightning-quick swirl of steel, and all three coyotes fell, two bisected through the middle and one with half a head. From behind her, Anita heard a lupine snarl, and turned to find a coyote on Simon's back, teeth sunk into him. Before she could even think to help, Simon pitched the attacking predator off him onto the snow and his strong jaws snapped on its throat like a bear trap.

Her hands clenched involuntarily, and Anita finally remembered the pistol in her hand. She brought it up, trying to take aim, but the four coyotes ringing Simon were too close; she was terrified of hitting him instead. She didn't dare try to help Salem; he was moving too quickly for her eyes to follow as he carved a path of destruction through the rest of the pack. One latched onto his leg, but Salem kicked it so hard that it soared away through the air.

Spinning back toward Simon, she saw a pair of coyotes heading her way. Simon saw them too, but when he tried to head them off, his opponents snapped at him, ringing him in. Anita leveled the pistol and fired, but her shot went wide, and the explosive report was much louder than she had expected. She cringed as it assaulted her eardrums, and the first coyote sprang.

Scrambling sideways, she dodged its claws by inches, its fur brushing her coat. Her heart leapt into her throat as she whirled and fired three quick shots. Two missed, but the third lodged in the coyote's hip just as it was pivoting on the spot. The animal yelped and collapsed.

Anita heard the second coyote coming, charging low to the ground instead of springing. By the time she turned it was within a yard, and she kicked at it without thinking. The animal dodged, but Anita had overextended, and as she landed heavily on her kicking leg, the coyote sank its teeth into her ankle. The tough leather of her boots blunted some of the attack, but she still felt a stab of pain as the teeth pierced her skin.

She cried out, but rather than recoiling and trying for a better bite, the coyote tried to drag her instead. Even hopping awkwardly on her free leg, she wasn't going to miss at point blank range. The bullet went straight into the center of the coyote's back. It released her, falling onto its side with a whine, and she shot it through the head.

Pulse racing and lungs dragging breath in before forcing it out again, Anita landed hard on her bad ankle, and the pain intensified. Unable to balance, she stumbled and came down on her side. She looked up in time to see the first coyote limping toward her through the fog, saliva dripping from its muzzle. There was nothing natural about the way it snapped its teeth at her, and Anita swung her pistol hand up just as the coyote broke into a staggering charge. Shooting one-handed, she grazed it the first time, but the second shot went just under the coyote's jaw and lodged in its chest. It collapsed, gargling blood in the back of its throat, narrow jaws working against the snow as its three good legs scrabbled on the ground before growing still.

For a second, Anita rested.

A light pressure scratched her leg. She whirled up to a sitting position, shifting her pistol into a two-handed grip with her arms locked out, eyes wide. But there was no coyote. Even as the fog swirled around and over her, blocking out the images that went with the sounds of Simon's snarling, snapping fight and the occasional splatter she associated with Salem, she was sure none of the pack had gotten close to her. No teeth latched on to her to drag her away to be devoured.

Her ankle tickled.

She glanced down, and her frown of confusion became horror. A rat was crawling up her pant leg, tiny claws scrabbling for a hold on the denim. She screamed and kicked, trying to flail it off, and the movement dislodged it—but it landed only two feet away and charged right back at her like she was a magnet.

Scrambling back, her right hand digging into the snow behind her, she felt it come down on something warm and soft, followed by a brief but intense pinch in the back of her hand. She looked down and saw she was all but gripping another rat, her blood on its teeth. She had barely begun to shriek again before the darkness around her surged, countless beady eyes fixated on her, bald tails wriggling, and long gnawing teeth chomping the air.

They dug into her jeans for a hold, clawed for purchase on her leather coat, and slipped into the legs of her pants where they draped over her boots. Clammy paws slapped on her thighs, and Anita cried out in sheer terror. Dropping her pistol, she tried to roll away, but her arm slipped and she fell on her stomach. They surged onto her, burrowing under her jacket and against her turtleneck, scratching her bare hands, and sneaking under her coat as their naked tails stroked the small of her back. Pinches of pain popped up all over her body as their teeth and claws found purchase.

They were lodged in her hair. They scrambled over her neck. She screamed until she felt a tiny paw on her lip and clamped her jaws shut, the idea of it darting into her mouth and eating her tongue overriding any thought or sane reaction. She got to her feet, heedless of the dull throb in her ankle, swatting at herself and moaning through her clenched teeth every time her bare palms met those little hairy bodies. She grabbed at them wildly and threw them off, but for each one she hurled away there was a lance of pain in her hand and another rat took its place. The paws scrabbled over every inch of her, invading her, their squeaks in her ears and—

"Freeze!"

Salem's voice was so icy cold, so filled with overpowering authority, that it pierced even her blind haze of horror, and Anita locked into place obediently. In the next instant, the air whirled around her like she was trapped inside a tornado. The rats squealed and shrieked, warm blood leaking onto Anita's neck and face and hands, but she dared not open her eyes. The wriggling all over her body grew still, one cluster at a time, until the only thing shaking was Anita herself. She forced her eyes open.

Salem stood before her, blood dripping from both swords. A pile of bisected and decapitated rats lay all around her. She staggered back, and two dead rats toppled from the inside of her coat. The movement stirred something inside her, and she felt a frantic scrabble between her coat and her turtleneck.

Salem frowned. "Missed one."

His katana flashed, an adder-quick stab at her chest that she had no chance of blocking. The point slipped through the leather of her jacket and back out without cutting her skin, and the wriggling stopped. The vampire stepped forward with a three-fingered grip on his gladius and shook the lapel of her coat with the other two fingers, and the dead rat fell among its brethren.

Salem winked one emerald eye.

Anita's mouth was still hanging open, the memory of those tiny bodies all over her fresh in her mind, when Salem stuck both his swords through his belt and pitched forward onto his hands and feet. His transformation was smoother and faster than Simon's; in barely more than a second, he was another wolf, darker and burlier, and he dived into the wave of oncoming rats. His jaws snapped up three of them before they were even aware of his presence, and a feral snarl ripped through his blood-soaked teeth.

The coyotes might have felt safe in the strength of their overwhelming pack numbers against a wolf, but the rats clearly had no such confidence. They squealed, racing off in all directions with their bald tails snapping behind them. Salem pursued them, his sharp claws and teeth making quick work of any that got within range. He disappeared into the fog, his growls growing more distant, and the rats did not come back.

There was pressure on Anita's back and she whirled around, bringing her hands up to protect her face. Simon stood there, bite marks healing on his chest and arm, a pile of dead coyotes in the snow behind him. He recoiled, eyes wide, but then his hands shot out to grab her upper arms. She struggled in his grip until he spoke. "Anita!"

She grew still for a moment, looking into his eyes as she struggled for control. The images kept forcing themselves into her mind—a dying heart pumping blood out of the stump of a coyote's neck, the beady little eyes advancing toward her face—and every sting and ache on her flesh reminded her of the scrabbling, naked paws and the teeth that had found purchase there. Something warm ran over her eyes, and acid bubbled in her stomach as she tried to identify it. Lurching away from Simon, she wiped at her face with the palms of her hands; they came away dripping red that was not her own. Her coat was half-shredded, her turtleneck and jeans damp, and her legs shook.

"Anita . . ." he started warily.

Anita forced herself to take deep breaths until they slowed. Her brain had needed a reset after whatever happened in the alley, but she couldn't afford that this time. *They were just animals, and they're gone now.*

She, Simon, and Salem were here for the monster influencing them, the one who had killed Miguel and Heidi and twisted Christine into a mockery of herself. The thoughts steeled her, and her hand was steady as she took Simon's.

"I'm okay," she promised, willing it to be so. His gray eyes probed her face, looking doubtful and concerned, but she squeezed his icy fingers and he nodded.

Salem's voice, right behind her, still made her jump. "'Okay' might be overstating things," the vampire commented, and as Anita spun around to look at him, she saw he had both swords raised again. "Tender moment later. Not being eaten now."

"Eaten?" Anita asked faintly. She felt something cold, hard, and familiar in her left hand; Simon had pressed her fallen pistol into her grip. But he wasn't looking at her, and he drew his knife again as he stepped forward to Salem's side. Anita forced herself to swallow and move to Simon's other side, and as she listened, shuffling, heavy steps and low grunts reached her through the fog.

Someone gasped to their left, then ahead and to the right. But they weren't quite gasps; the sound reminded Anita of a medical special she had seen of a sucking chest wound, the patient drawing in air through a gunshot in his lung rather than his mouth. Then figures surged out of the fog, and she couldn't restrain her scream. Simon hissed at her side, his knife held out like a warding torch.

Salem rolled his eyes and said, "Ah, Shafax. Always the melodrama."

A group of people was closing on them . . . but they weren't quite people. Their faces were sunken and hollowed and their flesh was putrefied, warped, and various shades of blue and gray. They were fully dressed, but their bloated bare hands and faces showed blisters that had burst and leaked green and yellow fluids. Their eye sockets were hollow, but they seemed to know exactly where they were going. They plodded forward more slowly than living humans, but faster than Anita would have expected from . . . from . . .

"Zombies?" Simon asked, disbelief in his voice.

"The least of the undead," Salem said disparagingly. "Shafax has to resort to them because none of us will serve him willingly anymore."

He looked past Simon at Anita and asked, "Maybe you'll contribute to the fight this time, Dinner?"

Anita remembered the pistol in her hands and raised it. The things shambling at her looked human in the swirling mist, but they were clearly not alive. They moaned through the hollows of their torn-out throats, and the sound sharpened her focus. She aimed at the nearest zombie's head just long enough to see her sight picture wobbling all around it; she would never land that shot. Instead, she pointed it at the thing's chest, gritted her teeth, and pulled the trigger.

Hands trembling from the cold and lingering nerves, her first shot missed entirely. Overcompensating for her aim, her second shot grazed its arm. Pulling the trigger more slowly, she put the third shot in its stomach, but the thing slogged on without even slowing down.

Through the ringing in her ears, she heard Salem snap, "Oh, Mars and Bellona, let me do it!"

He stuck his katana point-first into the ground and wrenched the pistol from her hands. He fired one-handed, hardly pausing to aim, pulling the trigger again and again until the firing pin clicked on an empty chamber. For every shot, a zombie lurched back, a hole in its forehead or right between its eyes. One thing's head exploded.

Simon turned to stare. "You always said—"

"I said using guns is beneath me," Salem cut him off, tossing the empty pistol back to Anita. "Not that I can't. Let's—"

But he stopped in mid-sentence, because the enemy was still advancing. The bullet wounds did not heal, but nor did they have any discernable effect. Even the headless revenant continued forward. A second wave appeared behind the first, and the reinforcements were markedly less human. Several were all but skeletons with only thin strands of tissue connecting joints, and most were missing body parts; one skeleton was gone from the waist down, and dragged itself forward with its arms, its bony jaws clacking. Other zombies wore a variety of outfits, but Anita saw several in the shredded remains of gang colors with bullet holes through their shirts. One shambling corpse wore an undershirt, underwear, and a burlap sack tied over its head with a bloodstain on the front and duct tape still clinging to one wrist. Anita suspected people had been making use of the cemetery long after it closed.

She and Simon fell back, but Salem had his eyes on a male zombie with half a head and a revolver clutched in its dead, decaying hand. Salem sprang at it and ran it through the heart with his katana. It raised the gun and shot him, but as Anita gasped, Salem just lopped off the gun arm with his gladius before swinging it around to chop off the head, too.

"Didn't I kill you once before?" he demanded.

What was left of the head landed in the snow, but the teeth still gnashed. The zombie's remaining arm grabbed at Salem, fingers scraping his bare chest, until the vampire hissed and chopped that off too. Its legs continued to plod forward, pushing the torso farther onto the katana.

"Salem!" Simon barked, pushing Anita back with one hand as he held out the knife in his right. The zombies had formed a loose semicircle and were starting to close in.

Salem drew his katana out and amputated his target's legs at the knees, then kicked another zombie away as it came at him from the side. The rib cage squished when it cracked under the blow. "Go around, come at them from the other side!" he called, chopping off a pair of hands reaching for him. "Cut them into as many pieces as you can!"

Simon pointed to the gap in the zombie ranks and Anita followed him through. His kukri flashed and a zombie head rolled away, but its headless body got a grip on his arm. He shoved it away with his other hand and darted through the space between two of the groping, groaning bodies. Anita raced toward the same hole, but the lingering pain in her ankle slowed her, and dead fingers brushed across the back of her jacket. She broke through before they got a firm hold and ran after Simon, weaving and dodging around headstones. The moaning was all around them now, and it echoed off the cold stones until it sounded like the graves themselves were calling her home to them.

The snow at Anita's feet erupted and a hand seized the cuff of her jeans. Too petrified to scream, she pointed her gun into the dirt, but the trigger wouldn't pull; she remembered a second later that it was empty. Stomping on the hand with her other foot, she broke it off at the forearm. The whole burial plot churned, and Anita knew she didn't want to see what was coming through. She hobbled after Simon, the hand still clinging to her leg until she kicked it off against a headstone.

Simon had stopped in the middle of two skeletons with only shreds of tissue keeping the bones together; even as she watched, one's arm fell off on its own. Simon jammed his kukri through its rib cage, grabbed them both, and smashed their heads together; the skulls disintegrated into shards of bone. The vampire ripped his knife back out and hacked both his attackers in half through their spines.

They retreated toward a pair of mausoleums, and Anita glimpsed the outline of a taller building in the distance, which had to be the chapel Miguel had mentioned. A number of the zombies turned to pursue them, and as Simon waded into them, Anita pulled out one of her spare magazines and examined the pistol frantically, trying to remember how to load it. Across the graveyard, mist whirled around Salem as he tore through the crowd of the dead, wheeling his two swords like a combine harvester and hacking everything in his path to shreds of bone and necrotized flesh.

She ejected the empty magazine, but then jammed the replacement in the wrong way. Pounding from behind her drew her attention, and she turned to see the door of a mausoleum rattling on its hinges. She tried to focus, finally slamming the magazine home, and managed to pull the slide back, but her finger caught in the ejection port.

"Ow!" she yelped, pulling it free; it had already turned to a blood-filled purple blister on her skin. The door in front of her cracked, a fault line ripping from ground to frame, and Anita backed away, glancing behind her. Simon was still knifing his way through zombies, and disembodied limbs were crawling after him.

The door dissolved into splinters, and the three who had been hammering on it tumbled out, each on top of the next. Anita shifted her aim down, but as the half-smashed face glared up at her, the pentacle necklace beneath glistening with blood, recognition kicked in and Anita's finger froze on the trigger.

Sarah was glowering at her, her good eye starting to decay, the other caved in along with the left side of her head. Tony's head lolled to one side, the snapped neck bone unable to support it, but his frost-covered face was fixed on her and his blue lips peeled back from his snapping teeth. The girl beneath them both sat up with an animalistic snarl, her shirt half-shredded from the stab wounds on the flesh below.

They got to their feet as more poured from the mausoleum. Anita backed away, but she couldn't make her finger tighten on the trigger. She had seen these people less than two weeks before, alive and healthy, together like a mismatched family. Even as one of Tony's powerful hands reached for her, she remembered his fond smile as he ruffled Heidi's hair. They were closing in on her, moving faster with their recently dead bodies still intact, their undissolved eyes glaring at her, their strong fingers on her coat—

"Snap out of it!" Simon roared, and he barreled into Tony, sending him sideways into the mausoleum hard enough that his collarbone cracked and one side of his body slumped. Anita blinked and scrambled back to give him room. The girl with the stab wounds grabbed him from behind and bit the side of his neck, and Simon grunted in pain; somehow her teeth had managed to puncture his tough skin. Another of Miguel's friends, his body strangely flattened, latched onto Simon's knife arm.

Anita tried to summon the will to shoot one of these people who still looked like people—people who might've become friends—but before she could, Sarah's hands clamped onto Anita's shoulders and pulled her in for a bite. Her foul corpse breath invaded Anita's nostrils, but Anita managed to throw her arm up against Sarah's chest, holding the snapping jaws at bay by inches and leaning her face back from the chomping, hungry teeth. She pressed the rosary against Sarah's wrist without effect.

Then Sarah's head was gone, bouncing off through the snow. Her pentacle necklace slipped over the stump, brushing Anita's jacket as it fell to the ground. Simon grabbed the headless undead and hurled it away. She backed away as he turned into a heel kick that ripped the flattened boy's jaw off.

A dark flash of movement against the fog and snow was her only warning.

"Simon!"

He turned a second too slowly, and Christine hit him like a wrecking ball. He flew into the wall of the mausoleum and smashed right through, the roof caving in as the wall gave out. As the bricks rained down to bury him, Miguel's reanimated friends started toward Anita, but Christine raised a pale hand. "No! She's mine!"

They faltered, then obeyed, trudging off to the sounds of Salem laughing in the distance. Anita stared at Christine, raven hair swirling around her inhumanly lovely face, her blue eyes glimmering with their own light. Her red lips peeled back from her fangs as she took a step forward.

Instinct bypassed thought and Anita brought up her hand, the rosary still wound around her wrist. Christine lurched to a stop, and the predatory grin on her face contorted in fury. She hissed, but Anita stood her ground. The fog twisted around Christine as she glared.

"Chris . . ." Anita gasped. Anticipation of this moment had haunted her mind every hour since Christine and Shafax had fled the ruins of Christine's home, and now she had nothing to say.

"It's over, Anita," Christine said, her voice too tense to be smooth. "We're past you now."

"Past me?" Anita asked blankly.

Christine laughed; the hideous twist to the familiar sound made Anita's skin crawl. "This was never about you. My king wants Flavius, and Simon led us to him. That's it."

Anita stared. "He turned you into a monster . . . he made you kill your own parents just for that?"

Christine rolled her eyes. "Made me? Please. Nobody makes me do anything. I wanted him, and now I can be with him forever."

"Christine, what did he do to you? This isn't you!"

"You don't get it, do you?" Christine asked, shaking her head. "He's given me everything. I'm immortal, Anita. I'll never die, never age, never be as weak and defenseless as you are. Look what I can do!"

She raised her hands, and thunder roared directly above them. The clouds swirled and writhed.

"Christine, you can't listen to him!" Anita begged. "They told me what he is! He's killing vampires!"

"I know," Christine replied. "He'll be all-powerful soon. Maybe as soon as he finishes with Flavius."

Her eyes darted across the graveyard, then back. She smirked again as her eyes blazed. "I'll take care of Simon, though. Maybe I'll even get a taste of his blood myself." She winked. "Have you had any of it? I could kill you first so you could come back. You were a great court jester when we were kids; you'd make a good little attendant when I'm queen."

Anita had been afraid, sick at heart, and broken inside as she watched the vampire king command Christine like she was his slave. She had been so determined to save her friend. If they could just pry her away, she had hoped, maybe they could redeem her, convince her to abandon the monster. Even if she couldn't become human again, Simon was a vampire, and he wasn't like her.

She knew now that she had been deluding herself all along, willingly turning her face away from the truth. Salem and Simon had been right. There was nothing left here to save. This wasn't Christine.

Swallowing hard, she held out the crucifix in her hand and took a step forward. Behind Christine, the rubble of the broken mausoleum stirred.

Christine hissed and backed up a pace. "Oh, please," she spat. "Suddenly you're a believer?"

"It saved me from you and that thing last night," Anita fired back. Her vision swam, but she blinked the tears away. "It won't let me down now."

"It's a piece of plastic and a fable!" Christine spat. She seemed far too intent to notice the bricks shifting and toppling off the rubble.

"Yeah?" Anita demanded, and she took another step forward. Anita didn't know where the rush of confidence was coming from, but strength surged in her arm. Christine almost stumbled in her retreat. "Then take it from me."

Christine lurched forward as if she planned to do that very thing, but her hand trembled as it got closer, and her fingers curled in toward her palm. She screamed in frustration, and it was more of an animal yowl than any human sound Anita had ever heard. The vampiress glanced around and ripped a stone wing off an angel sculpture. She drew her arm back to throw it, and Anita's eyes widened; she doubted the power of the cross was going to stop a blunt piece of carved concrete.

Simon exploded out of the mausoleum, the cuts on his torso and above one eye still sealing shut, but he caught the tip of the angel's wing just as Christine started to throw. She cried out in pain as her body wrenched forward and her arm stayed in place, and Simon kicked her in the back.

She went down hard, sprawling on her hands and knees in the snow. Gray eyes alive with fury, Simon shifted the stone wing into both hands and brought it down on the back of her head, but Christine managed to roll onto her back and kick him in the gut with both feet. He flew back before his crushing blow could connect, dropping the wing and tucking into a roll.

Ignoring Anita, Christine launched herself at Simon, claws flying for his throat. He slipped aside and kicked her in the face. She dropped, but kicked his legs out from under him. They grappled on the ground until Simon got her in an armlock and threw her off him. He jumped to his feet and Christine was on him in a second, slashing at him with her claws. He blocked and diverted her blows, jabbing her in the face and kicking at her legs to break her rhythm, but he barely slowed her down.

Anita's heart raced, but she knew the contest was beyond her. She looked for Salem and saw him mowing through a pack of the living dead. She jumped, waving her arms, trying to get his attention. Her injured ankle buckled when she landed, and as she fell, the rosary slid off her wrist and the gun dropped into the snow.

Christine turned, sensing Anita's vulnerability, her jaws opening wide beneath her glowing red eyes. In the next second, Simon's fist crashed across her jaw. She went down on her hands and knees again, and this time Simon kicked her in the ribs before she could recover. The blow sent her hurtling through the air; she bounced off one headstone and smashed into another, then sank to the ground in a daze, chips of cracked marble in her sable hair.

"Simon!"

Salem's voice was so casual it was nearly chipper. Anita got up to a sitting position and saw through the fog that he had a severed head on the end of his gladius. A gleam of steel pinwheeled through the air before the katana fell to earth, its blade planting in the ground and waving like a victory flag.

Simon turned toward it, but the crunch of stone drew his attention, and he turned to see Christine hurling half the monument at him. It broke against his forearms, but the blow knocked him back and off-balance. Christine dove through the shower of dust shards, rolled, then drop-kicked Simon with both feet, sending him into another mausoleum. Christine spat in his direction, then fixed Anita with her hellfire eyes.

Anita patted frantically in the snow for the fallen rosary, but her cold-numbed fingers couldn't find it. Christine wrenched the katana out of the ground and sprang, but Simon tackled her in midair. She rolled free of him and swung the blade around in a ferocious but inexpert slash. Simon turned in, trapping her wrists against his side, and forced the blade out of her hands. She flailed and kicked it in Anita's direction.

Christine snapped her teeth at Simon. As he leaned away from the bite, she wrenched her hands free, boxed his ears, and struck him across the face. He went down, and she leapt for the blade, but Simon caught her ankle from the ground and sank the claws of his free hand into her calf. She shrieked and kicked him in the face with her other foot; Anita cringed as his head snapped back. Still kicking at him, Christine dragged herself forward by hand, reaching out for the fallen katana.

Anita got to her feet, adrenaline burning away the pain in her ankle, and she went for the sword too—until Christine's eyes froze her in place. The red glow faded to bright, pleading blue.

"Help me, Anita!" she begged. "Don't let him hurt me! We're friends! We've been friends forever!"

She sounded near tears, and the misery and fear on her face were convincing. Without looking, she kicked Simon in the head again and screamed, "Anita, please don't let him kill me!"

Her fingers groped as she stretched her arm as far as it would go, and her shiny claws scraped the sword's hilt. Anita wrenched her eyes away from Christine and saw Simon's expression, rigid as he struggled with Christine, panic on his face. And not, Anita realized, for himself.

"Anita . . . ?"

The voice of an angel on the lips of a monster. Anita kicked the sword out of Christine's reach. The vampiress shrieked, and her eyes turned fiery red again. The smooth lines of her face twisted with rage. "No! I can't fail him! Not now!"

She kicked back again, but this time Simon was ready. He caught her leg with his claws and slashed through the flesh. As Christine howled, Simon grabbed her around the waist, got to his feet, and tossed her five yards away; then he dove for the katana.

Christine rolled out of the fall and rushed back, screaming. Simon slipped the toe of his boot under the katana's blade and flipped the sword up into his grip, snow spraying in the air as his hand clamped on the hilt. He turned to meet Christine's charge, stabbing between her outstretched claws, and ran her through the heart.

She froze in place, her jaw trembling and her claws grasping the air as she sank to her knees. Her wide eyes gazed up at Simon as he looked down on her, fury in every hard line of his gaunt face. Her claw marks were still healing on his cheek and chest. At the end of the sword, blood leaked onto Christine's shirt, turning the flowers in her paisley blouse to roses. More blood overflowed her lips, dribbling down her chin. A single drop of blood slid from the corner of her eye.

Anita had never seen anything so pitiful. "Simon, please," she begged, voice breaking. "Please don't make her suffer."

He drew the blade out and Christine's back arched. Her eyes squeezed shut and her mouth opened wide, but Simon swung a two-handed blow and struck off her head before she could scream. His blow was so fast and precise that her head simply dropped sideways, landing faceup in the snow as her body collapsed the other way.

Anita was afraid to look, but she forced her eyes open and was glad for it. The long fangs in Christine's mouth shrank back to normal teeth. Her beauty faded just a bit—still radiant, but in the way she had always been beautiful, with no magic or preternatural charm in her flesh. The harshness melted off her face, her ruby lips paled to pink, and the strangest expression of peace settled on her snowy features.

HANS RICHTEIN had noticed the Master hissing and snarling to himself, but it was the sound of cracking stone that finally drew his attention. The vampire's gnarled hands had been gripping a plinth built into the wall, and it broke in his grasp, dust and stone chips falling to the floor. The hands seemed more withered than before, and Hans was fairly certain the scab festering between thumb and forefinger was new.

Hans hadn't been paying close attention to the Master's frustrations; instead, he'd been thinking about Christine, longer than he could remember thinking of anything but the Master since . . .

since he couldn't remember when. Since *before*. Usually, thoughts distracting him from the Master were brief, lasting only until the soothing balm of the Master's voice brushed them away. But these past minutes, the assuaging fog hadn't come, and discomfiting ideas were taking shape in his mind, new things he hadn't considered and old ones he had forgotten.

"And so she fails," the Master rasped poisonously. His voice was harsher than Hans remembered.

"Christine?" Hans asked, blinking. His maimed eye stung, but he ignored it as he looked up from the floor.

"Of course Christine!" the vampire lord snarled. "Failed and destroyed. My blood wasted on that worthless harlot."

That sounded wrong, and Hans thought it out. Worthless? Admittedly, she hadn't been his favorite person. But worthless? Everyone had worth, didn't they? Hans was confident he had heard that somewhere. And now she was gone—perhaps turned to dust, as he had seen so many vampires do when Shafax was done with them.

Dust thou art, and unto dust shalt thou return.

Why did that sound familiar, too? And why was it painful to remember?

He looked away from the vampire, trying to concentrate. Part of his mind rebelled against the awkward and shameful feeling, like he was breaking a rule, delving into *before*. But he struggled until his subconscious found the voice that went with the words, a man in robes of brighter colors than Shafax's. A high, vaulted ceiling went with the memory, and a hand on his forehead, smearing . . . dirt? No, ashes, that was it. He was young—he remembered two older people holding his hands as the bright-robed man looked down on him solemnly.

There was a cross on the wall behind the man in the robes, and Hans's mind tried to shy away from it. Shafax hated crosses—they had left a wake of broken ones behind them. Some Shafax had smashed himself, and others Hans had destroyed for him. He remembered striding through another graveyard half a world away with a sledgehammer, removing the symbols wherever they occurred. The memory gave him a new, nauseating feeling he couldn't recall experiencing at the time.

"Drained, and still they come," the vampire hissed aloud. There was definitely something different about his voice; where was the melody, the gentle caress that wiped away concern and fear?

Hans got to his feet, his head aching as he forced himself to remember. The visions (memories?) ached in his heart, a phantom pain, like he was bleeding in sympathy for a character on a movie screen. He thought there might have been a time before Shafax. A time with the man and woman (parents?) from the church. A time in a desert, surrounded by other people (comrades? friends?) in uniforms just like his.

Yes, it was him in the church, he was sure of it. But was he wearing the uniform? There was a casket (Anja) with flowers (she had liked Dutch tulips, but her parents had insisted on white lilies—*weiße Lilien*—instead). People were crying. Hans thought he might have been one of them; the wetness on his cheek was so real that he patted his flesh, expecting it there. It didn't make sense, though; there was no pain that went with the memory . . . no, that wasn't right. There was no injury, but there *had* been pain . . .

The glowing red eyes in the hood turned his way, but Hans barely glanced at them. "There are many to be enslaved—many who are still whole." Part of Hans felt ashamed at this taunt, but the majority of him was too lost in memory to bother with what the vampire wanted. "You may render me one final service."

Hans wasn't particularly interested in service. Why had he been in pain? This woman (Anja) who had died ("I'm so sorry, *Unteroffizier* Richtein. Her motorcycle took the turn too quickly.") had meant something. She hadn't been worthless either.

One of Hans's powerful hands brushed the long knife still strapped to the back of his belt. He had taken it with him to hunt down the two escaped prisoners (Heidi and Miguel; he had heard them talking, they had names), intending to . . . kill them? Why? What had they done to him?

The girl had stabbed him first, that was it. He couldn't see. But why had he grabbed them in the first place? Why had he wanted to drag them down into this place that was rank and dark and full of death? What could they have done to deserve this?

He had stabbed another girl in the graveyard, stabbed her far more than any body would require to die. It had felt good then, but he searched in vain for that feeling of pride and triumph any-where in himself now; he found only shame. And a boy, trying to escape the other way—Hans had slit his throat. He had begged in the second before the knife bit into his flesh, but Hans hadn't cared then . . .

Why not? He cared now.

Strong hands grabbed his shoulders and pressed him to the wall; he saw the fire within the cowl. This was the reason. Some-thing in that fire and the hideous, horrible voice that went with it took away guilt and shame and reason and meaning and put itself in their place. But now the something was gone, and he remembered the man and woman (*Vati und Mutti*) and the . . . Anja. She was not just a woman who had died, she was Anja. Of course she was Anja! How could he have forgotten her?

Hans didn't notice the slash of pain in his neck or the weariness settling over his limbs, robbing him of his strength. He was on the verge of a breakthrough. Her face was hazy, but her eyes had been blue . . . green? Maybe gray, but they looked green in the right light (light was fading now). Her smile. He remembered that . . . almost.

His vision was hazy, turning black, and he blinked impatiently. He just needed a few more moments, and he would remember her . . . just a . . . few . . .

SIMON WATCHED Christine's corpse topple into the snow, then

looked across the graveyard. The moans had ceased, and the revenants lay still where they had fallen. The fog was settling back to earth, revealing a pile of twitching body parts surrounding Salem. The elder vampire was covered in slime and bodily fluids—it glistened in his short hair and dripped down his bare chest—but none of it seemed to be his own blood. Taking time only to kick away what looked like an arm, Salem started toward them.

Anita knelt on the ground, staring at Christine's remains. Crying and falling in the snow had smeared away some of the rat blood on her cheeks, though there were streaks of red in her hair and down her neck. Her jeans and jacket were cut in several places where Salem had slashed through them with his swords, and he smelled the coagulated blood around her ankle where the coyote had bitten her.

"Anita?" Stripping the coat off an inert zombie, Simon draped it over Christine's head, then knelt down next to Anita. He stuck the katana into the ground and touched one of her hands; she didn't recoil. "Are you all right?"

She blinked and looked at him. She licked her lips, another blink sending another tear down her cheek. But she brushed at it and said in a tone that was both bewildered and relieved, ". . . yeah. Actually . . . I think I will be."

"Delightful," Salem's brusque voice cut in, and he was suddenly beside them, wrenching his katana out of the ground and flicking it in a practiced way. Christine's blood splashed onto the ground at his side, and the blade gleamed. "Shall we?"

Simon got up and helped Anita to her feet. While she looked around in the snow for her fallen rosary and pistol, Simon kicked through the rubble of the collapsed mausoleum, tossing aside bricks until he finally dug out his kukri knife. The blade was scuffed and blunted in several places, but salvageable.

"Why did we have to dismember them?" Anita was asking as he walked back.

"He was trying to reanimate everything," Salem said contemptuously. "More things to hurt us, but also more effort for him every time we chopped something off. Too many pieces made it more effort than it was worth. Even Shafax has limits. For now."

"I can't find my rosary," Anita said uneasily. Simon looked as well, but he didn't see the discomforting strand of beads anywhere.

"Well, we don't have time for a scavenger hunt," Salem declared, starting toward the chapel. "Let's not lose the momentum."

Anita's eyes were wide, her heart galloping. He reached out and squeezed one of her hands. "Don't worry," he said. "We'll keep you safe."

"'We?'" Anita repeated, but she held his hand as they started toward the chapel.

Simon rolled his eyes, but said, "I will keep you safe. I promise."

"I didn't see you playing rat exterminator," Salem's voice called from inside the chapel.

Simon gritted his teeth; it had been uncomfortably frightening watching the coyotes advance on Anita and the rats bury her under their wriggling bodies. Fear did not come to him naturally, and he was horrified that his exposure to Anita and the emotions she triggered might be opening him to the dangerous ones too; his distraction over her had already led to the coyote bite in his shoulder.

The trusting smile she forced for him muted his unease for the moment.

"I know you will," she replied, as if Salem hadn't spoken.

They found Salem in a corner in the chapel, drawing a deep breath and nodding. Simon joined him, and he too smelled the dried blood on the ground, only hours old. Salem met his gaze for a moment, then looked at Anita.

"Maybe you should sit this one out, Comestible." The customary mocking smirk on his lips didn't match the sudden iron in his voice.

Anita's heart leapt and her throat moved as she swallowed, but she shook her head. "No. I have to see this through."

Salem studied her for a moment, then sighed. "Stay out of the way."

He raised one boot and smashed it down on the bloodied tile. It broke, the pieces toppling down the stairs beneath, and a pair of dead, slightly discolored faces leered up at them. Anita flinched backward, Simon raised his knife as he stepped in front of her, and Salem spun both of his swords into stabbing positions. But the two corpses were unmoving, and Salem slowly lowered the blades.

"Looks like a couple zombies missed the party," he observed, kicking them down the stairs and out of his way.

"That's the guy . . . the drama major," Anita said, staring down into the hole.

"It's all right," Simon reassured her. "They're dead—completely. They can't hurt us."

Salem went down the stairs in the space of one of Anita's too-fast heartbeats, and Simon was right behind him. The underground crypt was cramped, its ceiling barely taller than Simon. A stone sarcophagus was built into the floor right in front of the stairs, and a few more coffins were wedged into recesses in the walls. Simon smelled blood that he recognized as Miguel's and Heidi's coming from a small room to the right of the stairs, but Salem set off down a narrow hallway in the other direction, the points of both swords held in front of him.

Simon gave Anita his hand to help her down into the darkness, then pressed a finger to her lips. Still holding her hand, he tugged her after Salem, brushing spider webs out of her way.

The hallway branched off at a right angle, and Salem stopped at the corner, his back to the wall and gladius point aimed past his body at face level. A dim glow brushed the far wall past the bend; Simon imagined Anita would be seeing his and Salem's profiles in silhouette. The older vampire carefully glanced past the corner, then looked back at Simon with a grim expression. Nodding, Salem led the way, and Simon tugged Anita after him.

At the far end of the short corridor, Shafax was waiting for them.

He sat on another stone sarcophagus built up against the wall, his back to the bricks, the hood over his face, and his fingers laced together. The brackets in this room had torches, and they burned with low orange and yellow flames. A dead man lay in the corner, bloodied bandages and gauze over one eye. The room was more or less square, perhaps the length of two of the sarcophagi placed end to end. The cracked floor had once been a mosaic; Simon thought he could make out a figure of a skull amidst the fragments. Whatever had been on the ceiling had been deliberately effaced.

Salem stepped into the room with his swords raised, and Simon was beside him in the next instant, holding his knife to guard. Anita crept in behind him, and he was intimately aware of her every heartbeat, the smell of her dried blood, and every scuffle of dislodged dirt or brushed stone pieces as she stepped.

"So." The deathly voice was acid in his mind. "You have survived to come to me."

"I always survive," Salem returned.

"I was not speaking to you," the voice corrected, and the cowl turned to stare unmistakably at Anita. She cringed.

Salem didn't take his eyes off Shafax, but he tipped the katana toward the corpse on the floor and said coolly, "I don't throw away my soldiers' lives needlessly."

The twisted, choppy sound coming from the hood's darkness, like a snake having its breath forced out in gasps, might have been a laugh. "And that is what makes you weak, Flavius."

Shafax unlaced his fingers and gestured to the floor. "Come, prostrate yourselves before me and your sufferings will be few. Except yours," he added, looking back at Anita as murder oozed into his voice. "You will scream for an end to your torments long before I relieve your agony, mortal."

Anita's heartbeat doubled its pace, and Simon took a step forward, baring his fangs as he pointed his knife. "You won't lay a hand on her without coming through me."

"Then she had best savor this last moment without pain," Shafax replied, and he rose to his feet. A negligent flick of two fingers sent his hood to pool at the base of his neck, revealing his ravaged face and the almost palpable hate in his eyes. His blistered lips peeled back over his jagged teeth.

Salem said something then, a mix of long vowels and harsher sounds in the back of his throat. It was no language Simon knew, though it sounded vaguely like snippets of Hebrew and Arabic he had heard. Whatever Salem said must have been horrendous, though, because Shafax's eyes widened.

"You owe me useful lives, Flavius," Shafax hissed, opening and closing his clawed hands in anticipation. "Your blood will be due recompense for your defiance."

"You owe me a couple lives as well," Salem sneered back.

"I?" Shafax's face twisted with sudden, ballistic rage. "I am beholden to no being! All life exists for me, and for me alone! I am lord! I am god! I am—"

"Ozymandias, King of Kings," Salem suggested.

"Silence!" Shafax shrieked, and the force of his fury propelled them all a step back. It crawled on Simon's skin like a thousand stinging insects. Anita gasped behind him, but he dared not take his eyes away from Shafax to check on her. "You will not escape me now!"

"Christine did."

Anita's voice was so unexpected that they all blinked, but Shafax snarled, "That unworthy slut died worshipping the spittle that falls from my lips, you simpering wretch!"

"Better to die than to spend one more night as part of you," Anita fired back, and Simon was impressed by the steel in her voice.

The frenzied look on Shafax's face froze in place, and Simon felt the fuel in the air ignite. Shafax's mouth emitted a long, gargling groan that barely sounded like language, and he slowly raised one hand. The index and little fingers were pointed at Anita as the middle and ring fingers curled back to meet his thumb. The air shivered like a heat mirage, and Simon's eyes widened in horror.

He threw himself in front of Anita just in time; the brunt of the curse struck him without effect, but his vision blurred and his body convulsed for a second. In that instant, Shafax's hand flashed back down and ripped the lip from the sarcophagus on which he had been seated. He hurled the stone through the air, and Simon raised his arms just before it smashed into him. The force of its impact threw him backward, the stone shattering into fragments. Still standing behind him, Anita couldn't get out of the way in time, and she flew into the wall. Simon heard her head connect with the stone, and as he collapsed to the ground, she fell beside him, unconscious.

When he blinked away the blood running in his eyes from the new cut on his forehead, he thought for a moment he was still disoriented from the curse.

Shafax and Salem whirled around each other like tornados of black and white, and Salem's blades singing as they smote the air, all but invisible with speed. Simon struggled up to his hands and knees, but he had no idea where to even start.

He had a sudden and vivid memory of sparring with Salem years ago, trying out the techniques the elder vampire had taught him. Now and then, his fist or foot had slipped past Salem's guard and connected. Simon would gloat, and Salem would roll his eyes and insist that he'd been toning his skills down to give his protégé a sporting chance. Simon had snickered to himself at Salem's transparent attempts to save face.

If they survived, he would have to apologize.

There was a sense of unreality in watching Salem fight. Every technique was precise, every movement and shift of weight balanced. He worked the two swords in concert like they were extensions of his will. No blow went farther than necessary, and every miss was retracted the instant Salem saw it would fail. He flashed around Shafax with a speed that had even the deformed vampire hissing in fury.

But it was a good thing Salem was fast, because Simon could tell he was pushing himself to his limits just to survive. Shafax's claws ripped toward Salem from every angle and gouged furrows into the stone walls when he missed. Salem tried to cut at Shafax's limbs with his swords or shunt the blows sideways, but once in a while he had no choice but to block, and the force of the blow threw him staggering back.

Simon leapt into the fray, stabbing at Shafax's back, but an invisible blow caught him in midair and propelled him into the wall. He bounced off in time to see Shafax catch the katana and twist it out of Salem's hands. He swung it ferociously this way and that, but it was clear he knew little more about swords than Anita knew about guns, and Salem scored a jab with his gladius. Black drops of blood sizzled and smoked on the stone floor.

"All those memories of all those vampires, and you're still swinging it like it's a club," Salem taunted.

Snarling, Shafax slashed, and Salem threw himself out of the way. The katana blade hit the wall and snapped in half, and Salem bellowed, "You son of a bitch! Muramasa made that!"

Shafax threw what he had left of the blade in his hand, and Salem dodged again, switching his gladius to his right hand. The katana stuck in the wall, embedded to the hand guard. Simon darted up to Salem's side and the two of them came in together.

Salem stabbed low while Simon slashed high, going for the kill on Shafax's neck. Shafax pulled his leg away from the low blow and kicked Salem back. Then, so quickly Simon had no idea how it had happened, Shafax had him by the wrist with one hand and the throat with the other. The hooked claws dug into his neck.

"Your human will beg for you as I ravage her body and soul!" the vampire king hissed. Simon tried to pull the hand off his neck, but its strength was impossible.

Then Salem was there, cutting at Shafax's side. Shafax's body turned to smoke for an instant, and Salem's slash passed through, but the hands restraining Simon vanished as well, and Simon launched himself backward. By the time Shafax became corporeal again, Simon had returned his knife to guard.

The blood glutton weaved around them, slashing at them both with his claws as they cut at him with their blades. As Shafax's talons raked through the muscles on Simon's off arm and he cried out in pain, Salem took advantage of the instant of distraction to slice a cut into Shafax's shoulder. Shafax's answering scream and the telekinesis that accompanied it hurled them both away.

Shafax streaked toward Simon, but screeched in frustration as Salem came at his unprotected back, spinning in a swirl of black cloth to face the greater threat. His forearms struck Salem's so forcefully that Salem dropped his sword, gnarring in pain. Shafax's hands clawed at Salem's throat, but Salem twisted away and Shafax's nails cut five lines of red into his cheek instead.

Simon dived on Shafax's back, kukri poised to impale the taller vampire through the chest. Shafax raised a hand to intercept, and Simon's knife scraped down the arm, ripping back the sleeve and carving off a chunk of flesh. Roaring like a tiger, Shafax reached that maimed arm up and over his shoulder and sunk his talons into the bare flesh of Simon's back like he meant to tear out his spine.

But instead, he threw Simon onto the floor before him, and Salem hesitated as the blur of Simon's body interrupted his frontal assault. Before Salem could recoil, Shafax slapped him into a wall. An invisible force then seized Simon, and he saw the ceiling approaching him for an instant before he smashed into it. The impact dug him six inches deep into the stone, so hard that he tasted the dirt above it and his skull cracked. Hooked on an unseen line, he flashed back to earth, and his back pulverized the floor below to dust as his pelvis and ribs fractured in stabs of agony.

He finished drawing the breath for a scream just as Shafax kicked him, breaking another two ribs, and he soared into the far wall. He smashed the stone and collapsed to the floor, splintering agony in every part of his body, blood running in his eyes and pouring from his mouth. He heard Anita's heartbeat nearby, but muffled, as if she was underwater, or behind several walls of a building.

He forced his head to turn the other way, rolling his face against the ground and registering with a new stab of pain that his nose was broken too. Lethargy weighed him down as his immortal body struggled to heal all his injuries at once. Orienting his face away from the wall, he saw Salem and Shafax fighting hand-to-hand.

Salem was obviously the better fighter, and his claws were stained with bubbling black blood. But Shafax pushed him from side to side with invisible blows, and Salem's face was grim. He caught a blow from an angle and tried to turn Shafax into a wrist lock, but the vampire just raised his arm, lifting Salem into the air, and hurled him into a wall. Salem bounced off and rolled to his feet, panting, raising his claws to defend.

Salem fought on, but it was Shafax on the offensive now, chivvying Salem toward a corner. Every time Salem slipped toward the side, a magical force threw him back. Shafax's blows started to land, lines of red materializing on Salem's chest in time with snarls of pain and defiance. Simon looked around desperately for his kukri or Salem's sword; the knife was missing, and the gladius had fallen beside Anita. She was awake, rubbing her head and squinting.

There was a crunch of stone, and Simon looked back to see Salem bouncing off the cracked corner column, blood on his face. Two of the fingers of his left hand were curled in, broken. Shafax's blows were slowing down, but Salem didn't have the coordination left to deflect them. He was reduced to blocking, and every block smacked him back. Then Shafax grabbed him by the upper arms, and Salem grappled with him instinctively, his arms trembling with the effort of holding Shafax's snapping teeth away as the vampire leaned toward his throat. Stone chips rustled at Simon's side, but he didn't look.

Without warning, Shafax dug his talons into Salem's biceps like hooks and then ripped them free, leaving flesh and muscle dangling in the air. Salem screamed, and Shafax backhanded him down so brutally that Salem bounced on the ground once before he came to rest, curling his arms in to his chest. He gritted his teeth and kicked at Shafax's leg, but Shafax stomped down and pinned Salem in place.

Suddenly, Simon smelled blood. Not Salem's blood, pouring from his arms even as the maimed muscles started to knit back together, or the acrid odor of Shafax's blood, bubbling on the ground like overheated oil. It was fresh, human blood, and a flavor Simon recognized. His head spinning at the motion, he twisted enough to meet Anita's eyes.

A smear of red on the blade of Salem's gladius matched the oozing blood blister on her thumb. She held the sword in her free hand, eyes wide, and pointed at Shafax frantically. Focusing on the fear in Anita's face and trying to think past the waves of torture wracking his body, Simon started to rise.

Shafax leered down at Salem. Salem snatched up a broken piece of his katana in one wounded hand and swiped half-heartedly, but Shafax stepped down on that limb too.

"Do you see now?" the vampire king gloated, and though his voice was ragged with exhaustion, there was undisguised glee in it. "Nothing is beyond my reach! Nothing will not be mine!"

Simon had gotten up to one knee, and he extended his hand. Supporting the blade with both of her hands, Anita stretched and placed the hilt in his grip. Salem's green eyes flicked to them, but they did not widen, and he looked right back at Shafax and spat on his robes.

Shafax shrieked with fury and stomped down on Salem's ribs; Simon heard the crack from across the room, along with the muted hiss through teeth that was the only satisfaction Salem would give his enemy.

"Defiant to the end," Shafax sneered. "Receive, mighty Flavius, the reward of defiance."

He laid his claws on Salem's neck, and Simon was out of time. He forced himself to his feet, hefting the gladius like a spear. Dirt and rubble scraped under his boots, and Shafax started to turn, but in the second of distraction, Salem grabbed the katana fragment again and buried the blade in the other vampire's knee. Shafax jerked in the middle of spinning around, maw stretching wide as he roared in pain, and Simon threw the blade.

And missed.

The gladius point pierced Shafax's chest two inches below his neck and off to the right, lodging at an angle along his collarbone, though Simon heard the top of the sternum splinter. The sword sank in to the hilt, the blade bursting out of Shafax's back with a splash of blood against the wall. Shafax's eyes widened in rage and his limbs jerked spasmodically, but Simon had no strength to cross the room and finish him. The force of that insane glare pushed him to his knees, and he stared at the face of his destruction.

"I will . . . kill her first!" Shafax pledged hatefully. His voice sounded like he had gargled broken glass, and blood spilled over his lips as his twitching hands groped for the sword handle. "Make you watch . . . as I peel her skin from muscle . . . muscle from bone . . . and then I will take this sword . . . and I will cleave you to pieces . . . bit . . . by . . . bit . . ."

His long fingers brushed the gladius's hilt, and the blood-smeared lips stretched into a feral smile. Anita reached out and Simon caught her hand. Futile as it was, he dragged himself in front of her to shield her from the promise of horror in those eyes.

And then, with a furious roar that echoed off the walls, Salem shot to his feet behind Shafax, reached over his shoulder, grabbed the handle of the sword, and ripped it backward.

The blade tore out of Shafax's shoulder and ripped his chest cavity open. Blood overflowed the gaping wound as Shafax's right arm slumped and his head lolled left. More black fluid burst from his mouth, staining his teeth ebony, and the vampire's screech of agony was lost in the gurgling sound. His arms flailed as Salem's other hand came down on his left shoulder and forced him to his knees.

Salem threw the gladius aside and stood over Shafax, naked hate carved into every line of his face. He plunged his right hand into Shafax's wound, ignoring the vampire king's struggles, then ripped it back out again, clutching Shafax's withered heart in his grip. It was scabbed and rotted, the colors of rust and wax, and black blood dripped from it.

Shafax's body grew rigid, fingertips twitching as his arms curled like he was having a seizure, hideous eyes wide and jaw trembling. His tongue protruded from between his sharp teeth, and his lungs forced a strangled gasp from his throat. Salem hooked him by the eye sockets and wrenched his face back so he was forced to look into Salem's eyes, which glowed red. Salem extended his arm to hold the heart over one of the torches on the wall.

"Long live the king," Salem whispered, and he dropped the heart into the flames.

The orange and yellow flared to purple, sparks flying from the torch bracket. Shafax's arms shot out and his back arched. His eyes caught the same purple fire as his heart; the flames engulfed his eye sockets and burst from his mouth, and smoke curled out of his nostrils. He jerked and writhed as if nailed to an invisible cross, and the talons on his fingers cracked and dropped off one by one. His long fingers all bent backward, the bones inside powdering to dust as the digits pressed to the backs of his hands. His arms wrapped around his chest, and he lurched forward, the flames racing over his face and melting his flesh down to charred skull. A single, awful wail crawled its way through the flames in his throat, like a thousand tormented souls shrieking at once from perdition.

Then he collapsed forward as the flames engulfed his torso, pouring from his sleeves and smoking under his back for an instant before he impacted the floor. His blackened skull shattered, the flames were extinguished, the empty robe flattened to the floor, and Shafax the Ancient One, King of All Vampires, was gone.

Salem slumped against the wall as the torch flames turned back to yellow and orange, their fuel exhausted. He sank to the floor, boots sliding out and pushing Shafax's empty robe away. Simon watched as Salem stared down at his half-healed arms knitting themselves together again. When he was whole, Salem looked down at the empty robe and breathed something so quiet that it couldn't make its way through Simon's still-muddled hearing. Then a weak but recognizable version of the older vampire's usual smirk touched his bloodstained lips, and he added, "But better late than never."

Simon toppled sideways onto the ground, staring vacantly at the ruins of his enemy. Anita dragged herself over, curling up against him and pulling his arm around her. It felt faintly pleasant, but her blood called to him. He was so weak . . . "It's okay," she told him. "It's over. It's over . . ."

For a moment all three of them lay there unmoving, Anita's panting and her heartbeat the only sounds.

Then Salem struggled to his feet, clawing the wall more than once for support and coughing roughly while clutching his abdomen. His skin was undamaged now, but paler than usual from blood loss and still marked with his own dried blood where he had been injured. His biceps looked like they had been painted red. Leaning on the stone wall for a long moment, testing his strength, Salem finally shambled over to where his gladius had fallen. He groaned as he stooped to pick it up; Shafax's blood had evaporated from the blade.

Salem shuffled in their direction, and Simon tried to rise to meet him, but his limbs refused to cooperate. The stabbing pain was fading, but the ache lingered, along with a strange churning in his stomach that he thought a human would call nausea. His vision swam, and he wondered if some aftereffects of Shafax's magic still clung to him. He felt weak and frail, and he slumped against Anita, her pulse taunting him.

Salem stood over them, and though he was haggard, the unnatural light still shone in his emerald eyes. "You realize," he pointed out in an exhausted voice, a wicked smile tugging at his lips, "that with Shafax gone, I don't need your help anymore? So there's really no need to keep either of you alive."

Horror gripped Simon, and he struggled against the torpor weighing down his body. He had come this far, invested so much, only to lose her to Salem? The fear he had known as they prepared to enter the crypt returned with terrifying force, but he barely managed to prop himself up on one elbow before Salem nudged him down with the toe of his boot. Anita tried to rise, but Salem casually rested the point of his sword on her throat, and she froze. Swallowing, she looked up at him, and he fixed her with his gaze, measuring her for a long moment. His eyes went to Simon's, and Simon glared back at him, all the force his body would not exert concentrated in his gaze. Salem glanced back at Anita thoughtfully.

Then he smirked, and took the sword point away.

"This won't end well," Salem said, as he had in the cathedral alley, "but not by my doing. You're brave, little human, and I admire bravery. And I hold to my word, Simon. Whatever fate comes for her, she's safe from me."

He paused, then winked. "As are you . . . my old friend."

His laughter echoed from the hall long after he was gone.

ANITA DIDN'T know how long she lay there, her back to Simon's chest, shivering on the cold floor. But eventually she got to her knees and looked Simon over. His body bore the dried bloodstains of his fight, and the bruising beneath the surface reminded her of the way he had looked after whatever Salem had done to him two weeks before. His face was discolored, his mouth drooped open, and the reflective sheen in his gray eyes had dulled.

"Come on, Simon," she said, taking his cold hands and tugging him up. "We have to go."

He just wheezed, neither protesting nor helping, a lifeless mannequin against her side as she struggled to her feet under his weight. She dragged him down the hall, her ankle aching from the added burden, stopping only to pick up his long knife and stick it back in its sheath on his belt.

They reached the narrow staircase, and Anita's legs and arms burned with the effort of hauling him up into the chapel; when she draped him onto the dirty floor, she collapsed on top of him, panting. She had seen so much—she could still feel the rats' paws on her body, the coyote's bite through her boot, and the chilling force of Shafax's baleful gaze. But her mind kept drifting back to the last, lingering calm on Christine's features. She was free. The monster was destroyed. Anita's part in this whole horrific episode was over, and she could awaken from the nightmare at last.

Except she couldn't leave Simon.

She had watched him throw himself in front of Shafax's curse. She didn't know what it would have done to her, and she didn't think she wanted to, either. He had battled with Christine for her, dared Shafax's fury to divert his wrath from her. His strength had given her the courage to speak her hate to the monster's face, and hers had given him the force of will to help bring the thing down forever. Simon was nothing like the creature that had destroyed Christine, and whatever he was, Anita wasn't going to abandon him.

"Simon, we have to go," she told him, sitting up and pulling on his arm.

He didn't look at her as his head flopped from side to side. "Too . . . weak . . . got nothing . . . left . . ."

"Simon, it'll be dawn in a few hours!" she said urgently, remembering Salem's words. They hadn't used it against Shafax, but it could kill Simon just as easily, and there were windows all around the chapel. "You have to move."

"Can't . . . rest . . ."

She took two deep breaths to keep desperation from clouding her mind. "You said this is your native soil, right? If I take you back down, you could sleep?"

The thought of descending again into the crypt made her skin crawl, and she wanted nothing more than to forget the place had ever existed. But if it helped Simon . . .

He blinked and peered at her blearily. "No blood. If I . . . sleep now . . . I won't wake up."

Anita's heart felt like a block of ice in her chest, and panic started to leak into her voice despite herself. "Tell me what to do!" she begged. "How can I help you?"

The vampire looked like he was struggling just to comprehend her words. "Blood . . . need . . . need blood. Go find somebody . . ."

That was too much. Anita knew she could never go find some innocent person and bring him or her in here like a lamb for slaughter. Even saving Simon didn't justify murder. "Simon . . ." She heard the tears in her voice. "Simon, I can't do that. I can't. I'm so sorry . . ."

"Blood?" he asked vacantly. She wondered if he could even hear her anymore.

It was tearing her in two; she was desperate to help him, but unable to condemn some innocent person. Her eyes fell on the statue of Saint Brigid against the wall, red tear tracks dried on her marble cheeks, and she shuddered. The path she envisioned had no clear end, and she thought of Salem's warning with dread. But as she looked down at Simon again, she took a deep breath and said, "Bite me."

Apparently Simon could still hear her, because he blinked and focused on her with obvious effort. "What?"

She pulled back the collar of her turtleneck, leaning over him. "Take some of mine. A little. Enough to get through the night."

Simon shook his head slowly, breathing in sharp gasps. "Anita . . ."

"Trust me," she said, bending down, and she kissed his cheek.

She had the sense that it was her eyes hypnotizing him this time. After a long moment, he reached up to cup the back of her head with one shaking hand, opening his mouth and baring his fangs.

"Just a little," he whispered against her flesh, and she shivered, her hands curling around his body. "It'll only hurt . . . a second. Just enough to . . . see me through . . ."

There was a faint stab of pain in her neck, and she flinched on instinct. But it passed, and a comforting warmth stole over her body as she let herself relax into the vampire's kiss.

EPILOGUE: PART I

Madrid, Spain

"*BIENVENIDO, SEÑOR Rothard. ¡Próspero Año Nuevo!*"
"*Y tu, Inés, gracias. ¿Esta aqui Señor Massont?*"
"*Si. Él y los otros estan arriba. Se estan esperando.*"
"*Gracias.*"

Timothy Rothard headed up the stairs to the private office wing, and the guard at the door gave him a respectful nod. "Welcome back, Director."

"Thank you."

He stepped through the door, and the lobby's music faded to quiet as the guard closed it behind him. The double doors at the end of the long hall were open but, as he expected, the Council chamber itself was empty. The door leading out the back of the chamber into the smaller meeting room was ajar as well, and Timothy heard voices inside. He headed right in.

Smiles and wishes for a happy new year greeted him all around, but as he took the vacant seat between Gerard Massont and Luther DiNapoli, the jocularity faded.

"We've missed your perspective in your absence, Tim," DiNapoli observed grimly.

"What news?" Timothy asked.

"Commander von Gratz and his team raided a location in Marseilles, but there was nothing to find," Diego Azevedo reported from DiNapoli's other side. "If Shafax was there, he's long gone now."

"We have a connection in the customs office, do we not?" Pierre Charron inquired from the other side of the table.

"He is just a low-level man, Pierre," Klaus Schreiber reminded him. "It is very difficult for him to access the information we need. It will take time."

"Time we don't have," Charron replied. "He must take the risk. The King of Vampires must be stopped."

"Any luck locating the other ancients?" Timothy asked before it could turn into an argument. "Their whereabouts might provide likely targets."

"Nothing concrete. Von Gratz and his people are on standby, but there's too much conflicting information," said Joshua Anderson. "We can't dispatch that team on a whim."

"Any vampire in Europe or Asia with any sense at all will be lying low," Amir al-Hasan grumbled.

"Perhaps we need to turn our eyes to the Americas, then," DiNapoli suggested.

"Perhaps to Chicago," Timothy muttered.

Silence fell on the table as the other directors looked at each other. It was a moment before Azevedo spoke. "Do you know something, Tim?"

Timothy's mind went to that meeting with Anita's boyfriend—Simon something or other—but he knew the stress had been getting to him on that restless vacation. He was jumping at shadows. "No," he sighed. "No, I just . . . worry for my family, in times like this."

One or two of the others looked disappointed, but Anderson nodded sympathetically. "As do we all."

"But America might be worth the look," DiNapoli mused. "There are a lot of cities where disappearances go overlooked. New York, Chicago, Los Angeles . . ."

"Rio," Azevedo put in pointedly.

"I do not think there will be anything to draw Shafax to Los Angeles," Hideo Tajinata said. "Commander von Gratz assured us he devastated that coven. He does not make mistakes."

A grim silence followed this until Schreiber said, "The Americas."

"Worth further investigation."

"We should get analysts on it immediately, see if there are any new trends since we lost track of Shafax."

"We can send recon teams to likely targets . . ."

"Have von Gratz and his squad follow the leads we get . . ."

The discussion stagnated, and all eyes went to the head of the table. Gerard Massont looked at each of them in turn, brushing his neatly trimmed beard thoughtfully, before he spoke.

"The King of Vampires is unaccounted for, and we have only years until the Corona. As always, time is on the side of our enemies, and we're a step behind." He drew a deep breath, then nodded. "Begin the investigation at once."

EPILOGUE: PART II

Chicago, Illinois, USA

BRITTANY MICHENER looked down at the picture in her hands and couldn't strangle the sob that hitched in her throat. They had been at the Grand Canyon; her mom and dad were waving at the stranger they had gotten to take the picture, the sweeping brown and orange of the desert behind them, and seven-year-old Heidi was standing in front of her, looking up at Brittany with a grin while Brittany beamed right back down. The glare of the bright Arizona sun had made them both squint, but the sunlight glinted off their smiles. Heidi was wearing her Hello Kitty shirt. She had loved cats . . .

Brittany remembered Heidi romping through the house when she was six, wearing cat ears they had bought at a dollar store. She had worn the silly things everywhere until they were little more than felt scraps on wire. Of course, she had been a cat for Halloween that year, and she had smiled all night long.

It overwhelmed her then, sudden and remorseless, and Brittany leaned against the pillow on the couch, the tears pouring freely. Why bother pretending? Her baby sister was gone.

It had been a whirlwind of horror. Heidi, missing on Christmas Day, no note or explanation, no answer on her cell. Brittany and her parents frantic with worry, calling every friend of Heidi's they knew. Terror growing as Carlotta Jimenez reported that her son Miguel was missing too. And finally, the knock on the door, and two uniformed Chicago police officers looking sad and grim as they reported that an anonymous tip had led them to an alley where Heidi's and Miguel's bodies had been found.

Endless interviews had ensued with the detectives. Who was Heidi friends with? When had they seen her last? Did she hang out with the wrong kind of people? Did anyone hold a grudge against her? As if there could be any rhyme or reason to this nightmare. As if anything could explain why two people had been brutalized, dehydrated, and frozen to death.

The mortician had smiled as he led them into the funeral parlor, clearly hoping that the perfect beauty he had restored in Heidi's face might be a comfort, but Anne Michener had dissolved into wails and screamed that her baby girl wasn't really dead. Her listless husband had just held her, jaw trembling, and Brittany had been forced to greet the mourners alone.

She had been buried this morning. A short conversation with Mrs. Jimenez had revealed just how fond Heidi and Miguel had been of each other, and Brittany had been filled with shame that she hadn't known Miguel's name before. Miguel and Heidi had been interred side by side, even as the police continued to search for several of Miguel's other friends, who had all been reported missing too.

And now the long, hollow emptiness stretched in front of her, and Brittany just shook against the pillow, picturing her happy little sister and wondering what she could have done differently. She had heard what the detectives said, what the handful of high school visitors had remarked: sad, withdrawn, painfully shy. The words speared her. She remembered the bad years before leaving for college, Heidi in the hospital with jagged cuts on her wrists, but she had hoped her sister was getting better.

Why hadn't she known? How could she have made it right? Brittany thought the questions would hound her until she died.

"H-Honey?"

Wiping her eyes with the back of her hand, Brittany looked at her mother in the door and struggled to keep some semblance of a brave face. "Hey, Mom. I'm sorry, I know I said I'd work on dinner . . ."

Her voice was thick, and she knew her eyes must be red, because her mother's quavering composure fractured and she stumbled to the couch, wrapping her arms around Brittany and sobbing as Brittany sobbed back.

"Oh, Britt . . ." Anne wept. She pulled back, her face the picture of misery. "I h-h-hope you kn-kn-know how m-m-much I love you."

Brittany squeezed her hands. "Of course."

"I know I haven't b-b-been . . ." Anne trailed off, then whispered, "She was my baby."

She dissolved again, and Brittany held her for a long moment, wishing there was anything she could do to have her little sister back. She would gladly have suffered for a century for one more day with her. She would have died herself to bring Heidi back.

The doorbell rang.

Brittany and Anne straightened in surprise, and Brittany glanced at the clock. It was after eleven, and the family members who lived nearby had all seemed to sense that being close wouldn't be helpful. Who would intrude on this worst possible night?

Anne got to her feet, her breaths shuddering as she tried to bring herself back under control. Brittany started to get up. "Mom, I'll—"

"N-N-No, you stay, sweetheart. You've done so m-m-much already . . . my brave girl . . ."

She touched her daughter's cheek with a watery, fragile smile, then stepped into the hallway to answer the door. Brittany rocked back, her face in her hands, and tried to contemplate how this was ever going to get better.

"Oh my God!"

Anne Michener's scream from the hall was so unexpected that Brittany froze in place, her blue eyes wide with shock. She got jerkily to her feet, but a plaintive voice followed her mother's scream, and the sound of that voice nailed her feet to the floor.

"Mom?"

It was quiet, soft, like the speaker was on the verge of tears. It was sweet and light and kindhearted and everything Brittany knew she would never hear again. It hollowed her in a strange, frightening way, and she wondered if she was having a dream, or a nightmare.

"Oh God! Oh, my baby! I knew you couldn't be gone!"

"I . . . I had to come home," the soft voice said, sounding confused. "I felt like I had to come home . . ."

"Of course you did!" Anne blubbered, sobbing new tears. "Of course you came home!"

"Mom . . . can I come in?"

There was something off in the voice now. Anxiety, even fear, but something darker, too. Brittany's mind caught up with her frozen body, and she remembered that Heidi was dead. She had seen the body. She had watched them bury it. This couldn't be reality.

"Of course! Come in! Oh, my baby! My baby's come home!"

"Can Miguel come in?"

Miguel?

"Yes! Come in! Oh, sweetheart, I was so afraid . . . oh, honey, you're so cold . . . honey?"

ENJOYED READING?

Leave a review on Goodreads and Amazon!

Goodreads

Amazon

ACKNOWLEDGEMENTS

This book—the off-and-on writing and refining of which spanned the better part of two decades—would never have seen the light of day without the support and encouragement of so many people.

I thank God for all the many blessings He's given me, especially my loving and supportive family and friends, and the inspiration and motivation to write (and keep writing). They say "man plans and God laughs," but at least now and then I see the humor.

No thanks are sufficient for my loyal alpha readers—Liz Dean and Dr. Monica Nentwig when *Old Scores* was in its infancy, and Gabriel Darke and Mandy Paulson for Version 2.0. From editing and advice to picking my brain on the lore of the world and making me consider things I never had, I couldn't have done this without you.

Thank you to Courtney Rae Andersson of Elevation Editorial, who sanded down the rough spots and sharpened the blunt edges throughout *Old Scores* to make it the best it could be.

My mom, Kathi Harrison, not only inculcated a love of reading in me from childhood, but also employed her forty-year experience as an ICU and ER nurse (and that of her occasionally bemused colleagues) answering my various and sundry questions about traumatic injuries; if I had a nickel for every time I started a text message with "This question is for writing, not practical" . . .

Thanks to my mom again, along with my sister, Megan, for consistently encouraging me to publish.

Christine Ripsky not only allowed me to borrow her given name, but suggested Christine Stokely's surname, too; thanks, old friend.

Thanks to Florian Klitzing for tweaking my German; any errors which persist are mine alone.

My many English teachers at St. Mary School and Marian Central Catholic High School helped me develop a strong foundation as a reader and writer that has served me well ever since. Sue Heider, Carol Wall, Gina Jayko, Jessica Horwath, Sharon Adams, Chris Connell, Mary Kennelly, Darlene Gorski, Kay Hansen, Judy Sowinski, and Debra Vachuta—thank you. Thanks also to Frederick Pollack of the George Washington University for both some insights in writing and a hefty dose of critique that gave me a much-needed critical assessment.

Sincere thanks to Kristen Lindstrom for declining to represent *Old Scores* 1.0 in 2005; it wasn't ready, and I'd be embarrassed today if that version had been published then.

ABOUT THE AUTHOR

Andrew J. "A.J." Harrison has had a lifelong love for classic monsters, but especially vampires. A retired officer of the United States Army Judge Advocate General's Corps, he lives in the Chicago suburbs with his calico cat, Vandal, who lives up to her name. *Old Scores* is his first novel.

 immortalvendettas

 immortalvendettas

 @imvendettas

9 798988 636458